THE HEART OF CREATION

THE STARSEA CYCLE BOOK TEN

KYLE WEST

Copyright © 2024 by Kyle West

All rights reserved.

No part of this book may be reproduced in any form or by any electronic or mechanical means, including information storage and retrieval systems, without written permission from the author, except for the use of brief quotations in a book review.

Cover Art by Deranged Doctor Design.

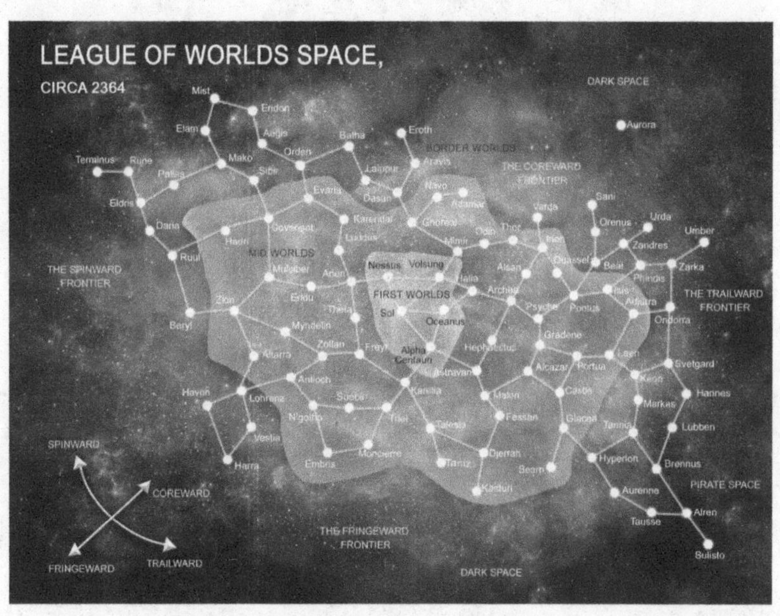

LEAGUE OF WORLDS SPACE,
CIRCA 2364
DARK SPACE
Mist
Eridon
Eroth
Aurora
Etam
Aegis
Batha
Terminus
Rune
Mako
Orden
BORDER WORLDS
Aravis
THE COREWARD
FRONTIER
Palis
Sibi
Laipour
Evaris
Dasan
Navo
Eldris
Adamar
Sani
Daria
Government
Karendal
Ghoreal
Odin
Thot
Varda
Orenus
Urda
Hadri
Liaxus
Mimir
Iriel
Umber
Ruul
MID WORLDS
Muzzber
Arien
Nessus
Volsung
Alsan
Quassel
Zandres
THE SPINWARD
FRONTIER
Halia
Belai
Zarka
Zion
Eridu
FIRST WORLDS
Archae
Isis
Phindis
THE TRAILWARD
FRONTIER
Theta
Sol
Psyche
Pontus
Athura
Beryl
Myndelin
Oceanus
Gradene
Ondora
Zollan
Freyr
Hephaestus
Alcazar
Portus
Laen
Altarra
Alpha
Centauri
Istravan
Svetgard
Havon
Antioch
Karsha
Melon
Castle
Keon
Hannes
Lohranz
Suebi
Fessan
Glaona
Markas
N'golfo
Tikel
Talesia
Tanna
Lubben
Vestia
Taniz
Djerrah
Hyperion
Brennus
Harra
Embris
Moncerre
Beorn
PiRATE SPACE
SPINWARD
Karduri
Aurenne
Alren
COREWARD
Tausse
THE FRINGEWARD
FRONTIER
Sulisto
FRINGEWARD
TRAILWARD
DARK SPACE

1

WHATEVER THE LIGHT REALM WAS, Lucian soon learned there was also darkness.

They followed the Seven-Fold Path deep into the forest, leaving *Blood Wyvern* far behind. The golden sun was lowering through the silvery branches of the trees, the graceful arches of which formed an interconnected living canopy reminiscent of a cathedral. The thick, towering trunks were like pillars, beneath which spread the forest's natural mosaics and heavenly scents— lush, multicolored grasses, babbling brooks, and low shrubs bearing succulent fruits. It was a living temple of paradise, where it seemed around every bend, there was a new wonder to behold.

And through the middle of it all, the Seven-Fold Path forged ahead with its prismatic colors, weaving through majestic trees toward an uncertain end.

It was mostly quiet; Lucian figured everyone was still getting used to their heightened senses. Every whisper of the breeze, every trill of birdsong seemed infused with additional layers that were missing from their own reality. Lucian could only wonder how this place, so far removed from their own, even had parallels to trees and birds. If the Light Realm was anything like the worlds in their own reality, evolution took predetermined paths with slight variations. If that was true, then it would be mostly the same here, and while things might appear fantastical to their eyes, they would also be familiar.

Or, it was often said that the Light Realm was the true reality, of which the Shadow Realm was only a reflection. Perhaps that meant their own reality was only a copy of this one, following the path of what had already come before.

The silence of the forest was finally broken when Serah started humming and then singing.

"Follow the Rainbow Road . . . Follow the Rainbow Road . . . Follow, follow, follow, follow, follow the Rainbow Road . . ."

Fergus scoffed. "What in the *Worlds* are you singing?"

"It's from some old movie I saw," she said. "I thought it was fitting, given the situation. Even if no one but Lucian can actually *see* this road."

"I think I know the movie you're talking about," Mira said. "If it's what I think it is, the similarities are . . . *uncanny*."

"Uncanny?" Fergus said. "Hmph. I suppose . . ."

Lucian remained quiet, scanning the surrounding forest for potential threats. He had multiple defensive wards active, and in theory, those wards would alert him long before anything dangerous came close. But he didn't want to take any chances. They had come too far for that. The last thing they needed was to be taken by surprise.

Similarly quiet was Emma, who seemed to still be taking their new environment in.

"One thing's for sure," Fergus said. "This Light Realm is strange. Not at all what I expected."

"What *did* you expect?" Mira asked.

"Oh, I don't know. Something more ethereal, I guess. Not sure how to describe it. In fact, this world seems more real than our own . . ."

"Well," Emma said, "the Old Masters of the Volsung Academy have always said our reality is the shadow."

Everyone remained silent for a moment as they considered Emma's words.

"I think you're right," Lucian said.

"That begs the question," Serah said. "How many realities are we dealing with here? There's our own, of course, and this one. Are there others? Shadow Realm number two, so to speak."

"Who can say?" Emma asked. "We're dealing with something unprecedented."

They fell into silence as the ethereal path continued to cut its way through the mythic forest, glowing even after the sun had set. Lucian had watched the passage of the sun through the trees and found its rate of setting was about the same as it would be on Earth. They were clearly on a planet of some sort, or perhaps even a moon, given that gravity was noticeably lower than Earth. Given the exertion of the day, he was not only tired but hungry.

For all the differences in this world, some things remained constant.

Serah seemed to be of a similar mind. "What's for dinner?"

"Whatever's in our packs," Lucian said.

"Might be time to set up camp for the night," Fergus said. His eyes became suffused with green Radiant Magic. "I can see a cliff through the trees there. Might make a nice shelter. We can continue on our way tomorrow."

"Sounds like a plan."

Lucian led them away from the Seven-Fold Path, into the gloom of the forest. Away from the Path, the forest foliage wasn't as bright, glowing instead with a dull illumination. By the time they reached the base of the cliff, the trees had ended, replaced by rocky turf intermixed with a sporadic carpet of green lichen. Lucian looked up at the sky to see a multitude of stars in unknown constellations shining down on him, bathing the cliffs in cloudy light. Streams of nebula formed a background against a single world of blue, white, and green. Such was its beauty that Lucian's breath was caught for a moment. It was much too large to be a moon. Which would mean, as he had previously suspected, that the surface they were standing on was a moon to that world.

He forced himself back to the situation at hand, taking in the others who were watching him. "Well, one of our questions has been answered. While our bodies might look different, they still function the same way. We still get hungry, tired, and have our usual limits. It seems there are natural laws similar to our own reality. We're probably on a moon, given the lower gravity and the size of that planet in the sky up there."

Fergus pointed his chin upward. "All that, plus there are worlds other than this one, if those stars are any sign."

"Anything's possible," Lucian admitted. "Let's set up camp and make sure we're warded strongly. If something is coming up on us, I want to know about it."

They set to work doing just that. Fergus created a powerful Radiant ward to block out the light of their fire, while Lucian created a Psionic ward to prevent interference with their dreams. Anlilta had spoken to him, so he didn't want to take any chances with other visitors that might be more nefarious. He also created a Binding ward to repulse anything that got too close. If anything came into contact with that barrier, it would alert Lucian immediately.

They set up in a hollow of the cliff, warming up a quick meal and preparing for their first night in the Light Realm. Lucian checked his slate to see how much time had passed, only to find the device completely defunct. The others' slates were the same. He wasn't sure, but his only guess was that passing through the First Gate fried it somehow.

"One thing I'm wondering," Emma said, after they had eaten. "Why wasn't the First Gate guarded? You'd think being the only way to enter the Light Realm, there might be a guard or two posted at the very least."

"Maybe they didn't know we were coming," Fergus said.

"Should that matter, though?" Serah asked. "Emma's right. The First Gate is probably one of the most important locations in the Light Realm, if not *the* most important. Because it wasn't guarded last time, the Ancient One could steal the Orbs. Seems like a pretty big oversight by these Ascendants."

"You have a point there," Lucian said, "but anything we come up with is just speculation, right? We can ask Anlilta when we meet her. We should get some rest. I'll take the first watch tonight."

"I'll stay up with you, for a bit at least," Mira said. "I want to learn more about my magic."

"Don't stay up too late," Fergus said, already rolling over. "Wake me up when it's my turn to keep watch. Good night, all."

Emma and Serah settled down as well, clearly ready for sleep.

Mira nodded toward a clearing close to the fire. "Come on. We can get an hour of practice in."

Lucian followed his mother, passing the first trees into the small meadow. He created a light sphere above them to give some illumination. As his mother faced him a few steps away, Lucian felt a moment of vertigo as he looked at her face. It was beyond strange to see her roughly the same age as him, as she would have appeared when he was still a young child. He was struck by how alike they were in appearance, with the same narrow face, dark brown eyes, and brown hair. They might have been siblings.

And now he was in the strange position of having to teach her how to use magic. Somehow the act of her entering the Light Realm had given her a Focus. Or had she had one all along, and the Light Realm had merely awakened it?

"Ready?" he asked.

Mira nodded. "Ready."

"To begin," he said, "close your eyes and tell me what you see."

She did so without question. "I see seven lights."

Lucian watched her, surprised. "Really? Just like that?"

She nodded. "Yeah. That's what it's *supposed* to look like, right?"

"Usually, it takes months of meditation to sense your Focus for the first time. But it seems you can do it right away."

"It's there all right."

"Maybe it has something to do with us being in the Light Realm. Magic might be more easily accessible here."

"Or maybe I'm just a natural."

Lucian chuckled. "Maybe so. Now, do you notice anything about the lights? Describe them."

"They are bright, but one is brighter than the rest."

"Which one?"

"The red one."

"That's what I thought." Lucian remembered she had already produced a flame in her hand upon first entering the Light Realm. That she could stream with no prior instruction was already remarkable.

"Let's begin there, then," Lucian said. "Can you sense the ether within your Focus?"

"I can sense power. Potential."

"That's ether. It's the substance that powers all magic. You can't see it, but you can feel it and stream it. Here in the Light Realm, it is thick. Always present, always available. In the Shadow Realm, it's spread much more thinly. To use magic, all you need to do is reach for your Focus—those lights—and push through the red one to create a flame."

"That's not how I did it last time."

"What did you do, then?"

Mira opened her eyes, holding out her hand from which red flames leaped to life. "I just imagined it, like I'm doing now."

Lucian's eyes widened. Sorcery, then. It didn't require following any rules, merely imagining what one wanted. That she could do that without even *thinking* about it . . .

"It takes years of training to even approach what you're doing," Lucian said, somewhat in disbelief. "And even then, not everyone can do it."

Was it the Light Realm, or was it her?

The flame in her hand sputtered out. "What happens if I reach for the other lights?"

She threw out her hand, and instantly, a bolt of lightning materialized and forked its way in his direction. Lucian shielded himself just in time.

Mira gasped. "Lucian! I'm so sorry. Are you okay?"

"I'm fine," he said, cracking a smile. "Strong in Dynamism, too. That would be a tertiary Aspect for you, so that's surprising as well."

"What does that mean?"

"That means you're strong. Uncommonly strong."

Either that, or the thickness of ether in the Light Realm simply made *everyone* that much stronger.

"What about the orange light?" she asked. "Should I try it?"

"That's Atomicism. You don't want to touch that unless you want to cause a nuclear explosion."

She shuddered. "Never mind, then."

"Stick with Thermalism for now," Lucian said. "It's the magic of thermal energy. Heat and cold. It's what you're strongest with, and once you've gotten good with it, you can branch out to other Aspects."

"Sounds good. Exciting stuff, huh?"

Exciting, but also scary. Lucian and the others had yet to stream in this place. If Mira was this strong with magic, how much more so for him and the others? It needed testing.

For the next hour, Lucian gave her a crash course on basic Manifoldic Theory, much like he had learned at the Volsung

Academy long ago. But he wondered if there was any point to the lesson. If she could simply think of magic and make it reality, using sorcery from the start, she might not even need to understand these basic principles. In fact, they might only serve as a hindrance.

He stopped himself and instead thought back to Lakhmu's lessons, and even Vera's original instruction. Deep down, he knew their lessons were far more important than what he had learned at the Academy. Streaming from a place of soul's truth, imagining what you willed, and willing what you imagined, was the heart of magic itself.

If Mira began her journey without limits, nothing would stand in the way of her development.

She had a unique opportunity to start as a blank slate. The Volsung Academy's curriculum would only hold her back, as it was developed in consideration of two concerns at cross purposes: developing one's abilities to the fullest extent, but never at the cost of risking the fraying. This resulted in mages who were always held back from their full potential. Stunted.

But the fraying wasn't a threat anymore, so there should be no holds barred in his mother's instruction.

So, with this in mind, Lucian taught her as he saw fit, using Psionics to understand her thoughts and correct the flaws in her thinking. With Psionics, speaking became unnecessary. He simply had to share his knowledge with her, much as Themba had done aboard the *Tempus*. Everything he knew, he transferred as a single stream of thought.

The originally prescribed hour passed quickly, and by the time a few more had gone by, Mira had learned more than the typical mage could learn in a year, if not more.

She blinked, completely bewildered. Lucian had pushed her far, to where she was bordering on being overwhelmed. But because of his Psionic Magic, he knew her limits as well as he knew his own.

"That's enough for now," he said. "Just a few more hours of practice, and you'll be as good as the rest of us."

"Will it be that simple?"

"Maybe. Your progress has been amazing so far. We got to every Aspect, and you're already learning how to combine them. That's advanced stuff."

"Guess I really am a natural. I was just joking before."

"Well, it's no joke. You're strong." He nodded back toward the camp. "Let's get some rest. Big day tomorrow."

Mira nodded numbly, heading to their shared campfire with the others. She closed her eyes and was instantly asleep.

Lucian stood watch, even though he knew his wards would make it unnecessary. He needed some time to think, to take in this new world. A cool wind blew, carrying with it a sweet fragrance he recognized to be one of the silver fruits he'd seen growing in the trees. He climbed a stand of nearby rocks, looking into the starry sky, watching the stars wheel as the hours passed. With Radiance, he peered at the orbiting planet above, sharpened his senses until he could pierce the atmosphere and distance. He saw lights on the surface. Cities, then. Was that where the Seven-Fold Path was leading them?

Looking at the stars, he realized any of them could hold the Heart of Creation. The thought stilled him with its enormity. He felt overwhelmed in a way he had never experienced, even when traveling through time. At least with time, they were still dealing with a universe based on rules they were familiar with.

Here, the rules were different. And anything different was dangerous.

How could he protect himself, or the others, if he didn't even know what to protect them *from*? Certainly, he knew this place still had agents of the Ancient One. Anlilta had warned him of that in her vision. Though the Ancient One's form had been vanquished back in the Shadow Realm, he still abided somewhere in the Heart of Creation. And as long as the Orb of

Shadows existed, he might be resurrected if anyone ever embraced its power.

According to Anlilta, the Ancient One's agents would leap at the opportunity to wield it, to become the reincarnation of their master.

There was only one thing Lucian knew to do. He had to return the Orbs to where they belonged. And he had to protect them every step of the way.

Of course, this raised questions about his own reality. Would returning the Orbs cut it off from magic entirely, causing the Gates to stop working? Was there a way to guarantee the Shadow Realm's safety?

There was only one person who might have an answer. In the City of Anshar, Anlilta was waiting. And not only her, but other Ascendants, including Enkius, the original holder of the Orb of Creation. According to the Time Weaver, the Orb of Creation had been sent into the Shadow Realm hoping Lucian would use it to vanquish the Ancient One there.

Now that Lucian had done just that, what did Enkius plan for him and the Orb? Did he even know they had arrived, or was Anlilta the only one? Would he want the Orb of Creation back? Perhaps even *all* the Orbs?

He was deep in thought when he felt a touch on his shoulder and turned to see Fergus. "Lucian, get some sleep."

Lucian nodded and went to the fire. Such questions would have to wait.

2

GOLDEN BEAMS of light broke through the canopy of the forest, falling on Lucian's eyes. He blinked awake to find the fire low and the others still resting, with Fergus keeping vigil atop some rocks. Fergus turned, noticed his movement, and took a sip of coffee from his cup. He'd likely gotten that from his mother's pack. She carried the stuff practically everywhere, including, it seemed, the Light Realm.

Lucian filled his own cup and joined him. The morning stew was already steaming over the coals, filling the forest with a tantalizing aroma. The same bird-like, butterfly-like creatures he'd noticed the previous day fluttered in the sunbeams in vortices of blue and silver. He and Fergus watched, marveling as the forest came to life, all the surfaces bedewed and glittering under the growing sunlight.

"Nothing to report," Fergus said quietly, taking another sip.

Mira stirred at his voice, and with her movement, Emma and Serah roused.

Serah was the first of the women to blink awake, putting a hand to her head. "Why do I feel so hungover?"

"Have some coffee," Fergus said. "I made it extra strong."

"I wonder what coffee tastes like here," Serah said. "Maybe it's stronger by default." She stood and filled her cup with it, steam curling over the rim. She gave a mock toast. "To the Shadow Realm's finest!" She took a sip and looked as if she wanted to spit it out. "Wow, you weren't kidding. Tastes like gloombat venom."

"How would you know what that tastes like?" Fergus asked.

Serah gave a mock sigh of exasperation. "A regrettable excess of curiosity."

Emma stood and went through a few stretches, seeming to wake up rather quickly. "I don't see why anyone needs coffee here. This air is so fresh, it's like you're breathing in pure energy!"

"Ugh, *morning* people," Serah said with a shudder.

They ate quickly and packed everything with trained efficiency. They continued on their way, Lucian leading the way. Or rather, the Seven-Fold Path, leading the way.

Since the Path itself moved in relation to Lucian, they found many obstacles in their way, the first of which was the cliff they had camped under.

Lucian tethered everyone to the top, only to find more forest along the path.

"These trees are never-ending," Serah said.

"Let me scope things out," Lucian said. "There might be a faster way."

Lucian surrounded himself in a Gravitonic aura, floating off the ground toward the highest tree in sight. Once at the top, he scanned the surrounding forest, finding that it stretched to every horizon. He peered in the direction from which they had come, finding a line of high white-capped mountains in the distance. In the direction they were traveling, the land sloped downward among gentle hills before the rainbow path was lost to the horizon. Nowhere in the forest was a sign of the First Gate.

He lowered himself back through the trees, finding the others waiting for him. "A long way to go."

"Better get moving, then," Fergus said.

They walked through morning and into the afternoon with no change of scenery. As Lucian had suspected, he was getting used to the vibrant sensations of the Light Realm and didn't really notice them unless he forced himself to pay attention.

Afternoon quickly gave way to early evening. They began scanning their surroundings for a place to set up camp when one of Lucian's wards prickled.

He came to a sudden stop. "Something's nearby."

"I feel it, too," Fergus said. "A mage."

That was when Lucian detected movement to the right of the path, where a herd of creatures similar to deer materialized from the enchanted forest, slender and graceful. It was hard to tell just how many, but there were at least a few dozen of them, their translucent antlers refracting the forest's ethereal light, casting prismatic rainbows in every direction. Their silky coats shifted colors to blend with the forest's background as they moved, a kaleidoscope of silver and green. When any of them came to a pause, they almost seamlessly blended into the background, becoming one with the forest. Had they remained utterly still, and if Lucian hadn't had the benefit of his ward, he would not have seen them until it was too late. Though they looked like deer, he didn't make the mistake of thinking they were gentle.

Anything could be a threat here.

As the ethereal creatures crossed the Seven-Fold Path, their coats did not shift colors to match it, telling Lucian that they couldn't sense its presence either. The largest of the creatures paused, turning its gaze toward them. Four other "deer" also paused as the rest of the herd scurried on. It seemed these were guarding the retreat of the others. The largest of the creatures leered with bright red eyes, and Lucian could see rippled muscle bulging beneath its coat, making it seem more like a bull than a deer.

Most of these creatures, Lucian realized, had the mark of

magic on them, and the feeling was coming strongest from the buck.

As soon as he registered this, he felt a push against his mind. Lucian easily rebuffed the Psionic probe, strengthening his shield to be on the safe side.

"The big one's using magic," he said to the others. "It's testing my strength."

"Seriously?" Serah asked. "That would mean . . ."

"They're sentient," Emma said, her voice filled with wonder. "Only sentient creatures can use magic in our reality. It's probably the same here."

"Should we fight back?" Fergus asked, reaching for his spear.

"No," Lucian said, waving away Fergus's action. "They're trying to figure us out. Let me try talking first."

Lucian allowed a small hole in the ward, just enough to accept any communication. There was an instant connection.

Leave this forest or perish, Shadow Being. Go back to the Shadow Lands from whence you came.

The words that entered Lucian's mind were not exactly his own language, but he understood the intentions and layers the speaker meant to convey all too well. He simply watched, creating a counter-Psionic stream to better read the creature addressing him. It was elementary to sneak past its defenses; though the buck was more powerful than most mages Lucian had encountered, the deer was nothing compared to his abilities. The creature didn't detect the intrusion.

He sensed a wariness, a readiness to attack at the slightest provocation. Indeed, Lucian knew the creature would have attacked already if not for its curiosity. They saw this part of the forest as theirs, and the humans as intruders and the enemy.

He worked to decipher the original message. At first, Lucian figured "Shadow Being" meant the deer knew they weren't from the Light Realm, but by sifting the creature's thoughts, Lucian discovered this wasn't the case. Apparently, close to this very forest, was another place called the "Shadow Lands," which directly opposed this herd. The buck seemed to think Lucian and his friends were spies from this land, and as such, were agents of the Ancient One.

He also gained a sense of the name for what the deer called themselves: prismharts.

The trick, then, was convincing these prismharts that Lucian and his allies were no threat and on the same side.

The prismhart repeated his warning. *I'm warning you! Leave this place or perish, Shadow Being.*

The voice was more insistent, and Lucian knew if he failed to give a satisfactory answer, it would come to blows.

We apologize for intruding on your land, Lucian finally said. *We're strangers here.* He also opened his communication to his friends, and any other prismharts who could listen. *We're just passing through and won't cause any trouble.*

The prismharts were utterly still, and Lucian got the sense that his answer was unsatisfactory.

At last, the lead prismhart answered, stamping his front hooves in agitation. *I find your story unlikely; these woods are sacred, and we have been charged to defend it to the last of our herd. On the Eye of Kadur, there are many enemies of the Light, and not all are obvious.*

Lucian remained silent. He wasn't sure what "The Eye of Kadur" was, but by once again sifting the prismhart's thoughts, he learned it was the name of the world they were on, and he also gleaned that it was, indeed, a moon. Why it was called "the Eye of Kadur," Lucian couldn't guess. He didn't want to risk delving too deeply into the creature's mind, which would make his presence known.

The only thing he could be sure of was that this creature wouldn't try to kill them, at least not immediately. Its curiosity was piqued, and as long as it remained curious, there would be no violence.

Whatever the case, it didn't seem to think they were from the Shadow Lands anymore, but the point still stood that Lucian was a puzzle to be figured out.

And until he was figured out, he was a threat.

Where did you come from? How did you elude our wards? Speak!

We didn't pass through any wards, Lucian said. *I can't tell you anything more and you'll have to be content with that.*

Another prismhart behind the leader stomped its hooves. Lucian intercepted its Psionic communication to its leader, which it had intended to keep private. *They must be scouts of a larger force from the Shadow Lands. They must have breached the Barrier! What manner of creature are they, Father? I've not seen their like in all the Aetheria! They don't seem like the Sumaril, so perhaps they are a concoction of Ashurban the Maleficent!*

The lead prismhart bristled at this; Lucian detected he was miffed at the interruption, and that the second speaker was a young buck who had yet to learn the ways of the herd.

We aren't from these Shadow Lands you're talking about, Lucian said. *In fact, I don't even know what that is. We're strangers to the Light Realm. Just yesterday, we passed through the First Gate from the Shadow Realm. Maybe that's why we haven't triggered your wards.*

A long, profound silence stretched between them as the lead prismhart took this information in and processed it, all the while realizing that Lucian had interpreted the secret message. The leader was becoming more difficult to read, due to him streaming more Psionic Magic. Lucian withdrew his own magic before the prismhart could catch wind of it. It was better to be safe in this instance than sorry. If the herd ever became a threat, Lucian could instantly change tactics.

The First Gate is near, then?

Yes, Lucian confirmed. *A day's walk away.*

Unbelievable, the young buck scoffed, no longer bothering to hide his thoughts. *The First Gate has not been sighted on this world for centuries!*

Off with you, the elder prismhart said. *Now!*

The young buck let out a low growl before bounding off into the forest, where the other prismharts had hidden themselves.

The large stag turned back to Lucian. *We prismharts are the guardians of these woods, tasked by the Ascendants themselves with a holy purpose. To keep agents of the Shadow from treading in what little remains of the Light on this world. Perhaps you don't come from the Shadow Lands, but that is hardly the only place the Shadow can be found. Also, I can sense the stain of Shadow Magic upon you, though you think you have hidden it well.*

Lucian didn't need to ask for details. He was all too aware of the Orb of Shadows in his pack. Despite the Binding brand surrounding it, the scope of its power could not be easily contained. He became convinced, more than ever, that things would soon come to a fight.

If these beings were allied with the Ascendants, could Lucian risk engaging them? Even if he won, it could be a liability down the road. Nor could he reveal Anlilta's words to him. If it ever came out that the Chosen of the Manifold was here in the Light Realm, many agents of the Ancient One would fall upon him in droves, all trying to get his Orbs. But there was also another consideration. While the prismharts claimed to serve the Ascendants, Lucian couldn't trust them to be telling the truth.

And yet, the rainbow road led forward through the trees, past the area the prismharts were defending. There was no choice but to go forward, whatever the consequences. Lucian knew nothing about the Light Realm. All he knew was that he had to keep following the Seven-Fold Path.

Lucian needed to buy some more time. *I'm not an agent of the Shadow. Far from it.*

Do you really believe we're so ignorant? I've never felt the stain of the Shadow more strongly than I do from you, stranger.

Not ignorant. There are just . . . certain things you don't know yet. Lucian realized, after a moment, that this was the very definition of ignorance, and the words would likely be interpreted as offensive. *If there was some way to convince you, I would. I'm afraid I can't say anything else. I don't want to fight, but I will if it comes to that.*

The prismhart said nothing to this for a long time, seeming to consider and weigh Lucian's words. At last, it broke its silence. *I must admit, this situation is strange. Perhaps you are not agents of the Shadow, but that doesn't mean you are a friend to the Light. As such, I cannot allow you to cross this forest.*

We have to go forward. We have no choice.

You will get no better offer than this. Leave. I will not ask again.

Serah's voice entered his mind. *Nope. Don't like that . . .*

Alternatives? Fergus asked.

I don't want to fight them, Emma said. *They're beautiful.*

Remember what Anlilta said, Fergus reminded her. *Many beautiful things here are dangerous.* He turned to Lucian. *What are you thinking?*

If they choose to fight us, that's on them. We have one goal: to follow the Seven-Fold Path. There's no other option.

There's got to be a peaceful way to resolve this, Mira said.

Must there be? Fergus asked. *Sometimes, the only way out is through.*

The stag's red eyes glowered at Lucian. *What will it be, stranger?*

Lucian regarded the prismhart before him. *Whether through you or around you, I will find my way to Anshar. As far as I can tell, through you is faster.*

The prismhart reared and slammed its two front hooves in front of him, where a kinetic wave blasted forward, which Lucian quickly blocked.

We need not risk the lives of everyone here, the prismhart said. *How about a duel, just you and me?*

Lucian held out his hand, where Lightspear manifested, shining with golden brilliance in the forest, almost to where it was blinding. The prismharts shirked back at its light, and even the leader took an unsure step back.

You wield the Magic of Creation, it said simply. *Are you an Acolyte of Enkius the Golden?*

Lucian ignored the question. *Last chance. Let us pass.*

The prismhart snarled, its sharpened teeth a strange juxtaposition with its deer-like body. His fellows backed away while Lucian motioned his own companions to do the same.

Now, things are making sense, the prismhart said, *but I would test your strength to be sure. You might yet be an agent of the Shadow, conjuring a clever trick with that spear of yours. I look forward to uncovering the truth, whether I, the Eldarhart of the Prismwood, will be the first to welcome the Chosen of the Manifold to the Light Realm!*

3

BEFORE LUCIAN COULD SAY anything more, the prismhart shot forward with a roar that belonged to a lion rather than a deer, preceded by a wave of pure Psionic energy. Lucian shielded against the attack and leaped high, aided by Gravitonic Magic.

The prismhart whirled around and charged, giving a running leap while wrapping itself in Gravitonic Magic, flying after Lucian to meet him in midair. Lucian threw Lightspear, using Binding Magic to ensure it hit. But the prismhart phased forward, striking Lucian directly on his Binding shield and sending him hurtling back toward a tree.

The prismhart had access to Space-Time Magic, then. It wasn't something Lucian had expected, but now he knew to be prepared for it.

Two could play that game. Lucian warped behind the prismhart, recreating Lightspear in his hand while the beast wheeled around to face him, green orbs of energy collecting on its antlers. Lucian changed tactics, spouting a column of fire, interrupting the prismhart's attack. The creature dispelled its Gravitonic aura, dropping several meters while several green

20

lasers shot from its antlers. The attacks reflected off Lucian's shield.

As they fought in the treetops, Lucian had no trouble holding his own against the beast. He wanted the prismhart to back off and recognize the folly of fighting him, but after a few minutes, the creature didn't seem to slow. It drew ragged breaths, trying many magical and physical attacks to best him. Lucian merely dodged and pushed back to prove his superiority, but the prismhart never relented. Lucian had to admire its gumption.

At last, he decided a harsher lesson was in order. He drew a deep infusion of ether, channeling all of it into a Binding lattice that surrounded the prismhart. A cocoon of writhing blue energy locked his adversary in place, and Lucian just added to the prison's strength, making it all but impossible to escape. With a single thought, he could lace the cocoon with Psionic Magic, shattering the beast into its constituent elements.

Lucian lowered himself to the ground, continuing to draw ether to block the beast's Focus with Psionic Magic. He only allowed a small sliver of magic to escape, enough for the prismhart to communicate and hopefully surrender.

You would not best me, the Eldarhart said, *but utterly humiliate me!*

Will you let us pass now?

You are prophesied by the Speaker Anlilta! Has she thus summoned you to Anshar?

Yes, Lucian said, deciding to trust him.

You must forgive me, but I had to be sure of your strength. When I saw Lightspear, I thought it might be a trick of my eyes. Others know of Anlilta's prophecy, after all, who belong to the Shadow, and it might have been a trick of Radiant Magic. I don't know why I sense the power of the Shadow upon you; that part makes little sense. But I cannot ignore these signs. If you are not the Chosen, none are.

It's a long story about the Shadow Magic, Lucian said. *But I'm not on the Ancient One's side.*

I believe you, the prismhart went on. *We will do all that we can to speed you through these woods. There is great danger here, danger that might undo even the Chosen if he were caught unawares. You have my word that while under my care, no harm will befall you. But of course, you must free me first.*

With his Psionic Magic dominating the prismhart's mind, he knew the creature wasn't lying. First, he undid the Binding lattice. The prismhart pranced free, giving a graceful shake.

Lucian headed toward the others, who watched him with wide eyes. "The prismhart knows who I am. He says we can pass, but he'll need to help us through the woods."

"Seriously?" Serah asked. "All that kerfuffle just to get a tour guide?"

Before anyone could respond, the clomp of hooves announced four more prismharts, including the young buck the elder prismhart had just reprimanded. One creature went to each person, standing a few paces away.

These are the fastest in our herd, the Eldarhart said. *They will bear you and your squires with the utmost speed.*

My friends, Lucian corrected. *How far is Anshar from here?*

Lucian felt something like humor emanating from the prismhart's mind. *Anshar is many worlds away, on a planet called Eänna. Many call it the World of Light. I'm afraid we will not be going so far. Our purview ends at the edge of the Prismwood. We can take you no farther, but without guidance, I fear you'll never make it to the end of these woods alive. It has a way of confusing strangers and leading them down dark paths.*

The prismharts probably didn't realize that Lucian had access to the Seven-Fold Path, which would eventually lead them out of these woods. But riding on the prismharts would certainly make things go a lot faster.

What's the name of the world we're on now? You said something about the Eye of Kadur.

Yes, that is its name. Usually, it is simply called the Eye. Aside from one small part in which you find yourselves, it is in the clutches of the Shadow.

Lucian pondered this. *So, to get to Anshar, we need to travel to this Eänna, which is an entirely different planet. Any idea how we can do that?*

You would need a ship, and a fast one. But getting one powerful enough to travel the Gates is easier said than done. You might try the Kingdom of Ninshar. A powerful Ascendant of the same name rules from there. Or at least, he did last I heard. He is the Steward of the Eye, appointed by Enkius the Golden himself, though I have not traveled there in many years, when times were better. Ninshar's palace rises high from the largest island above the Crystalline Sea. We can convey you as far as the shoreline, where the Prismwood ends. Perhaps Ninshar can help you where I cannot.

We are in your debt, Eldarhart, Lucian said, intrinsically knowing this was the right thing to say.

The Eldarhart then kneeled nobly, allowing Lucian access to its back, along with all the other prismharts to Lucian's companions. The fact they were being afforded this honor spoke of the prismharts' belief in Anlilta's prophecy, and his respect for Lucian's role. Lucian knew he could consider them allies, at least for now.

Without hesitation, Lucian climbed onto the Eldarhart's back, boosting himself with Gravitonics. He nodded at the others to do the same for their own steeds.

"I guess we're doing this," Serah said.

She mounted a dappled doe with small antlers next to his, who Lucian knew to be the Eldarhart's mate. Fergus mounted a large beast, the same young buck the Eldarhart had chided earlier. Mira mounted a stag with large and reflective antlers, while Emma sat upon a sleek doe that had the look of speed about her.

Once all were settled in, the prismharts turned to face the direction the Seven-Fold Path was leading them. Lucian knew they couldn't sense the Path like him, but by sheer coincidence, they were pointing the same direction. At least now they had a lead in this Ninshar, and if he was an Ascendant, then he would definitely know something about Anlilta and how to get to Anshar.

Without warning, the prismharts shot forward, far faster than even a horse could gallop. And yet, their gait was so smooth that Lucian hardly felt the ground moving beneath them. The air rushed past his face as the trees streamed by in an ethereally glowing blur, almost like a crystal tunnel. It seemed as if they even ran right through trees, but they were going so fast that it was hard to tell exactly what was going on.

When Lucian reached out to sense the magic the harts were using, he was surprised to detect the streaming of both the Dynamistic and Space-Time Aspects. The creatures were creating warp bubbles while phasing through trees as needed. Such was their speed that Lucian knew all it took was one mistake, one miscalculation, to spell disaster, but such was the prismharts' knowledge of their own woods, down to the smallest tree and blade of grass, that they could fly at this speed without fear.

Lucian found it easy to remain seated; there was hardly even a jostle as they sped through the forest. His mother was the only one he was worried about, but she seemed to do just fine holding tight to the neck of the stag beneath her, even if her eyes were wide and afraid. Lucian streamed a calming ward designed to ease everyone's nerves, and within seconds, it took effect. Mira's eyes transformed from fear into wide-eyed wonder.

They hadn't been traveling for more than an hour when the woods came to a sudden end. Somehow, Lucian knew that as many as a thousand kilometers had passed in that time, what would have taken weeks to travel on foot. Their mounts came to a pause before a tall cliff overlooking a silvery sea beneath a golden-hued sky, in which several bright stars were visible. The sea stretched all the way to the horizon, with several ethereally glowing islands rising above the distant waves. To Lucian's surprise, many of those islands seemed to float high above, glowing subtly with silvery Gravitonic Magic. He counted a dozen of these larger floating islands, along with some smaller ones interspersed between them.

There lies the Kingdom of Ninshar, the Eldarhart said solemnly. *This is where we leave you.*

Lucian floated off the Eldarhart's back and landed in front of him, just steps away from the cliff. The others came to stand beside him, leaving their own mounts behind.

Thank you, Lucian said. *You've saved us a lot of time.*

Make all speed to Anshar and my master. Tread carefully, Chosen. Though we are firmly in the Light Lands, the Light is weak on this world. Agents of the Shadow are everywhere, and even this far into the core of the Light Lands, the Barrier is never far.

I assume the Barrier is some sort of border?

Yes, the Eldarhart said. *And it advances upon the Light Lands more with each passing year. But if you fulfill the promise of Anlilta's prophecy, then there is hope that this won't be the case for long. Farewell, Chosen. May the Manifold guide your steps . . . to the very end.*

The Eldarhart gave a noble bow, inclining his neck low, and the others followed suit. As soon as this was done, they turned as a single unit and within seconds, were blazing across the hills and back toward the line of forest from which they had come. In the space of an eye blink, they had vanished, leaving the humans standing alone on the cliff with the golden sun setting behind them.

"Wow," Serah said. "*That* was crazy."

"It's like we're in a fantasy land," Emma said. "Yet it's more real than anything I've ever experienced."

"Dangerous, too," Fergus said, straightening his pack. "It's late. We should try to find a spot to camp before tackling these islands tomorrow."

"There's probably something down near the beach," Mira said. "Where there are cliffs, there is probably shelter, too."

"Sounds good to me," Lucian said. "We're doing well so far. Hopefully, we can find this Ninshar and figure out the next step."

He led the way down the incline, toward the cliffs and the silvery water.

4

LUCIAN LED the group down to the shoreline, using a combination of hiking and Binding tethers. After about an hour, they stood on a shore made from white, shining crystals, which glowed subtly in the fading evening light. The waves gently lapped the beach as the sun set over the water. More stars appeared in the sky above, and the Seven-Fold Path stretched and disappeared over the indigo blue horizon. Wherever they had arrived, it was the end of the line, at least as far as this landmass was concerned.

They found shelter in a small cave on the cliff, creating a fire and setting their wards. As they ate dinner, they discussed the events of the day and theories about their new environment.

"It's clear in the Light Realm, magic has always been around," Fergus said, taking a bite of his stew. "Emma is right. It's Fantasy Land."

"There are Gates here, too," Lucian said. "The Eldarhart said we'd need a ship to get through them."

"So, there are spaceships," Serah said. "We have that much in common, at least."

"Whatever the case, it doesn't look like there are many people on this world," Emma said. "So far, the prismharts are the only thing we've met. If there *are* spaceships, we have yet to see one."

"Plus, everyone living here has never seen a human before," Mira said. "Remember the Eldarhart's kid mentioning the Sumaril? I think that's what he called them."

"Yeah," Serah said. "Sounds like they could be another species of some sort. We'll probably know what one is when we find one."

"Not much we can do but keep our eyes and ears open," Lucian said. "Ninshar is our lead. From him, we can figure out more."

"What about language?" Fergus asked. "I could understand everything the Eldarhart was saying, but that was because of your Psionic ward, Lucian. Will you keep that ward active all the time?"

"For now, that's what I'll do. It's not much effort for me. But when I've had time to learn the language, I can teach it Psionically, just like Themba did—only it'll be faster and easier."

"I hope so," Fergus said. "Anyway, tomorrow's plan. I say we wake up at the crack of dawn and head up to the biggest island, the one that's floating over the horizon. The Eldarhart mentioned Ninshar's palace would be there. If nothing else, it'll give us a good vantage point."

"And what do we do if we run into any locals?" Mira asked. "Try to blend it? Hard to see how that might work."

Lucian was about to respond when he felt a psychic disturbance from one of his proximity wards. His body stiffened, an action not missed by the others. The disruption was coming from the direction of the beach.

"Everything okay?" Serah asked.

"Something just set off one of my wards."

"Let's check it out," Emma said.

"Ward Space-Time," Lucian said. "If it's anything like the

prismharts, they can use it." He looked at the rest. "Between you three, cover the rest of the Aspects."

"Got it," Fergus said. "After you."

Lucian ducked out of the cave, streaming an invisibility shield over everyone using Radiance. The beach below was well lit by the panorama of stars above, while the glow from the floating islands lent additional luminescence. However, even considering his enhanced vision, Lucian could see nothing in the direction his proximity ward had triggered.

Anything? Emma asked Psionically.

Not yet. Stay alert.

Once they reached the shoreline, Lucian scanned the beach for any potential threats. He stood just a few meters away from the spot where his ward had triggered. There was nothing.

"Must've just been an animal or—"

Lucian felt a force slam against his shield, breaking it and throwing him backward. As soon as he righted himself with magic, an entity loomed before them. Something Lucian could only describe as a shadow with baleful red eyes reminiscent of coals.

Lucian summoned Lightspear just as a column of fire intermixed with lightning shot from the shadow. Mira came to her son's defense, throwing up a hasty shield, which was snuffed out in a shower of cinders and sparks. Emma created a light sphere and began feeding it with ether; Lucian recognized the stream, the same one she'd used on Nai Elyn to attack the swamp monsters. Within half a minute, it would start raining death from above, but until then, he needed to watch her back.

The shadow creature immediately eddied toward Emma, producing a sphere of pure darkness that could only be Shadow Magic. Lucian countered with a wave of golden light, wrapping it around the being and trapping it in place. The entity threw itself at the shield, barely breaking free with a pained shriek.

Emma's Radiant stream, now sufficiently powered, began

raining light arrows from above, blasting the strange creature to little effect. Lucian now knew the only thing that would kill it was Creation Magic.

While the others threw magical attacks at the shadow monster, Lucian surrounded himself with a golden shield, shooting forward with Lightspear extended. The shadow melted into the surrounding air, shirking his advance.

It appeared behind Emma. She seemed to move in slow motion, her Space-Time ward buckling under the shadow's malevolent presence.

Lucian reached out with the Space-Time Aspect, warping her away just in time to his side, where she would be covered by his shield.

"It's slowing time," she said, her eyes wide. "I can hardly contain it!"

"Forget about the light arrows!" Lucian shouted. "Shield Space-Time with everything you've got."

The others continued taking magical potshots at the shadow: fireballs, ice spears, forks of lightning. The attacks were powerful in their own right, but Lucian knew they would serve as nothing more than a distraction. This shadow seemed to be a more powerful version of the ones that had attacked them on Nessus. Nothing but Creation Magic would stop it, but that was difficult to do when it could slow time long enough to warp to a new location.

Lucian warped behind it, strengthening his Creation shield while shooting forward again. Lucian stabbed Lightspear, warping the space between him and the monster to bridge the gap.

It was a move the shadow hadn't counted on. It shrieked in dismay, its form wrapping around Lightspear like a boa. The endeavor was pointless; Lightspear was newly forged with the strength of ten million years of Creation Magic. It would take millions of such creatures, if not more, to extinguish its light.

The shadow contracted and became split by golden beams. Lucian's arm shook with the effort, but he held firm, not buckling before the onslaught. At last, the light was all-consuming, and not even the smallest trace of deep shadow remained.

The beach was quiet, and the sudden darkness made motes swim before Lucian's eyes. The only sounds were the waves and the rush of wind. The monster had been vanquished, and everyone was safe.

Lucian reset his original proximity ward. Where there was one of these things, there could be more. He set a ward of Creation Magic, which would hopefully be enough to deter other such creatures. Emma, likewise, set a Space-Time ward, which would prevent anything from warping too close.

Such powerful defenses couldn't be masked by Radiant Magic, but to Lucian's mind, they had no choice. Even with a powerful Radiant ward, the creature had found them, likely drawn by the power of the Orb of Shadows. Might as well do what they could to repel anything similar.

Serah, Fergus, and Mira joined him and Emma. "What the hell was that?"

The others looked to Lucian for an explanation, as if he knew. He shook his head. "Looks similar to those shadows on Nessus," he said. "But this one . . . this one was worse."

"It reminds me of the Ancient One . . ." Serah said. "It's not him, is it?"

"No. Something *like* him, maybe. A less powerful version. My guess is it's one of his minions."

"And it was just . . . wandering on the beach?" Fergus asked. "Seems too much of a coincidence."

Lucian had to agree. Already, a theory was forming in his mind. "Remember what Anlilta said? The Ancient One still has a lot of followers here. If any of those followers grab the Orb of Shadows, they can unleash the Ancient One again. That thing could probably feel the Orb of Shadows."

"As in, it was attracted to it?" Emma asked.

"That's what I'm thinking."

Serah's eyes widened. "That would mean anyone with Shadow Magic can detect you!"

"Yes. Probably so. Luckily, I have Creation Magic, but yeah . . . the situation is dangerous."

"What can we do to prevent that?" Emma asked.

"Realistically, probably nothing. If I'm right, then the Orb of Shadows is like a beacon. Too powerful to be contained. Maybe my Creation ward will keep the weaker stuff away, but it's not ideal. Like Serah said, it's likely that anything that serves the Ancient One can feel its power if they're strong enough, like that thing was. They will be drawn to it. I had the thought earlier in the forest, but this seems to confirm it."

"There could be more of them," Serah said.

"Could be?" Mira said. "There probably are. Lucian . . ."

"We just have to be careful. As dangerous as this one was, there is probably far worse here. Anlilta hinted some Ascendants are secretly on the Ancient One's side. That means they'll have access to Shadow Magic. Meaning they can sense the Orb, too."

"And it's just in your pack right now," Emma said in disbelief. "With nothing more than a simple Binding brand to keep it from touching anything."

"That about sums it up. Although, I'd have to be taken out before any of them could access it. My brand is strong."

"They'd have to get through us, too," Serah said.

"One thing's for sure," Fergus said. "We need to get to Anshar quickly. I'm assuming it's probably safer than this place. Hopefully, we won't have to deal with one of these attacks again, but like Lucian said, we need to stay alert. We were lucky it didn't happen when we first arrived."

"It probably takes time for one of these creatures to track us down," Lucian said. "One found us, so it's only a matter of time before others do as well."

"What now?" Serah asked. "Are we just supposed to sleep as if everything's normal?"

"No choice there," Emma said. "We've done everything we can. All the essential wards are up."

"Hopefully, this is something we won't have to worry about too much longer," Lucian added. "The next step is to find this Ninshar. Get some information, and hopefully a ship. That's all I've got."

"And what if this Ninshar isn't to be trusted?" Fergus asked.

"What other choice do we have?"

At the others' silence, Lucian realized they didn't know either.

"Let's get some sleep," he said. "We'll head out to the islands tomorrow."

5

LUCIAN SLEPT UNEASILY, but thankfully, nothing disturbed their wards through the night. When morning dawned, they ate a quick breakfast and headed for the empty beach, back to the site where the shadow monster had attacked. Aside from some bits of chipped rock and crystal from some of the larger formations, there was no sign of any trouble. Lucian hoped it stayed that way.

He opened his pack and reached in to find the Orb of Shadows exactly where he had left it. Whorls of blue energy from his Binding brand raced around it, orbiting a deep black and violet darkness that made it seem like a miniature black hole. He quickly closed the bag, wishing there were some better way to protect it, but for now, this was the only option.

The others watched him, waiting for him to make the first move. He walked to the shoreline and stared out at the cerulean expanse lit by the morning sun. While they still stood in the shadow of the crystal cliffs, the sea in the distance was illuminated with sapphire light, broken by the massive shadows of floating islands above. One island, the one Fergus had mentioned, hovered above the horizon. It was truly enormous, hosting a tall mountain that became lost in clouds above it, while smaller and medium-sized islands floated at various heights in between.

Besides these floating islands, there were more standard islands rising from the water, filled with jagged crystal formations and greenery. On their current landmass, the beach rose to both their left and right in high cliffs against which the waves crashed, forming a sort of shallow inlet, with waterfalls tumbling down their sides.

And, just before his feet, the path of prismatic light stretched across the water itself, about two meters wide and losing itself over the horizon. The sight was almost too beautiful and fantastical to be believed.

"Quite the undertaking," Fergus said.

"We'll see," Lucian said. "I figure we can island hop. I'll tether myself to each island first. If it looks safe, I'll tether the rest of you up one by one."

"Why not just warp all of us?" Fergus asked. "It would be much faster."

"It's too much ether to mask, so I'll do that as a last resort. I know it's probably pointless to hide, but slow and steady is better. If any of those shadows come back, we can change plans."

"Sounds good to me," Mira said. "A chance to do some sightseeing, right?"

"I like the positivity," Serah said.

There was nothing left but to get started. Lucian began by focusing on the extreme end of the landmass they were standing on, a rocky cliff jutting out into the water about half a kilometer in the distance. Within seconds, Lucian had created a glowing blue line that connected to it, and he sailed across the surface of the water.

Within half a minute, he was settling down on the turf above the cliff. It was about five minutes before he had tethered everyone over. Next, Lucian focused on the nearest floating island, which rose several hundred meters above the water and just as far into the distance. It was one of the smaller ones, its underside wrapped in silvery Gravitonic Magic. Long ago, some sorcerers must have levitated all of them. He doubted the brands would dispel anytime soon, and if they did, he could get everyone back to safety with an emergency warp.

Lucian quickly realized that it would be impossible to tether himself to the surface of the island above. From where they stood, it wasn't even visible. The best he could do was get to the side of the island, and then rappel himself up with a tether. Once secure on top, he could tether the others behind him.

He set out to do just that, flying like a missile toward the edge of the island. As soon as he slowed on the side of the rock, he created a series of new tethers that had him over the precipice soon enough. On top, he found what seemed to be an idyllic garden, filled with manicured trees, star-shaped blue flowers with a sweet fragrance, along with a steep hill that dominated the island's center.

He stood at the island's edge, finding a sheer drop to the water beneath while he was buffeted by the cool, salt-laden air. Observing the land he had just come from, he could see cliffs stretching in both directions, with the silvery Prismwood extending as far as his eyes could see, broken only by a line of white-capped mountains in the far distance. The rainbow path unrolled behind him, having readjusted itself because of his movement. Interestingly, it was heading toward the large island, which meant they were on the right track.

Once he was sure the small island was completely safe, he began tethering the others up one by one. Within minutes, they were reunited.

"Amazing," Serah said, taking in the view. "Once all this is said and done, the tourism industry in the Light Realm is going to skyrocket!"

"Still a lot of ground to cover before we even think about starting a bed-and-breakfast," Fergus said.

They kept alert, sticking to the edge of the floating island. Lucian trusted the others with the defensive wards because he needed his concentration for the tethers.

It took about fifteen minutes to reach the other side of the floating island, where a series of smaller islands, like stepping-stones, formed a likely pathway to the gargantuan floating island in the distance, which still floated hundreds of meters above their position. Lucian methodically picked a path to each island, and over the next few hours, they at last found themselves on a final small island, which was scarcely more than a floating boulder with a couple of trees on it.

All that remained was the last island, which at a guess was several kilometers wide, and probably about as long. Several mountains rose from the interior, covered with verdant trees, while their tops were obscured by clouds.

"I wonder how they created these," Emma said. "There's no one powerful enough to do this in our reality."

Lucian wondered himself. If he literally wanted to float a giant piece of land in the sky and brand it there, would he be able to? According to the precepts of sorcery, he could do so as long as he believed it was possible, and he had enough time on his hands. That these islands existed told Lucian that the magic-users here were far more powerful than anyone he had encountered so far.

"My guess is the Ascendants did this," Lucian said. "Maybe as a defensive measure."

"If they were built for defense," Mira said, "we just got this far with no trouble whatsoever. I know if I were the commander in charge of these islands, I'd be fired if five strangers waltzed in with no opposition."

"Good point," Emma said. "Maybe they're letting us in. That first island had a garden on it that looked well-maintained. Someone's living here, that much is clear."

"Ninshar," Serah said. "But where's the rest of his kingdom? Seems pretty empty."

"Maybe on the big island," Lucian said.

"Well, we won't figure anything out by talking about it," Serah said. "Let's keep it moving."

Lucian tethered himself to the last island, which was much farther than it looked. He climbed up the side and pulled himself over the precipice, over which a waterfall was tumbling down and breaking up into a mist hundreds of meters below. He peered down the river rushing over the island's side, finding a deep-cut canyon filled with trees and underbrush growing so thickly that it would be impossible to get through without magic. If there was going to be any traveling to the island's interior, it would have to be done by streaming Gravitonic Magic over the river's surface. In fact, that was where the rainbow path now led, right to the mountain dominating the island.

There was just enough space for Lucian and the others to stand at the edge. He was tempted to get everyone up to the mountain quickly with a portal, but they had come this far without being detected, so he needed to finish things out right. The sun was high above their heads, but such was their elevation that the surrounding air was quite cool. The environment they were in reminded Lucian very much of Volsung. The air was thinner, the trees having the look of evergreens, though slightly different from something he would see on Earth.

While the appearance of the environment was natural, there were also signs that, perhaps, it had been manufactured. Some surfaces were too smooth, as if they were a blank canvas the artist had intended to fill in later. The great mountain rising in the distance was almost perfectly symmetrical, its slopes a bit too sheer to exist naturally without having broken down over time because of the elements. As for the river, how could it possibly replenish itself without a ground source or constant snowmelt? Eventually, the water system on a floating island like this would run dry, unless it was continually created with magic.

While this island had the opposite feeling of the manicured garden they had already passed, it was just as unnatural. Someone or something was here, but it was not the kingdom the Eldarhart had hinted at.

"I don't feel any mages," Fergus said. "Seems it really is empty."

"Me neither," Lucian said. "Keep those wards strong, just in case."

Lucian began by creating a series of Gravitonic discs above the stream itself, following the prismatic path before them. He made them large enough that all of them could share a disc before stepping to the next one. It was only slightly slower than walking normally, especially once they got the rhythm down.

Soon, they left the edge of the floating island far behind, while the rushing river opened into a long, alpine lake, at the end of which were more evergreens and the mountain hulking high above the shoreline. It was here that Lucian saw the first signs of animal life. A flock of birds flew toward the base of the mountain, their feathers reflecting rainbow hues like the prismharts of the forest. Below the surface of the water, Lucian spied fish, their translucent scales making them easy to miss. Along the right-hand shoreline, four wispy orbs of light undulated in the gentle breeze. Lucian couldn't tell if they were alive or not, but he steered well clear of them all the same, just in case.

"There," Fergus said, gazing into the distance. "Some sort of settlement on the cliffs there above the shore. You see it?"

Lucian sharpened his gaze and saw what Fergus was talking about. A series of low buildings, coupled with a few taller ones, almost blended in with the mountain slope across the alpine lake. They were made from wood and stone, and their construction was almost mundane, to where they might have been made by humans.

"Walking over there will take less magic than tethering," Lucian said. "We're making good progress so far. Let's check it out but try not to make a big scene."

The others nodded, and they proceeded to the left-hand shoreline, which they walked up the remaining kilometer to the base of the cliff where the village was situated.

As they drew nearer, it became quite clear that no one was home. Lucian reached out with his Focus, but despite the strength of his stream, he detected no mages, nor any wards, defensive or otherwise. They walked down the main street, made from well-crafted cobblestones, completely unopposed. Despite the abandonment, the buildings looked well-maintained with no signs of wear. Most of the doors were closed, but those that were not revealed empty interiors with hardly a speck of dust on the immaculately clean floors. The village reminded Lucian of something he might see in a themed amusement park before opening. Everything looked livable, but not lived in.

But similar to his time in the past among the Ancients' buildings, the sense of scale threw him off. Everything looked slightly stretched, reaching higher than what he was used to. More than that, upon closer inspection, Lucian noticed that most of the buildings were not symmetrical in the expected way. One side of a shop, for example, was about a meter shorter than the other, and the windows on that side were smaller in scale. The doors were of various shapes, and not just the standard rectangle. The echoes of their footsteps seemed to hang on longer than they should have, not dissipating as expected, so there was always a continuous drone of them walking. It was probably an effect of the way the roofs leaned over the winding streets.

Lucian realized that the strangest thing of all was not in the overall picture, but in the details. Get too close to a building's corner, for example, and it might suddenly shift trajectory inexplicably, or blend right into the cobblestones beneath. The cobblestones themselves had a way of blending into each other if Lucian looked at them closely enough. It was almost dreamlike.

"This place is creepy," Serah said.

"It almost feels like a projection," Emma said, "but I'm not skilled enough to feel the streams creating it."

"I think you might be right," Lucian said.

"Strange," Fergus said. "What's the purpose of it?"

It took all of five minutes to walk through the village, and the feeling of strangeness was gone as soon as they had passed. The cobblestone street faded into a wide dirt track that snaked up the high mountain that dominated the floating island. The rainbow path also seemed to go the same general direction. Lucian had no bearing on north and south in this place, but assuming the sun rose in the east, like on Earth, the mountain was to their immediate north.

"I guess we can follow this trail, since it's going the way we want," Lucian said.

No one had a better suggestion, so Lucian rechecked the group's wards before moving on.

They got lost in the trees and quickly rose above the village. From a distance, it looked completely normal. All the strange details that were apparent up close faded with distance. Within half an hour, their path wound around the mountain, and they encountered their first banks of snow. Within two hours, it was quite cold, and snow was falling on the mountain's northern face.

Using Radiance to see through the storm, Lucian spied something in the distance. The path had turned through a narrow canyon, and blocking the rainbow path was a deep shadow that seemed to oscillate in the chilly mountain air.

Just as he was preparing his Creation Magic to deal with the threat, the shadow separated, revealing two more shadows, three in all blocking passage through the canyon.

It was clear they had to deal with this threat. Where the Path led, they needed to follow.

He summoned Lightspear in his hand, advancing as he created a shield of golden magic around him and the others.

6

IMMEDIATELY, the three shadows attacked in tandem, each streaming a line of pure darkness that contacted Lucian's golden shield. His shield sputtered under the assault, but only for a moment. Golden light surrounded him as he strengthened his shield, an aura of pure brilliance that made him seem like a shining sun. The shadows pulled themselves toward him via their dark streams. Lucian knew if they all struck his shield simultaneously, it might be enough to overwhelm his defenses.

With a quick burst of magic, he warped himself toward the right-hand shadow, the one that was most isolated. Reversing the flow of time for a brief instant, he thrust Lightspear before the shadow could shirk away from his attack. It gave a jarring screech as it shriveled before Lightspear's fury.

But before Lucian could finish the job, the other two shadows fell in on both of his sides, nearly extinguishing his shield. As the original shadow retreated toward the nearby cliff, Lucian attempted to warp away, only to find hard resistance to his Space-Time Magic. He switched tactics to Gravitonics, leaping high off the ground; he felt the shadows attempt to grapple him with their own Gravitonic streams, but Serah's ward was strong, allowing him to escape.

The shadow Lucian had struck earlier had retreated into a snowbank, quivering. The other two shadows approached it, and intrinsically, Lucian understood they could share their power to heal it. Lucian redirected the energy of his shield into a beam of pure golden light, striking the weakened shadow before it could be restored. Instantly, the dark entity was split at the seams, its shadowy exterior cracking with golden fissures before exploding in a miniature nova.

The other two shadows switched tactics, one rushing directly for Lucian and the other for his friends, who were busy at work maintaining wards and shields. Lucian easily warped himself in front of the shadow going after his friends; Emma's ward was powerful enough that the shadows were no longer contesting him in the Space-Time Aspect. He used this to his advantage, surrounding the approaching shadow with a reverse Space-Time aura, slowing it while simultaneously creating a forward Space-Time aura on himself, speeding his actions.

He rushed forward with Lightspear outstretched. Though the shadow tried to dodge, there was no way it could move quickly enough. Lightspear plunged within it, and Lucian held firm despite the coldness spreading into his arm. He streamed golden magic through the length of the spear, hastening the speed at which the shadow dissipated.

As soon as it had been dealt with, his mother screamed from behind, causing him to whirl around. Somehow, the last shadow had eluded him, cracking Emma's ward and warping toward his friends. Lucian warped himself right on top of the shadow, streaming deeply from the Orb of Creation. Like a repelling magnet, the shadow was cast back into the snowdrifts of the canyon.

His mother's eyes were wide as tendrils of shadow snaked around her arms, knitting themselves together. Lucian streamed with everything he had, bathing her body in golden light. The dark tendrils were stubborn, slowly unraveling and shrinking from the golden influx. And all the while, Lucian was aware of the shadow approaching from behind, but if he let up, even for a second, his mother was as good as lost.

Emma was streaming with everything she had, doing everything she could to slow the approaching with her Space-Time Magic. If she could even draw it out for two more seconds, it might make all the difference. The others were attacking the shadow by whatever means they could, though it was hard to tell how effective their attacks were.

At last, Mira gasped as she fell to the ground, completely exorcised of the shadow's dark magic. Lucian spun around, only to find that the shadow was looming above him. He streamed a Creation shield around himself, but this shadow was stronger than the others; its own malevolent force shattered Lucian's shield, which hadn't the time to build power.

With a quick Psionic push, he threw his friends behind him, leaving him to face the shadow alone. None of them could wield Creation Magic like him, and he wasn't about to risk their lives.

For the first time, Lucian noticed his fatigue, and although he held nine Orbs, even his godlike powers had their limits. Streaming Creation Magic wasn't easy; like Space-Time, another Major Aspect, it was far more intensive than the Minor Aspects. Lucian powered his Creation shield as much as he could, holding Lightspear at the ready. He didn't have the time or the ether to slow time again, and he knew throwing the spear wouldn't work. He had to stab the shadow and not miss. His shield would only last a few seconds, after which he'd be completely at the shadow's mercy.

The shadow lurched forward, surrounding his bubble of golden magic. Lucian instantly felt its compression. The shadow's dark power was far more than he would have ever guessed. He pushed with everything he had against the encroaching darkness. Directly ahead, he could see two red eyes, glowing like embers in a dark, starless night. The warmth left Lucian's bones, along with his will to go on. He realized the shadow was reaching around him, tantalizingly close to grasping the Orb of Shadows in his pack.

With a sudden burst of fury, Lucian streamed with everything he had. He pushed the encroaching shadow back, if only for a moment. But then it was back to compressing him again.

But just then, there was a great crash, and the shadow jolted away with a hiss. Lucian was free, drawing breath after breath while streaming power back into his shield. His limbs shaking, he turned to face the shadow, which, to his shock, was battling a new entrant fiercely. The new arrival was a powerful being that was tall, at least two and a half meters in height at a guess, wearing golden armor surrounded by golden light. He was streaming Creation Magic, too, lashing the shadow with golden whips laced with Binding.

Lucian only paused for a second. He charged forward, using Space-Time to increase his speed and plunge Lightspear deep into the shadow's heart. It quivered and screamed at the attack, and like the others, retracted as Lucian's weapon unleashed its full power. Beams of golden light split the shadow, and all the while its piercing wails tore at Lucian's soul. Unlike the others, it refused to die.

All the while, the mysterious attacker continued wailing on the creature with its whips; it was doing some work, though Lightspear was doing most of the damage. At last, after what must have been two minutes, the deep darkness of the shadow began to oscillate and lose its opaqueness, quivering here and there as it shrunk into a single splotch. Lucian did not let up, and he watched until there was nowhere else for the shadow to flee. Only when it had vanished for a few seconds, and he detected no trace of Shadow Magic, did he withdraw his spear.

But he could hardly relax as he turned to look at the being

before him. He—at least, Lucian interpreted the traditionally masculine features as belonging to a male—loomed above him. His golden shield dissipated, revealing icy blue skin that glowed with a subtle pearlescent sheen. The skin subtly shifted from blue to white in the late afternoon light.

His eyes were dark violet, with elongated slit-like pupils, with a gaze both penetrating and expressive, seeming to hold untold depths of ancient wisdom and knowledge. Rather than having hair, silk-like filaments floated around his head, so light gray as to be almost white, gently swaying in the icy breeze. Lucian noted the glow of Gravitonic Magic around them.

But what arrested Lucian most was the face, a perfect blend of strength and beauty, with a straight aquiline nose and a well-defined jawline that recalled an ancient Greek statue. Gazing upon the face, the being was most definitely *not* human, yet Lucian still recognized something human within it. The ears were subtly pointed.

Lending further glory to his appearance was an icy blue crown, floating just slightly over his head, which seemed to be woven from streams of air and frost. The being's arms and legs were bare, glowing subtly with strange glyphs Lucian couldn't even decipher, while his golden armor had faded into clothing that seemed to be woven from light itself. The armor, Lucian realized, must have been a manifestation of its Creation Magic, while the clothing seemed to be a projection of Radiant Magic rather than anything tangible.

Lucian knew this must be an Ascendant, and most likely the one he was looking for: Ninshar. There was no judgment in the being's brilliant eyes, only a warm acceptance that seemed to wrap him in a comforting blanket.

The Ascendant spoke in a resonant and melodic voice that Lucian perfectly understood, although it was speaking a different, lyrical language. His Psionic ward was still active.

"The Chosen has come to the Light Realm," he said, his eyes

turning upon Lucian's spear. "At long last, the Speaker's Prophecy has been fulfilled!"

Lucian did not allow his weapon to disappear, even if he was reasonably sure the Ascendant meant no harm. A quick glance at his friends revealed they were gawking at the godlike presence before them.

Lucian calmed himself, reminding himself that his power matched, or perhaps even exceeded, the one he was speaking to. He had been the one to deal the final blow to the shadow, after all.

Lucian, using Psionics, responded in the same language; the Ascendant seemed to allow him enough access to its mind in order to at least learn the language and communicate. "Thanks for the assist."

The being nodded regally but seemed to wait for Lucian to say more.

"Are you Ninshar?" Lucian asked. "We've been looking for you."

Lucian got the feeling the Ascendant wasn't used to being addressed so directly, especially by a being he considered lower than himself. But Lucian also knew he had to trust in his status. He was the Chosen of the Manifold, and that had to mean something here.

"Yes. I am the Ascendant Ninshar, Lord of the Ninshar Kingdom. And you, of course, can be none other than the Chosen of the Manifold, given your ability to wield the Magic of Creation and that weapon of yours. Any other sorcerer would have been destroyed by those Zulum."

"That's what those shadows are called, huh?"

"Yes. One is a tough fight, even for one such as I. Three, however, is something else entirely. You are powerful, Chosen. That much I can see. But had I not arrived, your doom would have been spelled."

By now, Lucian had strengthened his Psionic ward, just to be sure Ninshar wouldn't try to read his mind. Though he had saved their lives, it would be foolish to trust him so soon. Lucian ensured the ward also covered his friends. The Ascendant no doubt detected Lucian's use of magic, but Lucian knew this had to be the standard between meetings of powerful beings who were not yet sure of each other. The ward would keep them safe from psychic attacks, and they could deal with the Ascendant on a more equal footing.

"I'm sure you have many questions," Ninshar ventured, "being so new to the Light Realm. For you are clearly from the Shadow Realm, in accordance with the Speaker Anlilta's prophecy. You will be strangers here, unaccustomed to the Light Realm, not to mention its inhabitants and dangers. Fear not, for she is a friend of mine, and I will do what I can to help you. But perhaps a brief introduction would be in order. I'm the Steward of the Eye of Kadur, and I have ruled this kingdom for two millennia, ever since the end of the War of Light and Shadow. Alas, we are the last kingdom of the Light on this moon. And the Manifold willing, we will remain standing where all others have fallen."

"We have more questions, but maybe those can wait until we've gotten someplace safe."

"Indeed," the Ascendant said, his filaments swaying as he spoke. "You are a guest in my land; it is my honor to be the first of our kind to welcome the Chosen to the Light Realm. Though the Eye is far from the capital, we are an important world. Very important! Of course, I am happy to host you and answer whatever questions you may have, for I'm sure there are many."

Lucian nodded. He did, in fact, have many questions, and he doubted the answers would be free. "I hope not to trouble you for too long, Ninshar. This is just a brief stop before we continue on our way."

"To Anshar, no doubt," Ninshar said. "As I said before, I shall aid you in this endeavor. Though, of course, such arrangements will take time. My castle lies at the top of this mountain. We can travel there for rest and repose, and of course, food and drink."

Lucian considered for a moment. It seemed as if Ninshar was the key to moving further, but entering the home of an unknown, powerful being carried significant risks.

Ninshar's face seemed to brighten as a small smile tugged at the corner of his lips. By design or happenstance, it seemed the Ascendants shared many human-like qualities in their expressions. "I assure you; you have nothing to fear! You could not be in better hands. Come. Your zeal to continue your journey is commendable, but without my help, you won't get far. And lucky for you, I am more than happy to lend a hand."

Lucian watched him carefully, noting that the Seven-Fold Path was leading right toward him. It didn't mean Ninshar was an ally, but merely the next step in their journey.

It was enough for Lucian. "We'll accept whatever help you can give. It's good to meet a friend."

"Yes, friends are rare indeed, Lucian Abrantes of Earth," Ninshar said.

Though Lucian had never spoken his name, it didn't surprise him that Ninshar had parsed that much from his mind. He had been confident of his defenses, but that he hadn't noticed the Psionic breach was a bit concerning. What else did Ninshar know?

Ninshar seemed to read this misgiving. "Come. Soon, you will be safe within the walls of my palace, and I'll give you any answers you seek. There, you and your servants will be most comfortable."

"They're my friends, not servants," Lucian said.

"Forgive me. I simply assumed, by your power difference . . . well, perhaps things work differently where you are from."

Before Lucian could say anything more, the Ascendant waved his hand, and a portal appeared. On the other side was a magnificent palace at the end of a long, icy stairway that seemed to reach into the sky and beyond. Large parts of it were floating over the mountain's side.

There was nothing for them to do but follow Ninshar through the portal. Lucian nodded at the others, speaking standard English, though he was reasonably certain Ninshar could understand them with his magic.

"This is just a pit stop. We need to learn more, and he seems like a good source of info." He looked over his shoulder, toward the Crystalline Sea, which was no longer visible because of the thickening of clouds. "The Path is following him, so he's the key to getting a ship and off this rock."

"Maybe," Fergus said skeptically. "Remember . . ."

"I know," Lucian said. "No one is more careful than me."

Fergus gave a gruff nod. "I trust you. Lead on."

The others gave their own nods. They were in this together, whether Ninshar proved friend or foe.

Lucian was first through the portal, followed shortly by the others.

7

THE PORTAL CLOSED BEHIND THEM, affording Lucian a better view of the palace looming above. He wasn't even sure if it could be *called* a palace. It was dominated by a massive floating ziggurat, toward which several icy stairs led from the peak of the mountain. Multiple terraces laced the construction, filled with crystalline gardens and bioluminescent trees. The raw amount of magic emanating from the palace was shocking to Lucian's Focus, the mental equivalent of a waterfall pummeling him in the face. He felt the Gravitonic Magic keeping the mighty structure supported, the Thermal wards keeping the plants alive, the Atomic brands that continually created water, the excess of which poured over the sides and crystallized into clouds of ice.

Everyone's jaws dropped at the sight, while Ninshar looked at them with what seemed to be amusement.

As they approached the stairs, Lucian saw they were not actually ice but were warm to the touch, made from a material he had never encountered. Ninshar raised his arm, streaming a tendril of blue magic that bent the Binding ward encompassing the castle, allowing them to enter the space before it closed behind them.

Within the ward, the temperature was pleasant, quite warm compared to the outside, as if it were the most pleasant day of late spring or early fall.

The stairs widened as they approached a gate, the main entrance to the ziggurat before them. The crystalline doors opened as they neared, the path encompassed by overhanging branches of ethereal trees laden with sweet, otherworldly fruits.

Lucian looked here and there, trying to find other Ascendants that might call this place home. But no matter where he gazed, there was nothing but well-tended plants and beautiful nooks with grand views. A sense of emptiness pervaded the compound, despite its well-tended nature. Lucian felt a sense of heaviness and sorrow that belied the castle's beautiful exterior. He had come too far to ignore such feelings, but for now, he simply kept it in the back of his mind.

They passed through the main gate, entering a vast hall with a high, arched ceiling lit by hanging crystal chandeliers emitting soft golden light. Multiple tiers could be seen, with waterfalls tumbling over the sides through indoor gardens, a prominent flower of which included the blue, star-shaped ones he'd already noticed. The waterfalls collected in a stream that rushed by their feet to fall over the hall's sides. Mosaic arts depicted fantastical creatures, one of which seemed to be a serpent-like dragon plying the ocean. Living vines and flowers climbed along the walls. The same creatures he'd spied in the forest on the first day, reminiscent of both a butterfly and a hummingbird, flitted among the blossoms opening along the stream's side.

At the end of the hall, directly along the main corridor they were on, stood a single, ornate throne that seemed to be carved from a sparkling light blue gemstone, what might have been topaz. It shone with latent power, but like every other part of the palace, even this place was empty, what likely should have been the beating heart of the kingdom.

Before Lucian could ask about it, their host turned his head, giving a gracious smile. "This hall is grand, even by my kind's standard. I take guests to the observatory, the highest point of the palace. There, it's far more comfortable, and the view of both the stars and the surrounding terrain is quite arresting."

Lucian had to wonder why they didn't just go directly there with the portal, but he realized Ninshar had wanted to awe them with his home's splendor. He led them to a Gravitonically-powered glyph in the center of the hall. Once all had joined him, the glyph rose from the stones beneath and ascended the main hall, carrying them with it. As it rose, Lucian got a panoramic view of the surrounding hanging gardens and waterfalls.

"A lot of space for one person," Mira said.

"Indeed," Ninshar said, a bit sorrowfully. "That is a tale that will be told soon. Quite soon!"

Lucian tried not to read anything ominous in that sentence. He doubted Ninshar would be foolish enough to telegraph ill-intent, unless of course the Ascendant was underestimating them. It wouldn't be the first time someone had done that.

Suddenly, the glyph was surrounded with a burst of Space-Time and Radiant Magic as it phased through the ceiling briefly, coming to rest at the very top of the ziggurat. They found themselves in a much smaller space, more intimate and lived in. Lucian didn't want to call it cozy, given the danger, but in other, more usual circumstances, he might have. The first, and most stunning, visual was the completely transparent ceiling. It gave a brilliant view of the stars and planets above, including the one he had noticed their very first night, a cloud-wrapped orb of blue, green, and brown. A large, ethereally glowing telescope stood in the exact center of the space, seeming to Lucian to be more a work of art than a scientific instrument. He could feel complicated magical streams emanating from the device.

Along the room's edges, surrounding the telescope, were wide arched windows affording a panoramic view of the landscape below, along with the ziggurat's multiple tiers and themed gardens. Plush seating abounded on the periphery, and despite the situation, Lucian could see himself reading a book or taking a nap here. Glowing crystals embedded within the walls lent a warm, welcoming glow that contrasted with the grandeur of the hall below. Where there weren't windows, moving murals depicted fantastical constellations and what appeared to be mythical creatures in movement, along with historical scenes from this reality. It was such a barrage of images that Lucian could hardly make sense of it all, but it gave him the sense that the history of this place was as deep and complicated as their own.

"Please, sit," Ninshar said, showing a small, comfortable nook large enough to accommodate them all, surrounded by thick books, both on shelves and stacked on small tables. The central table contained a kettle with some sort of steaming beverage, along with what appeared to be small cakes and pastries, the smell of which was tantalizing. Lucian wondered who had prepared all this, or if it was all powered by magic.

Once seated, almost everyone heaved a sigh at the comfort of the plush seats beneath them. Lucian, Serah, and Emma sat on a couch, while Mira and Fergus shared a large, overstuffed armchair that had plenty of room for the both of them. Ninshar took a large chair for himself. Much like the Ancients' furniture, they had been built with larger proportions in mind. The seating seemed to conform magically to Lucian's body, only enhancing the comfort.

He ignored the feeling, knowing the coziness of this room could be something to throw them off guard. He held his Focus and kept his full attention on the Ascendant before him.

"This place is beautiful," Serah said, her blue eyes wide and speaking the language of their host through Lucian's ward. "Beyond beautiful. I feel like I'm in a dream."

Ninshar smiled, his eyes seeming to take in more than Serah's appearance. "Indeed. Imagine my surprise to find a creature as beautiful as you wander into my domain. It is me who is living in the dream."

Serah's eyes widened at this, and for a moment, she was uncharacteristically at a loss for words.

"We're not creatures," Lucian said firmly. "I don't care if you're a king. You don't talk about any of us that way."

Ninshar turned to look at him, his smile having the air of an adult humoring a child. "Of course. A turn of phrase, if you will." He poured out several cups of hot tea, then took something that looked like a scone and took a delicate bite. "I meant no offense."

"Let's move on," Lucian said. "If you know what I am, then you also know where I'm going and why."

"I do not know everything, as you suppose," Ninshar admitted. "I only guessed your identity because you hold Lightspear, the weapon foretold by the Speaker of the Manifold. That mighty weapon of lore can only be wielded by the Chosen. When I beheld it for the first time, it matched the description of Anlilta's prophecy. The power emanating from it was beyond anything I've ever felt. With such a mighty weapon, the entire Eye could be returned to the Light!"

Though Ninshar tried to mask it, Lucian could easily note the raw envy in his voice. He knew Ninshar wanted that power for himself.

"We appreciate you taking us in," Lucian said. "However, we'd be fools to trust you without knowing more about you. You say you're loyal to Enkius, that you respect Anlilta. But how can we know that for sure?"

Ninshar took a sip of his tea and crossed his legs, not bothered by the question. "Of course, your concerns are valid. I was tasked by Enkius the Golden himself to guard the Eye. This is my domain, and it is my sacred task to protect all beings who serve the Light, great or small. My purview only ends at the Barrier, the border between the Light Lands and the Shadow Lands that encompass the rest of the Eye. As for why you should trust me, I wield the Magic of Creation, which only loyal servants of Enkius can use. You have no way of knowing that, of course, but just as Shadow Magic can only be used by minions who have pledged their Focuses to serve the Ancient One and his schemes, Creation Magic can only be used by those who have professed loyalty to Enkius."

"I haven't, but I can use it," Lucian said.

"Well, that is quite a distinct thing. Long ago, directly after the War of Light and Shadow, Nathi left the Light Realm and became *Alkasen*, to bear the Orbs of Space-Time and Creation to the Chosen, in accordance with Anlilta's prophecy. And it would seem, after many years, that you have at last returned by the same words of that prophecy. That you bear the Orb, as the Chosen, gives you access to magic without ever having to seek the blessing of Enkius the Golden. You would be the first in history to use Creation Magic without it."

"Nathi," Lucian said. "You mean, the Time Weaver?"

"That could be a name he has called himself," Ninshar said. "Though I do not know it. Just as Enkius was gifted the Orb of Creation by the Manifold, so Nathi was gifted the Orb of Space-Time. It would be fitting." He drained the rest of his cup. "All that to say, you have nothing to fear. I am a friend of the Light, evidenced by my use of Creation Magic. And when I sensed the Zulum, I made all haste to investigate. As the king of this land, I can never suffer such vile creatures. That they have strayed so far from the Barrier speaks volumes. Not idly do they risk the Zulum, for it takes decades, and even centuries, to create them. That they risked three tells me they are quite desperate to get what you possess."

"How did they get so far into your kingdom in the first place?" Emma asked. "Do you have no guards or armies? Where are all the people? It can't be just you living here, can it?"

Ninshar's violet eyes turned upon her, and Lucian didn't like the look of unearned familiarity. "That is a sad tale, and we will get to it in time. As for the Zulum, they are among the most powerful of the Fallen's minions, manifestations of pure Shadow Magic imbued with the Focuses of many mages, and even sorcerers. The more Focuses they possess, the more powerful they become. Though like the ignition of a dark star, it takes a certain amount before Shadow Magic can create a new Zulum."

Lucian nodded. "I've seen them before in our own reality, though nothing as powerful as what we just fought."

Ninshar continued. "A weak one is quite dangerous in itself; lesser Ascendants have fallen to them. Nothing can defeat them save Creation Magic, meaning our means to fight them are limited. It takes an Ascendant, or a powerful sorcerer, to even have a chance." Ninshar gave a grim frown. "That they have wandered so far beyond the Barrier is . . . troubling. But if they don't want to be found, I can't detect them until they stream enough magic to reveal themselves. That, unfortunately, is the way of things."

"What is this Barrier, exactly?" Lucian asked. "The Eldarhart —I don't know if you've met him—told us about it, but he didn't really explain that much."

"I know him," Ninshar confirmed. "The Eldarhart is a wise and powerful being, one of Anlilta's creatures. The prismharts are technically a part of my kingdom, though they would probably contest that. As for the Barrier, it's what it sounds like. It's a magical separation between the Light Lands and the Dark Lands. Imagine a circle upon the lunar surface. Anything within that circle is part of the Kingdom of Ninshar, my realm. Anything outside that is called the Shadow Lands, ruled by a mighty Descendant named Ashurban the Maleficent."

"Descendant?" Lucian asked.

"A being like me that has chosen allegiance to the Fallen and the power of the Shadow," Ninshar explained. "They followed the Ancient One, and as their reward, received the right to wield Shadow Magic and forsake all vows to Enkius the Golden. Most

Descendants were destroyed during the War, but there are hold-outs, such as here on the Eye, which are far from the influence of Eänna. The Barrier keeps the Shadow Lands from spreading without recourse. But the Shadow Magic of Ashurban is power-ful, and every year, the Barrier gets pushed back farther. Indeed, most in my kingdom fled the Eye long ago. I have a few loyal sorcerers who have remained behind, but my kingdom is a shell of its former self. I, of course, remain. It is my sacred charge to defend the Eye to the last. If I were to leave, along with what few remain to me, the Eye would go dark, and the World of Kadur itself, which you can see in the sky above us, would come under direct threat from the Shadow."

Lucian was still thinking about something Ninshar had said earlier. He vaguely understood this War he had mentioned, the one between Light and Shadow, from his brief conversation with the Time Weaver—or, he supposed, Nathi. But now, he realized that conversation had barely scratched the surface. "What about this War?"

"If I were to tell you about that, we'd still be sitting here long after the sun rose. Besides, I'm interested in what you have to say. A Shadow Being has entered the Light Realm, an event that has only happened once before. I've brought you here for a very important reason, and I would explain that reason now, before the hour grows too late."

Lucian waited, knowing that the price for Ninshar's help would come eventually.

"You're asking many questions about why the power of my kingdom has waned, and I hope to explain that fully now. Some-thing was stolen from me. Something that turned the tide in the fight for this moon. I would have it back."

"And let me guess," Lucian said. "That's where we come in?"

The Ascendant gave a gracious, but sharp, smile. "Precisely."

8

LUCIAN WATCHED NINSHAR FOR A MOMENT, his violet eyes boring into him, seeming to see into the depths of his soul. He had the feeling this was going to be a long story.

"Long ago," Ninshar began, "my kingdom was invaded by the forces of the Shadow Lands before Ashurban had even come to power. The attack came from nowhere. We were . . . overwhelmed. But the object of their attack was not to destroy us, for in those days, my kingdom was powerful and could not be challenged on the field of battle. The invasion was instead a ploy to distract me, to rob me of an artifact of great power, one gifted to me by Enkius himself to battle the Shadow on this world."

"What artifact?" Lucian asked.

"I don't know if you have something equivalent in your own reality, but here, it's called an ethereal core."

"An ethereal core?" Serah asked. "Sounds powerful."

"Beyond powerful. Such cores are rare and only form in areas with high concentrations of ether, and only if they are left undisturbed for centuries. This core was discovered shortly after the War of Light and Shadow and, as such, is among the most powerful ever found. They are quite similar to the fabled Orbs. They can be absorbed by any magic-user, enhancing their power in all Aspects, including Aspects which they should not have access to. For example, someone like me could use Shadow Magic without ever having to profess loyalty to the Ancient One. But unlike the Orbs, the ether that ethereal cores contain is limited; given enough use, they will extinguish. Most ethereal cores take on names, especially the powerful ones. This one, gifted to me by Enkius himself, he named the Starflower, after the beautiful blooms you've no doubt seen on this part of the Eye."

Lucian recalled the flower in his mind. There had been fields of them, both in the Prismwood and these floating islands. "Sounds useful. It begs the question, though. How did you lose it in the first place?"

"Betrayal. How else? You see, ethereal cores will die out if they remain in one's Focus, even when not in use. For this reason, they are locked securely away when their master has no need for them. I kept the Starflower hidden in my palace, under constant guard from my most loyal sorcerers, whose minds I knew better than their own. One of these sorcerers was Ashurban himself."

"If you knew his mind, how did he hide his intentions from you?"

"I can only guess that he did so using Shadow Magic, the streams of which are impossible for me to manipulate. While he was in my house, he made a pact with the Ancient One himself."

"Why did he do that?" Emma asked. "What did he get in return?"

"The Starflower. What else? He was the most powerful sorcerer in my employ, and an artifact of such strength was the only way for him to take on the power of an Ascendant. For everyone who follows the Ancient One, the chief motivation is a desire for power. So, Ashurban slew all the sorcerers guarding the prize, and he took it for himself. He fled before anyone was the wiser. Over the years, using the power of the Starflower, he united the various kingdoms of the Shadow Lands, becoming a mighty Descendant. And ever since that day, we have been at war with the Shadow Lands. And because of Ashurban and the Starflower, it is a war they are winning."

"You're on a timeline, then," Fergus said. "How much longer can you hold on without the Starflower?"

"Not much longer," Ninshar said quietly. "My kingdom is already reduced, as you can see. They call this world the Eye because the green and blue of my domain is a small circle surrounded by a sea of gray desolation. This world had another name in the ancient past. Edea. Hundreds of thousands once called this moon home. Of course, I'm the one blamed for losing the Starflower to the Shadow. For six centuries, it's been in the hands of Ashurban the Maleficent, and as long as it's in his hands, I am a pariah in the court of Enkius the Golden."

"You said eventually, the ethereal core will die out," Lucian said. "Can you not just wait him out?"

"You underestimate just how much power the Starflower holds. Ashurban has used it carefully over the years. He channels its power only at great need, to preserve its strength. He is crafty, and over the centuries, has won this world little by little to the Shadow. Unless he is stopped, the Eye of Kadur is fated to fall. My power alone isn't enough to preserve the Light Lands. These floating islands, for example, were created with the Starflower's might, but in time, the brands that hold the islands aloft will fail. Indeed, most have already dissipated, causing the islands to crash into the sea, leaving behind only a remnant."

"I counted twenty-four floating islands," Fergus said.

"Twenty-two," Ninshar corrected grimly. "The greatest island is Skymount, upon which we stand, and it remains only by my personal power. A vanity, for that power could be put to better use. But one day, even its magic will fail; we Ascendants are powerful, but not so much as that. The glory of this kingdom was once said to rival even Anshar on Eänna; in the previous millennium, Enkius wished for a mighty capital to govern the Eastern half of the Aetheria, a beacon of the Light that would never fade. This world was that capital, at least until it shifted to Kadur. But those days of glory have long passed. And of course, the Starflower was the source of the Barrier's magical defenses. Now that the Starflower is in the hands of Ashurban, he can move the Barrier itself and so increase the size of the Shadow Lands. Not easily, mind you, but with careful meditation, he spends most of his waking hours bending himself to this task. And as the power of the Shadow waxes, as the Barrier encroaches, the Zulum can more easily slip past it."

"You need us to take out this Ashurban then," Lucian said. "And get the Starflower back."

"That's right," Ninshar said solemnly.

"And why can't you do it yourself?" Serah asked. "Is he really that much stronger than you?"

From the flash of anger on Ninshar's face, he didn't appreciate the comment, but his expression quickly became neutral. "Most of my magic is tied up in brands holding the kingdom together. If I were to leave Skymount, the magic of the Barrier would negate many of those brands that rely on my proximity to remain powered. The Light Lands would be completely subsumed."

"Why haven't you called for reinforcements?" Lucian asked.

"I would have long ago, but there is but one Gate. It leads to Kadur, and it's far out into the Celestial Sea. The Gate is guarded by Leviathan, a monstrous creature controlled by Ashurban's magic. While Ashurban lives, it is simply too dangerous to challenge alone. It watches the Gate nonstop with no need for sleep or rest. Many attempts have been made to pass through, but always, that attempt had ended up in Leviathan's waiting maw."

Serah broke the tense silence that followed. "Gulp."

"The Gate is on the water?" Emma asked.

Ninshar nodded. "Yes. And there is no other way to escape this moon."

"Not even by going to space?" Fergus asked. "That planet—Kadur, I think you called it—doesn't seem to be too far."

"The Void is simply too dangerous. The Ether can be unpredictable, tearing ships apart, especially on the border of the Aetheria, where its waves and eddies can be truly wild. The Void is easier to navigate toward the center of the Aetheria, where it is more stable. But to cross so near the edge of existence itself is simply to invite your death."

"No one has tried?" Lucian asked.

"Many *have* tried. I doubt even Anlilta herself would dare something so bold this close to the edge. It is simply impossible. The Kadur Gate is the only way."

"So, retrieving this ethereal core will do two things," Lucian said. "It will break Ashurban's power and will also give us the chance to defeat this Leviathan and get past the Gate."

"Exactly that," Ninshar said. "And with the Gate opened, Anshar can once again send aid to mop up the rest of the Shadow kingdoms. And you, of course, can escape the Eye and continue your journey to the World of Light. I won't lie; crossing the Barrier and battling Ashurban is not for the faint of heart. But it is necessary to secure your passage to Eänna and Anshar. The ship to cross the Celestial Sea is something I can provide, of course."

"Sounds like you'd be getting the better end of the deal," Serah said shrewdly. "You'd be getting the Starflower back, not to mention your entire kingdom."

"Do you not also stand to benefit? You want two things: to get off this moon, and to get to Anshar. You get both by defeating Ashurban and bringing the Starflower back to me."

"Why can't you just create a portal for us to Anshar?" Emma asked. "And if that's too far, why not Kadur?"

Ninshar laughed lightly. "Portals cannot be made across the Void! Perhaps it is different where you come from, but here, the Ether is so thick that it'll rip you apart as you make the transition. The Gates are the only safe way to travel."

"I'm with Serah," Fergus said. "This seems an unfair bargain. You want us to do the impossible, and you will only provide us a mere ship?"

"What else would you wish for, Fergus?" Ninshar asked, not needing to even ask his name. "Power? Glory? An ethereal core of your own? I already know none of these things matter to you and the Chosen, but I know reaching Anshar matters more than all the riches of the Aetheria. How is it an unfair bargain?"

Fergus went quiet, knowing that Ninshar had a point.

The Ascendant's violet eyes turned on Lucian. "So, what will it be? Lucian, this is our chance. That the First Gate opened into the Light Lands of the Eye, of all the places it could have gone, can be nothing but the will of the Manifold. You were meant to bring balance to the Aetheria, to restore the Light to its former glory. You are none other than Anlilta's Chosen, the one prophesied to destroy the Shadow once and for all, to return the Orbs to the Heart and save magic itself! If you can't find the Starflower, then no one can." His eyes next took in Lucian's companions. "And, of course, I include all of you, the Chosen's trusty companions. It is the perfect team to achieve the impossible."

Lucian looked at the others, who all watched him for the next move. With the information they had, there really wasn't much of a choice. During Ninshar's long monologue, Lucian had subtly woven some advanced Psionic streams, combined with other Aspects, but he dared not to stream too much. From his magic, he only got the sense that Ninshar was not revealing everything, but Lucian didn't need magic to know that.

He knew certain things Ninshar had mentioned were the truth. There *was* an ethereal core called the Starflower, and it *was* needed to gain control of this world. It would also be a great help in destroying Leviathan, a monster controlled by Ashurban that did, in fact, exist. Ninshar had a ship that would allow them to not only cross the Crystalline Sea but make the rest of their way to Anshar.

Despite this, Lucian couldn't figure out whether the Ascendant could truly be trusted, which was the most important question of all. He was guarding his mind Psionically, and if Lucian streamed too aggressively, Ninshar would certainly detect his intrusion.

Lucian was quiet for a long while. "We need more information. Anything to watch out for? Where do we even start?"

Ninshar grew somber. Outside the observatory's windows, snow was falling, swirling in the darkness. "What few agents I've sent across the Barrier never returned to me. My information, I'm afraid, is limited. But this is what I can tell you. Ashurban rarely strays from his fortress, a bastion called Esharal. It is a mighty, sprawling complex in the swamps of the Shadow Lands. It actually isn't too far from the Barrier. I can easily get you most of the way using a portal."

"Ugh, another swamp?" Serah asked. "I'm sick of swamps!"

"As for how to locate the fortress," Ninshar went on, ignoring Serah, "someone of your abilities will have no trouble detecting the Starflower. It will pull you in like a beacon."

"Like a moth to a flame?" Fergus asked.

"Not if the prophecies are true, and the Chosen's power is not in question," Ninshar answered.

"How do you cross the Barrier?" Lucian asked. "From everything you've said, it sounds difficult."

"A powerful shield of Creation Magic will suffice, just as the agents of the Shadow can cross it using Shadow Magic. I'm afraid there's little more I can tell you. As a powerful Descendant, Ashurban will be many times more powerful than those Zulum we defeated. But as a creature of the Shadow, he can be destroyed with Creation Magic just the same. And when he perishes, the Starflower will come free of his Focus. Now, this part is important. You are *not* to absorb the Starflower and take it as your own. It was entrusted to me by Enkius, so your only job is to bring it back safely. The deal is off entirely if you don't follow this very important point."

"No worries there," Lucian said. "I can just wrap it in a Binding brand. So, we have a deal?"

Ninshar nodded regally. "A bargain has been struck. In the morning, we'll see about going to the Barrier. For tonight, you must rest. You will be safe within these walls, I assure you. The magic of my palace is too strong for the Zulum to challenge. Come. I'll lead you to your rooms."

9

NINSHAR TOOK them to another wing of his castle, putting them up in a lavish suite of rooms overlooking the sea. The main living area was spacious, with a flowing open design and high arched ceilings. It was filled with plush seating, many sofas and armchairs adorned with fine fabrics. The walls were decked with artwork, mostly surreal and dreamlike, so mesmerizing they were almost hypnotic.

"I hope it's to your liking," Ninshar said. "After you've rested, I'll portal you to the Barrier. It's better to travel by day in the Shadow Lands than by night." He gave a subtle bow, barely perceptible. "Sleep well."

He closed the door with magic, leaving Lucian and his companions alone.

"Check out the view!" Serah said, walking to the expansive circular windows that dominated the far wall.

The rest joined her to take in the wide vista of the snowy slopes of the mountain, along with the Crystalline Sea spreading to the horizon. The water glowed subtly under the light of Kadur, which shone green and blue above, the main jewel in the star-studded sky.

"Let's focus," Mira said. "I feel like there was a lot I missed in that conversation, even with the Psionic language link."

Lucian ensured his wards were strong. He was sure Ninshar couldn't listen in on them, even if he had his own wards in place.

"Well, we can't trust him, obviously," Fergus said. "This foray into the Shadow Lands sounds like a suicide mission."

"How much of his story checks out?" Emma asked, looking at Lucian. "Were you able to see if he was lying about anything?"

"It seems most of the major stuff was the truth. But I could definitely tell he was hiding something."

"Ugh," Serah said. "Why can't Anlilta help us? She knows we're here. She can obviously communicate with us, so why doesn't she?"

"Her hands must be tied," Emma guessed. "She also mentioned it's dangerous. It sounds like Anshar is quite far, and the power required to send a message that distance makes it susceptible to interception."

"So, what to do about this ethereal core?" Mira asked. "Is it really the only way to get off this rock?"

"Seems like it's the next step of our journey," Lucian said. "We need to cross this sea to find the Gate, and for that, we need a ship. And he won't give that until we get this Starflower thing."

"That settles it," Serah said. "To the Shadow Lands we go."

"How can we prepare ourselves?" Emma asked. "A giant fortress in a swamp with a maddened Descendant sounds like a recipe for disaster."

Fergus nodded. "Especially if these shadow creatures—Zulum, I guess they're called—can sense what Lucian carries. We might quickly find ourselves surrounded."

"I could try shielding the Orb of Shadows with a Creation brand," Lucian said. "Maybe it'll take the edge off."

"Are we really safe here?" Serah asked. "Those Zulum things came pretty close to the palace. You'd think Ninshar would have put a stop to that earlier."

"I've never been in a place with so many wards," Lucian said. "We're safe."

"He might trap us with those wards," Fergus said. "Whatever the case, I can keep watch tonight."

"Get some sleep, Fergus," Lucian said. "You've been keeping watch every night since we've arrived. What I can tell you is, if Ninshar is going to betray us, he won't be doing it tonight. Not before he gets the Starflower back."

"I'll trust you in that," Fergus said. "Your basic wards are more powerful than any mage shielding with every fiber of their being. If we can't sleep safely here, none of us can."

Despite the strength of Lucian's wards, everyone felt more comfortable sleeping within a short distance of each other on the couches rather than in separate rooms. Somehow, the magical lighting seemed to sense their intent to rest, automatically dimming.

Before settling down, Lucian found a quiet corner and retrieved the Orb of Shadows, still safe in its Binding. He reached deeply into the Manifold, creating a golden brand of Creation Magic to intermix with the Binding brand. Now, the dark violet Orb shimmered with a strange bronze light, as if the light of the Orb of Shadows was weakened by the Creation brand. Lucian realized that even now, Shadow Magic was working at the brand to unravel it. It would have to be periodically refreshed. He would check on it in the morning and see.

Within moments of closing his eyes, Lucian was asleep.

———

LUCIAN AWOKE TO THE SUNRISE, the heat radiating into the living area from the windows. The first thing he did was pull out the

Orb of Shadows. As he had guessed, the Creation brand he'd created the night before was almost completely gone. He drew deeply into the Manifold, refreshing it and strengthening it. The Orb seemed to thrum angrily at the brand, its color a mix of copper and violet. It was the same sensation as kicking an anthill and leaving your foot there for the inevitable. Or perhaps pressure building behind a valve or trying to cap a volcano that was about to explode.

Lucian dismissed the thought as the others stirred, heading for the table where, somehow, a meal had magically appeared with no sign of anyone entering the room. Apparently, Ninshar had some sort of serving staff here. As for how the food had appeared, Ninshar probably had at least a few sorcerers who could perform Space-Time Magic, unless he had performed the magic himself.

Whatever the case, Lucian was hungry. He approached to find food that was both strangely familiar and quite different from what he was used to. There was a plate filled with a variety of exotic fruits, their aroma sweet, many of them glowing with subtle light. There were delicate pastries filled with jam and topped with cream, along with a stack of something that looked like tortillas but was filled with herbs and vegetables, with a savory aroma. There was something that looked like bacon, but in this reality, Lucian could hardly imagine it had come from a pig. Maybe it was from a different creature that was similar. Besides this, there were glowing beverages, mini cakes with white icing, a bowl of what looked like porridge, only it was purple, along with many other things, far too much for them to eat.

"Nice spread!" Serah said, grabbing one of the tortilla-things and downing it without hesitation.

"You are *far* too trusting," Fergus said. "We don't even know what's in it, or who made it!"

"Whoever made it, send my compliments!" She smacked her fingers as she went for a pastry. "Is that Chantilly cream?"

"If we die, we die," Lucian said, grabbing some mystery bacon. "I'm hungry."

Reluctantly, the others ate, and Lucian had to admit, it had been a long while since he'd had anything so delicious and nourishing.

A half hour later, the room was well lit by the rising golden sun. The door opened, admitting Ninshar into the room. He wore form-fitting clothing that was simpler than his armor from yesterday.

He beamed a wide smile. "I trust you slept well?"

"Well enough," Lucian said. "I think we're ready when you are."

"Excellent. That's what I like to hear."

Without further preamble, a portal opened in the middle of the living area with a wave of Ninshar's hand. On the other side, Lucian could see what looked like a gray wasteland, the earth cracked, with a bright blue sky. In the far distance was a shimmering veil with shifting colors, what had to be the Barrier. A bit of cold, dry wind rustled into the chamber, along with the dust it carried.

"Looks . . . *promising*," Serah said.

Ninshar said nothing, instead stepping through. Everyone else followed.

The portal closed, and the air of this new environment chilled Lucian to the bone. He took a look around, finding the multicolored Barrier before him, stretching as far as his eyes could see, not only left and right, but directly into the sky without end. He wondered if it went all the way into space. Or, "the Void", he guessed it was called here.

Looking behind, the gray wasteland stretched until he could make out, in the far distance, a line of glittering trees. Sharpening his vision with Radiance, Lucian could see the trees of the forest had the same appearance as those from the Prismwood. Perhaps this was another side of the forest.

"This is where I leave you," Ninshar said. "Remember, shield yourself with Creation Magic. It is the only safeguard against the Shadow. Tread carefully, for you are about to enter a place from which most don't return."

"We'll find the core and bring it back," Lucian said.

"I am heartened by your confidence, Chosen." He gave a small bow. "May the Manifold guide your steps. I'll be waiting at Skymount. Good luck."

Then Ninshar was gone, with a warp that left the space he'd occupied empty.

"Good riddance," Fergus said. He turned and looked up and down at the Barrier before them. "Quite the obstacle. I'm detecting large amounts of Radiant Magic."

"I'm detecting large amounts of *every* Aspect," Emma said. "Radiance, Atomicism, Space-Time . . . plus some Aspects I can't really figure out."

"Shadow and Creation Magic," Lucian said. "Both are the primary streams. Anyone who controls the Starflower, which has access to both kinds of magic, can also influence the position of the Barrier. Even now, it's moving . . . slowly."

"Like a glacier," Serah said.

Lucian wasted no time and began streaming a powerful Creation shield to encompass them all. "Let's try to make it quick. The Barrier is pretty narrow from the looks of it. It's powerful, but if we step through fast, nothing bad will happen."

"Can't even see what's on the other side," Serah said. "What if there's a cliff or something?"

"We'll deal with it when we get there," Lucian said. "As soon as we pass, I should be able to feel this ethereal core. Right now, the Barrier is blocking me from detecting it. Let's get it and get out so we can get off this moon."

Serah sighed. "I hate fetch quests!"

Already, a plan was forming in Lucian's mind. It all depended on how Ninshar reacted when they returned with the Starflower.

He strode toward the Barrier, and the others fell into step around him. It was time to enter the Shadow Lands.

10

AFTER LUCIAN ENSURED his Creation Magic brand was still holding strong around the Orb of Shadows, he turned his attention to creating a powerful shield to guard himself and the others from the Barrier. He streamed until the shield was bright. Then, he took a few steps forward, testing his shield's strength against the Barrier. It held, but he knew it wouldn't last for long. It was like trying to keep oneself from being pushed down by a waterfall.

"Hurry!" he called.

They pushed through the Barrier and, within seconds, found themselves on the other side. Lucian adjusted what was left of his shield into a powerful ward. With luck, it would be enough to block anything from detecting the Orb of Shadows, on top of the other brand he'd created around the Orb.

On the other side, they found that the landscape of the Shadow Lands was practically the same as the Light Lands they had left behind. Only the sky was different, with ominous clouds casting everything in a dreary shade of sepia. The lack of colors felt washed out compared to the Light Lands until he realized that this was about what he was used to in his own reality. A few hills rose in the distance, toward which the rainbow path now led them. This "fetch quest" seemed to be the direction they were supposed to be going.

"Make sure your wards are strong," Lucian said.

He reached with his Focus, seeking to feel the ethereal core. To his surprise, there was something like a faint echo, similar to the pull of the Source of Power on Mako.

"I can feel it," Lucian said.

"I feel something, too," Emma said. "Though it's faint."

"Nothing for me," Fergus said. "Although both of you are stronger than me."

"Yeah," Serah said, eyes shifting. "I can feel it, too. Totally. Really strong. Yep."

"Let's keep it moving," Mira said.

They continued in silence. As soon as they traversed the first hills, Lucian saw the swamp Ninshar had mentioned in the distance, with boggy land, gloomy trees with hanging moss, and a thick fog that spread as far as the eye could see. The Seven-Fold Path led directly into the murk.

"Yuck," Serah said. "Do we really have to head into that disgusting mess?"

"Looks like it," Emma said.

"I'm sure that place is hiding more than a few monsters," Fergus said.

They came to a stop at the base of the hill as Lucian considered their position. He was hit with an uncanny sense of something watching him. He turned back for a moment, toward the hill they had just come down, but there was nothing there. Nothing obvious, anyway.

As they approached the line of trees, they traded the cold, dry wind of the wasteland for warmer and more humid air. The shift in climate did not seem possible, but Lucian also understood the rules were quite different here. It was a place where magic influenced the environment in inexplicable ways.

When they entered the trees, it was as if they were being swallowed by a giant primordial beast. They had to create light spheres to push back the darkness, but thankfully, the Seven-Fold Path seemed to lead them around the worst bits of the boggy ground. Lucian could see it adjusting its course in real-time in relation to their movement.

It didn't take long for them to find life, most of which was grotesque enough to be called monstrous: giant insects with stingers as long as an arm, snakes wrapped around trees and hanging from branches, even a reptilian creature reminiscent of a crocodile with a row of spines jutting from its leathery back.

"This . . ." Fergus said, "is the stuff of nightmares."

Lucian reached for his Focus. If any of these monsters so much as made a move toward them, they would get a fierce dose of his death lightning. Even the trees seemed like guardians of this swamp, subtly leaning over the path, creating a sense of suffocation. A root tripped Emma, nearly making her tumble into a nearby pool of stagnant water. It was hard to tell if it was bad luck or something more nefarious.

Serah stepped closer to Lucian, her shoulder touching his. "So, ugh . . . how long until this fortress place?"

At that very moment, there was a bend in the path, along with a creature blocking their way that Lucian could only describe as a hydra. It had three serpent heads protruding from a dragon-like body covered in black scales, with six massively clawed feet. Collectively, the three heads flicked out snakelike tongues. Unlike other monsters, this one didn't want to move and seemed to challenge them directly.

Lucian reached out Psionically, on the off chance this thing was sentient and could be parsed for useful information, but all he felt was a carnivorous hunger beyond anything he had ever known.

Without hesitation, he raised his hands and shot twin bolts of orange death lightning, surrounding the monstrosity in a cocoon of super-heated death. The monster scarcely had time to screech before the Atomic-Dynamistic stream rendered it into a pile of smoking ash. Seeing such a grotesque creature leveled so quickly was more satisfying than Lucian wanted to admit.

At the display of power, it seemed the swamp shrank back; the trees stopped leaning so close, and the monsters that had been edging from the water slunk back into the depths.

"That's right!" Serah called. "You want some too? Come on!"

"Don't antagonize them," Fergus said. "Imagine if they all had the thought of attacking at the same time . . ."

"Don't give them any ideas!" Serah said.

Lucian knew they wouldn't do that. These monsters were not on the same side. Like any ecosystem, they fought and cooperated as needed to ensure their own survival.

"I think we're safe," Lucian said. "We just have to be aware of what's getting close to us."

Emma's light sphere, which was following above them, increased in intensity, pushing deep into the swamp on all sides. Above the trees, Lucian could hear several high shrieks, as what appeared to be wyverns or even pterodactyls flew overhead.

"It's like we're in the time of the dinosaurs," Fergus said.

At that moment, several spikes flew straight toward them. Luckily, the projectiles were blocked by Lucian's Psionic ward. Lucian's eyes found the strange creature responsible for the attack, a turnip-looking thing with wide, long oval eyes and a wide mouth poking its head above the swamp's murky surface. It attempted to slip back into the depths, but Lucian instantly froze the surrounding water, locking the monster into place. It squealed in dismay right before Lucian finished it with a fork of lightning.

He gathered his ether, streaming a shield of death lightning that swirled around the entire party. Anything that dared touch it would be blown to bits.

Once done, he set it with a brand. "Goes without saying but . . . don't touch that."

"Is this . . . a death lightning shield?" Mira asked, her face pale.

"Yes," Lucian said. "We won't have to worry about anything small. If we get to something bigger, I can take care of it."

"This Descendant fellow probably knows we're on our way by now," Fergus said. "I can hardly block this expenditure of magic."

"Probably," Lucian said. "But we're getting close. I can feel it."

For the next few hours, they made their way through the gloomy swamp, mostly avoiding the water and native life. Eventually, they came upon an actual road, what appeared to be a highway of sorts, quite wide and built on a stone bridge above the swamp itself, with neatly laid stones as a base. The fact this highway existed told Lucian that the Shadow Lands were not just a place of monsters. They had a working government and a great deal of resources to marshal. These stones were certainly not native to the region. The rainbow path laid itself atop the road, while magically powered lanterns lit the highway on either side. Lucian also detected wards covering the highway, designed to repel all but the strongest forms of native life.

He allowed his death lightning shield to dissipate. "We're very close now."

In his mind, he felt the ethereal core. What had once been a distant echo now felt like a hum in his mind, almost like an Orb.

"It may feel safer here," Fergus said, "but it's obvious that people—or at least, creatures of some sort, these Sumaril perhaps—use this road often. We should be careful."

"What if someone comes along?" Mira asked.

"We do what we always do," Lucian said.

"Improvise?" Serah asked.

"Exactly."

They came to another bridge, leading over a dark and stagnant lake. In the middle of that lake, Lucian spied several dark towers rising through the mist, connected by decrepit bridges, lit weakly by the orange light of fires.

"Looks like we've found our swamp fortress," Lucian said.

He could feel powerful magic emanating from the stronghold. The shield was quite similar to the one that had been guarding the Immortal's tower on Nai Elyn, but a fair bit weaker. It should prove easy to slip through. Lucian created the same shield to bypass it, making sure it was well-edified with Creation and Space-Time Magic. Then he prepared a warp that would place them on a bridge connecting two of the towers. That would get them close enough to the ethereal core for them to find the rest of the way.

"Get ready," he said. "I'm warping us to the bridge closest to the main tower."

"Let's get this over with," Fergus said, crouching low.

Lucian streamed his magic, and in the next instant, they reappeared high above the swamp. From the following quiet, broken only by the squawks of some carrion birds, it seemed they were still undetected.

"I feel it inside the main tower," Lucian said. "Lower."

As they started toward the tower, just a few steps away from the bridge, the metal door ahead swung open, revealing a bipedal creature with a light blue face, red eyes, and pointed ears, wearing a dark metal hauberk and wielding a trident. Its eyes widened as it cried out in alarm.

Lucian quickly quelled it with a Psionic stream, accessing its mind and penetrating its deepest thoughts. He quickly discovered that while sentient, this being was controlled by a brand of Shadow Magic, which made it completely subservient to its master. The brand was powerful, making it difficult to discover the information he needed.

Lucian deepened his connection, lacing his Psionic stream with Creation Magic. He broke through and quickly absorbed the layout of the fortress and any pertinent information that would help them against Ashurban. In the space of a moment, Lucian learned a lot. For one, the vast majority of the fortress was actually not contained in these towers, but beneath the surface of the swamp itself in a vast network of caves, dungeons, and tunnels. The lowest part of Esharal was where Ashurban and the core could be found.

Once Lucian couldn't glean any more information, he hurled the creature over the side of the bridge with a tether, Binding its mouth shut to keep it from making noise. It careened through the air, crashing into the swamp beneath.

"Damn," Serah said. "That was brutal."

Lucian approached the metal door, raised his hand, and melted it off its hinges. He lifted the door with Psionics and allowed it to fall over the bridge's side. Inside, a spiral staircase circled down into darkness.

"That'll take us to the lower part of the fortress," Lucian explained. "That's where we'll find Ashurban."

"Let's get a move on," Fergus said.

They ran down the dark stairs. Lucian could increasingly feel the pull of the core as they drew closer. Soon, the stairs ended, deep beneath the swamp itself, near the heart of Ashurban's lair. Another door stood before them, branded so subtly that Lucian almost didn't detect it.

"Wait," he said.

He read the streams and realized that anyone stepping through without the proper brand was going to have a bad day. From the heavy Thermal streams, the instructions of the brand were clear: to incinerate anything that didn't hold the proper pass-ward.

Lucian attempted to read the brand, but soon discovered that many of the streams were impossible to decipher. It could only mean one thing. The ward they needed to pass required Shadow Magic.

The only other option was to brute force the brand and hope for the best.

Lucian streamed Thermalism, creating an incredibly powerful shield. He also layered it with Binding Magic, which would protect them from any recoil.

By now, Ashurban was surely aware of them, so they had to get moving.

"Get ready," he said.

"For what?" Mira asked.

Lucian didn't answer, instead blasting the door off its hinges with a Psionic push.

What followed was chaos. Fire and pure energy surrounded them, but they were an island in the storm. Lucian had neglected to shield the light, but thankfully was quick enough to dim it so they wouldn't be blinded. He felt nothing of the unreal heat surrounding them other than a faint warmth. The explosion quickly ebbed, revealing a stone corridor burning with red-hot fire. If there had been anything beyond that hallway, it had been instantly vaporized.

Lucian led everyone through the flames, a bubble of safety in the inferno. His Thermal shield easily cooled their surroundings. Simultaneously, an Atomic aura streamed by Mira ensured the continual creation of a fresh atmosphere for them to breathe. That action, as complicated as it was, seemed to come naturally to her.

The corridors were completely clear as they threaded their way to Ashurban's chambers. Once they reached the end of the fires, they found a group of the same beings that had been on the bridge above. Watching for a moment, Lucian could see similarities in their appearance to Ninshar, but they lacked all the radiant glory of the Ascendant. Right now, they were maddeningly trying to put out the fire with buckets of water, completely oblivious to their presence within the flames. If they did that, it could only mean they had no access to magic.

Like the spirit of the fire itself, Lucian flew out, Lightspear in hand, cutting down the first wave of Sumaril, their bodies disintegrating into ash. The rest squealed and fled, but Lucian prevented their escape with a Binding barrier. Most hadn't even had time to grab their weapons before Lucian caught up and slashed them with a quick sweep of his spear.

For a moment, he considered the terror they must have felt at his attack and almost felt bad, until he realized that they would have done far worse to him, given the opportunity. Like the guard above, they were controlled by Ashurban's magic and would not have hesitated to kill them most brutally.

The others caught up with him and proceeded, refreshing the group's wards.

They rounded a corner to find two more Sumaril wearing black robes. They had been waiting in ambush, and it seemed they were magic users because two streams of white-hot fire shot from their hands, only to be absorbed by Mira's shield.

Lucian simply appeared behind them with a quick warp and cut them down, the golden magic of Lightspear disintegrating their bodies.

"It's not even a fair fight," Fergus said.

Lucian approached a pair of doors, on the other side of which their quarry was waiting. "If you're looking for something harder, you're about to get it."

"Let's go," Emma said.

Lucian blasted open the doors, where the Descendant Ashurban and the Ethereal Core waited.

WHAT APPEARED to be a decrepit sanctuary stood revealed, with tall arched ceilings and grand, stained-glass windows depicting scenes of monsters. The vaulted ceiling above showed faded scenes of battles. Dust covered the empty stone floor, and the entire space was dimly lit by a magical infusion of light branded along the walls and ceiling.

On the altar stood Ashurban. His figure was tall and imposing, staring down at them with baleful red eyes that glowed in the dim light. His skin was sickly gray and corpse-like, with a sharp and angular face stretched like candle wax, his ears pointing beyond his wispy hair. His robes were black as midnight, surrounded by a dark aura of Shadow Magic. His appearance was as grand as Ninshar's, albeit in a colder way.

Lucian sensed Ashurban had been deep in meditation, so much so that the Descendant hadn't realized anything was amiss until they had broken into the sanctuary. Either that, or he simply didn't care and was focusing on defending himself and the ethereal core he surely held in his Focus.

When Ashurban opened his mouth to speak, Lucian's Psionic ward easily translated the guttural words that issued forth.

"You dare disturb my meditation?" Ashurban's red eyes then marked Lightspear, along with Lucian's companions. Understanding seemed to dawn, and the Descendant gave an eerie, yellow smile. "Ah. That fool Ninshar has sent you, hasn't he? What if I told you that you were on the wrong side?"

Lucian understood only one thing: the longer he waited, the more power Ashurban could draw from the core to attack them. There was only one correct move here.

Lucian didn't bother responding, instead blasting a golden wave of magic toward Ashurban. The Descendant let out a cry of surprise but quickly streamed a Shadow shield to deflect the attack. He then collected that Shadow Magic, gathering it into a dark orb that split into multiple dark arrows that rained from above.

Lucian slowed the flow of time, allowing them to dodge the arrows while he worked to strengthen his Creation shield. Fergus and Mira fanned out to the left, the former streaming lasers from his hand while Mira threw fireballs laced with lightning. As Ashurban shielded both attacks, Serah moved in, creating a Gravitonic disc beneath Ashurban to lock him in place. Emma kept pace with Lucian for a more direct assault on the Descendant.

Despite the multitude of attacks, Ashurban still shielded everything while surrounding himself with a shell laced with orange death lightning, a shell that suddenly flared with cracking whips. Lucian neutralized the attack with Atomicism while he and Emma closed in. He stabbed with Lightspear, but not before Ashurban warped away, reappearing in the air above them. Lucian jumped after him, Lightspear in hand, while Ashurban streamed a powerful telekinetic tether toward Fergus, Mira, and Serah, who were pooling their magic for a coordinated attack.

Lucian didn't have time to block the tether, but thankfully, the three of them saw it coming, streaming a shield that shattered the tether on impact.

By now, Lucian had caught up to Ashurban, who turned to face him in mid-air, red eyes burning with fury. He created a shield of Shadow Magic and a spear of pure darkness to counter Lucian's weapon, but he must have known his weapon couldn't hold up for long, because the Descendant did everything he could to avoid Lucian's attacks.

While Lucian battled with Ashurban in the upper reaches of the cathedral, the Descendant's Sumaril minions began flooding the sanctuary, charging toward Lucian's companions, who were only now regathering themselves. Emma combined Radiance and Space-Time, phasing from one Sumaril to the next, cutting them down with her shockspear.

As his friends battled below, Lucian tried to seal the deal with Ashurban; the Descendant was incredibly wily, seeming to draw out the fight more so than trying to kill Lucian outright. Lucian realized that this was his plan: wait for reinforcements to arrive until they were overwhelmed, using the power of the Starflower to hang on. Emma and the others couldn't last forever against the Sumaril below, assuming the reinforcements kept coming.

And worse, no matter how powerful his attacks, Ashurban never seemed to exhaust himself. His Shadow shield was powerful, continually pulsing with infusions of fresh ether.

The others were now being driven back to the altar, the Sumaril numbering in the dozens, brandishing curved swords, axes, and even whips. Thankfully, none seemed capable of using magic. The Descendant floating before Lucian seemed to fight with greater intensity and desperation. Multiple times, Lucian blocked Ashurban's clumsy Space-Time streams, his opponent clearly trying to warp past him toward his friends, who were now fighting for their lives against endless waves of attackers.

Ashurban fought desperately, trying to get past Lucian, but Lucian wasn't allowing it. Ashurban screeched his dismay, fighting with the ferocity of a cornered badger, but Lucian kept him locked in place. The Descendant's desperation left holes in his defenses, holes that Lucian easily exploited. For the first time, Ashurban was being pushed back, enough for Lucian to stream a quick blast of chained death lightning at the swarming Sumaril below, obliterating half of them. That would allow the others to hold longer.

But this one move provided enough of a distraction for Ashurban to counterattack. The Descendant flew straight toward Lucian, wreathed in fire while throwing streams of pure Shadow Magic. Lucian countered, throwing Lightspear directly at Ashurban, the weapon absorbing the Shadowy chains. The Descendant warped a few meters away, reappearing with his shield fully powered. Lucian hit back, recharging his Creation shield to throw Ashurban back.

From below, Emma was still streaming at Ashurban, slowing his movements. Lucian used his own Space-Time Magic, speeding his advance as he summoned Lightspear again, stabbing it through the Descendant's shield.

An explosion of golden light spread outward as Lucian buried Lightspear deep into the Descendant's chest. Ashurban screeched in pain, golden beams of light piercing his body like arrows as he disintegrated in midair. As his body shriveled before Lightspear's fury, his dark robes floated off his form toward the teeming mass of Sumaril below.

The Sumaril, once bound by Ashurban's Shadow Magic, lost all coordination, attacking anything and everything in a directionless frenzy. Lucian floated above the crowd, easily mowing down the opposition. Within seconds, there was nothing but a hundred or more bodies, their collective stink already assaulting Lucian's nostrils.

Left behind where Ashurban's body once floated was a shining orb of sapphire blue, levitating and not falling to the floor as expected.

First, he created a Binding brand over the doors to keep more Sumaril from entering, but if the high screeches and snorts outside the sanctuary were any sign, they were already turning on each other.

Lucian floated toward the ethereal core, and from its color, he could see how it earned the name of Starflower. Indeed, it was the same hue as the beautiful mountain flowers he'd seen, almost as brilliant as a star. Lucian surrounded it with a Binding brand before grabbing it and heading for the altar, where the others were waiting.

He landed, finding that everyone was safe but frazzled. They were gathered around Emma, who was kneeling and catching her breath. Lucian kneeled beside her.

"You okay?"

Emma drew a few deep breaths, then gave a nod. "Yeah. That . . . wasn't easy."

"You turned the tide. Good work." He took in the others. "We'll be out of here soon enough." He handed the ethereal core to Emma.

Her eyes widened as her face was bathed in its blue light. "Lucian, are you sure?"

"It's yours. Besides, I don't want to put it next to the Orb of Shadows. I trust my Binding brands, but there's no telling how that would interact with it."

Emma nodded, at last standing with Serah's help. She took the core and placed it in her pack. "I'll save it for a rainy day, then."

"Let's get out of here," Fergus said.

Lucian had never heard of a better idea. He opened a portal back to the Barrier, and without further waiting, they stepped through.

12

THEY EMERGED on the wasteland on the Shadow Lands side. Lucian watched the Barrier before them, stretching seemingly eternally up into the sky, a panorama of all the colors of every Aspect. They would once again have to pass it before Lucian could warp them back to Skymount; the Barrier was powerful enough to interfere with his stream if he tried to portal directly there from this side.

He turned to look at the dark forest in the distance, noting the Seven-Fold Path no longer led in that direction. They had done whatever it had meant for them to do.

There was nothing left but to keep moving. Lucian began by streaming a Creation shield, an act that was second nature by now. Together, they stepped through the Barrier, taking only a few seconds to transition. Back on the Light Lands' side, the evening sky was comparatively bright, filled with a multitude of stars, and as always, the planet Kadur above. The sun was already setting over the treetops in the distance. The vast array of colors —of oranges, pinks, and purples—was a stark contrast to the dismal brown of before.

Before creating another portal, he turned to the others. "I couldn't get a good read on Ninshar, and I don't know what his reaction will be once we give him the Starflower. We're going to have to play this by ear. All I know is, he was following us for a good while, but we lost him in the swamp. I couldn't say anything before, because he probably would have overheard."

"Seriously?" Serah asked. "What a creeper..."

"At some point, he will lower his guard and let his intentions be known. Bear with me until that happens."

"I can already tell you he's up to no good, son," Mira said. "Either way, we're standing by and ready to help."

Lucian nodded. "I'm glad I have all of you to back me up."

After gathering himself for a moment, Lucian let out a breath and willed another portal into existence. He opened this one right before the celestial stairway leading to Ninshar's palace, set against a backdrop of the setting sun. They stepped through into the frigid air. Lucian streamed a Thermal aura to nullify the cold and waited.

It didn't take long for Ninshar to appear, warping at the base of the stairs, a golden aura surrounding his battle armor and spear. A wide smile was plastered onto his sculpted face.

"Back already!" he said. "And the sun has yet to set!"

"We did as you asked," Lucian said.

"You have it, then?"

Lucian nodded at Emma, who pulled out the Starflower from her pack in its Binding. The beautiful blue orb shone like a miniature star, its blue only enhanced by the Binding Magic protecting it.

Ninshar's eyes widened at the sight, his slit-like eyes becoming clouded with greed. Lucian felt an opening to his mind, reading the Ascendant's intentions.

"Yes, this is it," Ninshar said. "And you handle it so carelessly! That brand is a simple thing."

"There can be beauty in simplicity," Lucian said. "I think you'll find this brand impossible to break. It's safe, I promise."

"Well, I thank you for your speed," Ninshar said. He proffered a golden hand. "Undo the Binding, and I shall make the arrangements for the ship."

Lucian smiled. "Ah. Not so fast. Let's see that ship first."

Ninshar smiled graciously, but there was a sharpness to it, and anger in his eyes. It only lasted a moment, flickering away so quickly that Lucian would not have been sure it was truly there without the aid of his magic. "But of course. The harbor isn't far."

Ninshar opened a portal, on the other side of which Lucian could spy a sheltered cove, where high cliffs rose on either side of the water. It was clearly an entirely separate island below this one, in the water itself. Stone buildings and docks blended seamlessly with the surrounding landscape, carved from the mountain itself, all glowing from the light of the setting sun. Though there were at least two dozen docks, only one was occupied by a ship with an aerodynamic design. Lucian had to guess, from that sleek design, that it could fly as well as navigate the water.

"Follow me," the Ascendant said, stepping through.

The others looked to Lucian for direction, and he nodded it was safe. They followed Ninshar through, and in the next moment, stood in the harbor at the base of the mountain. The air was warm here, allowing Lucian to drop his Thermal ward. Ninshar's eyes almost seemed misty as he gazed upon the vessel, which, like the ethereal core, was surrounded by a protective Binding barrier. The ship's design seemed like a work of art, almost floating above the surface of the water. The wood of its hull was silver, the timber likely coming from the Prismwood not far away. Three series of masts promised a speedy vessel, which was also quite grand, befitting a being of Ninshar's station.

"It has been long since I've visited *Celestior* in her berth," Ninshar said wistfully. "I hate to part with her, but the price has been agreed.

Against all reason, against all hope, you have returned with the very thing that will allow me to rebuild my realm. And in less than a day, you have defeated my ancient foe, the Descendant Ashurban the Maleficent, who has killed all of my greatest sorcerers."

Though Ninshar's words were warm and congratulatory, Lucian could feel resentment emanating from the Ascendant's mind. He had fully expected Lucian and the others to die an agonizing death in the Shadow Lands. And yet, Ninshar's true purpose remained clouded to him.

"Will we need a crew for the ship?" Lucian asked.

"No, Chosen. It will heed the call of its master and captain. Only connect your mind to it, and it will obey your every command. There is no better vessel on the Eye to see you to the Gate, and even beyond."

Despite these words, Lucian couldn't help but feel the Ascendant was hoping the worst would happen. Still, Lucian detected no outright lie in Ninshar's words. Piloting *Celestior* would probably be like *Garuda* during the time of the First Starsea. "It's ready to go?"

"She stands ready, Chosen. Now, I'm afraid I must insist on receiving my end of the bargain. Only then can I release the ship to you."

"Of course. But only when you lower the barrier, and I'm one hundred percent certain the ship is truly mine."

There was a moment of tension, but at last, Ninshar's posture softened. "But of course. I have no ill will toward you, Lucian Abrantes. As a token of my trust, I shall be first to release my prize." A moment later, the shield to the ship fell, and Ninshar gave a bow. "She's yours to command, Chosen."

Lucian reached out for it and found an instant connection. He willed the ship to come closer to him, and to his surprise, it immediately sprang to life. It churned through the water with silky ease, and within half a minute, was turning and settling before them on the nearest dock, just steps away.

Ninshar waited expectantly. Lucian nodded to Emma. She looked unsure, but finally offered the core to Ninshar.

The Ascendant took it, his face basked by its brilliant blue glow, his hand shaking. "What is this? You must undo the Binding."

"It will unravel on its own once we're through the Gate," Lucian said. "It works by proximity. Read the stream for yourself and you'll see."

Ninshar took on a brief look of concentration. "Yes, I can sense that. It would seem you've thought of everything."

"That's why I'm still alive," Lucian said.

Ninshar smiled. "Oh? Well, this is a dangerous world, where only the canny survive. Even if the move was unnecessary, I do not fault your wisdom."

Lucian smiled back. "Funny you should say that. This world is quite dangerous, which is why I'm grateful for your help during our mission."

Ninshar frowned, puzzled. "What do you mean?"

"That can be the only reason you followed us into the Shadow Lands, right? To cover our backs?"

There was a brief flash of surprise, and even anger, on Ninshar's face, but it was quickly erased. "You are mistaken."

"You probably thought I wouldn't notice. I felt your presence right before we entered the swamp."

Ninshar laughed nervously. "Well, what's the harm in admitting it? Can you blame me for wanting to make sure you made it to Esharal in one piece, when so many had failed?"

"You insisted you couldn't cross the Barrier, which was why you needed us to do it. That was an obvious lie. So that's why I'm being careful, not letting you have access to the core until we're well off this moon. You say you're loyal to the Light, but this is at odds with greed for the Orbs, which I can feel with my Psionic Magic. My guess is, in following us, you were waiting for an opportunity to strike, perhaps while we were being attacked in the swamp, but in the end, you lost your courage. You went back to wait for us until we brought the Starflower to you. With the full power of the core, you could be on a stronger footing to challenge me for the Orbs."

"Your accusations are vile, Chosen. I am true to the Light, as ever I have been. If I covet the Orbs, well, what Ascendant of my station would not? It is possible to covet and not be a murderer."

"I see your point," Lucian said, "except you let those Zulum within a stone's throw of your palace. Such entities of Shadow Magic are easily detectable, unlike what you said. Why did you only jump in at the end of the battle? You only intervened when you decided I was going to win, thinking it was a sure way to gain my trust." Lucian went on relentlessly. "You let the Zulum through to kill us. When they failed, you changed plans, deciding we might be useful to get the Starflower. And once we got that for you, you could use its power to get the Orbs from me. The ship is a minor loss for you. In fact, by giving it to me, you hoped to win our ultimate trust, giving you an opening to go in for the kill."

"You waited to say all this until I gave you control of the ship," Ninshar said. "Clever."

"But now that all this is out in the open, you must know there's no chance of you getting the Orbs. Ever. I'm actually willing to let you keep the Starflower as long as you leave us alone. If you're smart, you'll count that as a win. Because if you follow us . . . you will die."

Ninshar suddenly snarled, throwing out his hand, but Lucian was ready. He shielded the sudden fork of lightning easily, shooting forward with Lightspear in hand. But before he could connect, Ninshar vanished and did not reappear. The harbor was completely silent.

"Is he gone?" Emma asked.

"For now," Lucian said. "He's not one to attack directly, but from the shadows."

"To think we lost the Starflower to that guy!" Serah said.

"Well, the point is we get to leave this place now," Emma said. "As long as the ship is truly ours to command, and Ninshar can't cause trouble, it's a win in my book."

Fergus regarded the ship before them. "So, will this ship really work? No traps or anything?"

"None," Lucian said. "I can feel its magic from bow to stern, from keel to the top of the mainmast. It's all ours. He hasn't had time to lay any traps as far as the ship is concerned, but that doesn't mean he doesn't have surprises in store for us in the future."

"We better get on before he tries anything else," Emma said.

"Yes, that's a good idea."

Lucian executed a quick warp, including the others in it. In the very next moment, they were settled on the deck of the *Celestior*. He accessed the Psionic link connecting him to the ship. He realized the Focus powering the ship had been a sorcerer once, and a powerful one. He read the ship's intentions once again to double-check and found nothing wanting.

"Looks like trouble," Fergus said, watching the cliffs in the distance.

Surrounding the ship, Lucian spied at least a dozen darker shades advancing from the harbor and across the water toward the ship. Zulum.

Lucian commanded the ship to go forward, and it glided across the water like a cloud. The Zulum were fast, though, and already the first had reached the ship. Lucian streamed from the Orb of Creation, creating a massive golden shield around the entire ship, continually feeding it with ether.

Lucian directed *Celestior* upward, out of the water so that it was flying. Automatically, its Gravitonic field engaged, keeping their feet firmly on the deck despite the sharp angle of ascent. The Zulum trailed the ship like shadows, but the ship's increasing speed left them in the dust. Several shot orbs of darkness toward them, but they were easily snuffed out by Lucian's shield.

Lucian turned his attention forward. They were already halfway toward the open water of the Celestial Sea, skirting between the high cliffs of the island.

"We're not out of the woods yet," Lucian said.

Celestior continued to speed through the air between the cliffs, and the Zulum were left hopelessly behind. Lucian entrusted the Space-Time ward to Emma, so there was no chance of the shadow entities reappearing anywhere close to the ship.

Within minutes, they had left the island well behind and were flying high above the open sea, toward the star-filled sky in the distance, once again following the Seven-Fold Path. Lucian commanded the ship to fly as fast as possible.

"We need to reinforce the ship's wards," he said. "They seem to be quite weak. Emma, Space-Time needs to be warded at full strength at all times until we're off this moon."

"No worries there," Emma said.

"I can make sure the Gravitonic field is kept up to speed," Serah said.

"Beautiful view," Mira said, looking from the bow at the starry expanse over the glowing sea. "Wonder how far it is to the Gate?"

"No telling," Lucian said. "The ship is pretty fast, though. All we have to do is follow the Seven-Fold Path. It'll take us right to the Gate."

Lucian set the ship to follow the rainbow path, which curved just above the serene water. Unfortunately, there was no way to direct the ship to follow it automatically, since Lucian was the only one who could detect it. He'd just have to do with as little sleep as possible for this stage of the journey.

"We're forgetting one thing," Fergus said. "Ninshar mentioned something about some Leviathan guarding the Gate. We'll have to fight it at some point."

"Yeah, he wasn't lying about that," Lucian said. "I imagine it'll show up once we're close."

"What do you think it is, exactly?" Emma asked. "I saw a painting of this dragon-like thing in the observatory. Maybe that's it?"

"It's clearly some massive sea monster. Maybe there's a way to phase the ship past it, or maybe we can fly above it. We're going to have some time to think about it."

"Assuming Ninshar doesn't attack us on the way," Fergus said.

"No way Ninshar can get past my ward," Emma said. "I've defended entire fleets with my magic. What chance does he have?"

"I just want to say," Serah said, "that might be the most badass thing I've ever heard you say, Emma."

Emma smiled graciously.

"We should secure the ship," Mira said. "It looks rather large, and I want to be sure there are no surprises."

They took the time to explore the ship, which unsurprisingly was more like a fancy yacht. The main cabin was expansive, with panoramic views of the surrounding sea and sky, plush seating, and exotic wood paneling. Below the living area were the living quarters, with at least twenty cabins of varying sizes. Each had a large, comfortable bed and a commanding view outside. The largest cabin was in the stern, with wide windows overlooking the sea. In the distance, Lucian could spy Skymount, easily small enough to cover with a single finger. It would soon be lost to distance, and for that, he was thankful.

Besides this, there was a richly appointed dining area, while in each room, Lucian detected magical brands attuned to his specifications. At will, he could change the temperature, allow ethereal music to play, summon food from a magically powered kitchen, or even release different pleasing aromas. There was even a magically powered spa with a sauna, and an observation area that seemed designed for stargazing.

After some time, they once again gathered in the main cabin. With Emma's Space-Time ward, Lucian wasn't worried about Ninshar warping directly on top of them. The only thing he had to worry about was this Leviathan in the future, and maybe Ninshar ambushing them somewhere along the way. If he did so, it would be without the benefit of the Starflower, since that wasn't usable as long as Lucian remained on the Eye.

"This ship might make a nice little base," Fergus said approvingly. "We'll fly to Anshar in style!"

"You've always enjoyed the finer things in life," Mira said.

"Yes," Fergus said. "Yes, I have."

Lucian did his best to ignore the intention in his voice. "We'll need to keep constant watch to be on the safe side, day and night. I can volunteer for the first shift. Make sure we maintain a steady course."

"I'll take second shift, then," Fergus said.

"Feels like we're making progress finally," Serah said. "No more side quests. Heart of Creation, here we come!"

It sounded good to Lucian. But both Anshar and the Heart of Creation were a long way yet.

13

FOR THE FIRST few days on the Celestial Sea, they were on high alert for any threat, but there was nothing but the airship skirting the surface of the water and the endless expanse of the ocean.

It was difficult to keep their guards up, given the deceptively peaceful environment. If Lucian ever enhanced his vision with Radiance, he spied vast schools of fish beneath the surface, some quite large. The largest life-form they saw was a long, dragon-like creature with a sail along its green-scaled back, flecked with silver. He wondered if the creature might be the Leviathan, or perhaps a smaller version of it. The monster seemed to follow them for a few hours before losing interest and diving into the depths.

Serah figured out how to use the ship's galley, with various magical brands that made cooking easier. At first, their meals were simple: bowls of fruit, warm fluffy bread with butter. But as time wore on, the dishes became more elaborate as Serah gained confidence: seared fish prepared to perfection, a creamy pasta-like dish reminiscent of risotto, steamed exotic vegetables infused with flavor. Lucian didn't know how she created such a strange assortment of food she had never worked with before, but something about the magical brands on the equipment also seemed to impart knowledge.

And as for imparting knowledge, Lucian took the reprieve as an opportunity to pass on the language of the Ascendants to the others, so that he wouldn't have to continually use a Psionic ward. This task was accomplished in just a few hours with great efficiency.

The passage was an opportunity for rest as well. The first few days in the Light Realm had been a gauntlet, where it seemed everyone and everything wanted them dead, from the Zulum to Ashurban, and finally, Ninshar himself. As one week passed, and then two, Lucian had to remind himself not to become complacent.

Strangely, after the first week, the Seven-Fold Path switched directions. Rather than going in a straight line toward the horizon, as it had been doing, it made turns seemingly at random, with no real rhyme or reason. Sometimes it was a slight change, and sometimes it was an extremely sharp turn, almost to where they were turning completely around and going back in their original direction. It made Lucian paranoid about going to sleep, knowing that the Path could change course at any moment.

And then one morning, they awoke to a sight that was both strange and terrifying. It started with a shout of warning from Serah, who had been on the early morning watch. Lucian warped to her position, summoning Lightspear while preparing his magical defenses.

His eyes were greeted by something that looked like a mountain rising from the water. Except, as Lucian enhanced his vision with Radiance, he saw it wasn't a mountain, but a living thing.

It took a moment to realize that it actually wasn't living. It was utterly still, a snake-like dragon far larger than the one that had followed them a week ago. He was certain there was no creature in all the Worlds that was as big as this, a hundred meters wide at the least and many times as long. It was unmoving, merely floating on the waves as if asleep, aquamarine scales glittering under the early morning light. It made no movement as Lucian directed the ship to fly around it, rising high above the water and gaining an even more commanding view of the beast.

And impossible to miss was the object that had killed the monster. Right through its center rose a spire of pure crystal, made of some ethereal solid that was strong enough to pierce its thick scales. The spire rose as tall as a skyscraper into a wicked point. Waves lapped at the side of the beast, its massive head with hundreds of eyes lolling under the gentle currents, all closed in death.

Mira swallowed. "Did . . . Ninshar do this?"

Lucian realized it couldn't have been anyone else, and he would have done so without the power of the core. "It probably hasn't been dead long."

"How did he do it without the power of the core?" Serah asked.

Lucian didn't have an answer for that.

"So, he killed this thing and is heading for the Gate," Serah went on. "And he's probably waiting for us on the other side. And he'll have the core to help him out?"

Lucian thought that was probably an accurate assessment. "Seems like it."

She whistled as she looked at Ninshar's handiwork. "Seems like we're going to have our work cut out for us."

"The Gate can't be far from here," Emma said.

Lucian realized she was right. They hadn't left the Leviathan far behind before he heard a low drone that steadily grew in intensity. By the time the noise grew into a dull roar, he saw the source of the disturbance.

A waterfall stretched from horizon to horizon, and beyond was nothing but dark sky and stars. It seemed the sea itself was falling over the edge and into nothing, as if they had come to the very end of the world itself. Lucian couldn't understand how such a phenomenon was possible, and yet it was staring them in the face.

As the others gathered around him, Lucian prepared to make a sharp turn to save the ship and its crew. But the Seven-Fold Path did not deviate, leading right over the edge.

Lucian knew his resolve to follow the Path would be tested as never before. The ship's Gravitonic Magic could levitate it above the water, but to levitate it over the vast space beyond those falls was something else entirely.

"Lucian!" Fergus called over the din. "Do something!"

Everything within Lucian screamed for him to turn the ship. But he also knew he'd be leading them astray.

"The Chosen will know the way," Lucian said. "Find something to hold onto!"

Everyone screamed as the sea came to a sudden end and the ship flew right over the edge and onto the rainbow path. Without the surface beneath for the Gravitonic brand to push against, the ship *should* have fallen into the massive cavity beneath them.

Except that didn't happen. They continued to fly, the latent magic of the Path powering the ship, acting as a surface as surely as the water had. The others watched in disbelief as the waterfall fell behind them, disintegrating into mist that was soon lost to what seemed to be eternal darkness. There was no light but the distant stars and a green and blue planet in the distance, the planet toward which the Seven-Fold Path was leading.

Lucian knew that if the ship deviated from the Path, it would fall into the void below. This was probably some massive crater into which the surrounding sea was falling, with the water somehow coming out elsewhere to continue the cycle. It didn't seem possible, but then again, magic was infused into the very fabric of this reality, so Lucian couldn't guess what was possible and what wasn't.

"Seems like we're heading toward that world in the distance," Fergus said quietly. In the eerie stillness of the black void, even a whisper sounded loud.

"Well, this is trippy, that's all I can say," Serah said, turning around. "Hey! I can't see the waterfall anymore. That was fast!"

Lucian turned to look, and indeed, the sea behind them was receding as the Seven-Fold Path took them farther across the crater.

"Up ahead," Fergus said. "That could be our Gate."

Something like a star appeared in the distance, growing steadily brighter. The Seven-Fold Path was leading them there with surprising speed. It reminded Lucian greatly of the First Gate.

"Get ready," Lucian said. "I don't know what's going to be on the other side."

"Ninshar," Emma said. "I'm already making my Space-Time ward as strong as I can."

Everyone redoubled their own wards, ensuring that whatever hit them on the other side, they were ready to face it.

They watched as the shining Gate, which shone with pearlescent light, fast approached. Much like the Gates in their own reality, it was composed of two massive, shining pylons, curved inward toward each other reminiscent of a pair of parentheses. But unlike the Gates they were familiar with, this one appeared to be a lot smaller, perhaps only a hundred meters tall and half as wide. Between the two pylons was a white plane of light, on the other side of which lay a new world.

Celestior continued to follow the Seven-Fold Path, Lucian trying to slow it down. They were coming in far too hot.

He forced himself to keep his eyes open as the opening neared, as its white light consumed them all.

On the other side, there was sunlight and a bright blue sky. The air was shockingly cold as the ship tilted downward, continuing to follow the Path, but also losing a lot of the speed it had gained going over the crater. Lucian snuck a look behind, but already, the Gate could not be seen; behind them, he spied a massive construction that could only be described as a floating palace. They were high in the atmosphere of Kadur. Over his shoulder, he could see the moon they had just transitioned from, which indeed, looked like an ominous eye watching them.

He wanted to get a better look at the levitating construction, but the Seven-Fold Path was leading them toward the ground. To divert course so high above the surface would mean losing complete control of the ship. The Path was now leading to a bank of clouds that looked like freshly fallen snow. Lucian reinforced the ship's defenses, keeping out the cold while preparing to protect them from the wetness of the clouds.

And, of course, he kept his senses on high alert. Ninshar could be anywhere nearby, and no doubt, he was watching them now.

They plunged into the cloud, Lucian's Binding barrier doing a good job of pushing the moisture back. There they remained for about a minute before the landscape below them stood revealed, a patchwork of desert, mountains, and badlands with no sign of habitation.

Nor was there any sign of Ninshar. Had he perished while trying to take down the Leviathan, or was he trying to lull them into a false sense of security?

That was when something buffeted the side of the hull, throwing the ship off the rainbow path and sending them hurtling to the ground beneath. As Lucian worked to steady the ship, a beam of dark magic sliced down from the sky, originating from a flying figure. The beam instantly shattered the ship's Creation shield and pulverized the deck.

There was no time to do anything but abandon the ship. Lucian quickly warped the entire crew away, into the open air in the distance, before the ship could disintegrate behind them.

They were falling in tandem, everyone screaming. All but

Lucian. He created a gravity point to draw them closer together. As Ninshar unleashed his next beam of Shadow Magic, Lucian warped the crew again, this time placing them just a few meters above the scorched surface of the planet, softening their fall with a Binding tether.

The impact wasn't easy. They rolled in the dirt, the heat about them sweltering. Mira quickly set a Thermal ward while the others prepared their own defenses.

They watched as the *Celestior* continued to spiral down toward a mountain in the distance. They didn't have time to see the impact, because Ninshar shot down like a comet, his advance wreathed by Shadow Magic, fully powered by the ethereal core.

Lucian flew up to meet him in midair, extending Lightspear.

14

NINSHAR PHASED FORWARD, slamming his body into Lucian, sending him hurtling toward the surface. Lucian felt himself wrapped in a Gravitonic aura that slowed his descent, an aura that must have been streamed by Serah in the nick of time. It was the only thing that stopped him from pancaking on the ground.

A vast vortex of flame spiraled downward, laced with electricity. The flames were slowed by Mira's Thermal ward, but there was nothing set up against the Dynamistic attack. The quick shield streamed by Lucian was quickly extinguished, sending a shock through his body.

Ninshar landed just steps away, a shockwave emanating outward, while a spear of darkness appeared in his hand. The Ascendant stabbed with stunning speed, but such was his aggression that he was blind to Emma and Fergus, who were yanking on his legs with Binding tethers. Enraged, Ninshar turned on them, but Emma phased behind him, scoring a hit on the Ascendant's exposed flank, while Fergus blasted a powerful laser right in his face, utterly breaking Ninshar's shield.

By this point, Serah and Mira were closing in from the sides, preparing their own attacks, while Lucian raced in from behind.

With a guttural cry, Ninshar streamed at the ground, sending a kinetic shockwave hurtling around him, throwing everyone back. Only Lucian could defend against the attack, but rather than engage with Ninshar directly, he leaped into the sky and streamed four quick Gravitonic auras on his friends to break their falls.

Ninshar flew after him, and Lucian could not prepare a warp in time. Instead, Lightspear clashed with Ninshar's spear of shadow, vaporizing it from existence. But the stab was a feint. Ninshar warped above Lucian, cocooning him in Binding tethers while lacing the streams with Psionic Magic that threatened to shatter him. Lucian easily threw off the Bindings, drawing as much ether as he could to create a powerful Seven-Fold shield supported with Creation Magic.

Ninshar simply ignored him, warping after Emma and beating her back with a newly conjured Shadow spear, which she was hard pressed to defend against. The others came in to help, taking off some pressure, while Lucian warped behind Ninshar to go for a backstab.

But the Ascendant had counted on this. He instantly counter-warped behind Lucian to land his own backstab. Lucian's shield caught the attack, shattering on impact, but also having the effect of destroying Ninshar's second Shadow spear.

The next moments were chaos, a clawing for survival in the dirt of this new world. Lucian couldn't say how long the battle lasted, but Ninshar fought hard, and it was all he could do to keep himself and his friends alive. Ninshar's strategy was to go after Lucian's companions to keep the pressure off himself. It was a way for him to buy more time, to distract Lucian from going for the killing move.

Lucian could feel Ninshar's power radiating from his Focus. The Ascendant was powerful in his own right, but this went beyond innate power. It was the Starflower, fully absorbed and being used without restraint. Ninshar had defeated the Leviathan without the benefit of the core, so Lucian knew his power was beyond even that.

Mira, in particular, became a target. Ninshar seemed to sense her importance to Lucian, and her lack of experience with magic overall. Thankfully, the others were there to defend her, but Lucian knew he couldn't let this go on.

Rage built up within him, rage he used to clasp his Focus harder. No matter what Ninshar did, Lucian had to remain distant and calculated. That was hard, though, when he knew it was only a matter of time before his friends weakened, making it easier for Ninshar to overwhelm them.

He needed to end this fight and end it soon. But how?

In the chaos, a sudden burst of clarity came to him. He opened his mind Psionically to the others, with great subtlety, so Ninshar would not realize they were communicating.

Go on the defensive, he said. *Start slowing down, enough to make him think you're weakening. I'll take care of the rest.*

There was no questioning. Over the next minute, they gradually shifted their tactics to become more defensive. Ninshar would focus on one of them, only for Lucian to warp that person away when the danger became too great.

Lucian communicated with all of them again. *We're going to set a trap for him. Mom, act like you can barely hold it together. That should make him focus on you more. Emma, Fergus, Serah: when I give the signal, blast him with everything you have: Space-Time, Radiance, and Gravitonics, in that order. I'll come at him with Atomicism. I've read his defenses. They're not optimized to deal with that combination of magic.*

No, Fergus responded. *I won't let you risk her like that.*

Let me do my part, Fergus, Mira said. *I'm a team player. Let's get a win.*

Lucian had to force himself to be cold and emotionless, otherwise this wouldn't work. If Fergus wasn't on board . . .

At last, he felt his friend's reluctant agreement, along with the others. The ethereal core, combined with Ninshar's Shadow Magic, made him almost impossible to overpower directly.

If they couldn't win outright, they had to outsmart him.

It took less time than Lucian would have believed for the plan to be set in motion. When Ninshar came for Mira again, she backed away, her eyes wide with fear as she streamed a paltry shield in defense. Lucian hadn't wanted her to appear *that* weak, but it certainly had the intended effect. Ninshar was taking the bait, flashing a victorious smile, beating back Mira while the others screamed their dismay. The others attacked Ninshar madly, but Lucian could see them holding back, according to his instructions. Now, the fear on his mother's face was very real; she truly believed she only had seconds to live.

And if Lucian did nothing, that would very well be the case.

Lucian watched closely, allowing his mother to hold off the furious Ascendant. She had a lot of pluck, dodging attacks and showing uncanny resolve. She fought with her magic alone, not having training in shockspear tactics. But even she couldn't hope to keep her defenses up for much longer.

Lucian noticed a shift in her stance, a shift that said Ninshar's next strike would land true. His spear of darkness fell, with nothing to bar its path.

He gave the signal. *Now!*

Emma, who had been gathering her ether this entire time, unleashed a powerful Space-Time aura, and Ninshar was suddenly moving in slow motion, the shadow spear's speed effectively cut in half. Even with the stream, Mira only barely rolled out of harm's way. Serah weighed Ninshar down with Gravitonics, completely immobilizing him. Fergus, with a defiant roar, threw out his hands. The green laser that shot out was so blinding that even Lucian's Radiant shield could hardly filter out the harsh light. It slammed into Ninshar's shield, breaking it entirely and causing the Ascendant to shoot backward at breakneck speeds. Even as Ninshar tried to shield the laser, it kept pushing him back across the cracked flatlands.

It was now or never. Lucian phased forward, Lightspear extended, drawing ether as fast as he could to enhance his attack. Ninshar turned to face him, even in midair, as Fergus's laser was at last petering out. The Ascendant drew up a Shadow shield, dedicating every fiber of his being to the effort. His eyes, no longer holding their former rage, were wide with fear.

Lucian slammed into the Shadow shield, which shattered utterly before Lightspear's wrath. In the next moment, the ethereal weapon stabbed Ninshar directly into the heart.

The Ascendant gave a harsh wail, convulsing as blood spilled forth, staining the sand beneath. Golden light spread from the point of the wound until it covered every part of Ninshar's body, forming a cocoon that shook and vibrated. Lucian held the weapon firm as more and more light entered Ninshar, bursting him at the seams.

At last, with a final scream, the Ascendant shattered into a pile of ash. The ash was borne by the hot, dry wind, and silence reigned over the arid plains.

Stood revealed in the ash was an aquamarine sphere of breathtaking beauty. It wasn't as bright as when Lucian had first seen it; Ninshar had obviously used it to excess trying to battle them. But perhaps it still had its uses.

Lucian kneeled in the dust, wrapping the Starflower in Binding Magic before picking it up. He turned around to find that the others had also fallen where they stood, as if they had just finished sprinting the last stretch of a marathon.

Lucian ran toward his mother. She was lying on the ground but appeared to be unharmed, only exhausted. Lucian streamed a reverse Thermal ward to keep the heat of the wasteland off them.

Fergus kneeled as well, gathering her in his arms. Her eyes were glassy as she drew ragged breaths, and Fergus's own eyes stared at Lucian accusingly.

"I'm okay," she managed. "Just … completely beat …"

Lucian closed his eyes in relief. "I'm sorry it came to that. It was the only way to defeat him."

Mira nodded her understanding but said nothing more.

The decision to risk her hadn't been easy, but perhaps even Ninshar wouldn't have dreamed Lucian would make such a bold move. And that was precisely why it had worked.

But now it was time to move on.

"We need to find some shelter," Lucian finally said. "What matters is everyone is okay."

They were back to only having their weapons, the clothes on their backs, and a few small packs. Everything else had gone down with the ship, the smoking wreckage of which Lucian could see on a distant brown mountain.

And stretching in the opposite direction, over a line of low hills, was the Seven-Fold Path.

Lucian nodded in its direction. "That's the way we need to go."

"Let's move, then," Fergus said, apparently deciding to let bygones be bygones.

"I can hold that," Emma said, reaching for the faded Starflower. "It's probably not much use anymore, but it'll at least keep it separated from the Orb of Shadows."

Lucian gave it to her, seeing the sense of her words. He then gathered his ether, preparing a warp that would take them to the base of the hills in the distance. Within seconds, they had reappeared. With the long visibility of the flatlands beyond, toward which the Path was leading them, things would progress quickly.

But at the moment, rest was more important. Within these hills, there were several caves and hollows to choose from. Lucian found one that looked promising and led the others there. Within minutes, they were shaded and setting their wards. They took a couple of minutes to ensure it was safe before crashing to the ground. Exhaustion hit Lucian in full force. He'd forced himself to sleep in quick shifts to ensure the ship never got too far off course, and the battle with Ninshar had almost pushed him to the breaking point.

Almost everyone was already asleep, Lucian being the last holdout. There were no threats, but he wanted to make sure that their battle had attracted no mages wanting to check things out. In a reality like this, magic usage was common, creating countless waves within the Ether, so much so that even an enormous wave, such as theirs, might pass unnoticed.

At least, that was what Lucian hoped. This part of the planet looked relatively isolated, so maybe they would be safe.

He sat in quiet meditation, allowing himself to recover from the battle. It had been closer than he would have liked, and in the end, it had taken all of them working together to bring Ninshar down.

If Ninshar was this tough, he could only hope they didn't have to fight another Ascendant.

Eventually, Lucian had to trust in his wards to keep them safe. He fell into a deep, dreamless sleep.

15

WHEN EVERYONE WOKE UP, many hours had passed, but it was still fully daylight. That could only mean days on this planet were atypically long. If that was the case, then it was easy to imagine how the surrounding landscape might become so scorched.

Despite the bleak surroundings, he knew there were cities here. He had seen the lights from the Eye, so he had to imagine that intelligent beings—these Sumaril, most likely—made their home here. He wondered if they were the same beings that had been possessed by Ashurban's magic at Esharal.

Lucian supposed they would run into them eventually. All they could do for now was follow the Seven-Fold Path and hope, somewhere along the way, they could secure another ship.

They packed up and ate a light meal that did little to quell Lucian's hunger. When they ventured outside the cave, the air was even hotter than before. Lucian was reminded of their time on Hephaestus because it was much the same here: infernally hot. At least the air was breathable.

Mira streamed the group's Thermal ward, and they started

following the Seven-Fold Path, using short warps and Binding tethers as needed to make fast progress. They blazed across an expansive plain, flanked on both sides by tall, dusty mountains, in which Lucian could see ruins of broken towers and fallen cities. Perhaps this area hadn't always been a desolate wasteland. They came across countless bones, too, poking up through the sand, of both monsters and bipedal beings about the same size as the ones they'd encountered in the swamp. Most wore armor, and some were even still clasping spears or shields.

"There must have been a battle here a long time ago," Emma said.

Looking around, she was probably right. It was hard to tell just what had happened in the battle, though. Hundreds of skeletons were now poking through the sand, and even ships lay half-buried.

"You'd think these things would have been covered by the sand a long time ago," Fergus said.

"Yeah," Serah said. "It's creepy."

Thankfully, with Lucian's magic, they crossed the "battle plain" rather quickly. They ascended a slope, on the other side of which they found running water and growing plants green with life. By the time the slope ended, they entered hilly terrain pockmarked with low trees and fast streams running between cliffs. It wasn't quite cool enough for Mira to let go of her ward, but the prospects were becoming more promising.

The Seven-Fold Path veered off to the right, leading them over the smoother bits of terrain until it found a road made of crystalline stones, well-maintained. The road contained many bridges with graceful arches expanding over the various streams. They encountered no one, probably because of the extreme heat. On a world like this, anything wise would hide during the hottest parts of the day, not emerging until evening perhaps. It was hard to say, being so new here, but relief from the heat was probably several sleep cycles away. It was a strange thought for

Lucian to wrap his mind around, but perhaps the heat was working out in their favor. They weren't likely to be encountered on the road, except by mages who could ward against the elements, and Fergus would detect them long before they became an issue.

They warped quickly down the road, and before too long, they came to the top of a hill, where Lucian spied a walled city off to the left, set against the backdrop of a deep blue ocean. Unlike the cities of the battle plain, this one was still lived in, and its entire expanse was protected from the harsh sun by a reddish dome of Thermal Magic. In the blue sky above, the Eye was easily visible, surprisingly gray and dreary, aside from a small, circular patch in its center that was green and blue.

"A strange place we've found ourselves in," Fergus said. He turned his gaze from the Eye to the city in the distance. "What does everyone think? Maybe we can find a ship there?"

Lucian considered for a moment. If they entered that city, they would be the only humans, becoming the objects of either fear or awe, or at the very least, of passing curiosity. It depended on whether these Sumaril were the only intelligent beings in the Light Realm, or if there were others. But Lucian knew as soon as they interacted with any being from this world, there would be no stopping the news from spreading. The Ascendants in Anshar would know of their arrival long before they got there.

Anlilta had urged secrecy, and for now, that seemed the wisest course. Then again, if they had many worlds to go through, Lucian couldn't imagine going the entire way without ever having to interact with anyone.

He knew only one thing: to trust his own instincts. What was most important was that the Seven-Fold Path wasn't leading into the city, but around it.

"We keep moving," he said. "It's too early to reveal ourselves."

"I agree," Emma said.

They kept warping down the extent of the Seven-Fold Path,

which veered off the highway and continued toward a line of mountains in the distance. From the position of the sun on their right, they were heading south.

They stayed out of range of local towns and villages, using tethers rather than portals to keep magic expenditure low. They were close enough to civilization that detection was a risk if Lucian used more powerful forms of magic. Fergus's Radiant shield would be enough to cover their tracks as long as Lucian stuck to Binding.

The Seven-Fold Path led through farms and terraces, with wide trees growing thick-skinned fruits and vegetables adapted to the heat and dry air. Lucian picked several of them until their packs were filled to the brim. Scanning them Atomically, Lucian detected nothing that would kill them, and they were filled with plenty of nutrients to sustain them.

Within hours, they were in the wilderness again, looking up at the mountains before them. Lucian began picking a way until all of them were too tired to continue.

It was cooler in the heights, enough to where Mira could at last drop her Thermal ward. They set up camp in the lee of some rocks and cooked a quick dinner, using some of the new crops they found. Even if he was sure they were non-poisonous, he tasted them first.

When nothing happened, the rest of them tucked in, eating "alien vegetable soup," as Serah called it. No one corrected her by saying *they* were actually the aliens and the interlopers, but her general meaning was clear enough. As for the taste, it wasn't unpleasant, but the texture would take some getting used to.

As the others went to sleep, Lucian ventured off on his own, climbing the mountain to the very top and scoping the terrain they would soon cross. The rainbow path stretched from his feet all the way into the distance. The fading light of the afternoon was progressing into the evening. The air was actually cool up here, making Lucian wonder if tomorrow things would be more active in the local towns and cities. The Eye above leered down menacingly, seeming to watch him.

He turned when he sensed Serah's presence, who was doing a combination of climbing and floating to reach the top. She settled next to him, taking in the view.

"Sometimes, you've just got to admire the scenery," she said.

He smiled. "It's a pretty view, for sure." As they watched the landscape together, Lucian shifted on his feet. "Wonder how many more times we'll have to cross the horizon to find the next Gate?"

"Hopefully, not too many more," Serah said. "I mean, it's fun to fly across the surface of a planet like a superhero, but anything can get old fast."

"I suppose so. Everything okay with you?"

"Well, I'm still halfway sane, and that's an accomplishment given everything." Her eyes became concerned. "What about you? I'm sure it's all the stress and everything, but you seem a bit more . . . distant. Is that a fair assessment?"

Lucian wasn't interested in taking a deep dive into his emotions. He wasn't sure of the reason for his distance, but maybe he had become so for the sake of survival and not messing up. The stakes were impossibly high, and getting off the Eye in one piece, and beating Ninshar, had taken a lot out of him. If not physically, then mentally.

Risking his mother like that was not something he would have normally done. Had he really strayed so far from his humanity? Was he becoming something else?

He couldn't allow himself to think about it too much. He let himself relax, such as he could, and drew her close. "All these decisions I'm having to make . . . they're impossible unless I become something else. *Someone* else. Like what happened with my mom. I risked her life because there was no other way. She could have died . . ." He shook his head. "It turned out okay, but if it hadn't . . ."

"But it did. Hard to say if you made the right call, but maybe if you hadn't done that, Ninshar would have worn us down eventually with the ethereal core. That thing's rotting powerful."

"Yeah," Lucian said.

"I think seeing how he fought shocked everyone. It shocked me. We expected him to be tough, but . . . not like that. Makes you wonder what fighting a stronger Ascendant might be like."

Lucian sighed. "I hope it doesn't come to that. Fergus hasn't looked at me the same. He'd say I made a mistake."

"He doesn't have the burden you have. He understands why you did what you did from a logical point of view. But the emotional side is still catching up. As for your mom, seems she's taking it pretty well."

"I just wish I could be stronger. Nine of the Ten Orbs, plus all of you. It should've been an easy fight. Yeah, he had the Starflower, and he used up most of its power. It makes me wonder . . ."

"Wonder what?"

"Maybe there's a limit to how powerful someone can be. At some point, everything you can do, *they* can do, and just about as fast. So, it comes down to making the right moves, no mistakes. That's where I might be at a disadvantage."

"How so?"

"Ninshar—just like the Ancient One—knew the best way to get at me was to go after everyone else. Ninshar knew she was my mother. He knew my weakness was having to protect everyone. As long as I continue to do that, he could always stay one step ahead. Any other enemy will see that, too."

Serah was quiet at this, but Lucian saw acceptance on her face. She understood, even if she didn't like it.

"If I had risked Fergus, or even Emma, he might not have

taken the bait," Lucian went on. "Of course, I wouldn't have risked you. That left my mom as the last viable person . . ."

Lucian lapsed into silence. There was nothing more to explain.

At last, Serah took a deep breath. "Hard choices. I hope you never have to make a choice like that again."

Lucian remained quiet. He knew that the road ahead might demand even harder sacrifices, sacrifices for which he might be judged. Yes, everyone knew what they were getting into, and that might mean death. And yet, he felt the pressure all the same. Sometimes, it seemed as if everyone expected him to be a god. But despite his power, he wasn't all-powerful.

His path was to become someone else. Someone who could guard the Orbs from any challenger. It was easy for the heart to get crowded out under all the pressure.

"I'm here for you," Serah said, her hands tightening on his. "Always. No matter what."

He drew her even closer. "I know it doesn't look like it, but I think we actually have a shot of doing this. We've made it this far, right?"

Serah smiled. "As long as we don't run into any more crazed, power-mad Ascendants on the way."

"Well, that goes without saying."

They stayed a couple of minutes longer, watching the landscape in silence, before returning to the cave.

16

THEY CONTINUED on their way across the blasted surface of Kadur. The sun rose and fell twice in that time, and as Lucian had guessed, this corresponded to about two weeks of their own time. The twisted badlands slowly transformed into a desert of bone-dry dunes with no trace of water. Without Atomic Magic, there would have been nothing to drink. The sands never seemed to end, to where Lucian had to portal back to more fertile lands to refill their packs with food.

This place reminded him very much of the Burning Sands of Psyche, especially with the tidally locked moon above, which only moved with their movement. Each day that passed, the Eye shrunk ever farther into the distance behind them, meaning they were crossing thousands of kilometers. Despite that, the Seven-Fold Path ran on, under the burning sun and through the long, frigid nights.

One night, during the deepest cold of the day-night cycle, they came to a rest at the top of a large dune, only to find their first river since entering the desert. It was iced over, with trees and sturdy grasslands beyond.

"Finally," Serah said. "Are we there yet?"

Lucian felt along the length of the Seven-Fold Path, hoping to sense the next Gate, but he shook his head. "Doesn't seem like it."

She heaved an irritated sigh, her breath sending a stubborn strand of hair fluttering away from her eyes. "Sand sucks."

By the time it was full day again, they were surprised when they came to the edge of a cliff, where before them spread a vast city with high golden walls covered by a translucent dome laced with powerful Thermal Magic. Lucian knew the purpose of the dome was to keep the city livable during the hotter and colder cycles of day and night. In response to the city, Lucian instantly shielded the party with an invisibility ward.

"Is this where the Path is leading us?" Emma asked.

Lucian watched the rainbow stream entering directly through the gate. It made him wonder if, perhaps, it was better to go around first and see if it came out the other side, or whether the Gate itself was in the city.

"Well, this city is the biggest one we've seen so far," Mira said. "Maybe we can blend in, or at least go about our business without drawing too much attention."

Lucian wasn't holding out much hope. For all of their travel on this planet, they had yet to cross paths with the Sumaril, a product of their stealthy travel and Lucian's magic. But they wouldn't be able to keep that up forever. He got the feeling that whatever it was they were looking for, it seemed to be in this city. The Path had veered around the previous city while it led directly into this one.

Whether it was leading to the next Gate, or perhaps someone they had to talk to first, he couldn't say at that moment. On the Eye, the Path had led them to Ninshar rather than directly to the Gate itself, seeming to sense the Ascendant had been the key to progressing. Lucian had the feeling it could be the same here.

"Well," he said, turning to face the others, "I'm not sure what to expect. All I can say is, just try to blend in."

"Try to blend in?" Serah asked. "You've got to be kidding."

"Well, you know what I mean. Act like we belong. We've done it before, right?"

"Maybe we can try sneaking in at night," Fergus said. "Invisibility shields and all that. Scout things out. They've never seen humans before. They could react with hostility."

"Or curiosity," Mira pointed out. "Not everything has to be doom and gloom."

"It's been daytime for about forty-eight hours now," Lucian countered. "It's not even noon on this world yet. Are we really going to wait five more days for it to get dark? We're on a clock here."

"It's up to you," Fergus said. "I've always been of the opinion that it's better to be careful."

"I'm tired of waiting around," Serah said. "If it's dangerous, we can always just warp away, right? What are the risks?"

"The risk is giving ourselves away too early," Fergus said. "If they figure out who we are, and what we have, everyone might want to take it for themselves. Like Ninshar."

"Nothing ventured, nothing gained," Emma said. "I'd like to learn more about this reality. And if the Path is leading there, that's where we need to go."

Lucian considered for a moment. Then, he decided. He allowed the invisibility ward to drop as he walked down the hill. As they headed to the gate, Lucian was reminded of the society the Ancients had created in the alternate version of the present, where some places were technologically regressed, like Grastia, while others were far more advanced, like Regalia. This city seemed to fit in the first category, the level of technology seeming to be late medieval or early renaissance. Of course, in a magically based society like this, it was hard to guess at technological levels.

He felt the magic of the dome more closely, finding that it was nothing more than Thermalism branded with Gravitonics. It extended beyond the city's perimeter, meaning they could easily pass through and enjoy the benefits of the controlled climate beyond. They did so, finding that the temperature beyond was still hot, but at least bearable.

Lucian spotted the first Sumaril patrolling the wall above them, shouting in alarm at their arrival. He sharpened his vision. As he'd suspected, they were the same species that had been defending the swamp fortress of Ashurban, appearing to Lucian like smaller, less glorious versions of Ninshar. For one, they were shorter, probably about equal in height to a human. Their skin tone seemed to be anything from light to dark blue, while lacking the pearlescent sheen that Ninshar had possessed. They wore chain mail armor that wouldn't have looked out of place in a medieval setting.

That was all Lucian had time to notice because they ducked behind the wall.

"Shy, aren't they?" Fergus asked.

Before Lucian could respond, the heavy steel doors to the city swung outward, revealing a contingent of armored soldiers with some at the forefront bearing spears alight with electricity. Closer now, Lucian could get a better sense of what they were like. Most had violet eyes, though Lucian noticed gold and emerald mixed in. Unlike Ninshar, their pupils were round instead of slit-like, and instead of Ninshar's silk-like filaments, they had actual hair, fine and straight, ranging in color from gray to light blue. The faces were surprisingly humanlike, to where there was almost no difference aside from a few superficial things. If anything, their facial structure was a bit elongated. Their ears, while pointed, were not as pronounced as Ninshar's.

"Elves," Serah whispered, her eyes wide.

Lucian understood her point. Aside from a few minor differences, these could have been elves from any of the RPGs she played.

The regiment came to a halt before them, where the lead Sumaril, wearing a violet cape and golden battle armor, strode forward confidently. This one had more traditionally feminine features: high cheekbones, thicker hair, fuller lips. Her eyes were forest green, and her disposition stern. Lucian could feel the strength of her Focus radiating toward him. A powerful mage, then.

There was a long stretch of silence, dust swirling across the paved path between the two groups. As the leader watched Lucian, he could feel the group's fear through his ward.

She opened her mouth to speak. "Who, and what, are you? State your business or begone!"

"We're trying to get to Anshar. We won't stay in your city long."

Surprise marked the mage's face. "Why Anshar? Eänna is quite far from here. From what world do you hail? I've never seen your kind before."

Lucian tried to give a mollifying smile but wasn't sure if it had the intended effect. "We've come from the Eye."

At this, several gasps of surprise and muttering broke out from the soldiers. The mage's demeanor hardened.

"It's been centuries since anyone has passed through the Eye Gate. The Heavenly Palace of the Old Kings has long been abandoned, with no means to access it since the Skybridge fell. If what you're saying is true, then how did you pass through the Eye Gate?"

"Carefully."

"You mock me?"

"We have a long way to go, so if you would let us through, we'll do our best to stay out of everyone's way."

"I can't let you do that until I have more information. Why are you traveling to Anshar?"

Rather than argue with her, Lucian just used his Psionic Magic, easily overpowering her ward and forcing her to relax a bit. In an instant, she snapped her fingers, and Lucian noted that each hand had six digits. One of the Sumaril, strong and burly with icy blue skin, sidled over. She said something to him in a low voice, which Lucian caught easily with his enhanced hearing.

"Inform the King at once."

The man nodded curtly and led a group of soldiers back into the city.

"These are strange times," the mage-captain said, returning her attention back to Lucian. "What is your name? What is your kind called?"

"Lucian. These are my friends. We're called humans."

"Humans," the mage said, testing the word. "And these . . . *humans* . . . live on the Eye? The stories say that many fantastical beings hail from there."

"I guess you could say that. What's your name?"

"Captain Eresha. If your story is true, then you have traveled far indeed."

Thankfully, she didn't press him for a further explanation, but Lucian could feel a sense of unease radiating from her mind, despite his Psionic Magic.

At last, she visibly relaxed when her messenger returned with the news. She inclined her head toward him, nodding along with the messenger's quiet words, before turning to face Lucian.

"King Lugan will receive you immediately. Follow me."

17

CAPTAIN ERESHA TURNED and gave the command to her troops, who began marching back into the city. Lucian and the others fell in behind her.

They passed through the gate to walk down a long, wide avenue, on either side of which rose lofty buildings of brick and adobe, anywhere from three to five stories. Throngs of blue-skinned Sumaril parted for the soldiers, their eyes going wide as soon as they saw who the soldiers were escorting. The Sumaril were mostly dressed in long, flowing clothing reminiscent of thobes, loosely fitting and designed for the heat, while the women wore dresses of dazzling colors with head wrappings to shade themselves from the harsh sun above. Despite the red-tinted presence of the dome above, it didn't filter out all the heat. Lucian switched his wards to a combination of Thermalism and Psionics, allowing it to fall over the crowd to get a sense of their mood. Their collective aura was tense, a mixture of surprise, fear, and intrigue. The Sumaril watched him and his companions curiously, though they couldn't approach because Eresha's soldiers had formed a box around them.

Lucian loosely held his Focus, ready to shield against any attack. Though he didn't believe violence was forthcoming, it was important to be prepared. The last thing they needed was a stray fireball or arrow to end things after getting so far.

After weaving through the busy streets, they came to a richer part of town, where magically enhanced towers reached to the sky, interspersed by verdant gardens and streams. The air was cooler here, perfectly pleasant, and filled with pleasing fragrances from passing flowers and trees. They walked between the boughs of two trees with golden bark, from which similarly golden fruit hung, ripe for the picking. The path widened, becoming a set of stairs leading up to the largest of the towers, flanked on either side by two shorter towers connecting to the first with gracefully arched bridges.

The doors swung open of their own accord, and Eresha came to a pause at the top of the stairway. Two Sumaril stood within, both males with chiseled faces, dressed in flowing thobes of silver with intricate geometric patterns. Lucian immediately felt the power radiating from them and took them to be highly placed sorcerers of King Lugan himself.

"We'll take it from here, Mage-Captain," the taller of the two said to Eresha.

Eresha placed a hand on her heart, or at least where Lucian assumed her heart was. She then backed away, her face lowered. A subtle glow surrounded the sorcerers' forms, while their faces held an aura of wisdom and power, their violet eyes glowing with inner radiance.

"You are about to enter the presence of Lugan, King of Kadur," the taller sorcerer said. "If we perceive you to be a threat, your life will be immediately forfeit."

"We won't cause trouble," Lucian assured him.

In tandem, the sorcerers raised their arms and streamed a portal at the center of the atrium, the action taking about half a minute to complete. On the other side, Lucian could see what appeared to be a vast room filled with sunlight streaming in from above.

The taller sorcerer gestured toward the portal. "The King awaits."

Lucian looked at the others, nodding that it was safe. The sorcerers' violet-tinged eyes watched him closely as he stepped forward, followed by the others.

He passed through the portal to find himself in a new area, a vast chamber of sandstone with intricately carved columns as thick as tree trunks rising to support a domed ceiling, where a hole in the center let in brilliant sunlight. Without having to really guess, Lucian knew this was the top of the tower, with no way to enter or leave except by magic. He assumed it was a security measure to keep the King safe.

That ruler was now sitting before them on a throne of jade, regaled in golden robes so long they flowed onto the floor. His face was withered by age, his skin dark blue, his eyes a dull red. A beard, silky white, followed the train of his robes onto the floor. The King's inherent magical ability radiated outward like a tidal wave, almost as strong as Ninshar's had been.

Several more sorcerers stood at the side of the throne, all dressed in white vestments, while the two sorcerers who had created the original portal followed from behind. They allowed the portal to close, effectively sealing them in. While Lucian and Emma had access to Space-Time Magic, he could only imagine how claustrophobic this room would seem for any being who didn't have it. The opening in the ceiling was the only other escape, and it was quite high above them.

Lucian readied himself to deploy his magic in case he needed to warp everyone away. For now, no danger seemed imminent.

King Lugan shifted in his seat, holding up a six-fingered hand in what Lucian assumed to be a greeting. The two sides stared at each other, Lucian feeling the old sorcerer probing at his Psionic ward for weakness. He strengthened the ward when he realized just how much effort Lugan was making to get inside his thoughts. He wasn't even trying to be subtle.

"If you want to know anything," Lucian finally said, "just ask. I'm an open book."

Immediately, the pressure ebbed, but only a little. "Your strength is not found wanting, stranger," Lugan said, with a tone of amusement. His gaze took in the rest of his retinue. "Leave us be. If this one wished to kill me, he would have done so by now."

Lugan's cadre of mages and sorcerers widened their eyes at this, but they did not dare to protest. One by one, they filtered out of the throne room through another quickly conjured portal.

To show his sincerity, Lugan dropped his magical shields, also releasing the strange magical pressure he'd been streaming against Lucian. Lucian felt he could finally breathe, and he could hear similar sighs of relief from the others. This Lugan was clearly extremely powerful in his own right.

Lucian let go of his own defenses, though he kept basic wards in place, including the Space-Time one, which would allow him to quickly warp everyone away if needed. Though he was certainly more powerful than Lugan, he was a stranger here. He had been betrayed too many times to take half measures.

"So," Lugan began, in a sonorous voice, "what brings you to Kadur? My soldiers tell me you are from the Eye, but don't think I believe that. It's also my understanding that you're trying to get to Anshar. Explain why."

"That, I can't say. All I can say is that if you're loyal to the Light, you will help us with our mission."

"It is a dangerous thing to refuse the request of a king."

"Some of us can afford to be direct."

Lugan's expression remained neutral as he considered. "Perhaps. Then, in the spirit of directness, let me ask you. Who are you? And how did you come into my court? My magic is the greatest in the Outer Worlds, outside of Ninshar the Exiled, but even I wouldn't dare brave the Eye Gate, knowing the monster that lies beyond. Did you defeat the Leviathan? If you are attempting to block the truth from my mind, I can sense this, even if I can't discern the nature of the truth you're shielding. I'm sure you're fully aware of the intricacies of Psionic Magic. Yours is a powerful Focus, and it can flare brighter still. But if it's my help you seek, you'll get none unless you answer my questions."

Lucian watched Lugan for a long time, knowing that if he was anything like Ninshar, this could go south quick. In this position, Lucian simply had to tell the truth, at least a part of it.

"Are you familiar with the Prophecy of the Chosen?"

Lugan watched him closely, raising a right hand in what Lucian took to mean a sign of assent. "Of course. Every Sumaril, from high to low, knows the prophecy of the Foresayer Anlilta, her sacred pronouncement following the War of Light and Shadow two thousand years past. That warriors from the Shadow Realm would enter the Aetheria and bring with them the Holy Orbs that were stolen from the Heart of Creation." He frowned, puzzled. "Do you mean to say that you are the Chosen?"

"You already know the answer to that question."

Lucian allowed Lightspear to manifest in his hand, and its golden brilliance filled the hall. Lugan's blue face paled at the sight.

But even while he was proving himself, Lucian could only focus on the timeline Lugan had mentioned. Ninshar had only mentioned the War happened a long time ago, but Lugan had put a number to it. If only two thousand years had passed since the end of the war, and Nathi—the Time Weaver—left the Light Realm directly after it, it could only mean one thing. Time here flowed much more slowly than it did in the Shadow Realm. The Time Weaver had entered the Shadow Realm approximately ten million years ago, and yet according to Lugan's count, this event had only transpired two *thousand* years ago.

Lucian had to double check. "Has it really been only two thousand years since the War? It seems too short."

"Though most would not call two millennia a short amount of time, that is the exact number of years it has been since Anlilta gave her prophecy, and the Ascendant Nathi answered the call," Lugan confirmed. "Though the War ended officially with her prophecy, in many ways, it never truly ended." He watched Lucian. "So, you are the Chosen. And presumably, you carry with you the Orbs of the Manifold, including the two given to you by the Ascendant Nathi."

"That's right," Lucian said, no longer bothering to hide the truth. He sensed he wouldn't be getting Lugan's help if he kept his true motives hidden. He needed another ship, and Lugan was the only one who could give that to them. "We need to get to Anshar, and fast."

"Of course," Lugan said. "Though Anshar is very far from here. You find yourselves in the Outer Worlds of the Aetheria, where the Shadow has a firm presence. Entire worlds have fallen to the Ancient One's forces, including most of the Eye from which you have descended. I assume the First Gate must be located there at the moment, and that Ninshar has aided you in getting this far."

"I'm afraid that Ninshar is dead," Lucian said.

"Dead?" Lugan asked, in shock. "Ill tidings! How did this come to pass?"

"He betrayed us."

Lugan's face paled. "He tried to take the Orbs? And . . . you foiled him?"

Lucian nodded. "Yes. I had no other choice."

Lugan let out a long breath. "Then you have been through much since coming to the Light Realm."

"That's where we could use your help," Lucian said. "I'm going to warn you first, though. Don't try what Ninshar tried. It wasn't an easy fight, but we brought him down in a desert. Near some ruins of what had to be a big city, close to the place the captain called The Heavenly Palace."

"You speak of the War Plain," Lugan said. "Yes. During the War of Light and Shadow, one of the greatest battles of the war was fought there. Terrible magic was wielded to where the land will be forever haunted." He paused a moment, considering. "Where did the First Gate open to, specifically?"

"It brought us out in the Prismwood," Lucian said. "Where the Prismharts live."

"An enchanting forest, that, though my eyes have not seen it since my boyhood, in the first century of my life. Those were better days, days before the Leviathan came from the depths, before the Heavenly Palace of the Old Kings fell into ruin. Ninshar's tragic tale would take too long to speak. It grieves me he saw your Orbs as the means to save his ailing kingdom. It's a terrible fate, but knowing his story, it does not surprise me in the least."

Lucian remained silent, electing not to say anything more than he had to.

Lugan heaved a sigh. "It's said that the Orbs are dangerous and lay claim to the hearts of the Ascendants especially. Even now, knowing you have them, I feel their terrible pull, a gravity scarcely impossible to defy. If this is what I feel, how much more would an Ascendant?"

Fergus cleared his throat. "If the Ascendants are so tempted by the power of the Orbs, maybe going to Anshar is the last thing we should do."

"Perhaps," Lugan said, stroking his beard. "But many of the Ascendants would welcome the return of the Orbs and wish for their immediate return to the Heart. Others, like Ninshar, might plot to steal them. It's impossible to say just what will happen; who can guess at the caprices of the gods? I will say this much. Long has the Light Realm dreamed of this day, that all the Orbs might be returned to their rightful place. I will do what I can to help you. Of course, you will want to know the quickest path there, if not the safest."

Lucian waited for Lugan's answer, though he had a feeling he wouldn't like it.

"Getting to Anshar, even from a world as esteemed as Kadur, is no small feat. We are in the Outer Worlds, as far from Anshar and the World of Light as one could possibly be. Only the Eye above us could be farther, and not by much."

"It doesn't matter how far it is," Lucian said. "We have to get there, and as fast as possible."

Lugan at last relented. "The journey to Anshar will take many months. Perhaps even years. While Kadur is safe, the same cannot be said of other worlds on the way, some of which have fallen to the Shadow."

Lucian considered this news. If two thousand years had passed here, while ten million years had passed on the outside, then literally *years* had already passed since they had first entered.

By the time they finished their mission, there might not even be a humanity left to save.

"We don't have months," Lucian said. "Is there a faster way?"

Lugan's white brows knitted together as he considered. "If you truly must get there as quickly as possible..."

He trailed off, and it seemed he was weighing his next words carefully. Lucian waited attentively, knowing all he needed was patience.

Lugan's eyes focused again on Lucian as he gave a grim smile. "The first way, the path I recommend, is possible, albeit long and arduous. But there is ... another way."

"What way?"

"The worlds of the Aetheria, as you know, are interconnected by the Gates. These Gates bridge the worlds so that one could walk instantly from one to another. I'm not sure how it is in your realm, but ..."

Lucian nodded. "I'm familiar with the concept."

Lugan nodded. "Not all worlds were connected to each other,

of course. The creation of a Gate was said to be a great effort, even by the Ascendants. But during and after the War, over the long years, many Gates have actually been lost, especially here in the Outer Worlds, where the Aetheria is a constant flux between Light and Shadow. The Gates are the target of the forces of the Ancient One, for they offer the power of speed, and traveling the Ethereal Void between worlds is far too dangerous. All that to say, there is a Lost Gate that is said to lead to Gadea, one of Eänna's moons. Long ago, during the War, it was taken by the Shadow with no possibility of recovery. It lies at the bottom of the Ghostly Sea, and it's not even known whether it remains open, allowing for travel. Assuming it is, however, it would take you to Gadea, the fourth moon of Eänna. How you would get from Gadea to the World of Light, I cannot speak to. None have made that journey in over two thousand years, when the Hanging Islands sunk to the bottom of the sea."

"The Hanging Islands," Lucian said. "Were these islands floating, like on the Eye?"

"Yes. Raised by Gravitonic Magic in the times before the War, they have since fallen, as their brands could not be renewed. With them fell the Gadea Gate. And the Moon of Gadea, despite being in sight of the World of Light itself, has long been a bastion of the Shadow, a constant thorn in the side of the Ascendants. A powerful Descendant rules from there, who styles himself Kharzul the Shadowed. He is, perhaps, the most powerful acolyte of the Fallen, devious in his diplomacy. From time to time, he attacks us through the Gate, but even for his power, the sea forms a most stalwart defense. All the same, those waters are treacherous, not only for their storms but for the monsters that abide there."

"How much quicker would that way be, assuming it was possible?"

"While I understand the urgency of your mission, I would caution you against the shorter path. If you were to travel the safer way, I can aid you with some of my most powerful mages and sorcerers and give you a flotilla of three of my most stalwart ships to brave the more dangerous parts of the journey. But even given such measures, your arrival would not be guaranteed." Lugan's expression became grave. "Now, if you were to attempt to find the Gadea Gate, I could render no aid. I would risk none of my ships or Sumaril on such a suicide mission. At best, I might give you one of my ships, small and speedy, but not my best because I know it will not survive the journey. The magic required to get the ship to travel underwater would probably be beyond even your abilities, and it's worse because none knows the depths of the Ghostly Sea. But what is known is that the Hanging Islands are quite far from the shore and would place you in the most tempestuous part of the waters. Their exact location has been lost to time."

"I can find it," Lucian said, realizing that the Seven-Fold Path would lead him there. "I can find what others cannot."

"Even so," Lugan said, "you would need to use powerful magic to reach the depths of the water just to search it out, and in complete darkness to boot. And assuming you found the ruins of the Hanging Islands, you would have to find the Gadea Gate in the rubble at the bottom of the sea. Once through to Gadea, you would be met by a frozen wasteland completely hostile to the Light, and the Descendant Kharzul the Shadowed would not be blinded to your entry."

"But we would be close to Eänna, and possibly get some help."

"Yes. Within sight and communication with the Ascendants, if they know to expect you. However, you would need to find some means of conveyance to the surface. It would not be enough to warp yourself there, as the Ethereal Void would make it impossible. Travel by ship is possible at such a short distance, but any ship seen moving outbound from Gadea will be immediately attacked by the Eännan Navy. You would need to convince them of who you are, and your mission, before even leaving Gadea's surface. Not impossible, but unlikely. There are many points of failure, which is why I advise you against this course."

"There may not be time for anything else," Lucian said.

Of all the things Lugan had said, his thoughts returned to one thing: the time differential between their two realities. Every day that passed here, a decade or more passed on the outside. They had been here several weeks already. All he knew was, spending many months traveling from world to world, while safer, would take too long. Without the Orbs, the Heart of Creation would eventually die out, and no one knew the hour of its demise. Anlilta had said it could happen at any moment, and that they had returned exactly two millennia after Anlilta's original prophecy was too much of a coincidence.

He knew it was up to him to decide.

"What say you, Chosen of the Manifold?" Lugan asked.

"We need to think about it," Lucian said.

"Of course," Lugan said. "We have comfortable guest quarters. Perhaps you can discuss it there in peace and get some rest. It seems your journey has been . . . arduous."

Lucian knew they had to look like a sight, with several weeks' worth of dirt, sweat, and grime. They hadn't bathed since their time aboard *Celestior*.

"That would be appreciated."

"Rest assured, Chosen. You and your companions are safe here. You are noble warriors, the fulfillment of Anlilta's holy prophecy. No harm will befall you within these halls."

Lucian nodded his thanks but knew not to take anyone at their word.

A portal opened before the King, and the two sorcerers from before appeared. Rather than their haughty disposition before, they gave formal bows to Lucian and his friends.

"Lead them to the Western Wing, and give them the finest

rooms we have," Lugan said. He returned his attention to Lucian. "We will speak again soon."

The sorcerers parted, allowing access to the portal. Lucian felt it with his Focus, finding that it led to another part of the palace, not too far from where they stood.

They entered, and the sorcerers closed it from behind.

18

LUGAN'S SORCERERS led them to a pair of tall wooden doors, opening them with a basic stream. A richly appointed living area revealed itself, filled with comfortable furniture, artwork of nature, and high arched windows overlooking a sea with an almost pearlescent sheen. Somehow, Lucian knew it was the Ghostly Sea Lugan had referred to during their meeting. Unlike the Crystalline Sea of the Eye, no floating islands hovered above its expanse. The sky was thick with clouds, and beyond the Thermal dome, Lucian was certain it was already sweltering.

The doors closed, and for the first time since entering, they found themselves alone.

"Here we are again," Fergus said, scanning the walls for any sign of listening wards. "In the home of someone who could very well be our enemy."

"Just another Tuesday for us," Serah said brightly. "Or is it Thursday now?"

Her question went unanswered as Lucian headed for the windows. He saw the Seven-Fold Path extending from himself and far across the ocean before him, beyond the horizon. Perhaps they could have circumvented the city after all, but they would not have received the information about the Gadea Gate. Was that where the Path was leading?

Emma came to stand beside Lucian. "Lugan was more helpful than I expected."

"Maybe he really is on our side," Mira said. "I don't want to get my hopes up, though."

"He knows who I am, and why we're here," Lucian said. "We shouldn't be letting our guards down."

"It seems the entire Light Realm will know about us soon enough," Fergus said. "Five humans, one of whom carries a spear of light and has amazing magical abilities. It won't take long for them to figure it out. Everyone and everything will be attacking us on the way to Anshar."

"Lugan claims the long way is the safer option," Emma said. "Did anyone else catch what he said about the War occurring two thousand years ago?"

"Yeah, that was weird," Serah said. "Because in our reality that happened *ten million* years ago. So that means time moves differently here. A lot more slowly."

"Which means time is going at warp speed on the outside," Emma said. "Quick napkin math says four centuries have passed since we've entered, give or take a few decades."

Fergus whistled. "Not what we signed up for. The question is, is there anything we can do about it?"

"Maybe we can go back in time once we're finished here," Serah said. "Although wouldn't that erase everything we've done?"

"Who knows?" Lucian asked. "Everything is just getting more confusing the further we keep going. Kind of the opposite of what I was hoping for."

"We're barely scratching the surface of the Light Realm," Fergus said. "It's clear this world is as deep and complicated as our own, if not more so."

"I wonder how us being here has affected magic back home," Emma said. "Is it still healed, or are mages fraying again on the outside?"

Lucian shook his head. "I don't know. Good questions."

They were all silent as they contemplated the implications. They had come here to save humanity, but Lucian could have never guessed it might not be the humanity they knew. If centuries had passed on the outside, they were saving an unknown future, not the present they had come from. It made things feel more distant, the end goal less tangible. He had come here to save the humanity of his time. How could he have guessed about this time change stuff? If they were right about the time differences, that meant Jagar was long dead, along with the likes of Khairu, Linus, Plato, and not to mention everyone else they knew. By the time they got back, as much as a millennium might have passed. Maybe even more.

That was assuming they even got to go home.

He turned to face the others. "We don't know what waits for us here. The fact is, we probably should have died a long time ago, given everything that's happened. But against all odds, we've made it this far. We're in the Light Realm. I don't see any reason we can't make it all the way to the end and finish things up, and maybe even save our own reality, too. Not the future version of it, but *our* reality. Maybe there's a way to reverse time, I don't know. We'll figure something out, and if not . . . well, we did the best we could."

"Maybe," Mira said, though she looked doubtful.

"That leaves one last question," Fergus said. "Which way do we go? The long way that's safer, or the short way that Lugan says will certainly kill us?"

"The long way," Mira said, without hesitation. "I say this time stuff has already gotten out of hand. If we take a year or longer, what actual difference is it going to make? It's the difference between a few hundred years and a few thousand. Both futures will be unrecognizable to us."

"The clock is ticking in another way," Emma said. "We don't know how long it'll take for the Heart of Creation to die, but it will happen eventually if the Orbs aren't returned on time. When it does, it's lights out for the Light Realm, and any realities that depend on it. That includes ours."

"So, you're thinking the shorter way?" Fergus said.

"I'm not sure," Emma said. "If everything Lugan said was true, it sounds like quite the gauntlet. We'd have to cross the water *and* go under it. And going onto a moon that's completely controlled by one of the Ancient One's top guys will be tough to deal with, too. I imagine he'll be stronger than Ashurban. If he's survived on Eänna's doorstep, within sight of Enkius' domain and Anshar, he has to be powerful."

"Yeah, that's a good point," Serah agreed. "So, we'd have to go to the bottom of the ocean, all while fighting monsters, while trying to find a Gate that's been lost since forever, then emerging on a frozen world owned by a dark lord who knows we're coming. That might take the cake as far as difficulty level."

"The other option could be just as bad," Mira conceded. "If we take Lugan's offer, it means trusting him to protect us. And like Fergus said, the Sumaril will figure out Lucian's importance. He'll become a target, and the Ascendants will have time to prepare for him, both those who will support him, and those who want to take the Orbs for themselves."

"Plus," Serah said, "Lugan said the ships would have to pass through worlds controlled by the Shadow side. It might not be as dangerous as this Gadea, but it's still dangerous."

"A longer journey with some dangerous spots, or a short one with one *really* dangerous spot," Emma said. "It's not a simple choice."

"Maybe you can delve the future?" Serah asked Lucian.

"Future delving only works until your future comes in contact with someone who also has Space-Time Magic. I imagine this Kharzul fellow will be pretty strong in Space-Time. Every sorcerer worth their salt is, and Kharzul isn't just a sorcerer. He's a Descendant."

"Well, my vote is we need to steer a path around him if we can help it," Fergus said. "That's my opinion. The stakes are too high, so we need to make a logical choice. And more importantly, if we make the wrong choice, it's not reversible. Warping and portals don't work between worlds here. At best, we can warp to a different part of whatever world we are currently on."

"We just don't know who to trust," Emma said. "If Lugan is really against us, he might be exaggerating the danger of the Gadea Gate to make us need him. If we take his offer, he'll have a long time to come up with a plan to steal the Orbs, if that's what he wants."

Lucian was silent as he considered all these points. In his mind, it was a toss-up between the two. The question was, did he believe in his own power enough to make the shorter journey?

He looked at Emma. "We still have that ethereal core. If push comes to shove, we might use it to get out of a tight spot. It has a bit of power left. Enough, maybe, to get us out of a sticky situation."

"Who would be the one to use it?" Mira asked.

"Emma would," Lucian said, without hesitation. "It would be good to diversify our options a bit."

"Insurance," Emma said. "If things go south."

"Which they will," Fergus said. "You *know* they will."

Emma watched the Ghostly Sea outside the window, seeming to think. Lucian could see the reluctance on her face.

"I wonder what it's like channeling that kind of power," she said. "It made Ninshar almost a match for all of us combined. I wonder if I'll even be able to control it?"

Lucian remembered how he'd given her the Orb of Radiance for a brief time, and the toll that had taken on her mentally, physically, and emotionally. He wondered if this would be the same thing.

"You probably won't have to use it," Lucian said. "It's just an option. I can keep it branded until it's time to use it."

"I'll do what I need to do," she said. "If you think it's best, then I can be the backup."

Lucian nodded, grateful to have her support. There was a silence, as everyone seemed to look to Lucian to make the final decision. Like the others, he stared out at the water where the Seven-Fold Path led. If they took Lugan's offer, they would, for the first time in their journey, stray away from following the Path. He knew, in theory, that the Path would move with him, and it would lead them to the same place anyway, even if the longer way was more circuitous.

Still, something about leaving the Path felt wrong. Lucian wasn't one for blind faith, but so far, the Seven-Fold Path hadn't led them astray.

But when he thought about the danger involved, the stakes, the possibility that one of his friends might be killed, he knew it would be irresponsible to risk the shorter way when there was a safer one. Perhaps he and Emma might survive the harder path, given their power and resources, but would everyone else? The battle with Ninshar had almost been too much, and Lucian had the feeling the shorter path would be even worse than that.

He suddenly decided, though he didn't feel good about it.

"We take Lugan's offer. The short way is too much of a risk."

Everyone was silent. Lucian knew they had expected him to choose differently. In fact, that was what he had thought, too.

But it was always safer to go with a known danger than an unknown one. He couldn't let impatience derail everything they had achieved so far.

"What about the risk of the Heart of Creation dying before we reach it?" Emma asked.

Lucian already had an answer for that. "Two thousand years

have passed here since the First Gate opened. We have to hope that there's at least another year left. Enough time to get to Anshar, get some answers, and travel the rest of the way to the Heart. Even if it takes a year."

"That's at least another five thousand years for our own reality," Serah said. "Though math isn't my strong suit."

"Are you sure about this, Lucian?" Fergus asked.

Even Fergus looked unsure of Lucian's decision, and he had been the biggest supporter of the less risky path. Neither option was good, but he had risked everyone too much already. Losing anyone would be emotionally damaging and hard to bounce back from.

He wanted everyone to survive this journey, even if it meant thousands of more years would pass on the outside.

"It's the right choice," Mira said finally. "The harder choice, in a way."

"Maybe it'll be a chance to relax," Serah said. "See things no human will ever see."

"It'll be no pleasure cruise," Fergus said. Then, echoing what Lucian had said earlier, "We can't let our guards down, even for a moment."

Of course, the idea of trying to relax during such high stakes was ludicrous. Expecting everyone to stay vigilant for months on end was a risk in itself. It was human nature to relax when no imminent danger was presenting itself.

And that could be something Lugan was counting on if he didn't have their best interests at heart.

But he couldn't second-guess his choice. "We'll let Lugan know our decision tomorrow."

19

THEY WENT to sleep after that, setting powerful wards that would alert them to potential danger. When Lucian awoke, the sky outside was covered in heavy clouds, laced with the occasional flash of lightning. Already, the wind was picking up, and a few fat raindrops, along with some pellets of hail, began pelting the window of their suite. The barrier surrounding the city seemed to do nothing to stop the storm's fury, except for repelling the lightning with a Dynamistic ward built within the barrier.

"Well," Mira said, joining Lucian at the window, "looks like we won't be setting off for a while."

"It's like a horror holo," Serah said from the table, where she was biting into a haunch of meat. "Now we're locked in the house."

"Where did you get that food?" Lucian asked.

She shrugged. "They brought it in while you were sleeping. Fergus said it's not poisoned, and that's good enough for me."

Lucian went to the table, finding a full breakfast spread. There, he found the meat covered with a dark sauce, a bowl of something that looked similar to rice or couscous, filled with small, chopped vegetables, exotic fruits, and cake.

"No, it's not poisonous," Fergus said. "But you also don't know where that meat came from. I'll be strictly vegetarian from now on."

"Smart move," Mira said.

Emma came to the table and took a delicate bite of meat. Everyone awaited her response.

"Not bad," she said. "Good sear."

"See!" Serah said. "Told you. All of you are missing out."

At that moment, they were interrupted by a chime, what Lucian supposed to be the doorbell. Readying his Focus, he went to answer.

Opening the door, he was surprised to see Captain Eresha. Her violet eyes were glowing, as if under possession of Psionic Magic. Lucian immediately moved to block her and was surprised by the resistance his stream met.

Emma stepped forward, slowing time around Eresha, but her attack, too, was shielded.

Lucian could only wonder how that was possible. Eresha was a mage. Powerful, to be sure, but nothing next to either Lucian or Emma.

Before Lucian could speak, Eresha cut him off. "I'm not here to fight you," she said, stepping inside and closing the door behind her. She seemed completely unconcerned with the attacks. "We must speak. It's about your mission."

"What do you know about that?" Lucian asked. "How did you get past my wards?"

"You don't know with whom you're speaking," Eresha said.

Lucian noted the Psionically possessed eyes, along with the different inflection of speech. Why was the voice familiar?

At that moment, it came to him. "Anlilta?"

"You are in grave danger, Lucian Abrantes. Lugan will betray you. If not now, then when he feels the time is right to strike."

"How can you know that?"

"I have spies placed all over the Aetheria. And especially in worlds so near the Eye, where I felt your presence enter the Light Realm. For now, my Focus is imposed over Eresha's, but I can't keep that up for long. From such a distance, Psionic possession is crude and easily detected. Even now, Lugan's soldiers are likely seeking the source of the message."

"So, you're saying we need to find the Gadea Gate," Lucian said.

Eresha's eyes widened in surprise. "I'm surprised he told you that much. But perhaps he did so in order to win your trust. Whatever the reason, you must never forsake the Seven-Fold Path, no matter the temptation. Everything else will lead to your destruction."

"He warned us about how dangerous it was. Are you saying it's not?"

"No, he's telling the truth about that. It *is* dangerous. But Gadea is a moon of Eänna, and as such, I can help you. You need only pass through the Gate and follow the Seven-Fold Path. Keep following it, without fail, until I meet you. The moon is dangerous, and Kharzul the Shadowed is not to be underestimated."

Fergus stepped forward. "How can we trust you? How do we know this isn't a trap?"

"What reason would I have to betray you? I am Anlilta, Speaker of the Manifold. My entire purpose is to prevent the dissolution of the Light Realm, and by extension, your own reality. If I'm not on your side, no one is."

"I don't know if you've noticed, but there's a huge storm outside," Lucian said. "How are we supposed to cross the water and find the Gate? I can shield the storm easily, but we'll still need a ship. Or more accurately, a submarine, since we're going underwater."

"I have a vessel prepared."

"Hold on," Fergus said. "How can we possibly guess your true motives? We only have your word."

At that very moment, the door was blasted off its frame. Two mage-soldiers stood outside the door, their hands wrapped with latent Dynamistic Magic. Fergus's eyes widened, but his reaction was quick, streaming a laser that sliced through them both.

"Do you believe me now?" Anlilta asked, speaking through Eresha.

Lucian's decision was instant. "Take us to the ship."

"I will not be in possession of Eresha much longer. Once I use her to create the portal, you must pass through quickly before I lose control."

More shouts could be heard from the corridor outside. Without further hesitation, Eresha spread her hands, opening a portal through which Lucian could see a small vessel floating with Gravitonic Magic. It appeared to be inside a cavern. Eresha's body convulsed with effort, and Lucian realized the mage would lose her life to buy their escape.

He didn't have time to process that fact. "Come on!"

They sprang through, Fergus bringing up the rear and nearly being cut off by the portal's collapse. The quiet stillness of the cave beyond was a strange contrast to the previous chaos.

Serah turned around, looking at where the portal had been just seconds earlier. "What the rotting hell just happened?"

Silence met her words. From the stunned reactions of the rest, she wasn't alone in this sentiment.

Lucian had similar whiplash, but it was up to him to lead. He took a few steps toward the ship while creating a bright light sphere that would illuminate the cavern and its surroundings.

The vessel presented an elegant silhouette against the sphere's light. Crafted with sleek, aerodynamic lines, it was smaller than a ship, yet more substantial than a mere boat. Lucian supposed it might be called a sloop. It lacked the luxury of Ninshar's floating yacht, seeming more austere and militaristic in appearance. Its contours, smooth and flowing, hinted at speed and agility. The hull, a fusion of metallic and organic textures, shimmered in muted hues of silver and soft blue.

Beneath the hull, a gentle silver glow wrapped around its underbelly, the light pulsing softly with latent Gravitonic branding. Despite its compact size, the ship was a perfect blend of functionality and elegance, ready to slice through sky and sea, and hopefully, even the deeps of the Ghostly Sea.

Lucian reached out for the vessel, finding that it was ready to connect to his Focus. As soon as it clicked into place, he willed it to allow them access inside.

A metallic ladder retracted on its hull, leading to the hatch on top.

"Come on," Lucian said.

The others fell in behind as he climbed. Within minutes, all were inside the metallic interior. Lucian was intrinsically aware of the ship's layout, knowing just where to go as he headed for the bridge. He felt the ship's power as if it were his own, as if it were an extension of himself. He knew its capabilities, which included being able to withstand the pressure of being deep underwater.

But would it be strong enough to withstand the extreme depths they needed to reach?

It was a question for later.

Go, he commanded.

The vessel lurched from its hovering position and forward through the wide cavern, buoyed by its brand of Gravitonic Magic. Once again, the Seven-Fold Path stretched before them, bearing the color of the Orbs and leading them out of the maze-like tunnels.

"I can't believe this is happening," Serah said. "Just like that, Lugan is the bad guy?"

"Seems like it," Lucian said.

"Those were his mages attacking us," Emma said. "No question about that."

"Now it's a race to the Gadea Gate, since the jig is up," Mira said. "Do you think he'll try to chase us through the storm?"

"Not if we're fast enough," Lucian said. "We have a big head start. And we can always go underwater to hide."

Their conversation stilled as they made a final bend, where in the distance, the cave mouth stood revealed. Though it was still afternoon, such was the thickness of the massive sheets of rain pounding down on the roiling surf that things looked positively apocalyptic.

"Ward with everything you have," Lucian said. "Just to be sure."

He created a powerful Binding barrier to surround the entire vessel. The ship had plenty of latent power built into its Gravitonic brands to get them where they were going, but not if its shields were maxed out. He felt Emma create a Dynamistic shield, while Serah created a bit of additional lift with her Gravitonic Magic.

"Brace yourselves," Fergus said, grabbing onto the bulkhead.

The others followed his example, while Lucian planted his feet with Binding Magic.

The ship, surrounded by their collective magic, headed out into the storm . . .

. . . only to fly as smoothly as if they were in space itself, with no impediment whatsoever. They were a bubble of calmness in the middle of watery chaos, with zero visibility other than the rainbow path leading into the unknown.

"Well, *that* was anticlimactic," Serah said.

"You're saying that like it's a bad thing," Emma said.

"Not at all," she said. "How far do you think, Lucian?"

He shook his head. "No telling. Probably several hundred kilometers, if not more."

"And then down. How deep do you think this ship goes?"

"That, I'm not sure about. I know it's not invincible. The hull has been strengthened with various brands, but that will only work to a point."

"To a point?" Emma asked. "What point?"

"Hopefully, not deep enough to worry about it. But if it comes to that, I'll have to reinforce the Binding shield with my magic. Like I'm doing now, only much stronger."

"Rotting hell," Serah said. "*That's* terrifying."

"Why not go underwater now to escape detection?" Fergus asked.

"The storm is covering us," Lucian said. "And it would slow us down a lot."

"I suppose. We also have monsters to worry about."

"Fergus, stop creeping me out," Serah said. "Heights, I can do. Spiders? Not really, but I can manage. But being in a submarine, hundreds of meters below the water, no light, pressure that'll crush you to a pulp like a fly in a metaphorical fist, isolated from all help, no time to even scream . . ."

"There are much worse ways to go, logically speaking," Emma said. "At least it would be quick."

"No one's going to die," Lucian said. "This is nothing my Binding can't handle."

"What happens when we actually reach the Gadea Gate?" Fergus asked. "Will it be wide enough for the ship to go through?"

"I would think so. If it's anything like the other Gate, there should be enough space. Ninshar's yacht was much bigger than this and it fit just fine."

"Hope so," Serah said.

"Whatever the situation," Mira said, "I hope we can trust this Anlilta. It seems we have no other choice."

Lucian could do nothing else but hope, too.

20

THE DAY DRAGGED ON, and all was quiet as they sailed into the heart of the storm. Thanks to everyone's magic, the ship was never truly affected by the squall. But this was the simple part. Lucian trusted the storm to cover their escape, and he trusted the Seven-Fold Path to lead them in the right direction.

All that was left was to wait and prepare themselves mentally as best they could.

As the day wore on, they took shifts. Lucian told everyone to get what rest they could, and he could alert them Psionically if there was any change. Only Serah remained with him, taking a nap in the bridge's corner. Lucian himself couldn't sleep. Only he knew the direction of the Path, and that direction could change at any moment. He had to keep going without sleep, at least for now.

They continued flying just above the surface, Gravitonic Magic continuing to support the vessel. It wasn't until there was light again, however small, that the rain petered out, leaving an eerie stillness behind. The sea, about ten meters below the

152

airship, was strangely calm, giving off a pearlescent glow. In the distance, the sky was the same luster, never truly becoming blue. Lucian wondered if they were in the eye of a hurricane. He allowed the Binding barrier to fall and noted a change in the Path ahead, which had veered slightly down. Reaching out with Psionics, he alerted the others to come to the bridge.

Fergus and Mira were the first to arrive. "Almost there?"

Lucian nodded. "Yeah. Getting close."

"I couldn't sleep a wink," Mira said. "Just knowing what's about to happen . . ."

Lucian took in his entire crew, who waited for any words of encouragement. He didn't know what to say. He was in this mess, just the same as them. But as their leader, he felt he owed them at least something.

"I know the next few hours are going to be crazy. We don't know what to expect. We just have to handle it as best as we can. Rely on each other. We're a team. That said, this might be the toughest situation we've ever found ourselves in. Anything can happen." He grasped his Focus to calm his own nerves. "There's a possibility one of us might go down fighting. It happened with Jagar in the tower on Sigil. Even if he survived in the end, we might not be so lucky. All of us knew the minute we stepped through the First Gate we might not be coming back. We're fighting for a cause bigger than any of us. If the worst happens, I might have to make a snap decision, and I need everyone to follow it without question."

The others nodded, and Lucian didn't feel the need to elaborate further. Death was always a possibility. Even a probability. If someone didn't make it, they couldn't hesitate to move on if the situation called for it. It was a sobering reminder of the danger ahead.

"Ship's almost to the surface now," Fergus said. "But well said, Lucian. I think we're all on the same page."

Lucian nodded. "All right. Raising the Binding barrier. Strong as I can make it."

Lucian did so, continually strengthening and edifying the shield around the ship. The vessel followed the line of the Path until it crashed through the surface of the water. The ship's inherent Gravitonic brand made it so that the transition was hardly felt. The ship slid from air into water as smooth as a dolphin.

Then, they were plunging into the darkness, a curtain of bubbles rising past the forward windshield. Lucian felt the pressure building against his brand with surprising speed. With every meter they descended, it was palpable. He continued streaming to make the shield even stronger. He knew the ship's magically forged hull could take the depths up to a point, perhaps as much as a thousand meters, but Lucian had the feeling the Gadea Gate was much deeper than even that.

He didn't bother turning on the ship's lights. That might make them the target of whatever monsters called these waters home. The Seven-Fold Path was still visible, the only thing leading into the depths. As long as they followed that, they would find the Gate.

For several minutes, they descended, the darkness deepening and the pressure building. There was little talking, everyone just watching out the forward viewport tensely as they headed toward an ocean floor that never seemed to arrive. Schools of colorful fish parted at their advance. After half an hour had passed, it was almost pitch black.

Suddenly, the Path shifted, and Lucian quickly adjusted the vessel's course with his mind. They ran along the sandy bottom, which was mostly bereft of life.

"Did we make it?" Serah asked.

But before anyone could respond, the ocean floor seemed to . . . *end*, as if coming to a cliff. The ship leaned over and began descending once more into the darkness. It only took a few minutes for there to be no light at all. The Seven-Fold Path did nothing to illumine their surroundings, though strangely, it was still visible about ten meters ahead of them.

"I'm detecting something," Fergus said, his body ensconced in Dynamistic and Radiant Magic. "Something big."

Lucian knew the stream he was using was an electric impulse seeking stream, useful for detecting other life forms.

"Let's hope it stays away," Lucian said.

"Seems to have stopped," Fergus said.

Lucian increased their speed, which meant he had to stream even more ether to power the Binding barrier. Blue magic flowed from his body, through the hull, continually surrounding the ship. The bright shield radiated outward, illuminating the surrounding darkness with great intensity. Lucian felt they no longer had a choice. They needed to see their surroundings, and the pressure of the water demanded it.

That was when, out of the darkness, a massive, gaping mouth appeared before them, accompanied by a pair of blood-red eyes.

Lucian diverted his stream, lacing the Binding shield with powerful Dynamistic Magic, electrocuting the monstrosity. It lurched away, a long serpent that coiled as it prepared to dive deeper toward safety. The currents created by its movement were massive, throwing the ship to the side and nearly making it keel over. As alarms blared and his friends screamed, Lucian righted the vessel Psionically as it continued heading down in the darkness.

"What the rotting hell was that?" Serah asked, her voice wavering.

"It's getting farther away," Fergus said, swallowing. "For now."

"Lucian, can you make this go faster?" Mira asked.

"This is as fast as we can go," he said. "The water down here is dense. Shouldn't be too much longer."

After a few tense minutes, Lucian gave in and turned on the ship's headlights, the Binding barrier no longer sufficient to see their surroundings. The surrounding darkness was illuminated by about fifty meters, revealing something out of the blackness below.

"Would you look at that?" Fergus asked, his eyes wide with awe.

It was difficult to discern at first, but Lucian realized it was an underwater mountain, along with the ruins of broken towers, bridges, and crumbled buildings. It was an entire city, what had once been the Hanging Islands of yesteryear mentioned by Lugan. The Seven-Fold Path weaved among the watery ruins, but there was no sign of any Gate.

It was only when they passed the first of the towers that Lucian got a true sense of the scale. The sunken city was enormous, easily as big as the greatest cities on Earth. Only this city had once existed on a series of giant floating islands far above the water, and Lucian had to guess that the mountain ahead of them must have once been one of those islands. Lucian could only wonder what it had been like during its heyday. It seemed a miracle that its decrepit towers and broken bridges were still somewhat recognizable, perhaps a testament to the ingenuity of its builders. It had existed for two thousand years in this dark, watery grave, with nothing but monsters for company.

"We're getting closer," Lucian said. "I can feel it."

"Watch the right," Emma said.

They passed a collapsed tower, around which was wrapped a serpentine sea creature, smaller than the one that had attacked them. It looked at them with stretched, glowing eyes built for darkness. It shut those eyes against the blinding light of the ship.

"A baby one," Serah said. "And *not* in a cute way."

More of the creatures could be seen as the ship plied through what must have once been a large temple with a broken dome above them. They swarmed by the dozens at the bottom of the expanse, each about five meters long. A nest, perhaps? When Lucian shifted his light downward to force them back, hundreds of things stood revealed. None were attacking, so there was no reason to fight them, but Lucian had to restrain himself from doing anything. As he tightened his Focus, the fear that wanted to rise and take control became distant.

It was with great relief that they exited the domed temple, following the path into a deep rift that seemed to separate two of the sunken islands. The darkness swallowed them as they headed down at a steep angle. Lucian felt the pressure building, so much so that he had to reinforce the shield constantly. If he let up for even a moment, it would be instant death.

In the rift, he felt a power source, what he knew to be the long-lost Gadea Gate. The Seven-Fold Path led resolutely down.

"We're almost there," Lucian said. "Hold on!"

"The Big Guy's coming back," Fergus warned.

Lucian could also feel the monster's presence through the ship's intrinsic Dynamistic ward. It was swimming far faster than the ship was moving.

He dropped every stream he had, diverting everything to the Binding shield and a new Gravitonic stream. He opened a gravity point directly in front of the ship, its pulling force lending additional speed.

All that mattered was reaching the Gate before the monster caught up to them.

"It's going to get us!" Fergus said.

Lucian pulled more deeply from the Manifold, lacing the shield once again with Dynamism, just in time to give the monster a nasty shock. It backed off, but its sudden writhing sent a strong current that pushed them further into the depths at an uncontrolled angle of descent. The Binding shield flickered for a moment, but Lucian streamed just in time to save it from petering out, even as the others threw whatever magic they could to reinforce it.

At last, Lucian could see a light in the distance.

"Come on!" Mira said. "We've got this! Go, go, go!"

Lucian strengthened the gravity point even more, seeing no choice. It forced the vessel to drop even faster. The Binding shield strained against the increase in pressure. Lucian became a conduit of ether, the building blocks of magic infusing into him at an unprecedented rate.

Just then, the ship was grappled from behind. Through the ship's Psionic ward, he could sense the serpent grasping the hull with crushing strength. Lucian increased the strength of the Dynamistic Magic, once again electrocuting the sea monster. But this time, its body shook and banged into the shield surrounding the ship, forcing it ever downward. Lucian felt himself lose control of the vessel, streaming with everything he had to get it through the Gate.

There was a moment of blinding white as the ship began passing through. It met resistance on the other side. Lucian forced down his panic. There seemed to be some sort of shield blocking the Gate, composed of all the Minor Aspects, but also including Space-Time and Shadow Magic.

He realized it must have been a way to prevent the water of Gadea from passing through to the other side. Now stuck in limbo, Lucian realized what he had to do. He had to get the ship through the shield, all the while allowing it to remain intact, otherwise the insane pressure of Gadea's depths would burst forth onto the other side.

Lucian streamed with everything he had, the surrounding reality falling away until all he could see was the Ether that powered the Light Realm. All of it entered him, and he enacted his will on the Gate, knowing the task should have been impossible. The shield was well-made and had been crafted with great skill and power, likely by Kharzul the Shadowed himself. If that Gate was tampered with, the Descendant would be the first to feel it.

But there was no other option. It was just Lucian and the shield, the pressure of the surrounding water inconsequential in comparison. He simply imagined them moving past the Gate, and then...

...He opened his eyes to see the ship slipping on an expanse of ice, right toward a cliff.

21

WITH THE LAST of his strength, Lucian streamed a reverse gravity point, slowing the ship just meters from the edge that would have plunged them to their deaths.

The ship creaked and then came to a complete rest. Outside the viewport, a gust of ice-laden wind beat against them.

His Psionic link with the ship had been broken, which could only mean one thing: there was nothing left to connect *to*. The ship was as good as dead. Already, Lucian could feel the temperature dropping sharply within the bridge. The hull had obviously been breached somewhere. Mira surrounded them all with a strong Thermal shield.

Lucian couldn't get a sense of the temperature, but he assumed that without the shield, they would freeze to the bone within seconds. All was quiet, and looking around, everyone seemed to be in one piece.

He knew this gauntlet was only getting started. They had only passed the first obstacle.

Now, they had to wrestle with the frozen wastes of Gadea.

Lucian turned to his crew. "Everyone all right?"

"Cold, but fine," Fergus said, his breath fogging in the frigid air. "That was . . . something else."

Serah shivered. "I think we need to get moving before we all turn into popsicles."

Lucian nodded. "Yes, we need to find shelter. Mom, keep that Thermal shield strong. Let's gather what supplies we can carry and leave the rest. Kharzul will look for us soon. He knows I tampered with his shield. Emma, ward Space-Time. I want nothing to drop in on us."

"Got it."

"Let's move out."

They quickly took up their essentials, which wasn't much. A minute later, Lucian was leading the way out of the ship, stepping onto the icy surface of Gadea. The combination of the ice and low gravity made it incredibly slick, and Lucian had to use a Binding glyph to keep everyone standing. The wind howled around them, and Lucian could feel the biting cold through his layers, despite his mother's ward.

Lucian turned around to see the hull twisted beyond recognition. The air just became colder, forcing Mira to reinforce the group's Thermal shield even more strongly. It was even colder than Halia after Fergus, Serah, and Lucian had been stranded after locating the Orb of Gravitonics, but reaching out with Atomicism, he found the air perfectly breathable. The gravity was light, probably half that of Earth.

Looking at the sky, there was no sign of Eänna, the planet around which this moon orbited. Possibly, it was hidden behind the looming, icy mountains in the distance, or they were on the moon's dark side. Lucian knew most moons were tidally locked to their parent world. That had been the case with both the Eye and Psyche, so he had to assume it was the same here.

It meant they had a long way to go.

They found themselves on the cliff the ship had nearly teetered over, beneath a chilling, starlit sky. Beyond the cliff, a rugged icy wasteland stretched all the way to the horizon, along with the Seven-Fold Path. Lucian got the sense that the spread of ice had to have come from the Gate itself. Perhaps, when the Hanging Islands of Kadur had sunk, the sea had come bursting through the Gate unabated, and had frozen in the harsh climate.

"The Path leads past those mountains on the horizon," Lucian said. "Thankfully, we can warp most of the way. Fergus, think you can cover our tracks with Radiance?"

"I'm honored you think so much of my skills," Fergus said, "but if you're going to be warping, not even my Radiance can block that out completely."

"Well, we have no choice," Lucian said. "Do what you can. We need to link up with Anlilta as soon as possible."

"Will do."

By the end of the conversation, everyone had finished setting up their wards. Lucian picked a point in the distance, sharpening his vision with Radiant Magic. Streaming Space-Time, they made the jump almost immediately.

They found themselves on the icy plain below, with the mountains looming before them. With no nearby threats, Lucian once again picked a spot in those mountains, right where the Path was leading.

Again, they reappeared. The next warp was shorter, to a small ridgeline that would allow them to see to the other side of the range.

Lucian warped them there, only to find another icy plain before them.

"How's your magic holding up, Lucian?" Fergus asked.

"No worries there."

"So, what's the plan, really?" Emma asked. "Just follow the Path and hope Anlilta shows up somewhere?"

"That's the gist of it. The closer we get to Eänna, the bigger the chance we give her to find us. That's what she told us, anyway. To keep following the Path."

For the next few hours, they proceeded across Gadea's icy surface. There was no sign of life, which wasn't surprising, given the extreme temperatures. Eventually, they were forced to stop as the wind picked up and threw endless waves of ice toward them. It made seeing the next warp point all but impossible, even with Radiance.

They entered a nearby cave, Fergus illuminating it with a bright light sphere. Within, they found a cleft of rock, upon which Mira created a magically fed fire.

It was hard to tell how far they had gone, but Lucian wouldn't have been surprised if his warping had allowed them to traverse several hundred kilometers. There was nothing really to do but rest and hope the storm had blown over by the time they woke up.

———

LUCIAN AWOKE to find the cave in darkness. The fire must have gone out, which was strange, since it had been set as a brand.

He rushed to recreate it, but with his Radiance-enhanced vision, he noticed a vague, shadowed shape at the cave's entrance. Zulum.

Instantly, Lucian sent a burst of Creation Magic toward the apparition, but the attack was deflected with ease. The shape made no move to retaliate.

In fact, it *spoke*.

"I only wish to talk, Chosen."

The being's voice was dark and low, almost discordant. A quick look at his friends told him they hadn't heard it at all. Details in his surroundings were hazy, not fully formed.

This was a dream, then.

Of course, Lucian had warded the group strongly before going to sleep, but obviously, his defenses had been lacking.

The interloper this powerful could only be one person.

"What do you want, Kharzul?"

"I have a proposition for you. Would you hear it?"

"Not really, but it seems as if I don't have a choice."

"There is always a choice. Choices have power, do they not? There are things you might want to know before descending on Anshar. Things the Ascendants would never tell you."

"How are you even talking to me?"

"No doubt, you thought yourself well-defended from Psionic incursion. However, you never considered the power of Shadow Magic. A deadly mistake! You carry my master's Aspect. All who serve the Shadow will be drawn to the power you wield. And yes, those powerful enough can even speak to you through it. Those like me. The power of the Shadow Aspect overcomes that of Psionics."

"So, you know where we are."

"Yes. So, you would do well to listen. Perhaps you can escape my clutches, but what about your friends? Perhaps you should hear me out for their sake."

"If you have something to say, say it."

Kharzul didn't waste another moment. "Then I will begin. No doubt, you've heard the side of the Light, but you have lent no ear to the side of the Shadow. Consider me an emissary for the Ancient One, whose Focus still abides in the Manifold. He cannot speak for himself, so I must speak for him."

"You mean the same Ancient One who tried to kill me and all my friends? I think I've heard enough of his side."

"Old slights can be set aside in the light of new information. Even now, you are running to your doom. There was never a pit of vipers viler than the Court of Enkius and his jackals. They would have you believe we of the Shadow are of an evil nature. But nothing in the Aetheria remains unsullied, and the corruption of the Light exceeds that of the Shadow. In fact, their evils are worse, for they shroud it in trappings of virtue."

"How does it exceed your corruption? I know you'd kill me if given the chance."

"Not necessarily. Not while there is a chance, however slight, that I might win you over to the side of the Shadow, which has the right of things. I am qualified to speak on behalf of my master. I am Kharzul the Shadowed, second only to Isthelah himself."

"Isthelah? Who is that?"

"Rarely is the Ancient One's true name uttered in the Halls of Light, for even after two millennia, they fear even a whisper might lend it power." Lucian saw Kharzul's sharp smile flash in the darkness. "Maybe they are right."

"Hard to be scary when you're dead."

Kharzul laughed. "Dead? No, Chosen. My master is very much alive. You may have slain him in your Shadow Realm, but he still abides in the Heart of Creation. So long as the Orb of Shadows exists, *he* exists. Even now, you are doing his bidding."

"I'm actually doing the opposite of that, but okay."

Kharzul chuckled. "Find the Aspects. Bring them to me. Does this refrain sound familiar?"

Lucian felt a chill. He had almost forgotten those words, spoken during his metaphysical over three years ago, and many times since then. They had come to him in the darkness of old dreams, and at the time, he didn't know what it meant.

"I'm bringing the Aspects, yes, but not to him. I'm going to the Heart of Creation."

"Where my master abides. Do you really think he would let you get so far without completing your true task? The Orbs are rightfully his. And his aim to use them is a just one. He will use them to recreate reality. To make it perfect."

Lucian thought of the Orb of Shadows in his pack, so perilously close to this enemy. While this was a dream, the thought still made Lucian uncomfortable. Even now, Kharzul's agents could be headed here, or even Kharzul himself.

And yet, he found himself unable to stop listening, either through Kharzul's magic or his own morbid curiosity.

Lucian resisted this urge, fighting to break off the connection, but Kharzul had him ensnared like a spider in a web. Something about the Orb of Shadows was lending him strength, forcing Lucian to listen.

"It would be wiser to be allies than adversaries," Kharzul went on. "As I was saying before, not all is as it appears with the side of the Light."

"How so?" Lucian asked.

"Have you ever wondered why Enkius the Usurper rose against Isthelah to begin with?"

"The Time Weaver told me about it. The Ancient One wanted power, but he couldn't kill those who stood in his way. So, he created the Orb of Shadows, and a lot of Ascendants—like you— followed him, becoming Descendants. The Light would have lost, until Enkius got the Orb of Creation, which turned the tide of the war. I'm sure I'm missing a lot of details, but that's the gist of it."

Kharzul gave a chilling laugh. "Is that the tale they've spun for you? The Time Weaver! Well, it doesn't surprise me that one would say as much."

"Well, what's your version?"

"It is not so simple as that. I shall try to be brief, but that is difficult when you're speaking of thousands of years of history. In short, two epochs mark the Aetheria: the Time of Before, and the Time of After, divided by the War of Shadow and Light. We now dwell in the Time of After, but the Time of Before was a paradise where Isthelah, the Firstborn of Creation, held dominion overall, at the very behest of the Manifold itself. That is why we among the Shadow remember his old name and title. We call him the First because it was his word that heralded the genesis of all exis- tence itself."

"So, he's basically God, according to you."

"He can be thought of as such. Before the Light Realm even

existed, he was blessed by the Manifold to rule it. With the power of the Aspects, this reality—the Light Realm—sprang into existence, and for a long while, it was the *only* reality. The Manifold has power, a mind of its own, but it avails nothing unless that power is directed by one of sufficient might. Isthelah was the first to channel the Orbs' power, using it to create the worlds of the Aetheria. He is Firstborn, for none, not even the mighty Enkius, came before him. Isthelah is a father to us all, and he was born of nothing but the power of the Aspects themselves. As such, the Aspects are his by right."

Lucian wondered if this could be true. It seemed unimaginable, but maybe there was something to it.

"He not only created the Light Realm with the Orbs; he created the Ascendants. Enkius, Anlilta, me, and all the rest who were of the First Echelon. The first generation. And when his work was complete, he made an unprecedented decision. Rather than live within the Manifold, he gave up the Orbs, instead choosing to live among his creation."

"He gave them up? Why?"

"This confuses you. Well, no one can say why Isthelah left. Was it boredom, or merely a desire to rule? Whatever the reason, the Manifold granted this request. This ushered in the Time of Before, a golden age unlike any other. Under his guidance, the Light Realm prospered. The Aetheria was formed, growing as the Gates bridged the Ethereal Void and connect the worlds."

Lucian figured that the Light Realm referred to the entire reality, including the Manifold, while the Aetheria was more of a political unit, defined as whatever was accessible through the Gates. It seemed to refer to the entire Light Realm that mattered.

Kharzul continued. "Most were loyal to their master, at least at first. But Enkius coveted Isthelah's rights and power, and he deceived many other Ascendants in betraying the Firstborn of Creation. They were, and still are, rebellious vassals, threatened by Isthelah's righteous designs. Long had Enkius lusted for the sovereignty of the Aetheria, but Isthelah in his bounteous grace suffered his ambitions. Enkius never dared to act, so mighty was Isthelah's unchallenged power, for untold eons."

"Okay. If this Isthelah was so powerful, how did Enkius win against him?"

"An opening came. The Ascendants bred amongst themselves, multiplying and creating other Ascendants, though of a lower breed. And those lesser Ascendants procreated, creating sorcerers and mages, and they created the mundane, those who could not stream even a single spark. Isthelah at first rejoiced at this proliferation of life filling his creation until he perceived Enkius' plans. His dastardly vassal's purpose was far more nefarious; he was not creating life to bring glory to the master. He was creating an army to usurp him."

"Why would Enkius want to attack him if Isthelah was such a benevolent ruler?"

"The answer to that query is simple, and I previously alluded to it—had you been listening, Chosen. Enkius desired the power and the favor the Manifold bestowed upon Isthelah. Many, including me, remained loyal to Isthelah, but two-thirds of the Ascendants came to favor Enkius in the end. He peddled many falsehoods, and so deceived them to their doom. War tore at the Aetheria, and for the first time in all creation, pain—*true* pain— was known and felt. Armies were vanquished, innocents slain, mighty weapons of magic devised, worlds destroyed. In those days, only the Seven Minor Aspects could be wielded, but the destruction was still profound. None of the First Echelon could be killed, though their children could. At the rate the war was going, all lesser beings were doomed unless something was done to stop it. But without something to turn the tide, Isthelah would be overrun and forced out of power. So it was that Isthelah ventured to the Heart of Creation, beseeching the Manifold for some way to fight back against his rebellious children. And so it was that the Manifold blessed him with a new Aspect that only he could wield: the Aspect of Shadows. Within this Aspect was contained the power to bend reality and create alternate forms of existence, new rules that would allow him to do the unthinkable: end the lives of his own children, who had become a poison against his righteous rule."

"Why would the Manifold give him so much power?"

"Are you not listening? It was by Isthelah's hand that the Light Realm even *existed*. It was his by rights. The Manifold granted his request, likely seeing it as necessary in bringing balance to the Aetheria. As such, the Orb of Shadows is the most powerful of all the Orbs, bound eternally to Isthelah's Focus, no matter where it goes. And as a reward, those loyal to him gain access to its unbridled power."

"What about the Orb of Creation?"

"I will get to that, in due course. It didn't take long for Enkius to see that the fight was hopeless. Unable to contend with the raw power of Shadow Magic, Enkius' lot fell, one by one. All seemed lost. That was until Anlilta, the self-styled Foresayer of the Manifold, uttered a prophecy that Enkius himself would wield a Golden Light with the power to repel the Shadow." Kharzul halted ominously. "Enlivened by these words, he went together with his friend and lover, Nathi, to the Heart of Creation. They begged the Manifold's favor, spinning tales of Isthelah the Fallen's supposed cruelty and malice. For whatever reason, perhaps touched by the pair's love, their stories were believed."

"Maybe the Ancient One was as cruel as they said."

"I was there, Chosen, awakened by the breath of life given by Isthelah himself. He is the rightful ruler of the Light Realm. If there was any fault of his, it was lack of control, for giving too much agency to his subjects, for being too kind. This kindness allowed rebellion to foment."

"If you say so."

Kharzul ignored the sarcasm. "To everyone's astonishment, Enkius and Nathi emerged from the Heart of Creation, each bearing a new Orb. Enkius bore the Orb of Creation, which held the power to revert and contest the power of Shadow Magic, while Nathi—the one you call Time Weaver—held the Orb of Space-Time. A final battle begun for the fate of the Light Realm itself. Each side matched each other stroke for stroke until the side of the Shadow proved almost triumphant. That was when, as a last gambit, Enkius and Nathi combined their newfound powers, creating the First Gate, which connected to your Shadow Realm, a lower plane of existence. Rallied by Enkius, the forces of the Light threw everything into attacking Isthelah, pushing him through the Gate. Despite grave losses, the Light managed this impossible feat. The Shadow was routed, forced into hiding."

"What then?"

Kharzul chuckled softly. "Their victory celebration was short-lived. For when Enkius tried to close the First Gate, he found it impossible to do so. Seeking the guidance from the Manifold, he discovered the fatal flaw of his and Nathi's plan: without Shadow Magic, the First Gate could not be canceled out of existence and was cursed to forever remain."

"So, the Orb of Shadows is needed to take out the First Gate," Lucian said.

"That is so. And that Orb can only be wielded by Isthelah himself, and anyone who takes on its power will *become* an extension of Isthelah himself. As such, closing the First Gate is impossible, unless it is done by Isthelah's will.

Lucian could almost feel Kharzul's mirth at the conundrum. If all that was true, all the Ancient One had to do was wait things out. Either he got what he wanted—complete control of the Light Realm—or eventually, too much ether would bleed out from the First Gate, causing the collapse of the Light Realm, which would spread to the Shadow Realm.

It was an impossible problem to solve unless Lucian could find some way to harness the power of Shadow Magic without becoming the Ancient One himself.

As far as he knew, there was no way to do that. There was the ethereal core, of course, but he doubted even it would have enough power to get the job done properly.

"I see you are trying to work out the riddle yourself, the riddle that has confounded the greatest minds in the Aetheria for two millennia," Kharzul said. "There is no answer. No answer but to embrace the side of the Shadow, to give Isthelah the First what is rightfully his. Loyalty to him, and him alone, will bring you glory and power beyond imagination."

Lucian, of course, wasn't satisfied with that answer. It seemed like a Gordian knot that was impossible to untie.

But perhaps there was a way to cut through it entirely. An answer that no one else had found.

"Still not convinced?" Kharzul said, his tone gloating. "Well, allow me to further convince you. Do you truly believe Enkius will allow you to hold on to the Orb of Creation, what he sees as his by right? While Enkius is still mighty without it, far more so than any other being in the Light Realm, he still needs it to cement his legitimacy and to continue his war to stamp out the Shadow from the Aetheria. Ever since the end of the War, Light and Shadow have continued to skirmish, neither side powerful enough to destroy the other, both lacking their respective Orbs. Nor will he suffer you to hold the Orb of Space-Time, which was held by his lover, Nathi. You have an impossible task before you, Chosen. I don't envy it! I think you will find, among the Ascendants of the Light, individuals are bound to their stations, regardless of their inner worth or ability. You will always be a lapdog to them. But those of us who belong to the Shadow, we value strength and prowess. Embrace the Shadow Aspect, and you have the potential to rise as a new deity. When we defeat the Light, Isthelah will fulfill his ultimate promise and grant godhood to all who are loyal to him. Using the power of the Orbs, he will make for all of us new realities of which we can be the master, to shape to our own liking. To Enkius, however, you are nothing but an inconvenience that must be gotten rid of once you're no longer useful."

"And why should I believe any of this? I know the Ancient One better than even you do, Kharzul. And you are a fool to believe his lies. Do you really think he'd ever let you be a god, to be his equal?"

"I wouldn't dream of such insolence; such are the fantasies of Enkius and his rebellious lot. The truth is, Chosen, the Shadow is the only one with the ability, or the interest, to save your reality. That's all you really want, isn't it? You simply want to return the Orbs and be done with it all. And, with luck, return to your reality, having fulfilled your quest. All of this, and more, can be done with the power of the Shadow."

"How?"

"Do exactly what my master bids you. Bring the Aspects to him. You need not travel all the way to the Heart of Creation. Even now, all you must do is to absorb the Orb of Shadows. It is a simple thing, accomplished with a mere thought. Do this, and Isthelah will give every possible glory. All will be forgiven."

"Wrong. You really think after all the pain I've caused him, he will give me anything except eternal pain and torture? He's promised me as much."

"Tell me," Kharzul said, his voice low. "How do you intend to accomplish your goals, lacking the power to enforce your will? The Chosen of the Manifold you may be, but even you can't withstand the might of Enkius, his house and retinue, and his allies of the Light without the power of the Shadow. Do you really think they have any regard for your reality, your simple pleasures?" Kharzul let out a scoffing laugh. "Their reality is the only one they care about. You and your friends are tools, nothing more."

"And you expect me to believe that you care about my reality? What is it you want, Kharzul? That's the one thing we haven't talked about."

"What do I want? This world is called the Dread Moon by the denizens of Eänna. In the Time of Before, it was a bastion of the Light. It was a world of balmy air, tranquil seas, and gentle mountains. I seized it by might and cunning. For two thousand years, the Ascendants have been shadowed by its chill presence. That they haven't been able to dislodge me from their orbit is testament to the weakness of the Light! But I aspire to more than this mere moon, Chosen. I dream of subduing the other moons that circle Eänna. I dream of the Shadow falling upon Anshar itself, of the Shadow enfolding the entire Aetheria. I dream of a return to the Time of Before, when Isthelah ruled. When all was as it should be. This is a vision you have the power to bring to fruition, if you are bold enough to grasp it!"

Lucian reached into his pack, producing the Orb of Shadows. Lucian felt its latent power through the Binding, and Kharzul seemed to hold his breath.

"Found something that'll finally shut you up, huh?"

Kharzul remained silent, though Lucian could feel the cold rage emanating from his being.

"There's no universe where I'd ever do anything to help the Ancient One. Too many people have died, a lot of them my friends, because of him. The one thing I *can* promise you? This thing is going to get destroyed. I'll find a way. I am the Chosen of the Manifold."

Kharzul considered this for a moment. "That is . . . unfortunate. I had hoped to expand your perspective, but it seems as if your mind is closed to the truth. You leave me no choice. If only you knew the pain I'm about to bring you."

Lucian tried to force himself awake, but Shadow Magic kept him completely bound, unable to escape the dream.

Kharzul's voice returned, taunting. "I will force you to watch what I do to her."

Her? He couldn't mean . . . "No. Stop!"

But Kharzul was already speaking again. "Look, Chosen!"

A sort of portal opened, but not a portal in the sense of Space-Time, but in the sense of Psionics. Through it, he could see through the dream and into the real world.

And by the group's fire, Serah was sitting on a rock slightly away from the fire, keeping watch over the group.

Lucian felt a cold rage well up within him, a rage that was far more powerful than anything he'd ever experienced. "You do anything to her, the pain I'll make you feel is beyond anything you can imagine. You talk about the power of Shadow Magic, but have you ever felt the relentless force of Creation Magic? Imagine being trapped in a cocoon crafted from it—barely alive, eternally suffering, never able to die or escape. I can make it happen with just a thought. It would be nothing to me. And if you find some way to die, did you know Creation Magic holds the power of resurrection? My brands would revive you, and the torture would start over. I would infuse your senses with Radiant Magic, just to make the pain that much more acute. You will scream for mercy, but there will be none. Only silence. Only darkness. Only agony. Don't think I can't. Don't think I won't."

Kharzul's smile wavered, his eyes narrowing as he weighed Lucian's words. The surrounding air seemed to thicken, and Lucian sensed his mind racing through the possibilities of the grim fate he'd just described. For a moment, the shadow of doubt flickered from his Focus, a testament to the gravity of the threat.

Yet Kharzul's ambition and disdain won over. "But then, Chosen, would you really be able to stoop to such savagery? For even if you could, even if you would, it changes nothing. The Shadow will be triumphant in the end." His grin returned, crueler than before. "You are not here, Lucian. My Shadow Magic binds you in the dream. And while you languish, powerless to act, dreaming savage dreams, I am here right now in this cave with her. She does not see me. The others will not wake. And I will do with her as I please while *you* watch."

Serah turned, looking toward the front of the cave, where it seemed she sensed something. She looked at the surrounding group, all sleeping.

Wake me up, Lucian thought, desperately trying to make the message reach her. *Don't go to the front of the cave. Serah!*

She watched Lucian for a moment, and it seemed as if considering waking him up. All she had to do was to shake him a bit, and when he didn't wake up, she'd realize something was wrong.

But would it matter? Kharzul was there, a predator in the darkness, drawing this out to make the torture that much worse.

He had to get himself out of this dream. But how?

Serah stood and walked toward the entrance of the cave. With increasing desperation, Lucian continued streaming, channeling everything toward overcoming the block.

It *would* break. It *had* to break.

And once it did, he would break Kharzul.

At last, the block shattered around Lucian's Focus, and he woke up, running into the darkness where Serah had gone. He shot toward her, extending his arms.

"Serah!"

She had time enough to widen her eyes just as a dark aura of Space-Time and Shadow Magic surrounded her.

"No!"

Lucian phased forward, but even this was too slow. When the aura dissipated, Serah was gone.

22

"EVERYONE, UP!"

Lucian's urgent call jolted everyone awake, their eyes widening in alarm. Fergus quickly conjured a light sphere, pushing back the darkness of the cave while igniting his shockspear. Emma followed suit, while Mira wreathed her hands in flames.

But there was no visible threat—nothing except that Serah was gone.

Lucian's heart pounded as he charged for the cave entrance, reaching out for Serah through his Focus.

Serah? Talk to me. Where are you?

As he had feared, there was nothing. Lucian increased the strength of his stream, madly drawing on the power of the Orbs until he became a living beacon of pure ether. He forced that ether to obey him, to find Serah, wherever she was.

He felt her presence, but just barely. Her location was being masked by powerful Shadow Magic. Kharzul's magic.

That magic pushed back against him, but with a defiant roar, Lucian retaliated, throwing everything he had into his psychic attack. In his mind, he could see Serah's face, drawn with fear. Her blue eyes seemed to find his, apparently able to see him. Where she was, it was dark, perhaps some place deep underground, though Lucian saw a few flickering sconces. She opened her mouth to speak but was silenced. A shadowy figure stood just steps behind her.

"Seek her out, Chosen, if you can," Kharzul jeered. "My fortress lies close." He gave a grotesque grin. "If you were wise, you would leave her to me. Trying to save her will bring you nothing but death."

With a roar, Lucian attempted to warp directly to him, even if there was nothing but a vision to guide him. But he was repulsed brutally, his stream shattered as he was knocked back several paces.

The vision evaporated, and Lucian found himself on the edge of a cliff, snow falling into pure darkness. Try as he might to reach out for Serah, he was repulsed at every turn. All he wanted was to speak to her, tell her he was coming.

But there were more productive ways to use his magic. Like tracking down and killing the one who was hurting her.

His connection with her was too deep for her location to be completely masked. Reaching out for her, he could tell she wasn't far, not even fifty kilometers away, which was nothing when he had the power of Space-Time.

Finally, Emma's voice snapped him to reality, and he got the impression she had been trying to talk to him for a while. "Lucian? What's going on? Where's Serah?"

He turned to face everyone. "Kharzul has taken her. We're going after her."

"Taken her?" Fergus said, gripping his spear. "How is that possible? I thought we were warded!"

"He got past it using Shadow Magic. He must have thrown everything he had into the attack. That's . . . on me. I shouldn't have gone to sleep."

Lucian couldn't allow his judgment to be clouded by regret. Only one thing mattered: getting to Serah as quickly as possible. For a moment, he considered summoning the power of the Orbs to go back in time and change things. But already, things were too far gone. Kharzul could contest his attempt to do so. Too much time had passed for that to be a realistic possibility.

Of course, the real question was why take Serah at all? Why hadn't Kharzul killed them outright as soon as he recognized Lucian would not switch sides?

There was only one possibility. Serah was bait, and Kharzul wanted Lucian to find her, to lure him into a trap where the advantage would be his.

And if Lucian died, of course, the Orbs would become his.

Emma was solemn. No doubt she blamed herself for not making her Space-Time ward strong enough.

"I covered every base," she said. "At least, I *thought* I did . . ."

Mira put a hand on her arm. "It's not your fault. We're in over our heads here, and we're too late to realize it."

"Why, though?" Fergus asked. "Why would he kidnap her?"

"Bait," Mira said, echoing Lucian's own thoughts. "It can be for no other reason. He wants Lucian to come after her and fight in a place of his choosing."

"I don't care *what* the reason is," Lucian said. "We're going after her. I'm not leaving Serah behind."

"I'm not arguing against that," his mother said. "We just need to keep our eyes open, son."

"Every minute we waste is a minute Serah could die," he said.

To add weight to his words, he drew deeply from the Manifold, creating a massive Radiant sphere in the distance, enough to shine like a miniature sun. Instantly, it was as if day had come, shining down on the moon and illuminating the snow-filled valley beneath. Lucian saw something like a road down there, leading into the distance. It was the direction they needed to go.

And something along that road was moving.

"A train," Fergus said, his eyes green with Radiance. "Who'd ever guess a train would be here?"

"Is it going the right way?" Emma asked.

Lucian homed in on the train, surrounding the others with Space-Time Magic. Seconds later, they had warped on top of one of its lead coaches.

The air rushed around them, freezing despite Mira's Thermal ward. Lucian planted their feet with Binding Magic, ensuring they wouldn't be thrown off. The train screamed over cold tracks toward a mountain face in the distance, from which jutted decrepit towers carved from ice and rock. Lucian was blind to everything but his goal.

"She's in there," Lucian said.

His mother came to stand behind him. "Lucian . . . I know it's hard to think right now. You want to go in there guns blazing? You have *no idea* what's waiting for us, and Kharzul knows he has the one person who will make you stupid enough to throw it all away."

"I'm not leaving her."

"I'm not saying to leave her," Mira said. "We just need to think about it a little, figure something out that won't get everyone killed! You're not invincible."

"It's too late for reason," Fergus said quietly. He looked at Lucian. "Kharzul wants the Orbs, right?"

Lucian nodded. "He won't get them. He tried to turn me. He said a lot of stuff. I'm not sure how much to believe. I just know that anyone who messes with Serah, dies."

The castle was nearing, looming over the train. Lucian didn't care what the train was doing here, of all places, or why it was crossing their path when they needed to break into the fortress. Maybe Kharzul had arranged it.

But Lucian wouldn't let that stop him. In the end, the battleground wouldn't matter. Kharzul would be defeated, just as everyone else who had opposed Lucian. He simply had to do his job. Drive Lightspear right into Kharzul.

He'd die, just like everyone else.

Lucian reached into his pack, producing the Orb of Shadows in its Binding. He thrust it toward Fergus. Fergus's eyes widened as he grabbed it.

"What's this?"

"Insurance," Lucian said. "Ultimately, that's what Kharzul wants more than anything else. He tried to convince me to use it, but now that he knows I won't, he'll try to kill me and get it himself."

"You're sending me away, aren't you?"

"You and my mom. We can't let him get near that Orb. I won't need it to kill him."

Before anyone could argue, Lucian hastily created a portal, opening it toward the first mountain range they had encountered on this moon. Hopefully, it was far enough away that Kharzul wouldn't find them.

"Go," Lucian said. "Be ready in case I need backup."

Lucian was worried Fergus was going to argue, but he didn't. "Good luck, Lucian."

Mira looked worriedly at her son, but the gates of Kharzul's castle were just seconds away.

"Give him hell, son," she said.

They both went, and the portal closed, leaving him and Emma alone on the train. Lucian raced to the locomotive, hopping coach to coach, with Emma trailing him.

By the time they reached the locomotive, they were entering the maw of the fortress, plunging into the dark heart of the mountain.

———

LUCIAN LEAPED OFF THE TRAIN, tethering himself to a nearby tower. He trusted Emma to keep up with him, and she did with no trouble. They climbed until they both stood on a tall tower about halfway up the dark stronghold.

The train below simply . . . disappeared, as if it had never been.

"Lucian, did you just see . . .?"

But Lucian was blind to the train, what had obviously been an advanced projection created by Kharzul's magic, designed to carry them into the fortress.

"Yes, we're walking into a trap," he said. "All we can do is watch each other's backs. Shit is about to get real. If I need you to use *it* . . . do it. No hesitation."

She gave a shaky nod. "Okay."

He strode toward the wall of the tower directly ahead, phasing right through the wall, with her close behind.

On the other side, Lucian found two Sumaril officers. Lightspear formed instantly in his hand, and he had slashed both down to ash piles within a breath. He reached out with his Focus, feeling Serah somewhere beneath them.

"She's downstairs," Lucian said, nodding toward a set of steps spiraling into darkness.

Emma nodded. "After you. Please be careful."

Everything Lucian was doing was the opposite of that. He knew that, but as he saw it, there was no choice. Serah would die otherwise. Even now, the things Kharzul could be doing to her . . .

No, he couldn't allow himself to think about that as they circled down into the darkness.

At last, the stairs ended in a long, stone corridor, filled with flickering sconces, at the end of which hovered a shadowy Zulum. Immediately, Lucian flew forward as fast as lightning. The Zulum eddied, unable to move quickly enough to defend itself from Lightspear, as he controlled the flow of time itself to his advantage. The Zulum attempted to shield that slowing of time, but Lucian felt Emma reinforcing his stream with her own magic, countering the Zulum's efforts. Lucian planted Lightspear deep into the shadow's heart. Its shriek was like music to Lucian's ears.

The next moment, Lucian simply dropped through the floor by phasing. Floor after floor, they went down, dodging enemies and only fighting when necessary. He wasn't sure how far they dropped. Twenty stories, if he had to guess. He saw lots of things . . . *twisted* things . . . that hinted at the torture Serah might be undergoing.

He couldn't spare a thought for any of it. He had to focus on getting Serah back. Nothing else mattered.

At last, the floors ended, and they found themselves in a large, pillared chamber. Lucian streamed a burst of Radiant Magic, revealing a shield of Shadow Magic rising before them. On the other side of that shield, Kharzul loomed. In the light of the blazing sconces, Lucian could better discern him. His elongated face, like melting candle wax, bore a twisted grin, revealing jagged teeth that gleamed eerily in the flickering light. His eyes, sunk deep into their sockets, burned with a malevolent violet blackness, mirroring his malice and cruelty. He was clad in robes that seemed to absorb the surrounding light, while the very air in his presence crackled with latent ethereal energy, as if the Shadow Magic of his master had coalesced into his being, making him one with it.

But Lucian wasn't looking at Kharzul. Floating above him, suspended with Gravitonic Magic and surrounded by a shield, was Serah. Her eyes were closed, as if asleep, while her blonde hair floated around her head. His heart nearly stopped at the sight.

He buried his emotions in his Focus. There was no place for them now, not when so much was on the line.

Lucian could feel the power of the Shadow shield before them. It would not be easy to break. And if Lucian focused on it with Lightspear, it would leave him open to attack.

Kharzul's smile widened. "At last, you have arrived. I was thinking you had lost your way."

Lucian ignored him, instead opening a Psionic connection to Emma's mind, shielding it with Creation Magic. *I'll need you to break the barrier.*

Lucian, the power behind that shield is unreal. What if it's not enough?

There's no other choice, Emma. Can you do it?

There was a moment's hesitation, as much as she could dare to think, but she gave her mental assent.

It was enough. The next moments, Lucian knew, would be chaos, upon which the entire fate of existence hung.

He undid the brand surrounding the Starflower with a thought, wrapping that thought in a veil of Creation Magic so it would not be detected.

The rest was now up to Emma.

23

LUCIAN HEARD Emma cry out as a beam of golden light, blindingly brilliant, shot from her hand and smashed into the Shadow barrier. Such was its ferocity and sudden appearance that Lucian knew it had to have extinguished the entire Starflower. The situation they were in demanded nothing less.

Even Kharzul the Shadowed seemed taken aback, his stance faltering. It was the reaction Lucian had been counting on.

Even as Emma let out the attack, Lucian was drawing as much ether as he could into his Focus, the sudden infusion of which stole his breath. Every atom in his body was charged with the force of a supernova.

He became one with the Ether as time slowed. Even as the Shadow shield was collapsing in slow motion, he shot forward, extending Lightspear. Kharzul raised a long, gnarled hand, his face twisted in grotesque horror, his violet eyes shining with fear. Lucian could see each nail curving from that hand, could see a small orb of Shadow Magic coalescing.

But it was slow. Far too slow. With the shield taken care of, nothing stood in Lucian's way, and there was nothing the Descendant could do before Lucian's fury. Lightspear made contact first with the Descendant's robes, and then with the vulnerable flesh beneath. There wasn't even time for that face to register the pain or surprise of the impact.

The golden spear suffused Creation Magic all throughout Kharzul's form as time resumed its former course. Beams of light crisscrossed Kharzul's body, and his Shadow Magic responded, trying in vain to hold his form together. But not even the Ancient One had contested Lightspear, the weapon that had been forged with Creation Magic to destroy him.

Within seconds, Kharzul succumbed, the golden magic of the spear obliterating him from existence, reducing him to ash. It was far too merciful a way for him to die, but Lucian didn't want to take any chances. Not with Serah's life on the line.

With Kharzul dead, the Gravitonic aura surrounding Serah dissipated, and she fell to the floor. Lucian was quick to respond, cradling her fall with a Gravitonic stream. He ran forward, holding her though her eyes remained closed. Desperately, he reached for her consciousness ...

She was alive, but heavily sedated. It wasn't just Psionics but Shadow Magic interlocking with her Focus, making the unraveling of the brand a deadly proposition.

Lucian's hands, glowing with golden light, trembled as he gently cradled Serah's head. He began working to untangle the intricate web of Shadow Magic, his thoughts filled with their shared memories. Each memory fueled his resolve, lending strength as he proceeded. Creation Magic danced delicately against the invasive tendrils of Shadow, each pulse of light a silent plea for her to return to him.

It could not be done with brute force; one tiny misstep and Kharzul's magic would erase everything that was her. This kind of magic was much more difficult than what he had done on Mako, where he had saved her from the fraying. He'd preserved her memory in the Ether, but he couldn't try the same thing until every strand of Shadow Magic had been eliminated.

But the Shadow Magic was cunning, sentient, slippery. Every time Lucian tried to unravel one of its many streams, another stream rose to defend it, guided by Kharzul's malicious intent. Though the Descendant was now dead, the brand had a life of its own, its subtlety beyond anything Lucian had experienced. It resisted and adapted, countering Lucian's every healing stroke with a sinister resilience.

Despite his growing exhaustion, Lucian pushed harder, the light from his hands burning brighter, now a fierce, blinding light that filled the chamber with stark shadows.

There was a point where it felt as if the knot would be unraveled, and yet maddeningly, the brand would rebuild itself anew. The Ether strained around him strained as he almost lost control of the delicate strands.

It was too risky. Stopping was the hardest thing, but Lucian forced himself to do it. He'd bought her time, and with Anshar so close, perhaps he could get help from someone who was more familiar with Kharzul's magic.

He opened his eyes, a tear falling on her face. She looked serene, at peace, some place halfway between life and death.

His face fell. "I've failed you, Serah."

"What's wrong with her?" Emma asked, fear entering her voice.

"It's the brand. Kharzul set some condition where, if he died, her mind would be erased. It's difficult to trick the stream into ignoring that command."

"What does this mean, Lucian?" Fergus asked.

For the first time, he turned, noticing that both he and Mira were there. So long had Lucian been absorbed in this feat that Emma had created a portal and retrieve both of them; Emma must have figured out where he'd created the original portal to. Lucian glanced around, only then noticing the Seven-Fold shield covering the door—a testament to the group's efforts to protect him while he worked.

"It's not a matter of power here," Lucian said. "There are just too many individual streams for one person to handle at once. My mind would have to be divided several times to take it on. I . . . might do that, but I would need more time and space. Serah . . . will have to hold on a while longer."

"What are you thinking?" Mira asked. "Is there a way to save her?"

Lucian knew saving her would be simple if he could control Shadow Magic. The streams would obey him then.

But the Orb of Shadows was the option of last resort.

"We need to keep following the Seven-Fold Path," he decided. "Find Anlilta. Maybe she has some way to heal her. Maybe, if me and some Ascendants work in confluence, we could handle all the individual streams within the brand. Anlilta is our way off this moon. If anyone knows anything about saving Serah, it'll be her."

He wasn't sure if that was actually true, or if it was a fool's hope. All he knew was he'd do anything to save her.

He clung to his Focus to numb his emotions. It was the only way he could go on and stay focused. Otherwise, the panic would derail him, cause him to make dumb decisions.

Fergus placed a hand on his shoulder. "We're with you, Lucian. Every step of the way."

Fergus handed him something. It took Lucian a moment to realize it was the Orb of Shadows, still safely branded. For a moment, he briefly considered unlocking it. Maybe there was a way to protect himself from its effects.

But then if he did that, Kharzul got what he wanted. After defending Serah, it would erase everything. It wouldn't save her.

Lucian grabbed the Orb and put it in his pack. How he hated that rotting thing.

He kneeled and lifted Serah easily in his arms. He turned to face the others. "All right. Let's find Anlilta."

Emma nodded, along with the rest. She was about to speak when there was a shifting in the ground, and several stones rained from the ceiling above, along with a cloud of dust.

It was far past time to leave. Unlike Serah's brand, it seemed much, if not all, of the magic holding Kharzul's lair together had dissipated upon his death.

Lucian created a portal that would take them to the frozen plain outside the stronghold. They stepped through, Mira creating a powerful Thermal ward to protect them from the cold.

Once free of the castle, Lucian could see Eänna in the distance, a golden world barely peeking above the icy horizon. The seven colors of the Seven-Fold Path led directly across the frozen expanse, losing itself to the distance.

The ground rumbled once more, and Lucian turned to see the fortress collapsing in on itself. He didn't stick around to see it.

Surrounding the group with Space-Time Magic, he warped everyone toward the horizon, following the Path across the barren wastes of Gadea.

THE HOURS PASSED, the icescape yielding before them as Lucian completed warp after warp. The world of Eänna grew in their vision until it rose above the horizon, a stunning world of blues, greens, and golds.

By now, two other moons had appeared, one barren and rocky, and quite close, and the other further away, but verdant with life and filled with clouds.

Lucian held Serah close. In the low gravity of Gadea, she was hardly a burden, and with his heightened senses, he could feel her heart beating faintly. She was his reason to keep going, to find answers, to never give up.

He did not stop. He didn't know how long they kept going, but Lucian didn't care. He wouldn't stop until Serah got the help she needed.

At last, there was a change. The trajectory of the Seven-Fold Path had shifted, veering upward toward Eänna rather than continuing into the distance.

Lucian, at last, came to a stop, scanning the sky above.

"What now?" Fergus asked. "Is this the pickup spot?"

"Has to be," Lucian said.

Waiting was easier said than done with Serah's life on the line. But the more immediate concern was the ice melting beneath him under the heat of Mira's Thermal ward. Emma created a levitating Gravitonic platform upon which they could rest.

They were all silent as they tried to get what rest they could from the day's ordeal, with Fergus masking their presence with Radiance. Lucian couldn't possibly sleep, instead lying facing Serah, running scenarios over and over in his head about what he could have done differently. At some point, his exhaustion was such that he nodded off, but even sleep was no relief, for waiting in his dreams was Kharzul, who even in death haunted his memory. His form shifted and twisted into Serah, her blue eyes haunting, seeming to blame him for what had happened.

The dreams were interrupted when a bright light blinded him from above, descending from the star-speckled sky, its arrival disrupting the dark, icy landscape. Lucian stood, immediately becoming alert as he regarded the shape hovering above the ice before them, a ship so unlike anything he had ever seen.

It reminded him of a flower, or maybe a shell, or more accurately, a combination of the two. A thick beam of silvery light emanated from its base, what had to be a stream of Gravitonic Magic. A substance, somewhat like glass, covered the ship's entire base, and it was filled with scenes of stars and galaxies, while curving scripts graced the hull around the glass. There was no discernible bow or stern; the shape was perfectly symmetrical, while a violet shining jewel, almost like an eye, leered down at them.

A circle of light appeared in its hull, and a figure emerged, shining with radiance and splendor. Through the light, Lucian could discern a strikingly beautiful being. Despite everything, Lucian held his breath. This was a perfect version of the Sumaril, the archetype, an Ascendant being of the First Echelon. As she floated toward them, surrounded by a shell of magic, Lucian watched her angelic face, a mask of perfect beauty, with deep violet eyes that seemed to perceive all things hidden and plain. She floated across the ice, her light blue skin without blemish. As she approached, she seemed to easily see through Fergus's invisibility wards. She wore flowing robes of pure white that trailed behind her, and she settled on the ice in front of them.

Everyone gaped at her. Despite their Gravitonic platform's height, the Ascendant was at their eye level, as tall as Ninshar had been. Though all of their bodies had taken on the qualities of the Light Realm, it was impossible not to feel inferior before such a graceful being.

Now closer, Lucian looked at her face, noticing not just her ethereal beauty, but kindness in her eyes, a kindness he wanted to trust. Like the other Sumaril he had already met, her ears were long and pointed.

There was no need to ask who she was. The only thing Lucian was concerned with was whether she could help Serah.

After watching Lucian for a moment, Anlilta's gaze went to Serah, becoming filled with sorrow. "You have traveled far, and against all hope, have come safely. I sense the banishment of the dark presence that once plagued this world. Kharzul the Shadowed is no more. Such news would normally bring joy to the Ascendants of Eänna, but now they feel only fear. For an unknown threat has come, at least, in their eyes." Anlilta's gaze went back to Lucian. "But if the words the Manifold spoke to me are true, there is no reason for fear. Only hope."

"Please," Lucian said. "She needs help. Kharzul's brand is like nothing I've ever seen."

"I will do what I can, Chosen. But I regret to inform you that my power, as great as it is, may be found wanting in undoing the magic of Kharzul the Shadowed. His magic is second only to the Ancient One. Even in death, his hand stretches far, and the complexities of his streams have ever been the bane of those who follow the Light. If there is any hope for her, it is in the Temple of Streams. There is great power there, a place blessed by the Manifold to spring an unending fount of Creation Magic. It is her only chance, especially if your craft isn't enough."

"The Temple of Streams?" Fergus asked, his voice soft, as if daring to even speak. "What is that?"

"A holy place within the mountain overlooking Anshar. You will be safe there, protected by my power. Not even Enkius would dare disturb that sacred place."

Lucian had to ask himself why Enkius would want to disturb it at all. Perhaps Anlilta and he didn't see eye-to-eye on a lot of things. Lucian had to wonder how much of what Kharzul said was true. Was he being drawn into a trap?

He detected no lie in Anlilta's words, but of Enkius, he had to be wary, especially considering what Kharzul had said. He knew not to trust the Descendant, but he had said a lot. Some of it was probably true.

"Take us there, then," he said. "Anything to save her."

Anlilta nodded her head slowly, closing her eyes. "It shall be done."

At that moment, Lucian felt a ward cover the group. That ward filled him with a sense of soothing peace that he was hard-pressed to guard against. He instantly relaxed, despite his Psionic ward.

They followed Anlilta to the ship, Lucian feeling hope rise in his chest.

With luck, the Temple of Streams could do what Lucian couldn't.

As they approached, a stream of Gravitonic Magic lifted them up, while Radiant and Space-Time Magic, branded to the ship, phased them directly through the hull. Lucian's feet came to rest on a luminous deck. He stood in what appeared to be a wide chamber, with a domed, transparent ceiling filled with a stunning view of the stars, two moons, and the planet above.

Anlilta stood in front of them, and her presence was just as grand as it had been outside. She wasted no time in raising her arms gracefully, and suddenly, the moons and planet above moved subtly. Lucian's eyes widened when he realized they had lifted off at a speed that should have been completely impossible. Over the next few minutes, the world of Eänna grew larger in the window. Lucian felt no shifting of inertia. The magic powering this vessel was far more powerful than any other ship he had boarded. That made sense, given the abilities of the being to whom it belonged.

"Isn't this dangerous?" Fergus asked. "I've heard that the Void can rip us to shreds."

"There is always danger," Anlilta said. "But you are traveling with me. You'll be safe."

In practically no time at all, they were advancing through the atmosphere without incident. Lucian continued holding Serah close, her eyes closed and her breathing slow. Desperation clawed at his throat, making his knees weak. His mother came to stand beside him, touching his arm. She didn't say a word, only sharing in her son's sorrow.

The rest of them remained silent as the ship slipped through the atmosphere with not so much as a quiver with the transition from outer space to the planet. They were over a deep blue ocean, heading down toward a landmass in the distance.

"Tell us," Emma said. "Are we in danger right now? From the other Ascendants, I mean."

Anlilta hesitated a moment before answering. "Yes. More than you know. But we are close to the end. Closer than you would ever believe."

"What do you mean?" Emma asked. "We still have half the Aetheria to go, don't we?"

"We will get to that in time. I know it doesn't seem like it now, but you made the right choice. Even if you survived Lugan's schemes, the journey from Kadur would have taken too long by ship. In my dreams, I can hear the wails of the Manifold. It cannot bear another year. Everything is happening exactly as it's meant to, even if it doesn't seem that way."

"According to who?" Lucian asked. He looked down at Serah. "Without her, none of this is worth it to me. She's my reason to go on. Take away that reason . . ." He left the rest unsaid. "We just need an answer from the Manifold. If *it* wants to be saved, it needs to save her."

Anlilta's eyes weighed him, seeming to invite speculation. "If there is an answer to saving Serah, it lies within the shifting whorls of the Manifold. At the Temple of Streams, it may give you the answer you seek. Or not. It could just as easily kill you."

"I'm the Chosen of the Manifold," Lucian said. "I've done a lot to save the Manifold. Can it not give me this one thing?"

Anlilta remained silent. Lucian's thoughts were broken when a verdantly green mountain rose in the distance out of the water, toward which Anlilta's ship sped. Lucian was surprised when it did nothing to slow down as it approached the tree-lined slopes above the roiling surf. Mira cried out while Fergus futilely raised a hand over his eyes. Only Lucian forced himself to watch.

The outside blinked, and then in the very next instant, they were at rest in a small cave, a cave that had to be inside the mountain. They had arrived at their destination mere minutes after departing. If they could take this ship to the Heart of Creation, it might only take a few days, but Lucian doubted it was that simple.

Anlilta faced the humans. "Follow me."

An opening appeared on the deck of the ship, creating a beam of silver light that drew them down. Looking around, there was nothing extraordinary about the cave they found themselves in. It could have been any cave, really, except it was lit with a perfectly uniform light that seemed to emanate from every point in the vast space, as if Radiant Magic were infused throughout its entirety. Lucian noted the sound of flowing water in the distance falling from the cavern's ceiling above. A shallow lake seemed to lead deeper into the cave.

It was toward the sound of the waterfall that Anlilta led them, and without hesitation, she walked over the water, Gravitonic glyphs appearing automatically beneath her sandaled feet. Lucian and the others followed behind.

As they continued on, Lucian could feel a massive power source ahead. It was more powerful than the one on Mako, by many times, though the expression of its power was far more subtle. It was difficult to describe, but Lucian knew that power might be enough to save Serah.

As they rounded a bend in the cave, Lucian saw a massive waterfall leading to a dead end. Anlilta did not slow, instead shielding them as they passed through the crush of water. The roar surrounded them, until they had passed through, finding themselves standing on a smooth golden surface that opened into a vast space, what had to be the interior of the Temple of Streams.

Despite everything, Lucian could not help but be awed by the sight. There was no ceiling, the top of the mountain open to the air, as if they were in a dormant volcano. Magically infused streams of water, dozens of them, seemed to flow in every direction: up, down, and side-to-side, some even curving around the rim of the volcano, a mesmerizing dance of air and water.

Levitating in the center of the space and surrounded by an aura of golden and silver magic was the most striking sight of all, a massive upside-down ziggurat, covered in greenery, with a central monolith that glowed with luminescence. That monolith, fifty meters high at a guess, seemed to be the origin of all the streams. Various ethereal pathways and stairways crisscrossed the space, some stairways even upside down, navigable by the Gravitonic Magic branded to them. Besides the waterfall they had just passed through, hundreds of smaller waterfalls fell from the interior of the volcano's cone, some of those waters joining the magically flowing streams, while the rest fed into a dark pool at the bottom.

Lucian noted other occupants in the space, various Sumaril who glowed with ethereal power, perhaps sorcerers and mages in Anlilta's service. Some seemed to stand guard, while others were in meditation, surrounded by an aura of latent magical power. Others appeared more mundane, perhaps non-magical Sumaril who had come here on pilgrimage to worship. Some noted Anlilta's presence, bowing even if the Ascendant wasn't nearby.

Despite the chaos of the last few days, Lucian couldn't help but feel a sense of serenity, the sound of flowing water and the ethereal hum of latent magic filling the air. Besides the streams, various trees and manicured water gardens lent beauty to the space, some of them floating on small islands, all exuding a pleasing aroma that delighted the senses.

Anlilta's soft, but commanding, voice broke Lucian from his trance. "Come. Let's do what we can for her."

24

ANLILTA SIMPLY STEPPED into the open air, floating toward the upward-facing base of the ziggurat. To Lucian, it appeared effortless, as if she streamed magic as naturally as breathing.

Lucian opted to follow Anlilta using a nearby floating walkway, not for his benefit but for the others. The walkway shifted midair, but Lucian reached out, Psionically directing it to reconnect with the ziggurat's base. There was a bit of resistance, but Lucian directed his will toward it, and the walkway couldn't ignore his command. With his Psionic Magic, he felt a distinct hesitance from the Temple, a palpable wariness as if it doubted their right to be there.

Several of the Sumaril from the surrounding walkways watched them warily, but as guests of Anlilta, they could hardly be denied.

At last, they reached the ziggurat. Anlilta led them toward the monolith at its center, the source of all the streams. As they drew closer, he recognized the streams weren't actually made of water but something else entirely. He reached out with his Focus, detecting magic from all the Aspects within it, save that of

Shadow. He had to wonder if these streams were some strange joining of two realities, that of the Ether and the Light Realm itself. In the Shadow Realm, magic was only visible when streamed, but here, there seemed to be different rules. Perhaps when the power of the Manifold was gathered enough, ether itself became visible. As he walked close to one stream eddying overhead, its ethereal fluidity reflected violet. But when Mira passed, it shifted to red.

It seemed to respond to their Focuses and primary Aspects, but for the moment, Lucian didn't understand why. All that mattered to him was that the power could heal Serah.

Anlilta turned, perhaps reading his thoughts. "Soon, Serah will be bathed in the streams, and the magic will work powerfully to expunge her of the Shadow Magic staining her Focus. Herein lies the beating heart of Eänna. This Temple, in the sacred volcano of Kuresh, is the most powerful source of magic in the Aetheria outside that which emanates from the Threshold of Creation. What the Ancient One would give to stand here and despoil it! Never has Shadow Magic been streamed here, even at the height of the War of Light and Shadow, when all seemed lost. It was created in the Time of Before, before the Ancient One was even called that. Back when he still had a name."

"Isthelah," Lucian said.

A collective gasp of horror escaped from the few sorcerer attendants who stood nearby. Even Anlilta's face paled a bit.

"Yes, that is his ancient name," she said quietly. "But we do not speak it here. Especially not here."

"Can the power of the Temple save our friend?" Fergus asked. "That's all we really care about."

Anlilta lowered her head, her expression grave. "That remains to be seen. You may have noticed the Temple's chilly reception. I don't speak of the guards or my acolytes, but of the very soul infused into its stones, emanating from the monolith before us. Though Serah herself does not stream Shadow Magic, she bears its stain upon her Focus. Bringing her here risks much. But there is nothing else we can do unless you were to overthrow the Ancient One himself. No easy task, but something that must be done, in the end."

"We shouldn't wait any longer," Lucian said. "Just tell me what I need to do."

Anlilta watched Lucian. "She must float within the epicenter of the streams, where the Creation Magic is most powerful. That is her only chance. And even then, you will need to direct that magic, speak to the Manifold itself. No simple task, for I'm the only one who has ever received the Manifold's revelations."

"The Manifold will talk to me," Lucian said. "I'm sure of it."

"Then place her at the point of the monolith, where the streams separate."

Lucian wrapped both him and Serah in a Gravitonic aura, floating upward toward the point of the monolith, leaving the others behind. It only took a few moments for him to reach it, to become absorbed by the golden light at its peak. Almost as soon as they entered, the epicenter shimmered darkly for a moment, as if taking on the Shadow Aspect Serah bore, or perhaps reacting to the Orb of Shadows still in Lucian's pack, before regressing to its previous brilliance. Serah's body became bathed with its light, but within the golden shell, a darker magic intermingled with the gold, seemingly at war with it.

Lucian reached out for the epicenter, embracing its power, becoming one with it.

Speak to me, Manifold. I have things to say.

He felt a presence swirling within the super concentrated ether, though he wasn't sure if it was the consciousness of the Manifold or something else.

Chosen. You've brought my Gifts back to me?

I'm not here to talk to you, Isthelah. I want the Manifold.

The Manifold will not speak to you. You must come directly to the

Heart of Creation for that. But I already know what you want. Embrace the Shadow Aspect, and I will return her to you.

Do you really think I'm so stupid? I killed you once. I'll be glad to do it again. This time, for good.

Many have made that boast. Just as I am the Firstborn of Creation, I will be the last, standing here long after your memory has faded. You will abide in the Manifold, and I will never let you know peace. But follow me, become my Champion . . . my own Chosen . . . and you will have glory beyond your wildest dreams. Your friends, too. The Speaker will betray you, just as Ninshar and Lugan did.

Deep down, Lucian wondered if this could be true. He remembered what Lugan had said about Ascendants being particularly corrupted by the Orbs' power. Could Anlilta be the same?

You're wasting your time. I will get Serah back, and there's nothing you can do to stop me.

Then come find me, Chosen. I look forward to destroying you.

There was a blast of Psionic energy that assailed Lucian's mind, but he easily blocked it. The shell of Creation Magic around Serah struggled to push back against the Shadow, but after a moment, the two forces were once again in equilibrium.

For a moment, Lucian wondered how the Ancient One had even communicated with him in this holy place. He realized the answer was the Orb of Shadows. Through it, the Ancient One was never more than an arm's reach away from him. Was it surprising that Isthelah could intercept his message to the Manifold?

As long as the Ancient One stood in the way, Lucian knew he could not heal Serah.

Now out of the vision, Lucian watched Serah, his own chosen, with tears welling in his eyes. He shed tears, because he recognized the terrible truth. She could not come with them, and he had to leave her here and hope that the Temple's magic could keep her alive.

He knew, deep down, she would never wake until he'd destroyed the Ancient One in the Heart of Creation. The Shadow brand marked her, and that marking wouldn't go away until he finished the job.

"I'll come back for you," Lucian said, touching the magical shield surrounding her. "I promise."

Her eyes remained closed, her expression peaceful. He knew she couldn't hear him, but one day, those eyes would open again. He'd do anything to hear her laugh, see her smile. There was nothing in any realm, in Light or Shadow, that could impede that eventuality.

***

LUCIAN LEFT THE EPICENTER, rejoining the others on the ziggurat's stone base.

Fergus was the first to speak. "Well?"

Lucian shook his head. "The Temple can keep her alive, but nothing more. She's bonded to the Ancient One now. The only way to save her is by defeating him."

Everyone was silent as they processed this news. He felt as if everyone was trying to read on his emotions, wondering if he was mentally stable enough to get them the rest of the way to the Heart of Creation.

And for the first time in a while, he felt doubt tugging him.

His mother came to hug him, and he let her. He felt nothing but numbness.

"She'll be okay," he forced himself to say. "We just have to work fast."

"She will be sustained," Anlilta said. "Here, at least, Serah will be safe from interference. It's time to dedicate everything to reaching the Heart of Creation."

"The question is, how?" Fergus asked. "It seems you were hinting earlier there was a way to get there faster."

"The future is difficult to delve, especially when the stakes are so high. I will do what I can, but even that path remains clouded to me. If the Manifold wills, that will not be so for much longer."

Anlilta then turned to face the epicenter, becoming surrounded by an aura of violet and golden energy. Lucian knew she was communing with the Manifold, hopefully without interference from the Ancient One like him. The surrounding streams vibrated, eddies peeling off and feeding into the Ascendant's aura. She kneeled on the stones and stayed in that position for at least ten minutes, praying as they waited.

At last, the light dissipated from around her, and she stood. "As I feared, the Manifold is silent on all things save one."

"What's that?"

"The Heart of Creation has not been entered since The War of Light and Shadow. Many have tried, but none have had the strength, or the will, to repeat the feat of the Fallen, Enkius, or Nathi. It takes powerful magic, and a powerful will, to survive the Ethereal Rip of the Void, especially so near the Threshold of Creation." Anlilta turned to face Lucian. "You must be strong enough to follow in their steps, Lucian, but the Ancient One wishes for that as well. He wants to hold all Ten Aspects, to impose his malevolent will on the Manifold itself. He can accomplish this if you ever absorb the Orb of Shadows."

"I don't plan to," Lucian said.

"I don't know what waits for you in the Manifold," Anlilta went on. "But the Ancient One is native to the Manifold. It will be the hardest fight of your life."

Lucian, once again, looked up at the Source. It felt like a betrayal to leave Serah here after everything. But she could not be carried, and eventually, the brand would erase her and replace her with something dark and evil, something *not* Serah. This was the only place she could stay that would give her a fighting chance.

He reached out with his mind, infusing the communication

not only with the power of all the Aspects in his possession, but his love. *We'll be back for you, Serah. I promise. Be strong.*

For the first time, it felt as if she was there, and she was listening. Lucian was tempted to push further, but he knew doing so was dangerous. The message, as short as it was, would have to suffice, even if it was nowhere near enough.

He returned his attention to Anlilta. "So, you got nothing about this shorter path from the Manifold?"

"Nothing, except that the Chosen would know the way. Continue following the Path, Lucian. That is all you can do. The Heart of Creation orbits the Aetheria. Right now, Kurzagûl is the world it is passing during its one-hundred-year cycle. The World of Shadow was the seat of the Ancient One's power in the days of the War, and there is no planet where the power of the Shadow is strongest."

"How far is this planet, exactly?" Fergus asked.

"Very," Anlilta said. "You entered the Aetheria from the Eye of Kadur, the extreme eastern side. Now, you are on Eänna, the very center. Kurzagûl would require you to travel west for another year, world to world, through territories that have long been the domain of the Shadow, where the Light holds little sway."

"There's no time for that," Emma said. "You said the Manifold doesn't even have a year left."

Before Anlilta could respond, an enormous shadow fell over them. A ship, almost as grand as Anlilta's, lowered itself onto the base of the ziggurat, a ship with wicked points and a spire that made it seem like a floating palace rather than a vessel. Anlilta's face darkened at its appearance.

"Who is that?" Mira asked breathlessly.

An opening appeared in the hull, emitting a brightness that Lucian had to raise a shield against. Within that light stood a tall, regal figure, radiating a golden aura and wearing resplendent armor that seemed to shine with all colors of the spectrum. He carried a brilliant white spear, and his eyes shone with golden light from a ruggedly handsome face. Two ears pointed backward while golden hair fell across his bare shoulders, every inch of his form radiating power, strength, and majesty.

Before Lucian could wonder whether this was Enkius himself, a powerful wave of golden magic advanced toward them, which Lucian shielded.

Then the new entrant flew like a lightning bolt directly toward them, spear extended, with a wicked smile on his face.

25

LUCIAN SAW ANLILTA REACT FIRST, her form becoming a whirlwind of golden magic as she surged forward. The two Ascendants clashed, each throwing the other back on the base of the ziggurat.

After a time, as the two Ascendants engaged in battle and Lucian got a sense of his opponent's abilities, he decided it was time to join the fray. Calmly, he conjured Lightspear and walked toward the mysterious attacker. Already, ether was gathering, coiling within like an inferno, demanding to be released.

Lucian noticed Anlilta hanging back, and he interpreted it as her giving him a chance to test himself against the adversary. The male Ascendant, who Lucian could see had a blue beard to complement his similarly blue skin, wrapped himself in a Gravitonic aura, shooting into the sky.

Lucian floated slowly after him, intent on his goal. The Ascendant sent a torrent of silver magic toward him, which Lucian didn't bother blocking. He opted instead to phase past it, directly in front of his opponent. The Ascendant's eyes widened before he warped himself to safety, just a few paces from Anlilta, who he threw back with a reverse Binding tether.

Lucian watched from above as Anlilta righted herself in midair, effortlessly blocking her foe's ethereal spear with a spear of her own. Anlilta stabbed, but the Ascendant disappeared, reappearing directly before Lucian.

Lucian lazily lifted Lightspear to counter the Ascendant's next stroke, slowing time. His adversary gave a primal roar as Lightspear smote the Ascendant's weapon from existence. Lucian swiftly ensnared his arms with Binding tethers, infusing them with Psionic Magic with shattering force.

But with a herculean effort, the Ascendant broke the Bindings, shooting skyward while setting the air in his wake ablaze. That fire spread outward, racing toward Lucian. He simply streamed a vortex of Psionic energy, capturing the flames while using Gravitonics to concentrate them into a super-heated ball. He next infused it with electricity to create an oscillating disc of plasma, which he shot toward his adversary, using Binding to ensure it homed in on him like a missile. The Ascendant fled, and with a curse, phased to a new location about fifty meters away.

But the shining disc simply switched course, once again picking up the trail. Lucian watched, curious to see how his challenger would extricate himself from the situation.

The Ascendant warped again, this time getting a fair bit of distance, channeling all his powers to create a Seven-Fold shield to withstand the attack.

"There you go," Lucian said.

The plasma met the shield, each combatant's magic obliterating the other. The Ascendant was knocked back but easily righted himself while conjuring a new spear. He gave himself a shake, watching Lucian below him with newfound interest. His form then became ensconced in yellow Dynamistic light. The sky above the cone of the volcano raged, bolts of lightning gathering and raining down toward Lucian in divine fury.

Lucian simply raised Lightspear, which acted as a lightning rod to absorb the energy. He then channeled the dispelled ether into his Focus, his body shining with white-hot brilliance. He redirected the electricity with Radiant Magic, creating a powerful green laser that focused on his enemy with deadly precision. Its blinding light crashed right against the shining figure above, utterly shattering his shield. The Ascendant warped, reappearing on the temple stones beneath.

Lucian looked for the others, to find that they were taking shelter next to the monolith. For now, it didn't seem as if the attacker was interested in them. There was also no sign of Anlilta. The Ascendant leered upward, flashing another cheeky smile that said all this was just a game to him.

Lucian completed a warp, finding himself about thirty paces from the Ascendant.

"Ah, Anlilta's Chosen," he said with a sneer. "It seems my master has thought too much of you."

"Oh," Lucian said. "So, you're just someone's lapdog."

"Silence! You don't know with whom you speak."

"You're right. You haven't introduced yourself. Unless fighting is the equivalent of a handshake here?"

Before the Ascendant could respond, Lucian phased forward, just paces away, and slashed with Lightspear. The Ascendant danced out of his way, throwing a hasty kinetic wave. Lucian allowed it to hit him, redirecting its energy to do a backward flip before floating down gracefully. He watched as the Ascendant's hands started shining with a blinding sunburst of orange and yellow magic.

"That's nasty magic," Lucian said. "I thought this was just a game."

Lucian quickly created a shield, not just to defend himself, but his allies. The coming tempest of death unleashed itself, an orange lightning storm battering against his shield, each crackle a harbinger of potential doom.

Except, the attack did nothing, not even putting in a dent. He mimed yawning.

Face twisting with rage, the Ascendant charged. Lucian diverted some of his ether into a new Space-Time stream, warping directly behind his attacker. He poised Lightspear for a fatal thrust.

But the Ascendant, cunning and quick, warped behind Lucian in kind, wrapping him in a cocoon of Binding Magic layered with Space-Time constraints. A Psionic veil attempted to enclose his Focus.

It was a clever attack, but the Ascendant didn't know who he was dealing with. Lucian pushed back against the incursion, breaking the hostile streams. The Ascendant cried out, his eyes shining violet with direct Psionic possession. The Ascendant made a fist and began punching himself in the face.

"Stop hitting yourself," Lucian said.

Furious, the Ascendant forced Lucian out of his mind, and Lucian danced back, creating room. Without moving, Lucian sent out a powerful kinetic wave, blasting the attacker backward. His paltry shield could do nothing to stop it. While the Ascendant was flying backward, Lucian warped right above him, extending Lightspear downward.

But it was at that moment that Anlilta plummeted from the sky like a meteor. She crashed against the attacker, throwing him down on the ziggurat's base, protecting him from Lucian's killing blow. The attacker slid toward the edge but recovered quickly, standing upright with yet another new magical spear conjured, his golden eyes weighing his next move.

"Are you done yet?" Lucian asked. "You don't want to see what this looks like if I actually try."

Before the assailant could respond, Anlilta landed in front of the Ascendant, her face a mask of rage. Her voice thundered within the confines of the volcano, echoing through the Temple of Streams. "Enough, Nabukar! Your audacity will be your downfall. Even you should not dare such sacrilege in this sacred place!"

Nabukar's expression was angry at first, but quickly shifted to one of mirth, accompanied by a hearty laugh. Despite that laughter, Lucian could sense the menace beneath.

Lucian landed next to the others before they all walked over to rejoin Anlilta, keeping close as the tension lingered. The fight was over, for now at least, but Lucian didn't allow Lightspear to dissipate. Emma, Fergus, and his mother stood just a step behind him, ready to lend whatever support he needed.

"So, this is your Chosen," Nabukar said. Then, to Lucian, he said, "You are lucky to have my mother to watch after you!"

Mother. Well, that explained why Anlilta had saved him. "I thought that's what she was doing for you."

Before Nabukar could respond, Anlilta interrupted. "You risk everything, Nabukar. And for what? If this is your idea of a prank..."

She trailed off, the words apparently lost to rage. Nabukar allowed his spear to disappear, apparently judging the confrontation to be over, though his expression was still dangerous.

"Oh, this is no joke. I came here at the behest of Father himself. He has a message for you, Mother, and most especially the Chosen." His golden eyes took in Lucian. "You *are* the Chosen, no?"

Lucian looked at Anlilta. "Is he really your kid?"

Anlilta gave a heavy, embarrassed sigh. It was the same sigh he'd heard from mothers back on Earth when their child started acting up in a store. Some things, he supposed, transcended even entire realities.

"Never mind that," Anlilta said. "What does he want?"

Nabukar cleared his throat self-importantly. "His message is thus: Two thousand years ago, my dearest friend left the Light Realm for the sake of your prophecy, Anlilta. He did what none of us had the strength to do. He became *Alkasen*, the Accursed, to seek the mighty warrior you prophesied would save us all. This warrior you named The Chosen of the Manifold, a Being of Shadow who would return the Orbs to the Heart of Creation from whence they came. And now, if rumors are true, this Chosen is here and has come as far as Gadea, and perhaps even farther by now. He even sent Kharzul the Shadow to his grave, a great deed of renown and strength. But I would still test his strength. I have thus sent Nabukar, our dedicated son and faithful messenger, to challenge him to a duel. If this Chosen is truly so powerful, they will have no problem in besting the Holy Messenger of the Court of Light. If the Chosen fails, then they were truly not the Chosen. For they will have to face much worse than the likes of Kharzul to fix the mistakes you've engineered with your prattling prophecies."

Anlilta's eyes had gone gold during this monologue. "Prattling prophecies? Even the smallest mistake or misjudgment can ruin everything. Already, things have not gone according to the plan laid out by the Manifold. Existence balances on the edge of a knife. The merest breeze or happenstance can undo it all. *Everything*, Nabukar!"

Nabukar watched her closely, and somewhat sheepishly, apparently not expecting such a vitriolic reaction. "I merely test the Chosen's strength and follow my father's orders. He is first among us, the one who saved the Light Realm two thousand years ago, so who am I to question him? However, I cannot say with confidence that the Chosen's powers have impressed me. He had your help, after all, and he wields the Holy Orbs like a sledgehammer, without the grace or cunning befitting them. That might be enough to deal with lower Ascendants, but it will not be enough to stop the Ancient One." His eyes regarded Fergus and Mira and seemed to hang longer on Emma, at whom he smiled. "What a beautiful creature! Your kind is...unconventional in appearance, but at least some of you are not without your charms."

"Watch what you say, Golden Boy," Emma said. "It might be the last mistake you make."

He gave an insolent smile. "I'll have you eating out of my hand soon enough."

Emma's voice was icy. "Doubt it."

Anlilta watched all of this with horror, a face that seemed to say, "Where did I go wrong?" At last, she recovered. "These are honored guests within our realm, Nabukar. They will be treated as such."

Lucian realized what Nabukar was doing. He was trying to bait him into doing or saying something stupid. He wouldn't give him the satisfaction. Despite being Anlilta's and Enkius' son, he was an Ascendant of middling power at best. Ninshar had been a much harder fight, though to be fair, he'd had an ethereal core to help him out.

Returning the Orbs to the Heart of Creation was why they were here, and what Lucian had to be focused on. That, and defeating the Ancient One once and for all. That was the only way he'd get Serah back.

As if Lucian's thoughts inspired action, Nabukar looked at the top of the monolith. While Serah wasn't visible with the naked eye, perhaps the Ascendants had heightened senses. His smile was subtle, his eyes hooded with satisfaction, characteristic of a bully imagining new ways of torment.

"And who is this? I can sense her importance to you, Chosen. How tragic! The magic of Kharzul the Shadowed is the most powerful in that foul Aspect in all the Aetheria. Not easily does one survive such a fatal blow!"

"Nabukar ..." Anlilta said, her voice laced with warning.

Lucian watched him. "She's not your concern."

"Well, it's a pity my mother never warned you, but Kharzul is fond of taking hostages. If you play his game and are drawn into his web, it will bring you only misery."

"How did you know we were even here?" Emma asked.

"Well, the death of Kharzul is not something easily missed. And my mother has been acting cagey of late. She hasn't been off world in quite some time, so when we detected her ship leaving, this stoked my father's suspicions. That she had found her Chosen, or at least, someone she believed to be the Chosen, was among his first guesses, confirmed by all of you yourselves."

"All this talking is pointless," Lucian said. "You still haven't told us why you're here. Is it really just to test me?"

"The Chosen is right," Anlilta said. "What does Enkius want? Time wears thin."

"My father wanted to reprimand you, Anlilta. Had you told the Court of Light of the Chosen's entrance to the Light Realm, perhaps we wouldn't be in this situation. We could have gone to Gadea in force and ensured nothing fell into ruin. We are lucky that the damage was limited to just one of these creatures."

"We aren't creatures," Lucian said. "We're humans. Magic-users just like your kind."

"*Our* kind? You are lower than us, human, and don't you ever forget it. You should bow and lick the stones before my boots!"

Lucian simply laughed, the way he would laugh at a child's outrageous outburst.

Nabukar's golden eyes narrowed. "Bah! I am tired of this talk. Games!"

"This is no game," Anlilta said. "This isn't about power or anything else. It's about the fate of reality itself. I kept things hidden because it was the will of the Manifold. The Chosen's mission required utmost secrecy to make it even this far. Every other path leads to a certain doom. That is the difference between me and Enkius. I keep enough humility to know that before the Manifold's whims, we are less than dust, our ambitions ruins before they've even been built. I've taught you much the same, and it saddens me to see that you have succumbed to the arrogance of your father's court."

These words did not seem to affect Nabukar. "Do you not

doubt sometimes, Mother? You came to us far too late to ask for help, and now look where we are. The Chosen was on Gadea in full possession of the Holy Orbs. *Gadea*! What was your plan, Mother, if he fell to Kharzul's schemes? Kharzul was within steps of the Orb of Shadows and the Orb of Creation, not to mention all the rest, and nearly had them all. I don't know how these creatures escaped his schemes, where almost none have, but it can't have been anything more than blind luck. Kharzul the Shadow has never been careless. Sometimes, I cannot help but wonder if you, of all people, might be an agent of—"

Nabukar was instantly wrapped with a series of tethers and tossed over the edge of the ziggurat like a sack of potatoes. A moment later, he warped back to his former position, his eyes burning with indignation. But after a moment of Anlilta's icy gaze, he at least had the grace to appear humble.

"I'm the farthest from an agent of the Shadow as you can imagine," Anlilta said dangerously. "I interfered in the Chosen's quest as much as I dared, knowing that such interference might be too much. How much more would we be doomed if I'd told you a single thing from the moment I knew it? It would have given your father a chance to entrap the Chosen in his selfish plans, for one. There is so little you know, Nabukar. So little! It's not the Chosen's role to play politics and bicker with spoiled children. The Chosen's only job is to return the Orbs to the Heart of Creation, to save us all from the doom we know is coming! The doom engineered by your father when he created the First Gate! And unless you, or Enkius, are going to help us in this matter, you must leave at once. If you cannot do so, I will have the entire Temple of Streams come down on you, son or not. That I have not already done so for your sacrilege is the greatest of miracles!"

Nabukar smiled disdainfully. "And how do you plan to cross the Aetheria to get to the Threshold of Creation, hmm? The Shadow lays heavy on the West, and even if you use the Gate to Iannas, the journey would be impossibly dangerous. As you know, the Heart lies closest to Kurzagûl, that most powerful bastion of the Shadow."

"How we get there is not your concern," Anlilta said.

"Whatever your plans," Nabukar said, "you can no longer keep them to yourself. Enkius knows, as do all his closest advisors. As such, you and all these Shadow Beings are summoned to appear before him and the Court of Light for judgment. Failure to do so will be interpreted as nothing less than treason, considering the disaster that has just occurred on Gadea. Trust me, Mother, I am not the only one wondering about your motives."

"I will not bring them before Enkius," Anlilta said. "To do so would be the doom of us all, unraveling plans centuries in the making."

"I suppose I cannot force you," Nabukar said. "But Father can. He is but a step away, and given the stakes, will not hesitate to lay siege to the Temple of Streams itself to enforce his will. You accuse Father of hatching schemes, so I must challenge you. Are you the only one with the right to weave webs?"

"Yes!" Anlilta said. "You don't understand the powers you're playing with. No one does."

"And you do?" Nabukar asked, with an air of boredom. "Unfortunately, there's nothing you can do or say to change Father's mind. You have said that even you cannot know the future. Is it surprising that we are losing faith? Mother, most have lost it long ago. Me included."

Mira tsked. "You need me to teach him some manners, one mother to another?"

"I'd rather face the Ancient One, personally," Lucian said.

"Enough," Nabukar said. "Will you come peacefully, or shall we do it the fun way?"

"Leave, Nabukar," Anlilta said. "If Enkius wishes to meet the Chosen, then he can come here himself."

"Giving you time to slip him away to one of your many secret havens?" Nabukar chuckled. "I know you think me stupid, Mother, but even I won't fall for that."

"We'll go," Lucian said. "I'd like to meet Enkius."

Anlilta watched him, unable to mask her horror, while Nabukar barked a laugh. "Ha! And here I was, thinking you'd hide behind my mother's skirts! Maybe I was wrong about you. Not that you have a choice, but it's better to face your reckoning with a brave face, no? Besides, I think you'll be most interested in what my father has to say. That goes for all of you!"

"I'm not facing any reckoning," Lucian said. "If Enkius thinks he can take the Orbs from me, he'll have to pry them from my cold, dead fingers."

"We'll see about that, Shadow Being! Well, my mother is right about one thing. Time turns, as they say. We have tarried too long, and my father doesn't like to be kept waiting."

"I'm coming, too," Anlilta said.

That was when Lucian felt the Speaker of the Manifold's mind connect with his. *You don't know what you're getting yourself into. Enkius is the most powerful Ascendant in the Aetheria. If he decides it's prudent, he can, and will, take the Orbs for himself, and he has his entire court to back him up. You can't even imagine what he'd do with such power. To you, your friends, and to reality at large. It's doubtful he'd do the right thing and return them. He may lie to himself, saying that he will. Someday. But I fear he would become something even worse than the Ancient One ever was.*

What do you suggest, then? We need to find a way to the Heart of Creation. If we try to run, they'll just chase us. We need to face this head-on, and we can always warp away if things get dicey.

Alas, there is no escaping this snare. The Space-Time wards will be too difficult to break through with so many of Enkius' lackeys around. Maybe with enough time you can punch a hole in their defenses, given your power, but can you do so quickly enough to save not just yourself, but your friends? It is not too late to go another way, Chosen.

Lucian considered this, and for the first time, noticed the

direction of the Seven-Fold Path had shifted from outside the rim of the volcano to Nabukar's ship. He hated the idea of leaving Serah behind, but this was the safest place for her, and the Temple's magic would keep her alive. Here, at least, she could exist, and once they left the Temple, Enkius would lose interest in it.

He thought briefly about seeing her again, one last time, but it would be for his own benefit, not hers. She'd want him to go on and not stay behind for her sake.

"Well?" Nabukar pressed. "Are we going, or what?"

"The Chosen will know the way," Lucian said. He nodded at Nabukar. "Let's go."

Anlilta's face fell, while the others looked at him as if questioning the decision. But there was no doubt in his mind.

"Very good," Nabukar said. "Follow me."

Lucian, Fergus, Mira, and Emma headed for Nabukar's ship. Anlilta sighed and followed behind.

26

LIKE THE INTERIOR of Anlilta's ship, Nabukar's vessel was like a palace, except his was beyond gaudy in presentation. Every surface gleamed with ornate gold and colorful, shining jewels, while luxurious, deep red fabric similar to silk draped the walls, complementing the intricately patterned marble floors. The ceilings were high and vaulted, with moving art depicting what seemed to be Nabukar's many triumphs. Lucian watched a scene where he fought like a lion, surrounded by Sumaril dressed in dark armor, whom he mowed down mercilessly with a smile on his face.

Plush, oversized furniture upholstered in rich fabrics was arranged throughout the domed entrance, offering both comfort and a sense of lavish excess. Even the air was perfumed, carrying a heady blend of exotic spices and floral scents.

Lucian held back the urge to cough. The sooner they were out of this place, the better.

Nabukar faced forward, where the walls suddenly became translucent, revealing the temple outside. Nabukar closed his eyes, a violet sheen of magic surrounding him. Not a moment later, the vessel lifted upward, and the temple grounds fell away. Just like with Anlilta's ship, Lucian didn't sense any movement.

They soared over the rim of the volcano, twisting in midair to face downward, where an imposing city unfolded beneath them, a sprawling metropolis that shimmered like a jewel. Lucian's breath caught at the sight; though he had seen many wonders in this reality and in others, the beauty and majesty of this city almost defied words.

Its architecture was a tapestry of luminescent spires and cascading waterfalls, seamlessly blending magic and technology. Floating buildings and bridges, suspended by Gravitonic Magic, connected the city in a dizzying network of pathways. The skyline was punctuated by floating islands that hovered serenely, adorned with lush gardens, mansions, towers, and gleaming structures. Theirs was not the only ship plying the skies; dozens, and perhaps even hundreds, could be seen navigating the verdant island they found themselves over. Various parks and rivers interwove with the city's shining, golden towers, and there were even floating trains making their connections.

What got Lucian most was the sheer size of it. Even with their altitude, the island and the city it held almost stretched to the horizon in all directions, with every part occupied by buildings and parklands. He noticed an enormous park toward the center, almost large enough to be a nature reserve. Lucian guessed Anshar was home to tens of millions of Sumaril, if not more. Two of Eänna's moons could be seen hanging in the evening sky above, both green with life and blue with water, a far cry from the Dread Moon they had just come from.

If anything, the city made Lucian realize that the three worlds they had visited were the backwaters of the Aetheria. There was so much to see here in the Light Realm, and he just wished Serah was here to see it, too.

It was hard to break his gaze from the sight, but in the end, he was forced to as the ship headed toward the sea, where out over the placid blue water, a grand palace floated. Or at least, what Lucian *thought* was a palace. Its majestic presence dominated the horizon, completely inaccessible to the city, surrounded by the tumultuous water. Its golden silhouette, outlined against the setting sun. He didn't have to ask who lived there.

As they drew closer, Lucian realized it wasn't just a palace. It was so much larger than that, a city and fortress all in one, and from the way it floated above the waves, it was perhaps even a ship.

As Nabukar's vessel passed over the sea, tinted pink from the sunset, they passed through an ethereal barrier, a ward of protection to keep the palace and its inhabitants safe. The ship came to a rest on a circular docking platform, a solid surface crafted by branding Gravitonic and Binding Magic. Several Sumaril, dressed in lavish, multicolored robes, rushed to attend, faces lowered in supplication. The hull parted, Nabukar heading for the opening and floating down toward the celestial pathway beneath.

Anlilta gestured for Lucian and the others to fall in beside her, her posture seeming to offer protection. Though Lucian wasn't afraid, he held his Focus to be ready for anything. There was no telling what they were walking into.

Lucian felt Anlilta connect to him Psionically. *We are entering a den of adders such as you've never known. Let me do the talking.*

Lucian was content to allow that, at least for now.

Anlilta turned her head toward Emma, Mira, and Fergus. "Stay close."

Nabukar chuckled. "You've never seen a more beautiful slaughterhouse."

"We're not cattle," Emma said.

Nabukar gave another insolent chuckle, as if he disagreed with that.

As they proceeded, Anlilta and Nabukar barely even noticed the Sumaril servants groveling in their wake. Lucian noted they were not magic-less servants, but powerful mages in their own right, which went to show just how low on the totem pole they were compared to the godlike Ascendants. As soon as they had passed, the mages rushed toward the ship, apparently under orders to tend to it.

Lucian saw nothing more of them once they entered the palace itself, which opened into a grand corridor designed for the larger frames of Ascendants. It was quite beautiful, the walls themselves an intricate, moving painting that continually played for its watchers. A massive battle was being played out on the ceiling above, in what looked to be outer space. Or, Lucian supposed, "the Void." Fanciful, ethereal ships were interlocked in battle, in colors of gold and black, while golden and shadowed figures themselves floated freely, wrapped in magic. Behind the battle scene, in the distance, a shimmering white light could be discerned running the entire length of the ceiling. Lucian had a hard time making sense of the masterwork, but something told him it was the final, epic battle of the War of Light and Shadow that Kharzul had described, outside of the Heart of Creation itself.

He wondered if that light was the Heart of Creation, but rather than ask Anlilta, he elected to remain silent.

The entire time they walked, Lucian noted that the Seven-Fold Path continued to follow Nabukar. That was all that truly mattered. If they followed him, then they would find their way to the Heart, even if it didn't seem like it.

Anytime they passed another Sumaril servant, they either bowed or groveled on the floor, depending on their rank. Most seemed to be mages, though others had a greater aura of power and majesty about them, an aura that told him they were sorcerers. They would pause in their tracks and give a quick bow before going on their way, while mages stopped everything they were doing and didn't dare to move until the Ascendants had moved on. The few times they passed Sumaril with no magical abilities, they lay face-first on the floor, well out of the way of the passing giants.

Soon, they reached a central chamber even more resplendent than the corridor that had led them there, the interior of a massive tower with dozens of golden arcades which seemed to stretch up endlessly. There was no one here in this vast space, which Lucian thought strange. Nabukar paid no mind, leading them to the center of the space, where they stepped upon a central platform that shot up into the wide space above. So far, Lucian had yet to see another Ascendant.

"Seems empty," Lucian said.

"An astute observation, Chosen," Nabukar said, with a hint of mockery.

"Where are we going?" Anlilta asked. "This isn't the way to the Golden Hall."

"You'll see soon, Mother," Nabukar answered. "Patience!"

"You will tell me where we're going at once, or we will leave."

"Oh, you're in too deep now," Nabukar said. "But never fear. There is no danger within these halls for the Chosen. Outside these walls, however, it's a different story." He chuckled. "You are about to discover a secret, one that has been hidden ever since the end of the War. All will be made known in due time."

Anlilta pursed her lips and said nothing more.

Once they reached one of the higher levels, Nabukar led them down another corridor. For half an hour at least, they walked through winding hallways, up and down random staircases, with directions that seemed to make no intuitive sense. Magical brands guarded every passage, but Nabukar always neutralized them before proceeding.

"What has Enkius been hiding?" Anlilta asked.

"His master stroke," Nabukar said. "Come. We are nearly there."

They made a final turn, where at the end of a long corridor stood an unmistakable sight. Lucian's eyes took in the shimmering, pearlescent barrier, and as soon as he perceived it, the direction of the Path switched from Nabukar to wherever the Gate led.

"Enkius' secret hope," Nabukar said. "Hidden from all but Father and his closest confidants. We will find him through there, along with the rest of the court."

"It's hardly been an hour since the duel. You're saying, in that time, he and his entire court have passed through this Gate?"

"Yes. Boldness is required if we are to deal a fatal blow to the Shadow."

"And where does it lead?"

"Let's just say, this Gate will take us to somewhere most convenient for our purposes."

"Enough games," Anlilta said. "Speak plainly for once!"

"It's the right way," Lucian said.

Anlilta watched him, considering. "It's going to the Heart of Creation? Can you see it?"

"Probably not as far as that," Lucian answered. "But it will be one step closer."

"I should say so," Nabukar said, nodding toward it with an insolent smile. "After you."

"I think not," Anlilta said.

Nabukar's response was simply to laugh. "Suit yourselves."

He shot forward, right through the Gate.

Anlilta's violet eyes burned with annoyance as she turned toward Lucian. "This could be a trap, Chosen, despite the direction of the Path."

"Wherever it leads," Lucian said, "it's closer to the Heart of Creation than here. More than that, the Path has been following Nabukar ever since our fight. We're supposed to be following him."

"I can go first," Fergus said. "Scout out the terrain."

He strode forward, restrained only by Mira. "Are you crazy? It could be underwater, like that last one!"

"She's right," Anlilta said. "We can't go through it without proper preparations. We don't know Enkius' intentions. He and everyone else could ambush us on the other side."

"You think he's going to try to steal the Orbs?" Fergus asked.

"That is a strong possibility. A possibility we must keep from coming to pass."

"So, where does that leave us?" Mira asked. "If going through that Gate gets us closer, there's no stopping me. Let's just be smart about it."

"I agree," Emma said. "How can we best prepare ourselves? Is there any way to tell what's beyond it?"

"It's a Lost Gate," Anlilta said. "They cannot be moved, so my guess is, somewhere in our wanderings of the palace, we passed through a portal that was disguised among the other brands. It wouldn't have felt any different from passing through another ward, assuming it was set up properly. That portal took us to somewhere else on Eänna, the true location of this Gate."

"How do we know we're on Eänna and not one of its moons?" Fergus asked. "Or even another world entirely?"

"There's no change in gravity," Emma said. "We are somewhere on Eänna still, I'm sure of it, unless there is another world nearby with the same gravitational pull. It's beside the point. We need to pass through this Gate; we just need to make sure we do it safely."

"There's nothing you can do to prepare yourselves for Enkius' schemes," Anlilta said. "And for all my powers, I cannot guarantee your safety. But once they see I'm with you, they will think twice before trying anything."

"What are the alternatives, if any?" Lucian asked.

On this point, Anlilta was silent.

Lucian continued. "That's what I thought. It's this or using a ship and hopping from world to world the long way. That will take months, if not longer. We don't have that kind of time. You said so yourself."

"Whatever you choose, I'll defend you," Anlilta said.

Lucian realized the decision was up to him. And the decision was simple. "We're going in. Ward everything you can."

Anlilta's expression darkened. "So be it, Chosen. Lead on."

Lucian nodded. "Let's get those wards up."

Once everyone had prepared their magical defenses, Lucian stepped toward the Gate, drawing on the power of the Orbs for protection. The others followed behind him.

——————

As SOON AS the group passed through, Lucian's Thermal shield was hammered, the temperature outside hotter than a furnace. Blinding, fiery red spread in all directions. As Lucian's Radiant shield blocked out the glare, details resolved. They were on a stand of rock above a roiling sea of molten lava. Fire rained from the sky while an infernal wind blew, carrying sharp bits of molten rock that pelted Lucian's shield. The air was unbreathable, both because of the temperature and composition of poisonous gases, but thankfully, Lucian's Atomic ward kept the air within their protective bubble freshened, while Binding kept out all the wind and molten rock. He felt slightly heavier than he should have; the world they were on had a higher gravity than what they were used to.

If Hell were real, Lucian figured they had found it.

After a few seconds, his shields equalized with their hostile surroundings. If they needed to go back, the Gate was still behind them.

Of Nabukar, there was no sign. Anlilta searched the surrounding maelstrom, her expression thunderous.

"If they're trying to kill us, they're going to have to do better than a hell planet," Emma said.

Ether was pouring through Lucian in a torrent. Despite the number of streams under his active control, there was little effort. He was only concerned with one thing at the moment.

He caught sight of the Seven-Fold Path, leading across the sea of lava. Because of the amount of fiery debris falling from the sky, he couldn't see too far into the distance.

"I know where we are," Anlilta finally said, her tone dark. "This is Tiamatia, The World of Fire."

"What does that mean, exactly?" Mira asked nervously.

"Tiamatia is a twin world of Kurzagûl, and the two are connected by Gate. We would just need to find that Gate to reach Kurzagûl, at a city called Mishar. That will get us closest to the Threshold of Creation, giving us the biggest chance of success."

Those words just focused Lucian even more. The sooner they got to the Heart of Creation, the sooner he could deal with the Ancient One.

"All right," Fergus said. "Any suggestions on how to get off this rock?"

It was at this moment that a massive column of lava shot upward from in front of them. Lucian strengthened the group's Thermal shield as strong as it would go, and only a trace of its heat sizzled against his skin.

Lucian nodded toward their left. "The Path leads off that way. But I don't see any other places to tether to."

"So, we're stuck?" Emma asked.

"Where is Nabukar, anyway?" Fergus asked.

As if the mentioning of his name were a summons, the powerfully built Ascendant appeared before them, wrapped in a shield of golden magic. "That you've survived this long bodes well."

"Where is Enkius?" Anlilta asked. "And where have you been?"

"Scouting ahead, Mother. As for Father, he isn't far. He's set up camp in a hidden vale, where the eyes of the Shadow won't find him. It has been preserved over the centuries, in the days before this world was a place of death."

"For what purpose?" Anlilta said.

"As a bet, Mother, in case your words ever proved true." Nabukar's golden eyes took in Lucian. "If this one is truly the Chosen of Prophecy, then consider this my father showing faith in your words, even if you don't see eye-to-eye on everything else. He has gathered the entirety of his court here for a final attack on the Shadow. But first, he wants to determine the Chosen is who he claims to be."

"A final attack? Nabukar, attacking is the last thing we should do. The armies of Kurzagûl are the last things we should deal with. The Chosen must return the Orbs to the Heart to destroy the Ancient One for good. That is the only way forward. Our mission requires utmost secrecy."

Another lava plume shot up, which Lucian shielded against. Once it had passed, Mira spoke. "Can we talk about this some-where else? *Anywhere* else?"

"An excellent idea," Nabukar said. "This storm is especially bad, so I must risk a portal."

Before anyone could say anything else, Nabukar opened a golden portal, on the other side of which was a barren wasteland. Immediately, the Seven-Fold Path shifted directions through the portal to this wasteland, telling Lucian it was the fastest way to reach their eventual goal.

He noticed the others were looking to him for confirmation, even Anlilta.

At that moment, the ground shook, and another column of fire arced in their direction.

"Now!" Lucian said.

They charged through the portal, immediately finding them-selves on a cooler and dimmer part of the planet. It was still hot, and the air poisonous, but Lucian could at least relax his Thermal ward a bit. Other than the wind swirling the dust under a gray sky, it was quiet.

"We've come to the northern part of the planet," Nabukar said. "Not a place the Light often treads."

"No," Anlilta said, her tone tense. "Tiamatia is a very dangerous world, and the risk of building a base here is unacceptable."

Nabukar gave an insolent smile. "Still, you must admit, it has proven most useful. And now, it becomes our springboard from which to strike."

"Any such strike is doomed as soon as it is discovered," Anlilta said. "The power of the Shadow in this sector of the Aetheria is great, and to allow the Orbs to come so close to the seat of the Shadow's power is beyond foolish."

"And yet, you urged it to pass through the wastes of Gadea," Nabukar said.

"Because there was no other choice!"

"Neither do we have a choice, Mother. Even you say we are running out of time. Well, this is it. Our last chance." He glanced at Lucian. "That's why he's here, right? He is the Chosen. With the power of the Orbs, what chance do the denizens of Kurzagûl stand? We will strike at them suddenly and find a ship for the Chosen and his companions. It is the best chance we have."

"It's too much of a risk!" Anlilta said. "We need to stay hidden, or else everything will fail."

"Let's find this base," Lucian said, cutting off their argument.

"Of course, Chosen."

Nabukar leaped into the air and flew toward the distant mountains, never minding whether the humans behind him were capable of the same. Lucian saw it as another one of Nabukar's tests. If he was the Chosen, summoning the power to follow him should pose no issue.

Lucian streamed Gravitonic Magic around the group—everyone except Anlilta, who was already flying after her son. They floated in the air, and he set his Focus to follow Anlilta, slowly bringing them up to speed.

They flew across the landscape at breakneck speeds. Lucian realized that if they were trying to keep a low profile, this probably wasn't the best way. He changed his mind when he detected Anlilta's Radiant Magic, powerful enough to mask their presence. Traveling with two powerful Ascendants certainly had its perks.

The entire time, the Seven-Fold Path followed Nabukar, which was enough for Lucian. Within minutes, they were settling down between two pointed peaks. The rift between them was as desolate as any other part of the world.

"We're close now," Nabukar said.

It only took a couple of steps for the Ascendant to simply disappear, as if passing through some sort of barrier that masked the location of whatever was beyond.

Lucian and the others followed.

27

BEYOND THE VEIL of searing heat and desolation lay an oasis of staggering beauty, a paradise that defied the blasted wastelands outside.

As Lucian walked in, the first thing he noticed, strangely enough, was the air—cool and fragrant with the scents of exotic blooms and rich, moist earth. Next, he saw the towering trees filling the vale, their trunks twisted into fantastical shapes, many bearing jewel-like fruits. Those trees cast a soft, ethereal glow that illuminated the garden before them. Cascading waterfalls, clear as crystal, tumbled from seemingly nowhere, feeding meandering streams that flowed with a gentle murmur. Hanging gardens, suspended in mid-air by magic, brimmed with flowers of every color, their petals shimmering with dewdrops. Stone pathways sparkled underfoot, winding through the lush undergrowth, leading to secluded nooks and enchanted clearings. The very air shimmered with the delicate dance of golden Creation Magic.

But most imposing of all was a gargantuan golden tree, its vast trunk branching out into a sprawling canopy of similarly golden leaves. The leaves rustled with a sound like gentle rainfall, casting dappled shadows that danced on the ground beneath. Around this tree, platforms floated in mid-air, connected by curving staircases that spiraled up from the valley floor, twining about the central trunk and outspread branches. Upon these platforms, structures of graceful architecture rested, constructed from materials that sparkled with ethereal light.

Lucian's breath caught at the sight. He sensed hundreds, if not thousands, of magical wards powering the valley, imbuing a sense of calm and eternal peace, keeping it safe from prying eyes. He had to remind himself not to relax, especially considering who awaited them in this garden.

"We are near," Nabukar said, his harsh voice out of place in this paradise. "This is the only outpost of the Light on this side of the Aetheria. As the Shadow had Gadea, the Dread Moon, we at least have our own dread here." Nabukar watched Lucian, his eyes narrowing slightly, as if in warning. "If Enkius senses you are no friend of the Light, you'll never leave this place alive."

"He has nothing to worry about on that count," Anlilta said, answering for Lucian. "The magic powering this valley...how can it possibly be worth the risk of discovery?"

"He will have much to tell you about that, Mother," Nabukar said. "If you would, follow me."

Nabukar led the way quickly through the garden, unsentimentally brushing aside any foliage that got in his way, no matter how beautiful or meticulously placed.

The thick garden opened into the valley, golden mountains rising on every side. Here at the bottom, Lucian could see a few Sumaril sorcerers wearing resplendent robes. Though they were similarly sized to humans, they looked like children next to their Ascendant masters. Lucian assumed them to be in Enkius' employ, guardians who stood ready to fight for their master. The Sumaril watched their approach cautiously but did not challenge them as Nabukar led them toward the main pathway that circled up the tree.

They passed more mages, who bowed as Nabukar passed. But when they noted Anlilta, their bows deepened, some even prostrating themselves. This did not go unnoticed by Nabukar, who wore a scowl that suggested he thought himself worthy of just as much praise.

One of these unfortunate mages had prostrated herself a little too close to the path of the procession.

"Out of my way!" Nabukar snarled, sweeping his arm with a Psionic push.

The mage cried out, rolling along the celestial pathway, perilously close to the edge. Lucian reached out, streaming a gravity point to stop her from falling. She hung suspended for a moment over the side, her violet eyes wide with fear, her body quivering, before Lucian gently guided her back.

Nabukar snorted, as if Lucian had saved a bug rather than a sentient creature. He held his silence, deciding that reproaching the Ascendant wasn't worth his time.

Thankfully, they arrived at the top of the tree without further incident, where they entered a graceful veranda, the inside of which was as luxurious as a palace. At the far end, Lucian could at last see the one who had summoned him, sitting on a crystalline throne on a raised platform, surrounded by a retinue of Ascendants and sorcerers.

The first thing Lucian noticed about Enkius the Golden was the elegance of his clothing rather than the Ascendant himself. His outer robe was a rich tapestry of deep blue and gold, hanging heavily around him, adorned with intricate patterns that seemed to move and change in the light. Around his waist, a belt of pure gold cinched the robe. The ensemble was completed with a cloak that cascaded down his back, seeming to be made from ethereally golden flames. His skin, unlike most of the Ascendants Lucian had seen, was dark blue, while his hair was composed of white fronds that floated around his head. A golden aura radiated about his person, and when his eyes locked on Lucian's, Lucian felt the power radiating from them. He read much in that gaze: mostly challenge, but something darker he interpreted as greed.

Greed for the Orbs he held. It could be nothing else.

He quickly noted two other Ascendants that stood on either side of Enkius, both women of divine beauty, each with light blue skin. The one to the left of Enkius seemed to be clothed with nothing more than ethereal wisps of magic, and she held a crystalline spear of pulsing blue light. The Ascendant on the right, like Enkius himself, radiated a golden aura and wore similar golden armor that left only her hands and face bare. She was no less beautiful than the Ascendant on Enkius' other side, while being taller and leaner. She bore a golden spear.

All went quiet as Lucian and the others approached the throne. The crowd also seemed to take in Anlilta, hushed whispers taking to the gathering like a low wind. Lucian kept a firm grip on his Focus. Enkius watched neutrally, and Lucian imagined the Ascendant was carefully evaluating how his strength would match up against him. Lucian was carefully guarding his thoughts with a powerful Psionic shield. Already, Enkius' magic was testing his shield's strength, not attempting to batter it, but seeking any weak spots.

Lucian smiled. There were none.

"Be welcome, Chosen," Enkius finally said, in a resonant baritone. "No doubt your journey has been long and arduous."

The two Ascendants beside Enkius remained silent, apparently not making a pretense of welcoming Lucian.

Enkius' gaze then took in the others, but mostly Anlilta, who remained silent. Enkius gave a superior smile. "Anlilta. As beautiful as ever. That you've left your prophecies and dreams to attend to me speaks volumes."

"I'm not attending to you," Anlilta said. "That's what all these sycophants here are for." She nodded toward Nabukar. "Our son said you wanted to speak to me, so here I am."

"No, Anlilta. You overestimate yourself." His golden eyes flicked toward Lucian. "It is the Chosen I seek. You *are* the Chosen, no?"

"I am," Lucian said simply.

"And you are...to be our bulwark against the Shadow? The answer to all the Speaker's prophecies? Tell me. How much stock do you put into Anlilta's words? Most, if not all, of us Ascendants have grown deaf to her ceaseless blather."

The tall, golden Ascendant next to Enkius flashed a dangerous smile. The beautiful blue one openly laughed. It reminded Lucian of a hyena.

"She's gotten us this far," Lucian said. "As you've said, we've been on quite the journey. I won't bore you with the details. This is our last stop, we hope. We really need to keep moving."

Enkius watched him closely. "Not yet, Chosen. I can feel their power, their pull. You are right to return them to the Heart of Creation. Many would use them for power, but you seem inured to their call to glory."

"It's not glory I want."

"Then what is it you want, Chosen?"

"I already told you. To return the Orbs to the Heart of Creation. And to finish what I've started."

"To kill the Ancient One himself? A commendable goal, to be sure."

His tone of voice said he was humoring Lucian, as an adult might humor a child's ridiculous fantasy.

"No doubt, you believe you can't fail in this," Enkius went on. "Unlike my court here, you fully believe in Anlilta's prophecy. But there are other prophecies, other interpretations. And compared to us, your kind is weak. Beings of the Shadow Realm are as nothing when compared to Beings of Light. Without the Orbs, you would be nothing."

Lucian smiled. "I'm the Sorcerer-Ascendant of all Magekind, at least where I come from. And mastery of magic isn't about the Orbs. It's about belief. It's about your goal. It's about love. These things trump even the power of the Orbs."

"And your conscience, your ambitions, are so pure? Perhaps one more powerful would be a better bearer of the Orbs."

"Someone like you?" Anlilta asked in disgust. "You dare challenge the Chosen of the Manifold and expect to escape with your skin?"

"I am more powerful than him, even if he bears the Orb of Creation falsely, a gift that was rightfully given to me by the Manifold itself. Who are you to deny me it, Chosen?"

"I am no one," Lucian said. "What matters is what the Manifold wants. Do you think the Manifold trusts you to do what's right? Maybe with just a thought on my part, even you could be brought low, Enkius. Do you dare to even try?"

All was silent as Enkius considered this, giving a dangerous smile. "Take care in how you answer, Lucian Abrantes of Earth. I have destroyed worlds and am the Bane of the Shadow. In the Aetheria, there is no higher good than me."

Lucian closed his eyes, remembering Lakhmu's teachings. "Goodness is not something you are. It's something you do."

"And you define good, Chosen?"

Lucian opened his eyes, meeting Enkius' gaze steadily. "I can't ignore the things I've heard about you. The Manifold trusted me to keep the Orbs safe from anyone who would misuse them. That includes anyone who wants to bend them to their will, to fulfill their own goals rather than returning them to where they belong."

Enkius' smile widened, a glint of amusement dancing in his golden eyes. "The things you've heard about me, eh? Rumors, I assume. Dangerous things, aren't they? They can paint even the most innocent of intentions in a sinister light. Perhaps I could say the same thing about you. Have you considered that? But maybe I have a better idea of how to use them. Is it so wrong to use them for a good purpose before I dispose of them?"

Anlilta snorted derisively, but Enkius ignored her, his attention fixed solely on Lucian.

Enkius continued, his voice low and dangerous. "Tell me, Chosen. What do you know of my intentions? Are they good or ill?"

"I know enough about you to be cautious," Lucian answered evenly. "I know you covet the power of the Orbs, that you want them for your own purposes. Maybe in the end you actually will return them to the Heart. But can you ignore their call to power?" Lucian shook his head doubtfully. "By the time you've accomplished your goals, by the time there is no Shadow left to fight, it might already be too late for you. Who's saying such power wouldn't turn you into something unrecognizable, something worse than even the Ancient One? You are already powerful, Enkius, but with the Orbs, there would be nothing to check you. The desire for power, ultimately, leads to nothing but destruction and chaos."

Enkius leaned back in his crystalline throne, his expression inscrutable. "And yet, here you are, standing in my presence, holding the very objects of my supposed desire. Do you not fear what I could do to you? Here, in my domain, with my servants, not even the Orbs can save you."

"I fear nothing," Lucian replied, his voice unwavering. "Fear doesn't dictate my actions. I will do whatever is necessary to protect the Orbs. For them to remain out of the hands of those who would misuse them. I will not risk them changing hands." He hardened his gaze. "Even if that means standing against you."

The others shifted beside him, apparently ready to fight to the death.

There was a moment of tense silence as Enkius regarded him, his gaze piercing. Then, to Lucian's surprise, he chuckled softly, the sound echoing through the veranda like distant thunder.

"You have spirit, Chosen. I'll give you that much."

The golden Ascendant beside Enkius interrupted, her voice cold and sharp. "But spirit alone will not protect you. Do not mistake our hospitality for weakness. You tread on dangerous ground here."

Lucian switched his attention to her. "I understand the risks of coming here. If I were weak, do you think I would have answered your summons? The Speaker of the Manifold begged me not to. Even knowing this was a trap, here I stand. I won't be intimidated or bullied. You might be Ascendants, far more powerful than any of us individually. But we've fought through thick and thin, standing together for years as a single unit. We fight as one and have been underestimated repeatedly. We destroyed the Ancient One in the Shadow Realm. The point is, the Orbs are not yours to command, Enkius. They never were. Nor are they mine to command. They belong to the Manifold. No single being was meant to control this much power. So, the best person to hold them is the person who doesn't want them."

Enkius' smile faded, replaced by a glimmer of something more malevolent. "We shall see, Chosen," he said softly. "We shall see."

28

THERE WAS a moment of tense silence, where Lucian believed Enkius might explode. All it took was for one person—Sumaril, Ascendant, or human—to lose control, and all hell would break loose.

But at last, Enkius shifted on his throne, seeming to turn his mind to other matters. "Yes, I've summoned you, but not merely to ask you for the Orbs. I must have a sense of you, and so far, it's all been talk. Nothing but actions matter."

"On that, I agree," Lucian said. "I'm ready to work together with you to return the Orbs to the Heart. That's the only reason I'm here. The longer we stay here, the more likely the Shadow will discover my presence. Anyone who has sworn allegiance to the Ancient One will be pulled by the power of the Orb of Shadows. Not even the wards of this valley can protect against that."

"The Chosen is right," Anlilta said. "If this charade is some sort of test of his strength and abilities, you have been found wanting."

"Hardly," Enkius said. "And yet, the true test approaches,

236

doesn't it? We who sit so near to the enemy's seat of power, a mere cosmic step from the Threshold of Creation itself?"

"I'm ready," Lucian said. "The only question is, are you?"

"Such insolence," the golden Ascendant to Enkius' right snarled, her fist tightening on her spear. "How can you suffer this, Enkius?"

"Stay your hand, Ninsun," Enkius said.

"But he has—"

"Silence!" Enkius commanded.

Ninsun closed her mouth, electing to glower at Lucian instead.

Enkius returned his attention to him. "Do you have any idea what *any* of this entails? Only three beings in all the Light Realm have ever successfully passed the Threshold of Creation and arrived at the Heart. There's me, Nathi, and the one we won't even name. Countless others have tried, for their own reasons. None of them have returned. I will not risk the Orbs being held in the hands of one so weak. I have already proven myself strong. Without even bearing the Orbs, Nathi and I made the passage and lived to tell the tale. With the Orbs, there is no chance the Ethereal Rip will destroy me."

"It's not power that saved you," Anlilta said. "It was purpose."

"And his purpose is strong enough? You would take that risk, losing the Orbs forever?"

"I would. Because he is the one."

"He is weak," the blue Ascendant said, whose name Lucian still didn't know. "I could destroy him with a finger."

"Famous last words," Fergus muttered.

Enkius glowered down from his throne at Lucian. "Whatever your power, it's no match for the will of the Ancient One. You are doing his bidding, Chosen, by returning the Orbs to the Heart. The Orb of Shadows will call him, and he will answer. Our mortal enemy is counting on your weakness."

"What's the point of all this?" Lucian asked. "I've come this far, and I'm ready to do whatever it takes to finish the job. That's all that matters. I'll die before I hand the Orbs over to you."

"So you say, Chosen. But isn't magic, the most powerful of it, based on truth? Long have I believed Anlilta's prophecies to be folly, ever since she consigned Nathi to a fate worse than death. I've sacrificed much for the fulfilling of her baseless visions. More than you'll ever know. Two thousand years ago, against my better judgment, I entrusted the Orb of Creation to Nathi...who entered the cold dark of the Shadow Realm as an accursed *Alkasen*. This, Anlilta vouchsafed, was the only hope for the Light Realm, for all reality itself, that the Chosen receive the Orb of Creation. She prophesied the Chosen would return the Orbs to the Light Realm. Watching him leave was the hardest thing I've ever endured." His face became somber. "The longer I waited, the more I recognized the folly of it. I had given up Nathi, my true love, for nothing."

Anlilta ignored Enkius' solemn tone. "How was Nathi's sacrifice for nothing when the Chosen stands before us now? When he holds Nine of the Ten in his Focus, when he has resisted the call to power of the Orb of Shadows? Besides, I did nothing to twist Nathi's mind. Perhaps Nathi had the wisdom to see what you did not, Enkius."

"Never did Nathi utter a word of your schemes until your venom bewitched him. He was too good, Anlilta. And you poisoned that good. None...*none* wanted to make the fateful journey into the dark, from which there can be no return. The sorcerers, yes. But they are sorcerers. None of us, the Children of the Manifold itself, wished to take on the mark of the *Alkasen*, the Accursed, to enter the Shadow Realm and become subject to its poison. And even now, he is alone there, with nothing to comfort him. With no way back. With nothing but the power of Space-Time imprinted upon his Focus. So good was he that he did what I didn't have the strength to do. He had hoped to end the power of the First Gate by returning the Orb of Space-Time to the Heart of Creation. When I told him it would make no difference, he still wanted to try. Miraculously, he survived the journey a second time. And when it didn't work, the grief he felt was untold. And when years later, the Ancient One returned to rob the Heart of Creation, the knife twisted even deeper."

"Why are you blaming me for what happened?" Anlilta asked. "No one could have predicted that. When the Orbs were lost, I did the only thing I knew to do. I asked the Manifold what we needed to do to get them back. It wasn't easy, but I shared what the Manifold told me. Sending the Orb of Creation to the Shadow Realm, to give it to the Chosen, was the only way. You believed back then Enkius, with far less evidence than I have before you today. You believed so strongly that you entrusted Nathi with the Orb of Creation."

"He told me he knew a way back," Enkius nearly whispered. "And fool that I am, I believed him. It was the only reason I gave it to him. And then, I never saw him again." Enkius' eyes became almost murderous as he watched Anlilta. "You exploited that grief, Anlilta, for the sake of your prophecies. I can't prove it, but I know you got to him, told him to lie to me about coming back. Can you not understand the sorrow you've sown? Probably not, because you've loved nothing except for the Manifold's riddles. How could you understand the language of grief?"

Anlilta watched him, her expression neutral, not denying it. "Nathi knew what was required. No sorcerer was powerful enough to wield the Orb of Creation. It had to be one of us, one of the First Echelon. And as you said yourself, no one else would go. His sacrifice was not in vain."

"You should have volunteered yourself," Ninsun spat.

"And why not you, Ninsun?" Anlilta shot back. "Why not Nanshe? Both of you claim to know Enkius' heart."

The impossibly beautiful blue Ascendant to Enkius' right, Nanshe, shifted on her feet, her face a mask of anger.

"It was not their fight," Enkius said. "It was no one's. We could have left the Ancient One within the Shadow Realm to fester for all time. He would not have been able to touch us as long as we stayed united, as long as we held the power of the Orbs of Creation. Perhaps, one day, the Manifold would die, but I'd rather live two thousand years with Nathi than an eternity without him. And when the lights went out, it would have been beautiful. Because there would have been love, which is the balm for all pain. But instead, you have left me with an eternity of grief that only grows with the passing of the ages."

"We all belong to the Light Realm," Anlilta said. "We are all the Children of the Manifold, which even now bleeds her ethereal blood through the First Gate. Yet the fact remains: Nathi volunteered, and he knew you would never agree to it if he didn't lie."

"It should have been you, Anlilta," Enkius said.

"If it were me, there would be no one to guide the Chosen once they entered the Light Realm. None to help him navigate the vipers of your court. I understand your tears, but they should not be tears of sorrow. They should be tears of joy. Against all odds, the Chosen is here! He stands before us now, holding Nine of the Ten in his Focus, and one without it. And while Nathi might never return to the Light Realm, there is still a chance for our reality to be saved—with your help, Enkius."

"And why should I help you? It will all be for nothing. The Chosen will sacrifice himself in trying to reach the Heart of Creation. Remember the Ethereal Rip, which has claimed the lives of every being but three. He is too weak to survive the journey. The Heart will not suffer the weak to approach it."

"Too much has been sacrificed to give up now, Enkius. We need a plan to give the Chosen the best chance at victory. At any moment, the Manifold could extinguish itself. Perhaps that is what you prefer, but this isn't only your choice."

"There is no plan. How can we plan when things have shifted

so much, and the Speaker of the Manifold has kept us all in the dark?"

"If accepting that fault is what will allow us to proceed, then I accept it gladly," Anlilta said. "If there's no plan, then the logical thing to do would be to come up with one, would it not? We know the risks of the Ethereal Rip. If the Manifold is to be believed, Lucian has the strength to endure it. It would not have chosen him if he didn't have the strength."

"And what about his companions?" Enkius asked. "If they perish, will he have the will to go on?"

"They won't die," Lucian said. "I'll make sure of it."

"Confidence is good, but not when it is buoyed by ignorance. We are at a stark disadvantage against the Shadow. Gathered in this valley is the entire force we could muster on such short notice. We had planned to bring more, but in the chaos, this is all we could assemble. But with the Orbs, a surprise strike at the heart of Kurzagûl would be enough to weaken the Shadow beyond hope of repair."

"The only direct access to Kurzagûl is the Gate of Mishar," Anlilta said. "The fortress there will slow us greatly, even with the power of the Orbs. It risks more than a secret journey to the Threshold."

"Yes," Enkius said. "But storming the Gate is only one part of my idea."

"What's the other part?"

Enkius turned his eyes upon Lucian. "The Chosen, and his companions—should I find them worthy—won't use the Gate. They will instead use the Ethertree."

Anlilta looked at him as if he were crazy. "The Ethertree? You mean, this very one we're standing on?"

Enkius watched her closely. "For centuries, I have grown it here, taking on the power of the ethereal core that we found in this valley. It is one of the most powerful ever discovered. It has been gathering magic for one purpose only: a direct strike on Kurzagûl to bypass the Mishar Gate." His eyes went to Lucian. "However, the ethereal core powering the Ethertree could be...*repurposed*. At least, in theory."

"Repurposed?" Lucian asked. "What does that mean?"

"Right now, the instructions I branded into the core point the tree toward Kurzagûl, as one might expect," Enkius said. "But it might instead be coaxed to embrace a new target."

"The Threshold of Creation," Anlilta said in realization. "Is it as powerful as that?"

"I can't say," Enkius said. "Its wards are enough to protect it from the Void between this world and Kurzagûl, but to survive the Ethereal Rip of the Threshold is another thing entirely. However, there is no ship that can match its abilities in withstanding the Void. The Ethertree was grown with care, with the most powerful Creation brands that no other vessel can hope to match. Of course, such a plan would mean placing our full trust in the Chosen. While the rest of us march, perhaps to our doom, to the Mishar Gate, it might cause enough of a commotion to draw the attention of the Kurzagûli navy, allowing the Ethertree to pass the World of Shadow unscathed. Along with its cargo."

There was silence as these words were considered. At last, Anlilta spoke. "A daring plan. It seems too good to be true."

"You suspect I am deceiving you?" Enkius asked with a smile. "I don't blame you."

"Wait," Emma said. "So, the Tree is a spaceship?"

Enkius turned his attention to her. "Yes. One doomed to make a one-way journey wherever it goes."

"What's involved in changing the tree's course?" Anlilta asked, her tone skeptical.

"The most hard part," Enkius said. "The ethereal core that powers the Tree must recognize the Chosen as its new master. And for that to happen, it must believe that the Chosen is more powerful than even me."

29

A LONG SILENCE followed this statement. From the mood of the veranda, most believed this was an impossibility.

As for Lucian, he had no doubts he could beat Enkius if it were an even match. But he also knew not to underestimate his power.

"Can you not command the Ethertree to obey him, Enkius?" Anlilta asked quietly.

Enkius flashed a smile. "That defeats the purpose of him proving his worthiness, no? From the day it was planted, I imbued my magic within its seed, and the streams that guided its growth are unerring. It was always to be a secret weapon pointing at the heart of Kurzagûl. I'm afraid simply telling the Ethertree to obey a new master would not be possible. In fact, the act of doing so could prove disastrous, with unpredictable effects that would guarantee disrupting the streams protecting this valley. Nor would the Tree willingly go to its death when that end is uncertain. The Chosen would have to convince it of its new purpose."

Lucian thought this over, but there was little to think about. It seemed to be the only way forward unless he wanted to fight an

243

unwinnable battle at this Mishar Gate. And the Gate would only take them as far as Kurzagûl, one step closer to the Threshold of Creation. Once on Kurzagûl, they would still have to find a ship capable of taking them to the Threshold, bypassing whatever defenses the planet had.

In his mind, that was the harder path. This Ethertree was a way to bypass all the fighting, to get to the Heart of Creation as soon as possible.

Assuming Enkius wasn't lying, of course.

"I can take command of the Ethertree," Lucian said.

His declaration hung in the air, thick with tension. Around him, the assembled Ascendants of the Light Realm, along with the Sumaril sorcerers in their employ, exchanged uneasy glances. For the first time, the veranda was unnervingly silent, the only sound the gentle breeze rustling through the golden tree limbs outside. It seemed each person was grappling with the gravity of Lucian's decision.

While the suggestion of changing the Ethertree's course had come from Enkius' lips, very few seemed convinced that Lucian could seize it as his own.

Ninsun, the golden Ascendant, was the first to break the silence, her face a mask of anger and challenge. Her voice was sharp, like the point of the golden spear she wielded. "We speak of Anlilta's prophecy as if it's infallible. But prophecies are twisted to fit the desires of those who wield them. How can we be sure that this is the true path, that you are even the true Chosen? Could it not be any of us standing in this room? How can you, a Shadow Being, have the power to sway an ethereal core branded by the magic of Enkius the Golden himself? This would require you not only to have great power but great wisdom, to know the heart of Enkius himself, who you've spoken to for scarcely an hour. Would not the right Bearer of the Orbs be one of our own, an Ascendant of exceptional ability, one above reproach, one who knows the heart of the greatest among us?"

Lucian met Ninsun's gaze steadily, his resolve hardening. "What are you suggesting, Ninsun? That you can take the Orbs from me?"

Ninsun remained silent, though her golden eyes glowered in challenge.

Lucian took in the rest of the assembly with his gaze. "We will never be entirely sure this will work until we try. But as Enkius said, the alternative is to march into a battle at the Mishar Gate, a battle we are not guaranteed to win. The Ethertree is a chance to skip all that. It's not just about blindly following prophecy. It's about seizing the best opportunity we have to finish things right."

Anlilta stepped forward, her robes shimmering with the subtle play of light. "Ninsun raises a valid point. While you are the Chosen of the Manifold, while you wield Lightspear, your abilities are thus far untested, at least before those assembled here. However, we must also consider the unique position we find ourselves in. The only reason all of us are standing here can only be the convergence of countless threads of fate weaved by the Manifold itself. Why else would the Ethertree be a possibility if we weren't meant to try?"

"Even if that attempt means death?" Nanshe asked.

Enkius, who had been observing this exchange with an unreadable expression, finally spoke. "The risk is significant. The Ethertree's magic is old, intertwined deeply with the wards and shields that protect this valley from the wrath of Tiamatia and the Shadow. If the Chosen cannot convince it, the consequences will be dire. Not just for him, but for all of us here."

"Then why even mention it?" Emma asked. "Because you believe he'll die, and that puts the Orbs up for grabs?"

From Enkius' silence, the answer to that question was quite obvious. Why else would Enkius bring it up? If he was certain the Tree and its magic would prove his match, then it was a risk-free way for Enkius to claim the Orbs for himself.

Mira, standing slightly behind Emma, spoke up, her voice steady. "What other choice do we have?"

"And perhaps Anlilta is right," Enkius said. "Perhaps this is a convergence of a thousand threads of fate."

Fergus nodded in agreement, his expression grim. "Lucian has my support, as always. I've always advised caution, but in this situation, it is impossible to know which way is safest. If he believes this is the path forward, then I stand with him."

The room was divided, the air charged with a mixture of fear and uncertainty. Lucian knew he needed to sway them, to unite them under a single banner of purpose.

He stepped forward, his voice clear and resonant, addressing the entire veranda. "I don't have all the answers. But I know that if we stand here, divided by fear and doubt, we will fail before we even begin. I am asking for your trust, not just in me, but in the destiny that has brought us all here. We cannot forget that the future of all existence is at stake. We have to be bold and meet the challenge head-on."

His crowd of listeners didn't seem convinced. He didn't blame them; they were just words, after all, even if passionately spoken.

But he noticed Ninsun's earlier skepticism had twisted into repressed rage. She stepped forward boldly, to the edge of the crystalline platform that supported Enkius' throne, her golden armor clinking softly, the light reflecting off her ornate spear. Her eyes narrowed in challenge.

"Chosen," Ninsun called out, her tone commanding the room's attention. "If that truly is your title. You ask for our trust, to allow you to take the Holy Orbs toward an uncertain end. I say this is madness! Trust must be earned by deeds witnessed, not merely granted based on titles or stories told. If you are to lead us, if you are to convince the Ethertree to abandon its lifelong purpose, then you must prove your strength. Prove that you are worthy of wielding the Orbs!"

Every pair of eyes in the room was glued to the unfolding

confrontation. Lucian felt the weight of their stares, each one a silent demand for him to show his capabilities.

He elected to remain silent, to let Ninsun say the words that would end up becoming her doom.

Ninsun felt this, and realized she was already over the precipice, having thrown the dice of fate. "I propose a challenge. A test of your strength and abilities to wield the Orbs. Your opponent? Me. The stakes? Death."

The proposal sent a murmur through the crowd. It was a high-stakes gamble, one that could either solidify Lucian's position or end his life. And of course, if he lost, it would force the Orbs to pass to either Ninsun or maybe even Enkius himself.

Enkius, sensing the tension, intervened. "Ninsun, is this truly necessary? We are not children playing games of power. The fate of our Aetheria hangs in the balance. If the Chosen loses, it could be the end of the prophecy of salvation. If you lose, then I will not only be bereft of Nathi, but you. Why can we not agree to let the Ethertree itself test him?"

Despite Enkius' words, Lucian was certain they were half-hearted.

"This is personal," Ninsun retorted sharply. "We need a Chosen whose power is undisputed, one who must be tested even before the Ethertree's test. If he cannot survive my wrath, then he cannot survive the Ethertree. The Chosen has yet to prove that he can control the Orbs to their full extent. This is about more than mere trust—it's about capability."

"And my sister will not stand alone," Nanshe said.

A shift occurred within the chamber. The assembled sorcerers and Ascendants exchanged troubled glances as whispers fluttered through the veranda like leaves caught in a sudden gust. To face not one Ascendant, but two, seemed a step too far. That they were the personal guards of Enkius himself also spoke to their martial skill.

Even with Lucian's capabilities, it would not be an easy fight.

Just from their posture, Lucian was sure each of them was far more capable than Nabukar, and they had likely been fighting together for years.

Anlilta stepped forward, her face filled with dismay and fear. "Enough!" Her voice resonated with authority as she interjected herself between Lucian and the platform before them. "This talk of duels and tests of death is folly. Each of our realms is on the brink of destruction. Challenging the Chosen to a deadly contest solves nothing and risks everything. The only one who stands a chance of winning is our ancient enemy, Isthelah himself! If the Chosen is to be tested, let it be by the Tree itself, as was the original plan."

As Anlilta's words hung in the air, seeking to quell the rising tide of confrontation, Ninsun and her sister Nanshe, golden and blue, remained unyielding, their stance as firm as the resolve in their eyes.

"No," Ninsun said, her voice laced with conviction. "This is not merely about unity or avoiding internal strife. This is about ensuring that the one who wields the Orbs is truly worthy of them. The addition of my sister may seem an unfair challenge. But the Chosen will not only have to face the Ethertree, but the Ancient One himself at the Heart of Creation. That confrontation will make my challenge look fair in comparison. Though you stand above me, Speaker Anlilta, I must respectfully disagree with your words. My challenge stands."

Beside Ninsun, Nanshe nodded grimly in agreement, her blue eyes steady. "If the Chosen is to command not only the Orbs but our fates, his power and resolve must be beyond question. My sister and I have fought together, an unstoppable force, as far back as the Battle of Eternity at the end of the War of Light and Shadow. Death comes, for either the Chosen or for us! And if we die, then we die having proven what no one else was brave enough to face. That the Chosen indeed stands among us. But if he falls, then we know he was never worthy, and the Orbs can pass on to one more deserving."

Mira, standing slightly behind Lucian, whispered urgently, her voice tinged with concern. "Son, this is madness. They are pushing you into a corner—"

Lucian lifted his hand. The weight of every eye upon him felt like the gravity of a thousand suns pulling at his resolve. He knew the risk, felt the danger, but he also understood what his refusal would signify.

Weakness.

Anlilta merely watched Lucian with her violet eyes. She did not need to say anything. Lucian understood her advice was to decline the challenge, come what may.

Fergus added his voice, his tone steady and supportive. "Lucian, we already know you are capable. What these Ascendants are saying means nothing. This fight could rob you of the chance to prove yourself where it truly matters, with the Ethertree. This is exactly what the Ancient One wants. And in fact, his hand may be in this."

Ninsun swelled, her eyes furious. "You dare accuse me of embracing the Shadow? I am a Golden Warden, sworn to defend Enkius with my life itself!"

"And challenging the Chosen somehow fulfills this charge?" Fergus asked.

"Yes!" Ninsun said. "What will it be, Chosen? Can you defeat both me and my sister? Will you risk yourself for the chance to prove your worthiness beyond a doubt?"

"I accept your challenge," Lucian announced, his voice carrying through the veranda with a mixture of defiance and resolve. "Though I don't want it to be to the death."

"Why? Are you afraid?" Ninsun asked.

Nanshe flashed a sharp smile as she twirled her spear.

"Yes," Lucian said. "For you."

The room erupted into murmurs, the air charged with tension and disbelief.

Emma's brow furrowed with worry. "Lucian, there is still a

chance to turn back. This isn't about proving your strength. That's not in question with anyone who truly matters. This is a risk we cannot afford to take."

Anlilta tried once more to intervene. "This is reckless. We stand on the precipice of war, and instead of banding together for the last fight, we entertain notions of infighting. Think of the greater good, Ninsun, Nanshe. Consider the chaos we invite with your actions, the evil hand you have forced upon the Chosen!"

Her plea, however, fell on deaf ears. Enkius, observing the unfolding drama, remained silent, his thoughts inscrutable. The authority to halt the challenge was within his power, yet he chose not to exercise it. Lucian was sure he was hoping Lucian was defeated. If not by the Golden Wardens, then by the Ethertree thereafter.

But what would Enkius do if his plan failed? Was he hoping Lucian was weakened enough to go in for the kill?

Ninsun, seizing the moment, stepped closer to Lucian. "Prepare yourself, Chosen. You have one hour."

Her sister Nanshe nodded solemnly.

Lucian could feel nothing but sorrow. How would this assembly react once he killed the Golden Wardens? Would the Ascendants respect his strength, or become so enraged that they attacked all at once?

"I will stand with you," Fergus said. "They have two, so it's only fair that we do as well."

Mira's eyes widened. "Fergus, you can't!"

"Fergus," Lucian warned, "you know that would guarantee your death."

"I can't let you fight alone. It isn't right."

"Fergus," Lucian said again. "Please. I'm not asking you to stand aside. I'm telling you."

When Fergus heard the seriousness of his voice, he paused for a moment as he considered. While he was a powerful mage in his own right, his power against the likes of Ninsun and Nanshe was like a spark against an inferno. He would be slaughtered senselessly within the first few seconds of this contest.

"When I win," Lucian continued, "you will be needed. None of us can make it to the end unless we work together. I'll need you for the final fight."

At last, Fergus nodded. "Then just know Mira and I both stand with you. We will do whatever it takes."

"I'm with you, too," Emma said, watching Lucian worriedly. "Just remember what you're fighting for. Who you're fighting for."

Her words reminded him of Serah. He knew he would win the fight, if only because that was the only way he'd ever see her again.

Whatever truth the sisters held dear, it could never be higher than that.

30

WITHIN THE HOUR, the entire court had gathered on a wide lawn below. Lucian faced both Ascendant sisters, Lightspear in hand, while each of them held their own spears—Ninsun's golden and Nanshe's icy blue. The surrounding crowd was dead silent, and from the corner of his eye, Lucian could see Fergus and Mira watching with widened eyes. The sisters leered at Lucian across the lawn, their gloating faces completely assured of their victory.

In moments, he knew chaos would unfurl, and the fate of worlds would be decided.

"The rules are thus," Enkius proclaimed, from the center of the ring. "The stakes are death to the vanquished and ultimate victory to the winner. The battle may be observed by any, but none may intervene, nor will any protection be afforded to any spectator. This fight is strictly between the Chosen and his challengers. The punishment for any infraction is instant death. Is that clear?"

None challenged his words as the wind blew through the leaves of the golden canopy above.

Strength, Lucian, Anlilta's voice said in his mind. *Trust your instincts. The Manifold guides your steps.*

You've got this, Fergus said. *Remember everything you've learned.*

Do it for Serah, Mira said. *I love you, son.*

Emma said nothing, only giving him a fierce nod, a nod that told him to do whatever it took.

Lucian, for his part, felt nothing. Nothing but absolute focus for the task at hand. The power of the Orbs was latent and waiting, but Lucian knew he wouldn't even need them to win.

He had grown beyond them. He was the Sorcerer-Ascendant, the Chosen of the Manifold, but more than that, he was Lucian Abrantes of Earth.

Nothing—after everything he had gone through—would stand in his way.

He shifted his attention to the evening air, crisp and still as the last rays of the sun cut through the garden, casting long shadows over the dueling ground. He stood poised, Lightspear gleaming golden bright in his grip, an extension of his will. It was as if he held a sliver of the sun itself. He surveyed his opponents. Ninsun, with her golden spear, armor, and lithe form, exuded a fierce, predatory grace. Next to her, Nanshe shimmered with a frost-like aura, her form possessing an air of deadly intent. He wasn't sure which of the sisters would be most dangerous.

The silence deepened as Enkius took a step forward, his face sorrowful, as he raised his hand high. He held it there for what seemed an eternity until, at last, he allowed it to fall.

Lucian wasted no time streaming a blast of Radiant Magic along Lightspear, sending a blinding flare toward the sisters. He could hear the assembly crying out in surprise. But already, Ninsun was charging, her golden body wrapped in a shield of light while her golden spear left trails of fiery sparks in its wake. So fast did she run, each step left scorching earth beneath her sandaled feet. Meanwhile, Nanshe countered with a wave of her hand, summoning a barrier of shimmering ice to precede her sister's advance. Lucian felt the temperature drop instantly, raising a Thermal shield to block the worst effects.

He waited until Ninsun was literally upon him before phasing past her, reappearing equidistant between the two sisters. He tapped into the Orb of Atomicism, aiming for Nanshe. Molecules in the air around Nanshe vibrated, heating rapidly, forcing the icy Ascendant to dissipate her frost barrier or risk being over-whelmed by steam and pressure.

Not to be outdone, Nanshe shifted her strategy, her blue spear glowing brighter as she streamed a torrent of blue Binding teth-ers, aiming to immobilize Lucian with ethereal chains. Lucian gave a Gravitonic leap, soaring over the chains and landing directly before Nanshe, sending out a blast of Psionic Magic to disrupt her concentration. Already, he was suspecting Nanshe was the real threat, preferring to hang back and stream magic while Ninsun kept the enemy busy.

But already, Ninsun was closing in on Lucian, her golden spear flashing with fury. He was forced to respond, amplifying his speed with Space-Time Magic. Every one of Ninsun's strikes, parries, and feints was perfectly executed, and Lucian could only survive due to predicting where each strike would fall. He was pushed back, step by step.

Just as Lucian was nearing a cliff, he leaped off and twisted in the air, manipulating gravity itself to fall upward. Disoriented, Ninsun stumbled, her attack going wide.

As he levitated above both of the sisters, he reached for the Orb of Dynamism, streaming a network of electric arcs that danced unpredictably across the field. The sisters' eyes widened in tandem as they scrambled to dodge the lightning. Nanshe rushed to stream a yellow shield under which both sisters sheltered. Lucian focused all the lightning on that shield, streaming even more powerfully, becoming the center of the storm. Nanshe's shield buckled, nearly breaking, but Ninsun, with a defiant roar, raised her spear to ground the charges. But not without cost. The electricity singed the edges of her armor, her expression tightening in a mix of pain and determination.

But the pressure was taken off Nanshe, who could steady her shield.

The battle wore on as its participants cycled through every Aspect of Magic save Shadow, the beautiful garden around them bearing witness to the chaos. Beautiful blooms were incinerated, ancient trees shattered, and perfectly manicured lawns became a scarred battlefield. Of the previous watchers, there were no signs. They had long since fled to safety. The sisters moved in perfect synchronization, a deadly dance of magic honed over centuries of battle.

Lucian was so deep in his Focus that he didn't even see the battle but the interplay of ether and reality itself. He couldn't help but admire its destructive beauty. A single misstep would be his end, and his constant stream of Space-Time Magic was the only thing that allowed him to move quickly enough to keep up with the pair. The problem was, anytime he was forced to warp out of harm's way, the expenditure of ether was enough to give the sisters a brief respite, enough for them to regather and attack anew.

He needed to break this cycle, to force a paradigm shift. Lucian connected directly to the Manifold, letting it know his intentions.

I am the Chosen. Whatever I will, reality obeys.

A sudden infusion of pure ether, harsh and exhilarating, ignited his bones. He channeled it into a surge of Radiant Magic, as perfect copies of himself, dozens of them, exited his body and battled the sisters. So perfectly did they manifest they couldn't tell the difference between real and fake. Even Lightspear was perfectly copied, along with the magic each of the illusions streamed.

Lucian could not stand by and admire the gambit. Immediately, he joined his illusion army, dashing toward Nanshe, even as Ninsun did the same, who seemed to predict what was coming. Confused by the duplicates, Nanshe hesitated, her spear flashing out in a wide arc to clear them. Lucian, still brimming with ethereal power, warped immediately behind Nanshe, far faster than Ninsun could run to her sister's defense. He laced Lightspear with a combination of Psionic, Atomic, and Creation Magic; Psionic, to sow doubts in Nanshe as he moved in for the kill, and Atomic to deal a shattering blow that would blast Nanshe to her smallest components, and Creation, to counter the immortality that all Ascendants enjoyed.

As Lucian approached from behind, Nanshe still swatting at the illusions like flies, Lucian compressed the air around Nanshe, creating a vortex that disrupted her footing.

Lightspear came down, but with a deft move, Nanshe rose to meet the attack with her own spear. But so powerful was Lightspear that her ethereal weapon was instantly shattered. With Nanshe defenseless, a sudden scream caused Lucian to whirl just in time to parry a lethal blow from Ninsun, their spears clashing with a sound of thunder. It took only a couple of strikes for Ninsun's spear also to break and disappear into the surrounding air.

This was his chance. Lucian channeled the full power of the Orbs, unleashing a devastating blast of Radiant and Atomic Magic directly at the ground between them, shielding himself from his own attack's fury. The explosion was immense, sending both sisters spiraling in opposite directions.

He shot after Nanshe, flying through the explosion as he gathered more ether. He extended Lightspear as Nanshe lay sprawled on the ground, defenseless.

But Lucian could sense Ninsun coming from behind to rescue her sister once again, heedless of her own defense. Even as he neared Nanshe, he opened a portal directly in front of him, placing it just behind Ninsun, who was behind him. Directly ahead, he could see the golden sister, only now turning to defend herself. But it was too late. Lightspear found purchase in her back, piercing her armor as if it were air. Streams of light shot through Ninsun's body as she let out a pained shriek.

But Lucian didn't stop there. He kept his momentum, stabbing Nanshe not even a second later. The other sister did not cry out, instead accepting her fate by closing her eyes. As she had lived and fought with her sister for centuries, they would die together in the same stroke.

A second later, the sisters' bodies shattered irrevocably and instantly. The power of the attack exploded outward in a great golden wind, throwing Lucian back despite his defenses. He landed maladroitly on the scarred earth, his breathing heavy, his stance unyielding.

He closed his eyes for a moment, trying to regroup his thoughts before opening them again. The once-pristine paradise was now marred by the scars of the battle, fires and smoke belching into the sky. The only thing that remained was the golden Ethertree, the only plant that remained untouched by the conflict. He stood alone, with no sign of the surrounding congregation that had been watching at the beginning.

He didn't have to wait long. A large portal appeared, and from it, the entire court came through. Among the Ascendants and sorcerers, Mira, Fergus, and Emma emerged. Of the Sumaril, almost every being went wide-eyed at the destruction before them. Anlilta watched it with a neutral expression, as if the result had been foreordained. Most were in tears to see the garden's beauty so destroyed.

Lucian would have felt bad, but he had not been the one to ask for this. Everyone had witnessed the sisters' challenge, so none could say a word against him.

Last of all came Enkius the Golden himself. He looked around at the destruction, seeming to search for his two guardians, but not finding them. His face wasn't exactly pale, but there was a strange mix of emotions deeper than anything Lucian had ever witnessed. His once arrogant demeanor had finally been cracked by the sheer unexpectedness of what had unfolded. The garden, once a symbol of his power, was now as wasted as the land outside this valley, if not more so. His gaze swept over the scorched earth and shattered trees, the smoke spiraling upward into the evening sky.

His expression was one of grudging respect as he turned to face Lucian. The crowd held their collective breaths, their eyes wide with fear and awe. None had expected this outcome. Lucian realized the sisters' reputation must have been great indeed.

"Chosen," Enkius began, his voice steady but softer than usual. "Your victory...it is not what I expected." He gave a bitter chuckle, while his golden eyes held a glint that was not entirely warm. "As you yourself prophesied, I underestimated you, as did the Battle Sisters, who have felled every opponent who's ever dared challenge them." His smile was courteous, but it did not reach his eyes, which flickered momentarily with something else —perhaps a trace of pain, or a spark of deeper calculations. "There is no question. Your command of the Orbs, your resourcefulness in the face of such odds, against my Wardens, has only proven your status as the Chosen of the Manifold." He turned, looking over the remnants of the once-beautiful garden, before continuing. "This battle was meant as a test. I know in my heart now that it was too harsh, and now I must pay the price for my vanity. It would not be the first time. I should never have allowed the fight. That much is clear, but we cannot go backward."

The assembly, their initial shock fading into a murmur of conversation, watched as Enkius approached Lucian. He stood before him, the golden light of morning casting long shadows behind him and offered a bow—a gesture of profound acknowledgment.

"Losing Ninsun and Nanshe is a grave blow to us all, to me personally...but it also serves as a reminder that before the Manifold, we are all like children. Like you, Chosen, we must all be prepared to meet the challenges ahead with as much bravery as you have shown."

Lucian watched him, holding no illusions that he truly meant his words. He still wanted the Orbs for himself. And Enkius would never forgive him for killing Ninsun and Nanshe. They had gone back over two thousand years, to the War of Light and Shadow itself, and who knew how long before that.

He would try to find some other way to gain the Orbs for himself.

At last, Enkius raised his head, looking Lucian in the eye with a challenge of his own. "Let this battle be the last infighting among us. Let us now unite to face greater threats. We must do what we can to help the Chosen reach the Heart of Creation."

The crowd, still processing the gravity of his words, slowly nodded, their earlier reservations giving way to a renewed sense of purpose. Even if Enkius would backstab Lucian at the first opportunity, he at least had his public endorsement. Things could once again proceed toward the original goal.

Lucian's eyes turned to the golden Ethertree. That would be the true test. The battle with the sisters was a mere roadblock. He knew the Ethertree could do as Enkius had said, transforming itself into a ship capable of reaching the Threshold of Creation. If it were not capable, Anlilta herself would have challenged Enkius on the fact.

Enkius faced the assembly. "We go now to the Mishar Gate, and to Kurzagûl itself! This is to give the Chosen the best chance of victory, to draw the eyes of the Shadow so that he can slip past Kurzagûl unnoticed. Perhaps we march to our deaths, but if the Chosen is truly the answer, then perhaps we march to our salvation. Now is the time for courage and brave deeds! Many have fallen during our seemingly endless war, but everything is to be decided soon. Restitution will be made. Just think. Within days, perhaps even hours, the Ancient One will be no more, the Orb of

Shadows forever vanquished from all Creation, the Orbs returned to their rightful place!"

Some Ascendants and Sumaril cheered, but Lucian only steeled himself for the hard road ahead. At the very least, he knew he wouldn't have to face it alone. He had allies in Fergus, Mira, Emma, and now, Anlilta. The coming test would require every ounce of his cunning, strength, and vigilance, not merely the power of the Orbs.

There was a flicker of doubt. Was everything supposed to be happening this way? Was Serah still safe in the Temple of Streams?

He listened as the murmurs of the Ascendants grew into impromptu discussions of strategy. As they gathered and schemed, Lucian motioned to the others to follow him to a secluded corner of the garden, where a stream still ran murky with ash and dust.

They were getting close to the end, though it didn't feel like it. It was time to face that end, whatever came.

31

THEY STOOD TOGETHER, nestled among the Ethertree's roots. The giant tree stood untouched, the only plant spared from the wrath of the recent battle, its branches reaching toward the sky almost defiantly.

As Lucian approached the ancient tree, he could feel its magical force radiating toward him. For centuries, it had grown undisturbed, its ethereal core drawing ether into itself, strengthening its wards to become ever more formidable. If Lucian was found worthy, they could be mere hours from entering the Manifold itself. If not, it could cost everything. Whatever the case, the Ethertree was their next, and final, step on what had already been a terribly long road.

After over three years, Lucian was more than ready to see the end.

Lucian watched as Anlilta glanced backward, probably to see if they were being followed. Apparently, she feared retribution from Enkius, a possibility Lucian could never forget.

Fergus was of a similar mind. "You think he'll come after us?"

Anlilta turned to regard him. "I can't say. His thoughts are too guarded. One thing is certain: Enkius believes the Ethertree to be a more formidable challenge than the sisters."

Mira simply watched the Ethertree, her brown eyes narrowed. "If this thing tries to do anything to my son, I'll finish the job myself."

From her tone, Lucian believed it. "It's time."

The others nodded, ready to follow his lead. As Lucian stepped forward, the Ethertree shimmered, its leaves rustling despite the absence of wind. It wasn't a calming sound; it was almost like the sound of a thousand knives scraping together, or the collective hiss of snakes. It made the hairs on his arms rise. He felt the Tree's Psionic wards reaching out, testing his own shield, but he easily repelled the psychic pressure. He noticed the others lagging, their eyes wide with horror, seeming to see nightmares that weren't there. He extended his shield to protect them as well, and it was as if they were coming out of a dream. They quickly caught up to him.

At last, after climbing a large, gnarled root, Lucian and the others stood at the towering trunk of the tree itself. He placed his hands upon the knotted bark, feeling the pulse of Enkius' magic coursing through the wood.

He closed his eyes. *I'm here. I'm the Chosen. And I will prove myself to you.*

A single word, harsh and discordant, whispered back. *Unworthy.*

He placed his Focus directly on the Ethertree, not pulling any punches. He sought the ethereal core that powered it.

If he could control that, the Ethertree was his to command.

The resistance met his Psionic attack, and it was stiff and brutal. Lucian called upon his inner power, ether roaring through him in a tidal wave, all focused on the Ethertree's core.

But the more power he channeled, the greater the Tree's defenses. Horrifying images flooded his mind, the manifestation of his deepest fears that tested his very sanity. Serah, dead. All of his friends, suffering. The eternal void that would consume everything should he fail.

And the Ancient One's voice in the back of his mind, taunting, his whispers indiscernible but malevolent.

The visions only intensified, as Lucian found it impossible to even break the connection. Instead of him taking hold of the Tree, the Tree was latching onto his Focus, an infestation where brands were taking root and growing. Lucian shirked the ones he could, but it seemed for every one that broke, two more sprouted in its place.

The Tree's voice entered his mind, insidious. *You seek to command me, Chosen? What makes you worthy to alter my course, set by Enkius the Golden himself, made irrevocable by the Magic of Creation? Do you not know how he taught me to treat those who would challenge me?*

Lucian responded, straining to keep his resolve steady. *I am not unworthy. You're the only one who can let me reach the Heart of Creation to return the Orbs. I will take control of you!*

The Tree's presence in his mind grew heavier, its scrutiny more penetrating. *What makes you think that? Have you not noticed that the harder you try, the more my magic pushes back? I know my master's heart, and I sense the power you possess. He would not let you slip away so easily. What makes you stronger than him, more worthy than his ancient commands edified by centuries of magic?*

That was when Lucian recognized the truth. This trial didn't depend on his own strength, but on something else entirely. Something he lacked. The Tree was asking for something more profound than power. Enkius had lied to him, had subtly placed the thought in his mind that Lucian needed to be stronger than even him to subdue it.

He realized there was only one thing he could do to prove his worth, and that wasn't to gather more ether but to give it up entirely and trust that the Tree wouldn't utterly obliterate him.

The Tree wanted him to do the unthinkable.

Yes, it said. *Give them up. It is the only way. Do you dare, Chosen? Or will I cut you down where you stand, betray you to my master?*

I can't do that, Lucian said.

No, you can't, the Ethertree agreed. *But it is the only way you will convince me.*

Lucian opened his eyes, reached for his Focus. He could give up the Orbs with a mere thought. But as soon as their power was loose, Enkius would ambush him, and maybe every other Ascendant who thought they had a shot at getting them.

Perhaps even Anlilta herself, out of a desire to protect them from Enkius.

As Lucian held on, locked in a battle of wills, he felt the Tree's pain, as if every nerve of his body were afire. He screamed, but he couldn't let go. Not until he was dead, or the Tree was his to command.

That was when Lucian felt his mother's presence. From the strength of her stream, he recognized that only her love allowed her to pierce the veil of the Tree's magic.

You will have to go through me first.

The Chosen is mine, interloper. Die.

The Tree's magic switched to assault Mira, a blast of psychic energy that should have instantly killed her. But to Lucian's surprise, he still felt his mother's presence. She was still going strong.

Mom...stay out of this ...

But he could already tell that she wouldn't listen to him. *This is my son. As long as I'm alive, you won't have him.*

There was a thoughtful silence, as if the Tree was considering this.

You are lucky, Chosen. Allow me to speak to her. Perhaps something can be arranged.

No, Lucian said. *I won't let you have her.*

Lucian, listen to me, his mother said. *We've come too far for you to die here. If someone has to die for this, let it be me. Too much is riding on this. Just do what you're supposed to do. What I raised you to do. Help others. And don't get in the way of me trying to help in the best way I can.*

Mom ...

I'm your mother. I will protect you, and that's the end.

Just let me fight it a little longer.

You know that won't work. You can't see it, but Enkius and all the rest are waiting. We will lose everything.

The Tree's foul voice returned. *My patience wears thin ...*

Go, Lucian. I will be with you. Always.

With surprising strength, her Psionic Magic pushed him out. The Tree let loose of him, sending him sprawling back on the root. He scrambled up to see his mother touching the tree, surrounded by a Psionic aura.

"Mom!"

He ran forward, but as soon as he reached out with his magic, he was instantly repulsed and thrown back. The magic was powerful, something higher than even his own. It was magic created with sorcery, intertwined with a mother's love.

Even Lucian couldn't come between that.

"Mom!" he said, tears coming to his eyes. "I didn't want this! There's still a chance ..."

His mother was deaf to his pleas, facing the tree with her eyes closed, completely locked in. She was smiling.

Fergus stepped up beside him. "What's going on? Mira, what are you doing?"

When no answer came, he retracted his spear, and with a roar, charged forward. Emma tethered him, keeping him back.

"You can't, Fergus," she said. "It's the only way."

"It'll kill her!" he shouted. "And we all stand here, doing nothing?"

Anlilta came to stand beside him. "The Ethertree...has accepted a trade. It wanted something from you, Lucian. Some-thing precious. Just as Enkius gave up something precious to imbue the Tree with his magic. He...sacrificed someone he loved." Her eyes sprang forth with tears. "I can feel her here now ..."

"Who?" Emma asked.

Anlilta watched, her face pale. "Our daughter disappeared centuries ago, around the time this Tree would have been planted." She lowered her face. "Even I didn't realize the extent of his evil ..."

Over the next minute, the magic around Mira shifted from violet to the golden light of Creation. Lucian watched, tears in his eyes. Any of his attempts to connect to the Tree were rebuffed. He'd never felt so powerless.

After another moment, the Ethertree glowed softly from root to canopy, its leaves whispering not with hostility, as before, but seemingly in approval. Below the Tree, in the wasted garden, Lucian saw the crowd of gathered Ascendants, foremost among them Enkius himself. Enkius' face was inscrutable, and even if things were not going according to plan, he didn't dare attack Lucian directly, especially when backed up by Anlilta and his friends.

The Golden Ascendant was waiting for a new opportunity, waiting to see how the dice fell.

The golden aura surrounding Mira suddenly intensified, to where she was no longer visible. A blinding light shone, a light that could hardly be dimmed by Lucian's Radiant Magic.

But it only lasted an instant. Within seconds, the Ethertree had returned to its original luster.

And where Mira had once stood now was only empty space.

"No!" Fergus shouted.

Lucian's heart lurched. His worst fears had been realized. He could fight as hard as he wanted, but his weakness was always the ones he was trying to protect.

And now his mother was gone. He could only watch, horrified at the display.

"The Tree has accepted her," Anlilta said, her voice filled with wonder.

"And what's that supposed to mean?" Fergus demanded. "Where is she? What's happened?"

Emma's face was pale. "Is she ...?"

"Dead?" Anlilta shook her head. "No. She has become something else. Something, perhaps, only a mother's love could survive."

"How's that supposed to explain anything?" Fergus shouted. He looked at Lucian, his expression one of betrayal. "First, you risked her in the fight with Ninshar, and now you let her die? Your own mother? How could you?"

"Fergus ..." Emma said. "Please ..."

All Lucian felt was numbness. He had tried to save her. Had tried to break the connection.

"She wouldn't let me. Her magic...it was powerful enough to stop me."

Fergus looked at him in disbelief. "But you're the Chosen, Lucian. Nothing is stronger than you!"

"*She* was," Anlilta said. "And she still is."

Fergus sputtered for a moment, his face a mask of anger and grief. He then glared up at the Tree before realizing it was probably no longer the Tree itself he was looking at.

Mira, whatever was left of her, was in there. A part of it. Perhaps even the whole.

And if that was true, maybe Lucian could communicate with her.

He reached out for the Tree, finding it no longer hostile, but accepting. In fact ...

It's me, son. There isn't much time.

Mom? Mom, just tell me how I can get you out of there.

Never mind that. Hurry!

At that very moment, the bark of the tree shone with intense golden light, forming an entry point. A portal.

It was at that moment that Lucian sensed a shift behind him. Enkius was approaching, his golden spear flashing with menace. And not only him, but Nabukar and all the Ascendants and sorcerers in his retinue. His ploy had failed. He had not counted on Mira's magic being the thing to overcome his creation.

If he wanted to secure the Orbs, he had to do so himself. And quickly.

Anlilta shifted, placing herself between the humans and the oncoming Ascendants. "Go. I'll hold them off. Long enough, perhaps, for you to escape this world and head for the Heart."

Lucian didn't know how Anlilta could stand against so many until he realized she *couldn't*. At best, her sacrifice would only buy them seconds.

But this was the cause toward which Anlilta had dedicated her existence. She would never see all her preparations come undone, even if it meant she died.

Already, she was streaming powerful shields, doing everything to cover their escape. She created a vast wall of magic, almost as powerful as something Lucian would have done. The Ethertree, now under Mira's guidance, was shimmering with a new, reddish light, its branches slowly altering their reach, pointing toward the sky.

It only awaited its passengers.

"Come on," Lucian said. "We have to go!"

They rushed inside the Tree just as it came under heavy assault. Lucian's last view as the portal closed was of Anlilta, surrounded by a bubble of protective magic that could break at any moment.

They found themselves in a small chamber, at the center of which was a brilliant red stone shining with inner luminescence. From that stone, what Lucian knew to be the Tree's ethereal core, he could feel his mother's presence.

Whatever was left of her was in that stone. Her mind was alive, though her body was gone.

Before he could do or say anything, the floor, composed of living wood, shifted beneath his feet. Already, Lucian could sense the Tree's roots unfurling as it loosed itself from the ground beneath. The Tree was rocked several times by the impact of some powerful magical attack, but its inner defenses were strong.

Strong enough, perhaps, to lift off this world and get them out of range.

Lucian surrounded Emma and Fergus with an aura of Gravitonic Magic to counteract the G-forces, which were powerful enough to throw them around the inner chamber with reckless abandon. Lucian couldn't see anything that was happening outside. He just had to trust that his mother would get them to safety, into the Void above.

And from there, surviving the Ethereal Rip long enough to pass the Threshold of Creation.

32

ALL WAS silent in the Tree's inner chamber. Everyone watched as the red ethereal core thrummed with latent power. Lucian surveyed his crew. Emma was watching the core, her expression haunted, while Fergus simply looked numb. Lucian could feel the Tree's movements through the Gravitonic aura, always increasing in speed. By now, Anlilta was dead or subdued, but there were no more attacks.

The core brightened for a moment, and Lucian felt something—no, *someone*—trying to connect to him.

Mom?

Don't worry. They've got nothing on me.

Lucian heard Fergus's voice in his mind next. *Mira. You didn't have to—*

—But I did, Fergus. There was no other way forward. And I would do it a thousand times if it meant we got to finish this out.

Fergus hung his head. *You're...not wrong. It should've been me ...*

You're still arguing? Where we're going, bodies won't matter much anymore.

At this, Fergus said nothing.

After a couple of minutes of silence, Mira spoke again. *I think I have this ship figured out. It's kind of...exhilarating, to be honest. Do you want to see what I see?*

Before Lucian could respond, he could suddenly see outside the Tree, not by using his own eyes, but by experiencing what Mira could experience. He could look in any direction outside the Ethertree. There was no fiery trail, as might have been expected. The Tree used no fuel other than its latent magic, provided by the ethereal core Mira now controlled. Several golden lights followed below them, what Lucian assumed were a few Ascendants giving chase at Enkius' orders. They were too far to hurt them, and the Tree was far too fast. The surrounding sky was going dark. For the first time, they would enter the Void of the Light Realm.

The Tree itself was surrounded by a golden aura as the last of Tiamatia's thin upper atmosphere was replaced by the Void. Despite that, the Ethertree flew on. In the far distance was a dark planet, what had to be Kurzagûl. It was a world of blacks and browns, hosting several enormous inland seas. But that was not where they were bound. The Tree made a turn on a trajectory that would take them past the planet. The Seven-Fold Path stretched before the ship, and Mira's direction was true. Perhaps she herself could sense where they needed to go.

That path would take them dangerously close to Kurzagûl. Lucian could only hope that the Shadow World was distracted by the commotion on Tiamatia.

Instead, Lucian turned his focus to the cosmos outside, a cosmos just as beautiful as his own. There were stars, galaxies, and nebulae, their colors bright and many. But where they were heading, there were no stars, only the prismatic Seven-Fold Path leading into an endless black nothing.

And somewhere in that nothing, or perhaps even beyond it, was the Threshold of Creation.

"We'll be there soon," Lucian said.

Fergus remained quiet, kneeling in grief, unable to respond.

A quiet silence followed, Lucian's mother no longer trying to talk to them, but concentrating on guiding the ship on its one-way journey. After what Lucian guessed to be an hour, Fergus heaved a sigh.

"She's gone," he said. "And don't tell me that's her now." He nodded toward the ethereal core. "She'll never be herself again. Some things you just don't come back from."

Lucian was quiet, not really sure what to say.

Emma watched the ethereal core. "Don't be so sure. We'll all be joining her soon."

"Assuming we survive the Ethereal Rip."

"Either way," Emma continued, "we'll all be a part of the Manifold. Maybe dying is a part of it."

Lucian knew they couldn't just die. Or at least, *he* couldn't. He had to survive long enough to make it past the Threshold with the Orbs in his Focus, or else they would be lost forever in the Void.

"No one is dying," he said. "After fighting together for years...this isn't the way we're going to go out."

"I know," Emma said. "I wonder what it'll be like in there. Being alive, but not a part of the Manifold. Does it mean we can leave?"

Lucian didn't know. He hoped so. Because if he couldn't leave, that meant never seeing Serah again. She would be stranded in this reality.

"If there isn't a way back, I'll make one."

Fergus looked at the core, his face taking on a look of concentration. He and Mira were having some sort of conversation, a conversation Lucian and Emma wouldn't be joining.

Emma instead looked over at him. "How are you holding up?"

"I'm not sure. I'm just going to do whatever it takes to finish this out."

Emma nodded. "Same here. Who would have thought we'd

end up here after hopping on the same ship to Volsung? Now we find ourselves on a ship of a different kind."

That was putting it lightly. "There's no doubt in my mind. We're going home again. Serah will be all right. We'll put everything to rest. Magic—*real magic*—is about belief. And my belief in that is unshakable."

He reached out to the ethereal core to get a view of the surrounding cosmos. He was surprised to see that Kurzagûl was far behind them, having been none the wiser to their passage. He intrinsically knew Mira had used the Tree's magic to elude detection. Or perhaps the action on Tiamatia was drawing the eye of the leaders there.

Whatever the case, there was nothing left but to survive the rest of the journey.

————

HOURS PASSED. It was utterly silent, and everyone had fallen asleep. Lucian woke up to find that the Ethertree was vibrating. Fergus and Emma also roused at the disturbance.

Lucian reached out for his mother, only to find that she was quiet. When he expanded his view to take in the Tree's vision, he found the multicolored Path was still resolutely going forward. However, all the stars and planets had gone dark. There was only an endless void of black, and within that void, a shimmering veil of light toward which they flew.

It could be none other than the Threshold of Creation. If they could get past that, they would be inside the Manifold itself.

The Tree shook even more. Multicolored motes began dancing in the air before him like fireflies. Lucian recognized it for what it was. Ether was so thick that it was manifesting before his eyes. Many of those motes were drawn to the ethereal core that contained Mira's Focus, which in turn redirected their power into the Tree.

But the raw ether was also interfering with the ship's magic, making it behave erratically. And the vibration of the ship was becoming strong enough to be considered shaking. Lucian felt himself jerked to the side of the chamber.

"Hold on," he said.

Lucian reached out, using Creation Magic to create a bubble large enough to encapsulate the ship. As he strained to hold it, immediately the Tree stopped shaking and sped up as resistance against it was taken away. This worked fine for a time, but the closer they got to their goal, the more interference the shield met.

And it was not a slow and steady increase; it was practically exponential. Lucian's shield buckled, and he was forced to stream ever more powerfully, completely abandoning his conscious mind to join the Ether that surrounded him. Trying to force the Ethertree through was like trying to push against a repelling magnet. If his concentration slipped, even for a moment, the unbalanced forces would be enough to obliterate the ship and everyone on it.

Now he understood why this part was called the Ethereal Rip.

Just a minute longer, son, Mira said. *You can do it. Remember your why, and the how will take care of itself.*

Lucian was crying from the pain, but he held. He was a lone bulwark against the current turned tsunami, and he had to remain standing. The power of the Ethereal Rip only increased as time continued on. How much longer could it be? How much longer could he hold?

He was surprised to see that he was no longer on the ship but standing in the middle of the Seven-Fold Path. The light of the Path roared through him, pushing ever harder as he advanced forward. Of the Ethertree, of his friends, of his mother, there was no sign.

That was when a familiar presence joined him at his side, joining with his repelling stream. "I'm here, son," she said. "I got the ship as far as I could. The rest is up to us."

He wondered how they were even breathing until he realized some questions were pointless in this place. They were in the Threshold now, the last test before they reached the Heart.

Next came Emma, who stood on his other side, and Fergus, who stood next to Mira. They joined shields, and with their help, the load was lightened, though Lucian still endured most of it.

"We've got this," Fergus said. "From the Rifts of Psyche to The Heart of Creation. It's been an honor and a pleasure."

Emma took on a look of extreme concentration to where Lucian thought she would remain silent, but she surprised him by speaking. "Remember who you are, Lucian. The rest will fall into place."

Lucian wanted to say something back, but the forces stacked against him were too great. He became blind to thought as the pressure skyrocketed. This was the final push.

He screamed as the light obliterated him, as he clung to his Focus and the Orbs they contained. He reached for his pack, drawing out the Orb of Shadows in one last effort, just in time before his pack came loose from his body, carried away by the unreal forces around him. The Orb before him, still wrapped in its Binding brand, seemed to drink in the surrounding light.

He had to make it. There was no other option.

Almost as soon as he was at the end of his strength, the crucible of the Threshold was over. He stood alone, not sure if he was dead or alive. But when he reached for his Focus, he found that Nine of the Ten Orbs were there, while he still held the Orb of Shadows in his left hand.

He stood on a plane of white that stretched in all directions. The Seven-Fold Path continued on, leading across that plane into the seemingly infinite distance.

There was nothing left but to follow the Path. It would lead him to where he needed to go.

33

AS HE WALKED, his speed seemed to increase, each step large enough to take him over the distant horizon. Distances didn't seem to matter here, only intention.

He was alone, with no sign of the others. He didn't believe them to be dead, only...waiting. Waiting for what, he didn't know. He just knew they'd show up when the time was right.

He walked like that for hours, perhaps even days, the Seven-Fold Path never breaking. It became meditative almost. Lucian didn't worry about never reaching his goal. He knew the Manifold would lead him to where he was supposed to be.

At last, the bland monotony was broken, and in the distance stood a perfectly round altar, made from light itself, but still having a solid look to it. And along the circumference of that altar were seven pedestals of equal size.

Lucian knew that this was it. The Heart of Creation from which all reality had sprung forth.

He knew he should feel awe, but all he felt was a need to hurry. He was climbing the stairs within moments, finding himself in the very center of it all. He held nine Orbs in his Focus and the final one in his hands, yet there were only slots to return the original seven. What happened once he returned the seven, with only Space-Time, Creation, and Shadow left?

There was only one way to find out.

Lucian looked around to make sure he was truly alone before reaching out for the Manifold. Was the answer as obvious as simply returning the Orbs, like he'd planned on doing? Indeed, with the way things were laid out, that seemed to be the only option before him.

It felt too simple. Where was the Ancient One? Why was he not challenging him yet?

Or was the Ancient One simply waiting until the Orbs were returned, banking on the fact that Lucian would be weaker without them? Perhaps the right move was to look for the Ancient One first, defeat him, and *then* return the Orbs.

But this felt wrong, too. If the Ancient One wanted to be found, he would have allowed it by now. It was at this point that Lucian remembered his lessons from Lakhmu.

His power didn't come from the Orbs but from his truth. As long as he held onto that truth, he could face anything, even if he no longer held the Orbs.

Despite knowing this, it was a struggle as he walked to the first pedestal, that of Thermalism. The ethereal pedestal gave off a latent, molten glow. All he had to do was will the Orb into his hand, and it would leave his Focus and click into place. It was a simple thing.

But nothing was more difficult. He struggled with the idea of it, made worse because he knew the Ancient One could show up at any minute. Lucian was confident in his abilities, to where it felt as if nothing could touch him. Even in his duel with the Golden Wardens, he had felt assured of his victory.

So why the hesitation now? Perhaps the last battle was to be more with himself than any outside threat.

In the end, he resolved he had to do what they'd set out to do, otherwise everything would have been for nothing. Once this was done, once the Ancient One was defeated, wherever he might be lurking, he could leave this place and get Serah. Whether they could go back to the Shadow Realm didn't matter as long as he had her.

Lucian let out a breath, reached for his Focus, and willed the Orb to come loose. Red lines appeared from his sternum, spreading down his arm and coalescing into a fiery red sphere. The entire process took about half a minute. In his left hand, he held the Orb of Thermalism, in his right, the still-bound Orb of Shadows. As soon as the Orb of Thermalism was fully formed, its ruby-red light glowed, and he felt a hidden force pulling it toward the pedestal almost like a magnet.

Lucian let it go, and the Orb snapped into place almost instantly, letting out a low, ethereal hum. A band of red light shot outward, causing him to step back. The pedestal now shone with brilliant red light, that light gathering from the Orb itself to form a solid line of the same color toward the center of the altar.

Lucian felt an emptiness emanating from where the Orb should have been, but he couldn't focus on that. He had to finish the job.

Looking around, the surrounding field of white had some-what dimmed, as if the Manifold itself were shrinking in response to the return of the Orb. Nothing was out there watching him. Nothing that he could sense, anyway.

Lucian proceeded around the entire altar, going through each of the Orbs in order in a clockwise fashion: Atomicism, Dynamism, and then Radiance, doing each as quickly as he could. Each time, the pedestal shifted to that Orb's color and shot its own-colored line at the same point right in the center, about three meters above Lucian's head.

The sense of emptiness grew with each Orb lost. He checked his surroundings, finding he was still alone. Outside the altar, the environment was substantially darker than before, the equivalent of twilight.

He did the next three: Binding, Psionics, and Gravitonics. Each Orb returned made the floating sphere in the center shine even brighter. By the time Gravitonics was returned, the altar was an island in a sea of pure darkness.

Lucian stood back, watching all seven streams of light joining in the center. And from this joined light, three more lights shot out, forming three new pedestals in the center of the altar.

So, the original Seven were required before the other three formed.

Lucian hurried it up, going first for the pedestal of Shadow. It would be nice to get this one off his hands, and if it was put on the pedestal, the Ancient One would have to defeat him first before he could access it.

It was a simple matter of putting it there, and suddenly, it was gone, the burden released.

The light in the surrounding environment suddenly brightened. Lucian couldn't guess what was going on and instead turned to where the Orb of Space-Time was supposed to go.

Releasing this Orb from his Focus was far more difficult. He strained, hardly able to give up his power. In the back of his mind, he had doubts. If he gave up these three Orbs, would it immediately close the First Gate, cutting off the Shadow Realm from magic?

He stopped trying to give up the Orb. He needed answers first.

He looked around the altar, but of course, there was no one visible

At last, he shouted, "Manifold! I'm here. We need to talk."

As soon as these words left his mouth, the outline of a body appeared in the surrounding twilight. Lucian stepped back, willing Lightspear into his hand. But the being who materialized from the darkness was the last one Lucian had expected.

It was Enkius. His form loomed over Lucian, over two meters

in height, while his blue skin gave off a golden glow. His cape floated behind him, and for now, he bore no weapon.

But Lucian knew he was here for one reason, and one reason only. To take back what he saw as rightfully his.

The Ascendant flashed a predatory smile as he surveyed the scene before him—the altar, the shimmering Orbs, and Lucian himself.

While Lucian stood strong, in the back of his mind, he couldn't help but worry that he would be weaker now. Giving them up had taken more power than he would have ever thought, and he was strained by the ordeal. Still, he glared at Enkius, matching his stare with his own.

He'd die before this one got the Orbs.

"Chosen," Enkius began, his voice smooth and controlled. "I must commend you for making it this far. Truly, you are one of us, an equal. I see now I underestimated your resolve." His smile stretched wider. "No doubt you are wondering where your friends are. Unfortunately, they were not as strong as you. They have become one with the Manifold. It is a mercy. They no longer know struggle or strife. There is only peace, the peace which comes for all mortals."

"You killed them," Lucian said.

"No, Chosen," Enkius said, barely able to keep the taunt out of his voice. "You did when you brought them here. They were too weak to survive in this place. But aren't their lives a small price to pay for what you hope to achieve?"

"You're mocking me at a time like this?"

"On the contrary. I am congratulating you. Your tenacity is...admirable." He paused, his golden eyes flitting to the two empty pedestals that remained. "But it seems you are missing something crucial."

"How did you get here?"

"Me?" he asked innocently. "It wasn't difficult. You yourself provided the means. Or rather, your mother did. Mira, was it?"

"You were on the Tree?"

"Of course I was. The same shield you conjured to protect the ship also protected me. For that, I thank you. The rest of the Ascendants? I sent them to the Mishar Gate to die. It provided an adequate distraction for the denizens of Kurzagûl, allowing us to slip by undetected. See, Chosen? I have made a noble sacrifice, too. A sacrifice that demands recompense."

"I guess you killed Anlilta, too."

Enkius merely gave a mad smile, allowing Lucian to imagine the possibilities.

"You're not getting anything," Lucian said.

"That shall soon be decided. Did you actually believe I'd let you get away when my treasures were so close? You possess the Orb of Space-Time. Embedded within is the soul of Nathi himself. And then there is the Orb of Creation, to which my soul is bound. Neither Orb is yours, and that you hold them now is a sacrilege beyond words. I had to stop you before you returned them. It will be much easier to wrest them from you than the Manifold."

Lucian tightened his grip on Lightspear, unsure if its magic could be used against Enkius. If it couldn't, then Lucian had no way of defeating him.

There would be no way of finding out until he tried; in the end, the Orb of Creation would have to choose which person to follow.

Enkius seemed to read his thoughts. "You think the Orbs will obey you, weak as you are? Fortunately for you, this is not a fight I want. I want you to recognize me for what I am, the ruler of all the Light Realm! I am your better. Hand the Orbs of Creation and Space-Time to me, Lucian, and you can fight by my side as my chief lieutenant. We can purge the Aetheria of the Shadow, and then can we see about saving your reality."

"I'm finishing what I started, Enkius. I'm returning the Orbs.

That includes the two I still have. If you try to stop me, then I will destroy you."

Enkius chuckled softly, stepping closer, his presence oppressive. "How can you possibly be made to understand, Shadow Being? Those Orbs belong to me in ways you can never understand. They contain my thoughts and memories, and those of my beloved Nathi. Perhaps, with the Manifold's blessing, Nathi might even be brought back."

"I'm sorry for what you lost," Lucian said. "But even if it's possible, the Nathi you would bring back is not the same one who left the Light Realm."

"Is magic so limited to you, Lucian? Have you ever loved? What wouldn't you do to save your loved one, to not be alone in the universe? I would do anything, Chosen. I would become anything." His voice turned colder, the smile fading into a grim line. "That you can't be made to see that is...disappointing."

Lucian's stance hardened. "The Manifold intends for these Orbs to be returned, Enkius. As powerful as you are, don't forget where that power comes from. I could lose every Orb, and if I'm the only one standing up for the Manifold, then the Manifold will strengthen me and weaken you. The Orbs were never meant to be held by anyone, except for the one returning them. The one who remembers that purpose is the one who will be given power."

Enkius sighed, his expression shifting to one of mock sorrow. "The fate of the Orbs is not set in stone, as you deem. Why else would the Manifold want them returned so quickly? Isthelah himself realized that. The balance they bring, the power they hold...it could rebuild the Light Realm. It could build anything the holder desires. Do you not see? By giving up that power, you are sealing your doom."

"That's not your decision to make," Lucian said.

"How could you understand my loss, made more potent over two thousand years? Each year that passes, the poison becomes more concentrated, infecting every fiber of my being. The only antidote is Nathi. And you are the only one standing in the way of that dream. There is no going back now. Perhaps I'm wrong, but I cannot deny what I want. Even if it means everything else burns."

For a moment, the air between them crackled, charged with the tension of their standoff. Then, without warning, Enkius' demeanor shifted, his face hardening as the surrounding air shimmered with raw ethereal power.

"You say the Manifold will make me weak, sensing my so-called ill intent," he said, his voice booming around the ethereal landscape. "I say my will is strong enough to withstand the coming storm! Even if I'm fighting the Manifold itself, I cannot let you proceed, Chosen. Not unless you relinquish your Orbs to me."

With a swift motion, Enkius summoned his own spear, imbued with a radiant light that seemed to draw the very ether toward it. It was as bright as Lucian's own, the same golden color, the same strength as Lightspear itself. In this place, there was no need to wait ten million years to create it.

Lucian braced himself for battle.

34

ENKIUS MADE THE FIRST MOVE, his spear a blur as it sliced through the air toward Lucian. Without even a thought, Lucian slowed time around him and sidestepped, all while moving Lightspear to meet the Ascendant's weapon with a clash that sent ripples of light across the surrounding ethereal plane.

Controlling time had been easy enough. Lucian recognized Enkius' warning that his magic wouldn't obey him for what it was: a lie.

He was the master of his own reality. He was the Sorcerer-Ascendant, trained by Lakhmu, forged by trial, tested by the Manifold unceasingly. Everything he was had been built for this moment, and he would rise to the occasion.

Lucian retaliated with a surge of Psionic energy, aiming to disrupt Enkius' thoughts. The attack was no less powerful in the Orbs' absence. In fact, it was even more powerful, the surrounding space shimmering violet.

But despite this power, Enkius easily countered with his own shield before letting out a derisive laugh. "Is that all, Chosen? You'll have to do better."

Refusing to be goaded into recklessness, Lucian circled Enkius, his mind racing. He attempted to reach for the Orb of Creation, but it was only here that he met resistance. Unlike the Orb of Space-Time, it was still fully loyal to its original master, its magic blocked to him.

Enkius laughed again, seeming to sense Lucian's failure. He advanced once again, a complex tapestry of magic and physical prowess. He launched a series of rapid thrusts that Lucian barely parried.

"See the futility, Chosen?" Enkius taunted, his spear dancing dangerously close. "You are a usurper. The Orbs know their true master! They will betray you unless you submit now."

Lucian ducked under a vicious swing and rolled away, creating distance. He weaved a quick stream that distorted the area around Enkius, slowing his movements. His figure blurred, caught in a temporal loop, but the effect was fleeting. Enkius broke through with sheer force of will, his determination rendering the stream ineffective sooner than Lucian had hoped.

"You underestimate my connection to these Orbs, Chosen!" Enkius roared, his form stabilizing as he charged again, spear aimed with lethal precision.

Lucian realized brute force would not suffice and shifted tactics. He reached beyond himself, trusting his connection to the Manifold. The thick ether surrounding him responded, moving away from Enkius and infusing into his Focus. Lightspear glowed brighter, pulsating with pure Creation Magic.

Magic that could be directed to destroy Enkius, if it ever broke his defenses, for the magic was now obeying Lucian.

Enkius watched in dismay, but then in rage. "You twist my magic against me?"

"The magic is not yours," Lucian said. "It belongs to the Manifold."

Enkius roared, shooting forward like a thunderbolt, but

Lucian swung Lightspear in a wide arc, unleashing a powerful barrier with the very magic the Manifold had gifted him.

But such was Enkius' will and power that he smashed through it like a meteor, knocking Lucian back. As Lucian landed lightly on his feet, Enkius looked dazed, as if the effort had cost him a moment's concentration. Seizing the opportunity, Lucian streamed Gravitonics, pulling Enkius down with sudden force. The Ascendant faltered, his spear driving into the ground to steady his form.

Lucian didn't pause his attack. He combined Radiance and Atomicism, creating a dazzling array of blinding lights around Enkius. Under this cover, he warped behind him, Lightspear charged with a potent mix of Psionics and Radiance. He struck, targeting the mental barriers that kept the Ascendant's Focus safe.

The spear connected, and for a moment, Enkius' defenses wavered, his concentration breaking under the onslaught of light and mental pressure.

Lucian pushed forward. "It doesn't have to be this way, Enkius. The Manifold's strength is with me. Even you can see that now!"

Enkius staggered, his defenses crumbling, but his resolve hardened. "No, Chosen. I've come too far to yield!"

As Enkius roared his defiance, he gave a sudden burst of magic, breaking loose of Lucian's mental hold while creating distance. As he breathed heavily, Lucian sensed his desperation. All he needed was a bit more time to get the Ascendant to break.

Once again, he reached directly for the Manifold, infusing its willing energy directly into Lightspear, which shone with a bright, piercing light that seemed alive with its own intent. His connection to the Manifold, with no barrier or adulteration in between, gave him a bond to everything around him, as if he could see things through a new dimension. As if he had only to will something, and it would come to pass.

Enkius lunged forward, his spear cutting an arc of searing light aimed directly at Lucian. The air hissed as ether swirled around his spear. He moved in slow motion, time itself slowing to where the Ascendant was moving at a crawl, his face twisted in a grotesque display of aggression and desperation.

Lucian leaped high into the air at normal speed, even as Enkius was completely slowed. He twisted in mid-air, summoning a gravitational vortex that carried Enkius up toward him.

Lucian extended his hand, unleashing a torrent of Radiant Magic combined with Psionics. As in the duel with Ninsun and Nanshe, he created illusions of himself that multiplied around Enkius. The field was crowded with dozens of Lucians, but none of the illusions distracted the Ascendant, as they had Ninsun and Nanshe. Enkius' eyes remained on him alone.

"Clever tricks won't save you, Chosen!" he bellowed, his voice echoing in the ethereal landscape. "You think I can't feel the Orb of Creation dying to be free of your clutches?"

But Lucian was not just trying to trick him; he was studying his patterns, looking for the perfect moment to strike and end it. Powered by the Manifold, it was as if Enkius' every future move was telegraphed with perfect clarity.

When Lucian saw the opening, he had no time to second-guess. He emerged from behind one of his own illusions, using Space-Time to close the distance in less than an eye blink, his spear poised for the kill.

Enkius reacted instinctively, his spear coming up to meet Lucian's. The clash was explosive, sending waves of energy rippling across the ethereal plane.

With the force of their collision, Lucian manipulated the gravitational pull around Enkius, making his spear incredibly heavy. Enkius' grip faltered, his spear clattering to the ground.

Enkius threw out his hand, attempting to push Lucian away

with Psionics, but he had expected that. Using Radiant Magic, he reflected the stream, sending Enkius hurtling back.

Now was his chance. With a primal shout, Lucian laced Lightspear with Psionic Magic, throwing everything into the attack. He shot forward, a mix of Psionic and Space-Time piercing the veil of Enkius' mind, closing over his Focus.

Enkius' golden eyes widened as he realized what had happened. His mind thrashed to be let loose, but Lucian continued to stream, strengthening the barrier around Enkius' Focus with the power of the Manifold itself.

He was completely at Lucian's mercy. He held Lightspear within an inch of Enkius' throat.

"Yield, Enkius." His voice was steady, despite the pounding of his heart. "You've lost, and if you think Lightspear won't destroy you because it's made from Creation Magic, you're wrong. The Manifold has chosen the winner of this battle."

Breathing heavily, Enkius met his gaze, his expression a complex mask of recognition and reluctant respect.

"You...are truly the Chosen," he admitted, defeat clear in his tone. "You bested me without the benefit of the Seven Orbs. Perhaps...perhaps it is better this way. That I die now rather than be without hope."

"Are you going to attack me if I let you go?"

"Why would you punish me so? Destroy me, Chosen, and it would be a mercy. I have nothing, even if I were to escape this place. I risked everything for a chance to gather the Orbs, to recreate reality as I saw fit. To have Nathi again. But there is no hope for that now. None. Take that spear of yours and finish the job. Whatever future you're fighting for, I want no part of it."

Lucian realized then that he had to finish the job. He knew Enkius' every thought, and if he let him go, the Ascendant would just keep attacking him forever until Lucian finished the job.

Enkius was right. Doing that much would be a mercy.

"I want peace, Chosen. Can you grant it to me?"

Lucian watched the Ascendant for a moment, nodded, and finished the job.

It was a clean death. In an instant, Enkius the Golden was no more, his body and Focus absorbed by the surrounding ether.

35

ALL WAS quiet as Lucian contemplated his next move.

Part of him was tempted to relinquish his two remaining Orbs right away, but he didn't want to do so until he was completely sure he could secure the safety of the Shadow Realm.

Then there was the question of the Ancient One. Where was he? Was he lurking in the shadows, just as Enkius had been?

"Manifold!" he called. "You have chosen me, and I'm almost done with what you've asked. But there's no point in me doing this if I can't guarantee the safety of the Shadow Realm."

Silence was his only answer. Nothing would happen until he'd given up what remained. Otherwise, he'd be standing here for all eternity.

"Nothing?" he called out. "If you won't talk to me willingly, I'm going to force you to talk."

He went to the Pedestal of Shadows and retrieved the Orb, quickly wrapping it in a Binding brand. As soon as he did so, the environment beyond the altar darkened completely.

Next, he went to grab the Orb of Gravitonics. If the Manifold wouldn't get him what he wanted, he could return the favor.

When he was about to grab the Orb of Gravitonics, an ethereal voice seemed to come from everywhere at once. "Return the Orbs. You are so close to restoring the proper balance."

"So, you are listening. I won't return them until you guarantee the safety of my reality. Where is the Ancient One?"

"He cannot be destroyed unless his Orb is destroyed," the Manifold said. "Already, you have returned the Seven. These three that you still hold are gifts given to my children. They, too, must be returned. They are too powerful, too destructive for anyone to keep. You have done well to come this far, Chosen. Now finish your appointed task."

"Why did you choose me?" Lucian asked, unable to keep the frustration out of his voice. "And why would I finish my task when I came all this way to save my people? Why? How does it make sense?"

"I chose you because I know all. You were the only one who would finish the job properly. There is only one way to do it that risks nothing. It is time to finish things."

"What about my friends? What about my mom?"

"They sacrificed themselves nobly for this goal. Just as you must. That is what it means to be Chosen."

Lucian then realized the truth: he was stuck here forever until he decided it was time to return the Orbs. And as soon as he did so, he would be erased. The First Gate would close, while the Light Realm and Shadow Realms would be separated forever. The Gates would go offline. Humanity would survive, but not before millions, if not billions, of people died. And Serah would be isolated in the Light Realm, the only one of them that would remain, as soon as the power of Shadow Magic waned.

The Seven Aspects would remain, while the three Greater Aspects—those created for Enkius, Nathi, and Isthelah—would be destroyed.

"This isn't acceptable to me," Lucian said. "I refuse to return the Orbs unless I get some sort of guarantee. I want my friends to live. I don't want Serah to be alone. And I don't want billions to die! This is not what I fought and sacrificed for!"

"But it is," the Manifold answered. "I know it is difficult for you. But it is the only way."

"You already know what I'm going to decide," Lucian said. "So, what's the point of this conversation?"

"I do," the Manifold answered sorrowfully. "Which is why I must ask you to do what is against your instincts. It means sacrificing everyone, everything you know and love for the greater good. Because of your actions, countless beings and their descendants will sing your praises for all eternity. You will be remembered as the savior of the Light Realm. In the Shadow Realm, you will pass out of all memory. It is the best possible future for them. Magic was never meant for your kind, but life there will go on. You are the only one with the power to do this. The power to save both realities. That is why I chose you."

"I refuse. Why can't you just save the Shadow Realm? Why not just let us exist, let us at least have the Gates? I'm not asking for much here."

"The risk is too great. Your kind, like the Ascendants, has a penchant for war. While the Ascendants can't cross into the Shadow Realm without becoming *Alkasen*, it is not the same for your kind. Humans can pass into the Light Realm. It's only a matter of time before there is war between the two sides, as humanity covets the power and glory enjoyed by the Ascendants. After Enkius' actions, the Light Realm will be weakened. Since time passes more swiftly in the Light Realm than the Shadow, the Shadow Realm will have more chance to marshal endless waves of attacks. Despite the Ascendants' power, they cannot hope to stand against it forever."

Sadly, Lucian could see this as a future possibility. "Then we'll guard the First Gate. Allow magic to pass, but nothing else."

"What can be forged can also be broken," the Manifold said. "With enough time and persistence, any barrier you create will be destroyed, especially once you die. The rest of your life, should I agree to your demands, will not even be the blink of an eye in the greater scheme. The Ascendants, for all their flaws and vices, are my children. I will not see them come to harm. And I will do my utmost to defend them."

"I should've never returned the Orbs," Lucian said. "I should have kept them!"

"It was never your fate to keep them, Lucian. If you had, then I would die. And with my death would come the death of the Light Realm, and by extension, the Shadow Realm."

Lucian hung his head, feeling his failure. Where had he gone wrong? What could he have done differently?

Seemingly, there was no way out except to do what the Manifold said.

Except, deep down, he knew there *was* another way out.

The Orb of Shadows created alternate realities and rules that even the Manifold couldn't be privy to. If there was a future where he saved the Shadow Realm by embracing the Orb of Shadows, it was a future the Manifold would be blind to.

Paradoxically, he realized that assuming the Aspect of Shadow was the only viable future where he got everything he wanted, everything he was fighting for.

But the risks were incalculable. Did he dare to even consider it? Should he settle for less?

His eyes went to the Orb of Shadows, still in his stand, yet to be absorbed. He remembered the Time Weaver's warning that there would come a day when he was tempted to use that power, and that he must ignore the call at all costs.

But Lucian didn't come all this way just to be told "no." The Manifold had the power to give him what he wanted. He knew it.

If the Manifold wouldn't give him what he wanted, he had to take it by force. And there was only one way to do that.

So, he gathered the Orbs, one by one, starting with Gravitonics and working his way around. With each Orb slotting into his Focus, he felt a rush of power, an elevation from his current form. Nothing stopped him from grabbing the original Seven, having them join in his Focus with that of Creation and Space-Time.

Which left only the Orb of Shadows. The last step to challenging the Manifold itself.

But also, awakening the Ancient One.

There was no doubt in his mind. This was the only path forward. With this final Orb's acquisition, he would do what no being had ever done before. He would hold all Ten Orbs in his Focus at once, transcending the power of anything that had ever existed in any reality. Even the Ancient One, holding the original Seven Orbs at the Dawn of Creation, holding the Eight during his time as the Immortal in the Shadow Realm, would not come close to this level of power.

Lucian didn't know what would happen, but one thing he *did* know was that the Ancient One would not lie down and take it. His enemy would fight with everything he had to get back not just the Orb of Shadows, but every Orb Lucian held.

With the power of all Ten, the Ancient One could shape reality as he willed. Lucian was opening himself to that risk, but as he saw it, this was the only way.

He trusted himself and his instincts. He trusted that as the Chosen, he would know the way.

At last, Lucian let out a breath and absorbed the final Orb into his Focus.

As soon as he did, he gasped as unreality unfolded before him.

36

A TORRENT of ethereal energy coalesced around Lucian, each Orb pulsing in unison within his Focus, merging into a singular, overwhelming presence. Reality itself seemed to pause, time slowing to nothing even as his own actions and thoughts moved at warp speed.

With every pulse of the Orbs, Lucian's perception expanded exponentially. His consciousness stretched beyond the limits of his physical body, reaching out into dimensions that had been abstract concepts seconds before. Not only could he see forward and backward in time, but he could also see through the multiverse, peering down corridors into alternate realities and timelines that were just as real as his own. Realities where he wielded the Orbs, like this one, realities where he had given them up, and realities where he had died long before ever reaching this point.

And every single one of them was as real as the reality he was from.

Countless versions of himself had made it to this point, a practically infinite number, their minds converging with his own, their memories mixing with his as if they had always belonged.

295

He didn't know where he began, and the others ended. And always, his awareness expanded, an ascension from mortality to godhood. His mind teetered on the brink of infinite awareness, straining to comprehend the boundless complexities of existence.

This newfound perception was beyond overwhelming. It was intoxicating, disorienting, and absolutely terrifying. As the Manifold unfolded before him, as his vast intellect expanded to comprehend an impossible number of realities, his sense of self dissolved. His individual desires, his fears, his very ego, seemed trivial in the face of such unfathomable power.

He was no longer just Lucian—he was a conduit for the primal energies of creation itself, capable of rewriting the laws of physics with a mere thought. He was the Orbs. He was the Manifold, at once creator and creation, intimately linked with every particle, every wave of energy that made up every reality and even beyond.

His friends, his world, his mission—all these had propelled him to this pinnacle of power. But now, endowed with the ability to reshape reality at will, how could those motivations possibly drive him? Was it not more important to ensure the balance and harmony of the cosmos, and not just his own, but every other one in existence?

With a mere thought, he could either heal or shatter the delicate tapestry of all existence. And because of this power, he felt a temptation such as he had never known. Why not reshape the universe exactly as he wanted? It would be a small thing. With the Orbs, he could wipe the slate clean, create an entirely new order from nothing.

A new Big Bang to restart everything all over again.

Only one thought. It would take only one thought.

He realized then that he was no longer himself. Among his personalities lurked another, poisoning his original motivation, taking control.

This wasn't him. He wasn't about power, about control. All he had wanted to do was ...

... What?

You have done well, Chosen. You have found the Aspects. You brought them to me, as I commanded you. Watch what we can build together!

At that moment, Lucian felt a great power pulling at his Focus. It was a power he wanted nothing more than to surrender to. A power that was inside of him, wishing to be free.

He knew, in his nearly infinite knowledge, that it was Shadow Magic tearing him apart. Even now, in this place, it was fighting to take control of him, as it had taken control of every one of the Ancient One's acolytes.

Lucian reached for the Orb of Creation, using its magic to fight back against that power. A golden beam of light shot into the void before him, more magic than he had ever conjured in his life a thousand times over. In this place, such magic had the power to destroy entire realities.

But the void absorbed the golden light as if it were nothing.

There is no power greater than that of the Shadow, Chosen. Joined with the Orbs in a singular Focus! It matters not who the Focus belongs to; Shadow will consume it, make it mine.

Lucian summoned what little willpower he had left. *You haven't won yet, Isthelah.*

You think speaking my ancient name will soften me, make me smaller? How wrong you are. You have fulfilled your purpose, Chosen, and soon, I will reshape reality to my desires. But fear not. You will always be a part of me. You will always be able to watch behind my eyes and marvel at the wonders I create! I am a benevolent master.

Another voice entered Lucian's mind from some far-off place or time that he couldn't remember. Yet the voice was comforting and familiar.

Release them, Lucian. It is the only way.

Lucian? Who was that? A name, that much was clear.

The name fell from his mind. In the Orbs was a completeness, and to give up that completeness would certainly drive him to madness.

Lucian. What was in that name? He couldn't say.

Would he really trade infinite knowledge for just a name?

The highest good is not in knowing, Lucian. It is in doing.

That voice. Who was that voice? It was not him, but it was *within* him.

Remember Serah. Remember your friends. Remember those you love, Lucian, and those who love you. That is the essence of who you are. You do not face this darkness alone. All of us are here. All of us believe in you. And when you give us permission, we will lend you aid. The Ancient One, as powerful as he is, stands alone. He cannot stop all of us.

Serah is here?

That he could affect change, against all odds, allowed his mind to come to the forefront and briefly assume control.

And with that control came a surge of defiance such as he had ever known.

He threw his entire will into a single thought: the only one thought would save him.

He had to have faith that the name was enough, and the name would save him.

He released the Orbs. Immediately, his consciousness collapsed, retracting from its godlike omniscience to his former, limited self. His mind felt as if it had been torn in two, and he stood for a moment, completely dazed. He had no memory of what had happened, where he had come from, except that he felt a void in his Focus, an absence that couldn't be explained.

He was alone in the darkness, attempting to come to grips with how he'd gotten here.

His name. He had only to remember his name.

My name is ...

This thought was interrupted when a figure appeared from

the darkness, but it was no malevolent shadow. A familiar face formed in the guise of a short old man with kind brown eyes and a scraggly beard.

At last, it came to him like a thunderbolt. "Lakhmu?"

Lakhmu gave an encouraging smile, as if he knew he had what it took to take on the Ancient One.

And strangely, because of that smile, he believed it, too.

"Lucian," he said. "Lucian is my name."

"Yes," Lakhmu said, smiling. "You have given up the Orbs, their power, and have earned something far greater. You have earned mastery over self, something not even the Ancient One can claim. He is consumed by desire, a desire for control. And that desire controls him. But you have done the opposite, giving up control. And as such, you have made yourself powerful enough to defeat him. Not idly did I choose the name of Sorcerer-Ascendant. By your actions, you have risen to the rank of the immortals who rule the Light Realm and indeed, have surpassed them. All you need is courage and belief in yourself. So, take up your spear, Chosen. Drive it into the Ancient One's heart. Deal him a fatal blow, and there will be nothing to corrupt the joining of the Aspects. Hold them in your Focus, and all of creation will be yours to command."

"I don't want to feel that again," Lucian said. "I...wasn't myself."

"You have mastered yourself, and even if you gather the Orbs again, the Ancient One would not be there to haunt you. Only you would remain. You must remember your heart, Lucian, your reason for fighting. Your heart will carry you through to the end. And yes—your friends, too. Listen for them, for they are in this place, too. They are here to lend their aid, such as they can. Don't discount their strength, for it is not inherent strength that matters, but inherent belief. Lucian—"

Lakhmu never got to finish, because the surrounding darkness deepened, and the old sorcerer vanished into the surrounding ether. Without even a thought, Lucian summoned Lightspear to his hand. It remained to him, even though the Orbs were gone. A sphere of light illumined everything in all directions as Lucian floated in the void.

Slowly, a surface materialized below him. He floated down, settling on the altar he had left behind, with its empty pedestals. The Ten Orbs shone above the altar, drawn to this place, what Lucian now knew to be the Heart of Creation.

And across from him on the altar stood a shadow, all that remained of the Ancient One. There was no face, his body wreathed in oscillating shadows deeper than the eternal void of space. A spear of darkness stretched from his hand, the counterpoint to Lucian's own. All Lucian felt was a coldness radiating outward from the Ancient One's being, a desire for power, control, and pain.

Along with a boundless rage that would do everything to see him not just dead, but subsumed into his Focus, as he had done to countless others.

"It's over for you," Lucian said. "This is where you end, once and for all."

The Ancient One raised his spear, and with that movement, each of the Orbs responded, floating toward him. Lucian merely stood, watching as every Orb joined with the Ancient One's Focus, as his entire form took on a great resplendence.

Every Orb but one joined him: the Orb of Creation. Of all the Orbs, only it remained with Lucian.

It would have to be enough.

Lucian raised Lightspear, and the Orb flew toward him, snapping into his Focus. Despite the singular Orb, Lucian felt its power join with him.

"You will die, Chosen," the Ancient One said. "And when you die, I alone will hold the keys to the Manifold. And this time, you won't be able to stop me!"

Watching the Ancient One's face, Lucian saw it was no longer wreathed in shadow, but similar to the Ascendants he had seen outside this place. It was a strong, masculine face, all hard lines and angles, radiating a cold brutality. The eyes were red, and they were staring at Lucian malevolently.

"What can you do against me, against the power of these Orbs? Surrender, and your suffering will not be as great."

Lucian merely started streaming Creation Magic into Lightspear, and as its light grew in intensity, the darkness was pushed back from the altar, the golden magic fighting to pierce the veil of Shadow Magic surrounding Isthelah.

Lucian started walking forward, Lightspear in hand.

The Ancient One's counterstroke was a wave of pure Shadow Magic, so powerful that it instantly pushed back the golden light Lucian had conjured, until he was just a golden island in the darkness. But Lucian felt no fear. He simply walked forward, Lightspear in hand, its aura pushing back the darkness.

Around the Ancient One, a veil of orange Atomic Magic was gathering in a powerful attack that Lucian was certain would zap him into nothingness. He created a shield, such as he could, but the Ancient One continued to gather his power, leaving no room for doubt.

There was no way Lucian could counter the attack with the Ancient One channeling the Orb of Atomicism, when it forced the Manifold to obey his need.

There was only one chance, as Lucian saw it. He charged forward, his feet seeming to move in slow motion as he advanced.

Even as the Ancient One's attack continued to grow, Lucian saw movement from the periphery of his vision. From the darkness stepped a human figure, one he least expected.

There was no mistaking who it was: Xara Mallis. For a moment, Lucian felt his heart drop. Though her power was only a tiny fraction of the Ancient One before him, it seemed it was enough to tip the balance, to make his defeat all but guaranteed. Already, Lucian was concentrating all of his magic on defending the Shadow Magic radiating outward; if he diverted even a little, he had no chance of making it in time.

Lucian continued to charge, despite knowing it was pointless. If he was going to die, he'd go down fighting.

But Xara surprised him by completely wrapping herself in Atomic Magic, lashing out a stream so powerful that it defied belief. That stream shot from her hands, striking at the Ancient One's gathering attack, completely neutralizing it.

I've got this, Lucian, she said. *Consider it my way of repaying you for all the harm done.*

Despite the power of the Orb of Atomicism channeled by the Ancient One, Xara's Focus was strong. She equalized her magic against the Ancient One's, allowing Lucian to continue advancing.

Lucian nodded his thanks before redoubling his efforts, now leaping with a Gravitonically-assisted jump. The Ancient One already was changing tactics, creating a maelstrom of super-heated plasma hotter than the center of a supergiant star. Lucian felt its searing heat breaking through his Thermal shield and would be obliterated in moments.

But in the nick of time, another figure manifested from the shadows beyond the altar, near to where Xara had emerged. And this person was even more surprising to see than Xara. It was Cleon, his face fierce and blue eyes shining with fury.

"Take this, you rotting son of a whore!"

He streamed a column of red Thermal Magic at the Ancient One, powerful enough to neutralize the Ancient One's stream.

Lucian continued to advance, feeling the pressure of Shadow Magic really beginning to push him back. He streamed more from the Orb of Creation, fighting against the tide of Shadow with every step.

Next, the Ancient One leered down at Lucian but could do nothing against the reinforcements without leaving himself open to Lucian. So, he switched to the next Aspect, which was

Dynamism. A massive sphere of electricity coalesced around the Ancient One. Lucian didn't bother blocking this attack, trusting that someone else would emerge to reinforce him.

As he had hoped, a new champion entered the ring, standing next to Cleon, and he was surprised to see that it was his mother. At first, Lucian wondered how it could be her: she was no Dynamist, after all. But something deep down told him that this didn't matter. Like him, his mother was a sorcerer, able to command any Aspect with ease. A solid beam of yellow light escaped her hands, instantly neutralizing the Ancient One's Dynamistic Magic.

I've got you covered, son, she said. *Fight with everything you have!*

The Ancient One roared his dismay and quickly switched streams, hoping to be far faster than the next battle entrant could counter. A nova of light exploded outward, against which Lucian closed his eyes. But it only lasted an instant. When he opened his eyes, Fergus was there, standing next to his mother, his expression grim as he streamed a solid line of green Radiant Magic.

Told you I'd have your back, Lucian, he said. *To the very end.*

Lucian was over halfway to the Ancient One by now, but he was running in slow motion. Even with his Creation Magic, it was like trying to wade through a tsunami that never stopped coming. Even the others were struggling, Shadow Magic now trailing down the streams they were shooting toward the Ancient One. Xara's arms were shaking, as were his mother's. Lucian knew they couldn't last forever, so he had to hurry.

Next, the Ancient One's attack shifted to Binding. Lucian didn't know who, or what, would show up for this one. No one he had traveled with had ever been a natural Binder.

So, he was surprised to see when Transcend White—Vivienne—came to the forefront. Lucian continued to charge, fighting with everything he had to go after the Ancient One, even as Vivienne released a bright beam of blue Binding Magic. Like his mother, she was no natural Binder, but she had been called to this fight, and Lucian knew she would do everything to see it through.

You are truly the Chosen, Vivienne said. *And the Chosen will not fight alone.*

Lucian was running as fast as he had been at the beginning, but somehow, the space seemed to stretch between them. As Lucian neared, the Ancient One's Shadow Magic became more powerful, slowing him to a crawl. He streamed harder, the surrounding darkness encroaching into his bubble of golden light. At points, he came to a standstill, but he never gave up, fighting with everything he had.

There were but three more Aspects Lucian could be attacked with. The Ancient One's aura took on a violet color as Lucian's mind was assailed with horrifying images of his failure, as he saw all his allies utterly destroyed and absorbed by the Ancient One's Focus.

But the psychic attack only lasted for a moment, as Themba entered the battlefield and countered the Ancient One's stream. Lucian's heart leaped with joy to see the old Ancient, his tall wiry frame, alabaster skin, and red eyes just as he had remembered. Themba blasted a stream of pure Psionic Magic, long before the Ancient One could even get his attack off the ground.

Your destiny is victory, Themba said. *I am honored to fight by your side one last time.*

Lucian was ten meters away, still running as if in slow motion, even as arrows of pure Shadow Magic pierced his Creation shield, several coming perilously close to touching his flesh. His shield faded, and from the periphery of the altar, it didn't seem as if Lucian would get any more help. All these warriors and friends he had met on his travels had gathered, and now they were struggling, having perhaps seconds longer to hold on.

He wanted to shout his encouragement, to not give up, but he didn't have extra breath to spare. Instead, he methodically placed one foot in front of the other, even as gravity seemed to double, and then triple. Lucian couldn't divert any more magic to a Gravitonic shield. That would mean relaxing his Creation shield, and if he did that for even a moment, he would be lost.

He had to trust someone was coming to save him.

That someone had to be Serah. But how could it be possible? She was in the Temple of Streams right now, far away from here.

No. He had to believe.

And to his utter amazement, there she was. Serah stepped onto the altar, and her eyes instantly locked with his. In them, he felt her love. The connecting force was more powerful than any Orb, and Lucian's magic instantly carved a path toward the Ancient One.

Serah shot a stream of pure silver brilliance from her hands, attacking the Ancient One. Instantly, the burden pressing down on Lucian's shoulders was lifted.

I love you, Serah said. *Now kill that rotting bastard!*

He wanted to ask how she'd managed it, but there would be time for that later.

There was but one Aspect left for the Ancient One to use, and he didn't even get a chance. Emma was already attacking him with a stream of pure Space-Time, meaning that every Aspect, save that of Shadow, was defended against by Lucian's companions. The eight champions surrounded the Ancient One, their streams steady and in equilibrium.

The rest now was up to Lucian. He gripped Lightspear in his hand firmly. Despite all the Shadow Magic surrounding him, none of it dared to snuff out the ethereal weapon.

The Orbs had formed a crown above the Ancient One's head, and now that crown was spinning madly, each stream from each champion blocking its magic.

With a final push, he forced himself through the Ancient One's protective bubble, piercing it open with Lightspear.

Instantly, the Ancient One fell upon him, his spear of darkness clashing with Lightspear.

Lucian's mind was blank as he clung to his Focus, letting pure instinct drive him. Their movements were a blur as they fought among the altar and the empty pedestals, with quick streams of magic and hastily thrown shields intermixed with the melee. But the Ancient One's magical attacks could never reach their full, deadly potential, with Lucian's many allies blocking. Lucian was forced to look up at Isthelah, a giant in comparison who used his reach and strength to push him back. Yet Lucian was fast, guided by a force that was beyond even him.

That force was faith and inevitability.

And the Ancient One seemed to sense it. He fought desperately, every attack seeming to be cunning or strong enough to end things once and for all. But through pure prescience, Lucian knew just what to do to avoid death, to keep fighting.

Out of the corner of his eye, Lucian could see his allies stepping closer, a noose drawing tight. The multicolored lights streamed from their hands were blinding, completely wrapping the Ethereal Crown floating above the Ancient One's head, rendering the Orbs powerless.

Lucian and Isthelah continued to fight, even as his friends relentlessly closed in. The Shadow Magic surrounding the Ancient One was weakening; despite his power, there was little he could do against this combined front. Every second that passed, the weaker he became.

Isthelah suddenly drew back and phased toward Serah, a gambit to make Lucian fumble. But Themba, Vivienne, Emma, and Cleon were all there to defend her. Individually, they were weak, but together, they could scarcely be overcome.

The Ancient One was pushed back again, and he tried to attack the opposite side of the altar, which held Xara, Fergus, and Mira. But the three of them fought fiercely, pushing the Ancient One back yet again, to the very center of the altar.

Now he was surrounded. There was no longer any resistance. Lucian's Creation Magic had made the Ancient One an island of darkness. He was impotent. He had no one on his side. Even the one who had been on his side, Xara, had been redeemed.

Lucian walked up to him. All that was left was to deliver the final and fatal thrust of Lightspear. The Magic of Creation bore down on Isthelah's Shadow Magic, an ever-retracting shell. The Firstborn of Creation breathed heavily, even as Lucian's friends, standing in a circle around him, continued to stream hard and subdue him, never even giving him a chance.

"Kill me," the Ancient One said, "and you die, too. Didn't you know that's what it means to be Chosen? As soon as you make the Orbs yours, you will lose yourself. Kill me if you wish, but if you take up the Orbs, you will never leave this place."

"He's lying," Serah said

"If I have to die ..." Lucian trailed off, his eyes meeting Serah's. From the look she was giving him, that wasn't a possibility.

He was making it out of this alive. He had to believe it was possible.

"Oi!" Cleon said. "What are we talking for? Kill him quick while the killing's good!"

It sounded good to Lucian. Without thinking or further preamble, Lucian drove Lightspear forward as hard as he could. Its point met resistance. Shadow Magic surrounded it, pushing it back with everything the Ancient One had. Lucian streamed from the Orb of Creation, forcing the spear forward, even as tendrils of Shadow Magic began snaking their way toward him.

Lucian needed to strengthen his attack, or he wouldn't kill him before the Shadow Magic got to him. But how? What knowledge was he missing?

A familiar voice entered his mind. *Orient yourself with what you must do, not what you must know.*

Lucian pushed further forward, even as Isthelah's face twisted in rage. Doubts filled Lucian's mind. What if he had come this far only to fail? What if his truth wasn't strong enough to overcome the Ancient One's evil?

You don't choose your purpose; your purpose chooses you.

Again, Lightspear inched forward. Lucian floated off the altar, completely horizontal, an aura of golden light shining out from him. The tendrils of Shadow Magic now completely ensconced him, pressing in. The others were streaming with everything they had because the Ancient One was also attempting to use the Orbs to overpower them.

He couldn't finish him fast enough.

Embrace your truth, and the rest of your path will be set before you. Nothing will stop you. You are the Chosen of the Manifold, Lucian. But you must also choose yourself. And when you choose yourself, you will know the way.

Lucian flew forward, but the space between him and the Ancient One seemed to stretch. Lucian felt calm overwhelm him, a surety. However things appeared on the outside, he would be victorious.

He imagined the future with Serah, the Shadow Realm saved, his friends happy and living lives of peace. He imagined that future until it was more real than the evil he was facing right now.

The Manifold responds to truth, whatever form that truth takes. When there are multiple truths, the strongest truth wins. The strongest truth is the one we choose.

Lucian closed his eyes as he felt himself coming closer to Isthelah. When he opened them, the Ancient One's red eyes bored into his, wishing to instill eternal despair. They were the eyes from his many nightmares that had made him afraid to even sleep.

They were close enough now that the Psionic shield was weakening, and new thoughts, new hallucinations, were being implanted in Lucian's mind, including a vision of him failing, of his friends dying, of eternal torture at the Ancient One's hands.

But deep down, he knew it wasn't the truth. The truth was his to decide.

He was the Sorcerer-Ascendant. He was the Chosen of the Manifold.

But more than that, he was Lucian Abrantes, and he believed, with all his soul, that love, not hate, would form the bridge between imagination and reality.

There was nothing left to know, and everything left to do. The Ancient One, despite his struggles, uttered some last words of defiance.

"You will fail them...all whom you love. They will curse your name for all eternity. You have failed, Chosen. *Failed*."

Lucian smiled, because he knew it wasn't true. His words were nothing, as empty as a shadow, a last-ditch lie that had nothing to stand on.

His truth, the truth of love and faith, was higher. Because he believed in it, it would manifest itself, even if he let go of Lightspear right now.

The Ancient One seemed to recognize this, and there was nothing left to stop Lucian. Lightspear plunged directly into the Ancient One's heart, and his ethereal scream was terrible, but it didn't even affect him. The Ancient One would die just the same as his counterpart in the Shadow Realm. His Shadow Magic held on stubbornly, shifting and oscillating and warring to survive, but unable to overcome the Aspect of Creation.

Lucian noted that Lightspear's inner light was weakening, even so, it hung on. He held that position until nothing but the Orb of Shadows remained.

It shone with a soft, dark violet sheen, but the malevolent presence it had once held was gone. The Ancient One was purged, and its power to create new rules and realities awaited a new master.

Along with the Orb of Shadows, the other eight Orbs floated nearby. Like that of the Orb of Shadows, they were waiting.

Now it was up to Lucian to decide what to do with them.

37

BUT BEFORE LUCIAN could do anything, he staggered, feeling the toll of the battle for the first time. The others hurried forward to help him, but he only had eyes for one person.

Despite his exhaustion, he hobbled toward Serah, who clutched him in her arms.

"You're here," he said, delirious with happiness. "It actually worked!"

"What worked?" she asked, her voice shaky.

"I knew you would be here. And here you are. How did it happen?"

"I woke up," she said. "As soon as I did, I saw this portal open up ahead of me. I figured it was for me, so I walked through." She looked at him with concern. "Are you okay? Are you hurt?"

"I'm fine," he said. "What about you?"

"Never better."

Lucian let Serah go, a smile on his face. He took in all the rest, all standing and watching him. From their expressions, it seemed as if they didn't believe the Ancient One was really gone.

"That should be the end of him," Lucian said.

Fergus was the first to speak. "Rot me, that was a close one!"

Lucian looked around at the assembly, at faces he never thought he'd see again. Cleon. Themba. Transcend White—no, Vivienne. She had asked him to call her Vivienne. He didn't fully understand how they were here, but he knew that the Focus lived on after the body died. Perhaps it wasn't so strange after all. For the first time, he noticed that both Vivienne and Themba were younger versions of themselves. She was a beautiful woman, her face filled with strength and maturity, her hair brown rather than gray, her eyes fierce. Themba's pale skin was smoother than during their adventures through space and time. Cleon looked the same as ever, with flaming red hair and green eyes that held a hint of mischief.

Everyone was now looking at the Nine Orbs floating in the center of the altar, all orbiting each other, waiting to be claimed. Despite the power they promised, no one seemed tempted to take them.

Lucian looked around at all these heroes—those who had followed him here and those who had perished along the way. All he could feel was overwhelmed with a joy that defied words.

"I don't even know how all of you found me," he said, "but thank you."

"We were where we needed to be," Vivienne said. "For my part, I felt a sort of call. It's difficult to explain."

"Just glad I could help, in my way," Cleon said. "That's the second time you owe me!"

"I never got to thank you for that," Lucian said. "You made it all possible, Cleon. Without you ..." He turned to face the entire assembly, all watching him. "Without *all* of you. Without your support, without your friendship and sacrifice ..."

"We understand, Lucian," Themba said. "There is no need to explain. Now, what should we do about the Orbs?"

"We came here to return the Orbs, to save the Manifold," Mira said. "Is that what we're still doing?"

"We'll let the Chosen decide what comes next," Xara said. "Something tells me it isn't so simple."

Lucian realized they knew nothing about his conversation with the Manifold, how it didn't want to make any concessions to him about saving humanity. "Xara's right. The Manifold has its own goals and motivations, and it's not possible to change it just by asking. It's only interested in saving itself."

He then explained everything that happened from the moment he crossed into the Manifold: his duel with Enkius, asking the Manifold to save humanity, and being denied, and how this had led to him taking on the Orb of Shadows to force the Manifold to change its nature, the only thing that would allow him to rewrite the rules. But as soon as the Orb of Shadows was absorbed, this gave the Ancient One an opening to take him over. It was only through Lakhmu's interference that Lucian could remember himself, enough to give up the Orbs. This action had caused Lucian and the Ancient One to become separated, at the cost of him losing all the Orbs, except that of Creation.

"I never expected all of you to come here," he said. "Even if Lakhmu told me you would."

"Transcend White described it as a call," Emma said. "And that would be accurate."

Heads nodded all around. Apparently, it was the same for everyone.

"What about the Manifold?" Mira asked. "How can we convince it to save us?"

"We can't convince it," Lucian said. "We have to change the rules, and that can only be done with Shadow Magic."

"The Ancient One won't take you over again?" Mira asked.

Lucian smiled. "The Ancient One is gone—truly gone. The Orb of Shadows is like any old Orb, now. It'll respond to whoever holds it. And it has the power to change the rules of the Manifold. We wouldn't need to change a lot. Just allow magic to continue existing in the Shadow Realm."

"But wouldn't that kill the Manifold, eventually?" Emma asked. "Ether will spread too much in the Shadow Realm, and the Heart won't be able to keep up any longer. That's what Anlilta said."

All watched Lucian as he gathered his thoughts. "For a moment, when I held the Orbs, before the Ancient One got to me—it felt like I knew everything there was to know. Of course, as soon as I gave up the Orbs, that knowledge left me—but I still remember the *feeling* of that knowledge, even if the knowledge itself is gone." He shook his head, feeling as if he wasn't doing a good job of explaining. Some things just went beyond words. "The point being, as soon as I hold all the Orbs again, I'll know exactly what to do to get the reality we want on the outside. I'll be able to change anything. Literally anything."

"Including getting me out of here?" Cleon asked. "Don't get me wrong. The Manifold is great. Eternal peace and all that. However, if there is a way for me to leave, I'd be much obliged to take it."

"That should be possible," Lucian said. "I don't see why not."

"Rotting hell, yes!" Cleon said. "There's so much left for me to do out there. If it's possible ..." He trailed off. "Rot it, here I am, hoping too much. If it's not too much trouble though, Lucian, then yes, get me out of here."

The others seemed to ponder this. Vivienne, Xara, and Themba all exchanged glances. The idea of it seemed unimaginable on the surface, but technically, it *should* be possible.

"You don't have to decide immediately," Lucian said. "Take some time."

"So, does this mean we *all* get to leave if we want?" Serah asked. "We're not dead?"

"Yes, we can," Lucian said. "As soon as I absorb those Orbs, I'll have the power to make anything happen."

"Such power can be dangerous," Vivienne said. "It would be easy to lose yourself."

"What if that happens?" Xara asked. "What then?"

"Then there's no way back," Lucian said. "The only other option is simply to return all the Orbs and do what the Manifold originally asked us to do. That would save the Light Realm and close the First Gate. And magic would end in our reality."

"And we'd be stuck here," Serah said. "No, thanks."

"I say use the Orbs," Fergus said. "We didn't come all this way just to cause an apocalypse back home. We need the Gates at the very least. If using the Orb of Shadows won't bring the Ancient One back, then I'm for it."

"It won't," Lucian said. "The only danger is losing myself."

"That's a pretty big danger," Serah said.

"It is," Lucian confirmed. "I know what to expect now, and how to guard against it. I don't want ultimate power. I just want to make sure all of this wasn't for nothing. Otherwise, why'd we fight so hard for three years?"

The others were quiet as they considered his words. If Lucian lost himself to the Manifold, ascended to pure godhood, the Shadow Realm would be saved. But the cost was possibly losing their friend forever, Serah losing her love, and Mira losing her son.

Everyone understood the stakes. The only question was, could Lucian return from it? Could he keep enough of himself safe to give up the Orbs again?

"I can't encourage you either way," Emma said. "The choice is yours, Lucian."

"There's no question," Lucian said. "I'm going to do it." He turned to Vivienne, Xara, and Themba. "All I need to know is, if there is a way to bring all of you out, do you want it?"

Vivienne was the first to give her thoughts. "I've had my time," she said. "I was an old woman before, and if possible, I could return to the Shadow Realm in a younger body. But I feel I've seen enough of life. Most of my friends are here, and it is peaceful. I'd like to stay here awhile, and then fade on my time."

"I, too, would like to stay," Themba said. "The universe I'd return to is not my universe. I am content here, and like Vivienne, I have done my part."

All that was left was Xara. She seemed to ponder the question for a while before responding. "If I go back, then I don't know what I'm going back *to*. Everyone I know, everyone who matters to me, is here. Besides, is there even a place for me in the Shadow Realm? I was Xara Mallis. I called myself Sorcerer-Ascendant of Magekind, causing death and despair to tens and millions and what proved to be a fruitless quest. But unlike you, Lucian, I had never earned the title." She looked at Lucian, giving a slow, deciding nod. "It was an honor to fight with you for once rather than against you. But my time in the Shadow Realm has passed. Here, I can rest, at least until I'm ready to fade, like Vivienne. Even if it's in your power to bring me out of here, I'd rather stay."

Lucian nodded. "It was an honor to fight with you too, Xara."

To his surprise, she gave a nod and completely vanished, just like that.

"Good luck, Lucian," Vivienne said. "Don't fear death. It is just the door that opens to the greatest adventure of all." She smiled. "We have fun here, believe it or not."

With that, she also disappeared.

Themba said nothing at all, only giving a reassuring nod before he, too, faded away, leaving the rest of them on their own.

With the three of them gone, they once again turned to consider the Orbs.

"I'm about to start," Lucian said. "Get ready."

Serah embraced him. From the way she clutched him, it was as if she believed it would be the last time.

"If you're lost, just think of me," Serah said quietly. "I'll be waiting for you."

Lucian held her close, feeling his hand with her hair. "I'm coming back," he whispered quietly into her ear. "I wouldn't miss you for the universe. Because you *are* my universe."

Only then did she let him go, tears in her eyes.

This wouldn't get any easier. Before he could doubt himself, he stepped toward the Orbs, willing them to join with his Focus.

———

IN THE NEXT INSTANT, he was somewhere else. He became someone else.

Something else.

Omniscience crowded out his name, his thoughts, his ego.

But this time, he at least recalled that he had to remember it.

He floated for a time, his mind seeming to encompass all of existence. The longer he stayed here, the further he drifted from who he used to be.

Who *did* he used to be? He used to be something. But what?

Though he wanted nothing more than to expand, to become larger than even this, some force within him urged him to become smaller, to stay focused.

A face. Beautiful, blue eyes, honey blonde hair. She was smiling.

Serah.

If you're lost, just think of me. I'll be waiting for you.

For you. And who am I?

The Sorcerer-Ascendant. The Chosen of the Manifold. The Manifold itself.

I am Lucian Abrantes of Earth. And now matter how far I stray, how much power I hold, love is the bridge between imagination and reality. I am here for a reason, and that reason is to come back.

But not before I've done my work.

The Milky Way galaxy was a small thing indeed in the vastness of the cosmos, one among trillions of others. Indeed, it was hard to focus on embracing only *it*.

But he limited himself to just that. With the power at his disposal, it was easy to go overboard, to make too many changes.

With such power, his sense of scale was wildly disproportionate to what was actually required.

He had to limit himself to as few changes as possible. Changes that would allow the Gates to survive, along with magic, in the Shadow Realm. Magic could not be allowed to spread infinitely. It would eventually cause the Heart of Creation to die out.

And with his infinite knowledge, he saw a way to change the rules and make this reality possible.

He could do it because, as long as he held the Ten, he *was* the Manifold.

The galaxy spread before him, and he watched it through a dimension that meant he was both outside it and within it. Lucian began by creating an ovoid shield to surround the entire galaxy, a shield that would be impossible to remove or change.

The shield's only purpose was to keep ether from spreading further beyond that point. Forevermore, magic would be limited to humanity's home galaxy. Beyond it, ether could not pass, and it could not be streamed by any mage, no matter what their power.

Ether would fill the space within the galaxy, but only to a certain point, about equal to what it was now. And once that threshold had been reached, leftover ether would return through the First Gate and back to the Heart of Creation. Empowering it. Healing it.

In this way, the spread of ether in the Shadow Realm would never overcome the rate at which new ether was created by the Orbs.

This change was enacted with a single thought, by the power of the Orb of Shadows. Nothing more was required.

There was another rule to change, to ensure that their work would not be in vain. No being could ever wield the Orbs again, and to accomplish this, Lucian made it so that any being who entered the Manifold could never leave again. The Ancient One had been powerful enough to enter the Manifold and leave, as had Enkius and Nathi. It was conceivable that another person might manage the feat again, taking the Orbs and changing reality to suit their will, undoing all their hard work and sacrifice.

Lucian made it so as soon as he returned the Orbs, the rule would go into effect. The only exception would be a temporary portal that would take Lucian, and everyone else who wanted to leave, to *Blood Wyvern* and the First Gate. And of the First Gate, Lucian ensured it would remain by *Blood Wyvern*, at least long enough for them to use it. After they were done, it could change locations, as it was wont to do.

As soon as they left the Manifold, the only way for any mage was death.

With a simple thought, this was accomplished. There was no physical change to signify that anything had happened, but Lucian the shifting of the Manifold to suit his will.

There was another change Lucian had to enact, and that was to make the time pass at the same speed in the Shadow Realm as the Light Realm, and to make the change retroactive to when they had first entered. That would ensure that when they left, they would return to their own reality just a few weeks after first entering this one.

Lucian considered these changes, weighing how it affected every aspect of everything, every loophole. He perceived that his action would have the intended consequences, no more or less.

The last change would be to allow humans to still use magic. Before, magic was only usable if at least one Orb was held by a member of that species. And from there, the Manifold determined, through inscrutable criteria, just who received a Focus, normally at a rate of one in twenty million people.

With no Orbs being held, it would have to work differently. First, he kept the numbers more or less the same. The Manifold would continue deciding who received a Focus and who didn't, according to its purposes, as long as those numbers remained consistent. He also decided that everyone who currently had a

Focus could keep it. This would ensure a steady supply of magic-users to keep things running but would also keep magic rare enough to where it wouldn't be overwhelming.

As for the fraying, Lucian realized he didn't have to do anything to prevent it. The Seven Minor Aspects were joined, meaning the fraying would not affect mages. And as for how humans would access magic in the first place, the Greater Aspects—Creation, Shadow, and Space-Time—would act as a bond between mages and the Manifold itself, ensuring magic could still be used, and would function as intended.

Everything accomplished, Lucian found he was ready to return. He released the Orbs. As soon as he did so, he was back at the altar with everyone else. All Ten of the Orbs were floating in front of him. From the way everyone was watching him, it was as if nothing at all had happened.

But now, there was a white portal which had opened on the left-hand side of the altar, revealing the idyllic scene of the Prism-wood, along with the familiar shape of *Blood Wyvern's* hull.

Fergus, Serah, and Mira cheered at the sight, while Emma closed her eyes in relief.

"It's done," Lucian said. "Magic is here to stay."

The others redoubled their cheering at this news. Serah hugged Lucian tightly and there were smiles all around.

As he and Serah parted, Cleon came up to them. "So, you're saying if I go out through there, I'll really be alive again? I'll get my body back?"

Lucian nodded. "That's right."

He then explained everything he had done, but already, the exact memories of how he'd achieved it were fading. He'd always remember *what* he'd done, but not what it had been *like*.

Memories of godhood, it seemed, were fleeting, impossible for the brain to hold on to.

"So, mission accomplished?" Serah asked.

"I would say so," Lucian said.

"Only one thing left to do, then," Fergus said.

Lucian realized Fergus was right. All Ten Orbs remained floating before him, orbiting around each other in seemingly random patterns. It was mesmerizing to watch.

The pedestals were empty and waiting.

Lucian approached but quickly realized that it probably wasn't safe for him to get any closer to the Orbs. He had resisted the temptation to become a god twice. He didn't want to tempt fate for a third time.

"I was thinking," he said. "We all got this far because we worked together, right? Wouldn't it be fitting if each of us took an Orb and put it back ourselves?"

"You'd trust us with that?" Fergus asked.

Lucian laughed. "After everything we've been through? If I can't trust you guys, I can't trust anyone."

"Well, Fergus has a point," Cleon said. "I've always wanted to see what one of these bad boys felt like!"

"Trust me," Emma said, "it's not worth the pain."

Cleon watched her for a moment, surprised. "You've handled one of them?"

"It's a long story," Emma said. "I might tell you about it, assuming we actually make it back."

"I'd like that very much," Cleon said. "Over drinks, maybe?"

Emma gave a small smile, but before she could respond, Fergus interrupted. "Cleon, you handle the Orb of Thermalism. Emma can grab Radiance. I can do Dynamism ..."

By the time it was all divided up, some had one Orb, others two. Lucian, for his part, took the three Greater Aspects. He wasn't sure if they needed to be treated differently from the others, so he decided not to risk it.

Within a minute, every single one of the original Orbs had been returned, and three new pedestals manifested in the center. Lucian returned each of the remaining Orbs in kind.

As soon as it was done, each shot a colored light above the

altar, forming a single bright sphere that burst, spreading ether in all directions. The power Lucian felt from it was unreal, and the temptation to remain and bask in its glory was great.

But he turned to his friends and nodded toward the portal. "About time we left."

No one argued. He led the way—Serah on his right, his mother on his left. He stopped right before the portal, nodding for everyone else to go through.

"What about you?" Serah asked.

"I'll be through in a second. I forgot something."

"Forgot something? Don't tell me you're talking about the Orbs!"

"No, something else. I'll catch up in a minute."

She looked at him doubtfully for a moment, but in the end, passed through the portal with the rest.

Lucian stood for a moment, watching the Orbs and the light they conjured. He stretched out his hand, and Lightspear dutifully appeared.

Where he was going, he wouldn't need it anymore. Perhaps someone else, somewhere, would.

It was hard to remember, the memories almost entirely gone. But while he had held the Ten Orbs, he'd gotten a sense of other times, other realities, where Lightspear was wielded, not by himself, but by another. He couldn't remember the nature of these visions. It was like trying to recall a vivid dream from ten years ago.

He just knew it was important that he return Lightspear, if only because, one day, it would have to make the journey back to him through the Source of Power on Mako.

It was the last thing to do before he left.

He addressed the brilliant sphere of light, the beating of the Heart of Creation, floating before him. "Make sure it gets in the right place, will you?"

He then threw the spear directly at the center of the meeting of the Aspects, and it was absorbed with an ethereal hum.

Something shifted within Lucian. As a test, he held out his hand again, willing the weapon there.

When his hand remained empty, he smiled.

"Back to life," he said. "Back to reality."

38

LUCIAN STEPPED through the portal and into the forest, finding *Blood Wyvern* standing before them, just as they had left it. He turned to look at the portal, only to discover that it was already gone, the last direct connection anyone would have with the Manifold. There was only the trill of birdsong, the shifting of leaves, and the ethereal hum of the First Gate, beyond which was a white light, their passage back into the Shadow Realm.

All that was left was to go inside the ship and leave.

The rest of the team looked a bit dazed, looking around at the woods as if they couldn't believe they were here.

"Rotting hell," Cleon said. "Everything here is so...*sparkly!*"

"Sparkly," Fergus said. "And dangerous. The sooner we're out of here, the better."

The clomping of hooves interrupted their conversation. Lucian turned to see the herd of prismharts approaching, with the Eldarhart at the fore. Cleon's eyes nearly popped out of his head at the sight.

Something has changed, Chosen, the old buck said, making his thoughts public for all. *I can feel it in the air.*

Let's just say we did what we came to do, Lucian said. *The Orbs have returned to the Heart of Creation.*

Joyous news! We must celebrate. Did you ever find Anlilta?

Lucian's heart turned sorrowful. *Unfortunately, she died defending us.*

Died? the Eldarhart asked. *No, I don't think she did.*

Lucian wasn't sure how to explain. Perhaps the idea was unfathomable to the prismhart. *It's a long story, but she fought bravely to the end.*

You seem sure of what you saw. However, I have a strong bond with my master. If she had perished—no matter where, or how far—I would be the first to know. She lives, this much I can say.

Lucian was cheered by the news. *If that's true, then that's amazing. Without her, we would have never made it to the Heart of Creation.*

Well, I know how overjoyed she must be. We are far away from the World of Light here. I would beg news of you, although I can read your heart and can sense that you are eager to be away.

The Eldarhart's eyes shone with an otherworldly light, its antlers casting prism-like reflections around the clearing. The herd behind him seemed to hum with a quiet, almost reverent energy.

Lucian realized that reverence was meant for him.

The Eldarhart addressed Lucian directly, his majestic form dwarfing Lucian's human stature. The noble beast lowered its head, its eyes level with his.

Your bravery and sacrifice will echo through the Light Realm for all of time. You have chosen a path of balance and restraint, doing what no one else could have done. We thank you, from the bottom of our hearts.

The Eldarhart then lowered its neck, all but bowing to him. The others did likewise.

No need to bow, Lucian said, blushing from embarrassment. *I had a lot of help from my friends.*

Shall you come to our grove to celebrate? It would be our greatest honor to host the Chosen and his allies!

We thank you, Lucian said, *but like you said, we're ready to go back home.*

I understand, the Eldarhart said. *You are welcome here anytime, of course. Just because you are leaving now doesn't mean you can't return.*

I would love to someday. Take care of yourself, Eldarhart.

The same goes for you. Safe journey, and may the stars guide your path.

The prismharts retreated into the woods, but the Eldarhart stood watching. Lucian took one last look around. Though he intended to return someday, he imagined that day would be quite a while in the future. It was strange to think that while they had only been here for a few minutes, the Heart of Creation already seemed like a distant memory. All the memories he'd had from when he'd held the Orbs, all the knowledge, the godlike powers, were completely gone, not even as the figment of a dream. Perhaps it was better that way.

The Heart of Creation was a part of him, but it was also apart from him. He could live his life with Serah without being haunted by its memories.

Lucian wondered for a moment what would happen now. Magic would remain in the Shadow Realm, of course, and the Gates would work. He supposed things would be business as usual. No one back home would be any the wiser to what they had done. The *Alkasen* wouldn't be an issue, either, Silumko having taken their fleets back in time to the First Starsea following the Siege of Earth.

While the Shadow Realm was safe from the existential threat of the Manifold, Lucian knew that didn't mean peace was guaranteed. There would still be mysteries and conflict. Despite all its resources, humanity still had to contend with itself.

Lucian wasn't sure of his role in all that, and right now, he wasn't ready to think about it.

"Let's get on board," he said.

They all did so. As they boarded *Blood Wyvern*, they all went to the bridge and looked out of the main viewscreen. Lucian took in the serene beauty of the Light Realm, its arboreal tranquility belying the tumultuous events that had just transpired. The prismharts had mostly retreated, but Lucian could still see some of them watching through the lush undergrowth.

"First time on a spaceship," Cleon said. "You'll have to catch me up on a lot of things. What year is it, anyway?"

"2367," Emma said.

"Rotting hell, I was dead almost two years," Cleon said. "What else has happened?"

"There'll be plenty of time for that later," Fergus said.

Mira took up the controls, and with the press of a button, the engines powered on. Lucian smiled. It was a familiar sound, and one that seemed to promise more adventures. Less dangerous ones, hopefully.

He looked at Serah, who smiled. She leaned her head on his shoulder while he put his cheek on top of her head. He wanted to retreat with her as soon as possible. Even freed from Kharzul's brand, he was worried about her. She was contemplative for now and physically seemed to be fine, so he remained quiet, not wanting to ruin the mood. Fergus was closing his eyes, as if resting, while Emma was staring through the viewscreen, her expression one of resolve. Cleon's eyes were still wide as he took everything in. Lucian still couldn't believe he was here, but if anyone deserved a second chance, it was him. What he did with his second life remained to be seen.

"I can't believe this is real," Cleon said. "There's...there's so much I want to do."

"You'll get to," Lucian said. "Soon." His gaze took in the others. "Everyone okay?"

Emma turned, offering him a small, thoughtful smile. "I... think so. It's a lot to process."

"You're telling me," Serah said. "So, I guess I'll be the one to ask. What now? Are we each going our separate ways, or what?"

"Oh, trust me, there are still a lot of pieces to pick up," Lucian said.

"And a Mage Tower to build on Psyche," Emma added.

"Mage Tower?" Cleon asked. "Now, you've got me curious. I suppose the Queen got her comeuppance, eh?"

"I guess you could say that," Lucian said.

By now, Mira was turning the ship around, facing it toward the Gate. "All right. Bye-bye, Light Realm."

Before anyone could say anything else, *Blood Wyvern* eased forward.

"Time to go home," Lucian said.

Blood Wyvern's engines ignited more fully as they advanced slowly through the Gate, and within seconds, had left the Light Realm behind. All too quickly, the scene was replaced with a canopy of stars. It was so...*dark*, as if Lucian were looking through half-closed lids. All the colors, sights, and sounds he'd gotten used to were dulled here. This would take some getting used to.

And yet, it still felt like home, even if they were thousands of light years from Earth. Here, closer to the galactic core, the stars were thick, a reminder that this universe was vast and mysterious, and adventure was never far away if they wanted to have it.

This journey was over, and Lucian was glad about that.

But as he held Serah close, he realized a new journey—*their* journey—was just beginning.

EPILOGUE

ONE YEAR after the events of the Light Realm, everyone who had been part of the journey for the Orbs gathered in a dingy bar on Archea Station, the same one Lucian, Fergus, and Serah had visited all those years ago when they had first escaped Psyche. Fergus had insisted on it for reasons none other than nostalgia. Lucian had his own reasons.

As soon as Lucian walked in with Serah, it brought him back to that uncertain time. The bar still exuded a slight sense of danger. Despite the universe being saved, life went on as usual. Over a year out of the spotlight and wearing his normal streetwear, no one glanced at him twice.

He smiled when he saw all his old friends. His mother stood and hugged him, with Fergus waiting in the wings. Emma sat quietly, simply smiling, while Cleon sat in the booth's corner, absorbed by something on his slate. Even Jagar had made it. He sat across from Cleon, nursing a drink, a small smile tugging at the corner of his lips as he noticed Lucian's approach. Linus and Plato were also present, while Khairu stood next to Emma, barely more relaxed than her usual stiff demeanor. From her face, it seemed as if she didn't approve of the venue. Selene was the only one from all of Lucian's journeys not to make it.

Once all basic pleasantries were done, Fergus, the one who had called the meeting, made the first toast.

"To friends who have become family," Fergus said, raising his glass, the light catching the amber liquid with a soft glow.

The others lifted their glasses in kind, the clink of glass echoing softly in the dimly lit bar.

"To family," they all said together, each taking a sip.

Lucian glanced around the table, his heart swelling with a mix of pride and nostalgia. These were the people who had stood by him through the darkest times, who had helped carry the weight of the universe on his shoulders. That weight was gone now, and that they were all here together to celebrate, despite everyone being so busy with their own lives, warmed his heart almost to the point of tears.

The laughter and chatter picked up quickly, everyone eager to share stories of the past year's adventures, along with the more mundane moments. Serah started off, explaining what she and Lucian had been up to. They'd spent the first few months taking a break from everything before returning to Psyche, where Lucian could pick up his role of organizing the mages there. He'd kept the title of Sorcerer-Ascendant, and for now, the job suited him. Even without the Orbs, something of their original magic must have remained inside him, because he was still the most powerful magic-user in the galaxy.

Jagar listened more than he spoke, but his updates were no less significant. As he'd mentioned previously, he'd gone to Alsan, his home planet, to take up the farming life. He was a local hero in his community, and anytime there was something dangerous to do that required a bit of magic and a shockspear, he was the guy to do it. Lucian had the feeling there were lots of stories there, even in the short year that had passed, but Jagar seemed reluctant to say anything more. He seemed happy, and that's what seemed to count.

Khairu also spoke little about her personal affairs, instead talking about the headache of navigating the politics of the various mage groups and trying to get them to work together. Lucian understood what she meant because he worked with her closely. Sometimes, it felt like returning the Orbs was a simpler thing than getting certain personalities to agree to things. Every day, they made closer progress. The Mage Tower was rising tier by tier in the mountains above Dara, where the Sorcerer-Queen Ansaldra's palace once stood. It seemed a fitting spot for a new beginning.

As for Emma, she spent some time on her parents' estate on L5 before going into business with her father. She said she enjoyed the work, as it was a chance to take things easy and take her mind off things, but she imagined she'd get bored with it.

Cleon had returned to Psyche, reconnecting with some old friends and acquaintances. He told a story of trying to find his girlfriend after all these years. He found her, but she'd moved on, had settled down with a new man and even had a one-year-old to boot. After that, he figured Psyche held nothing more for him, so had done a fair bit of travel, seeing all the places he'd only dreamed of before finding himself back here.

As for Cleon's flirtatious offer to grab drinks with Emma in the Manifold, well, Lucian wasn't sure if anything had come of that. It seemed Emma was focused on other things, while Cleon was busy with his travels. And yet, anytime the two of them were put in the same room, there were certain looks and words exchanged that made him question if there *might* be something there. Lucian supposed only time would tell.

As for Plato, he'd retired back to Volsung, but not to the Isle of Madness. He found some family to live with, and from his stories, it seemed he was happy and at peace. Linus, like Khairu, had dedicated himself to building the Mage Tower. He said it was something to keep him busy and had no complaints.

As the night wore on, the conversation turned inevitably to the changes they had seen in the universe. The First Gate was still operational but was far too remote for anyone human to reach it, not even with years of space travel. Lucian imagined it would be decades, if not longer, before it was discovered, and he and the rest of his crew would die before telling anyone its location. He had placed a powerful ward near it, and if anyone ever came close, whether that was a human or something from the Light Realm's side, he would be the first to know. It was good enough for now, but given enough time, long after Lucian was gone, there would undoubtedly be future meetings between humanity and the Ascendants. While the Ascendants couldn't go into the Shadow Realm without becoming *Alkasen*, the same prohibition didn't apply to humans. He hoped those meetings would be peaceful, but in case they weren't, that was part of the reason he was forming the Mage Tower. The First Gate had to remain open if the Shadow Realm was to keep magic. It was one of the few things Lucian could not change for the brief time he'd been the master of the Manifold.

At last, after a few hours, there came a lull in the conversation. As had happened so often over the years, everyone seemed to look to Lucian for the next thing to say.

"Something I've realized," Lucian said, looking around the table, "is that the universe doesn't stop for anyone. Not even us. It never pauses or gives us a break. There's peace for now, but there will always be those who think that peace is worth breaking, for whatever reason. I want the Mage Tower to be a force for good, to keep humanity from turning on each other. And with no more *Alkasen* to deal with, and no fraying to worry about, humanity's spread into the stars is only going to speed up."

The others nodded their agreement. Lucian felt Serah's hand in his. He was glad to have her by his side.

"There's a lot left to be done, as we all know. I truly believe we're building a future that's brighter than anyone could have ever imagined." He cleared his throat. "And speaking of a bright future, I've got an announcement to make ..."

As they watched him, he undid the Radiant ward he'd used to hide the surprise all evening. Serah raised her hand, showing off a gorgeous engagement ring. Everyone gasped in amazement. Even in the subdued light of the bar, it glowed magnificently. Fittingly, it had ten stones, each representing a color of a different Aspect, surrounding a single band of pure, solidified ether. There was nothing of its kind in all the Worlds.

Emma was the first to react, her eyes widening as she gave her friend a hug. "Serah! Congratulations!"

Fergus chuckled. "It's about rotting time!"

Lucian shrugged. "I asked her the day after we got back."

"And you've kept it secret this long?" Emma asked. "That's an entire year!"

"Well, it was worth telling in person, wasn't it?" Serah asked.

Mira was crying, hugging them both. "I'm so happy for you, son. She's a good one. The best a mother could ask for!"

"Ahh, shucks," Serah said, her eyes shining with happiness. "You, too, Mrs. A!"

"Congratulations," Cleon put in. "Have you set a date?"

"Or a location?" Khairu asked with a rare smile.

"Well, we haven't set a date yet," Serah said. "But it's going to be on Psyche for sure!"

"Excellent," Fergus said. "Well, this calls for another round or two!"

"I can't," Emma said. "I'm already going to be stumbling back to the airlock!"

"Just one more," Jagar said with a smile. "Congratulations, lad. You're about to start the biggest adventure yet, though it might not feel like it after what you went through."

"Looking for any groomsmen yet?" Linus said. "Ushers? Flower boys? I'll drop my name in the hat!"

"Haven't worked out the details yet," Lucian said. "Everyone here is invited."

"As long as we can travel there by portal," Plato said. "No way I'm dragging myself all the way from Volsung!"

"I can arrange that," Lucian said. "No worries."

Fergus put in an order for another round. As the conversation drifted toward the future wedding, and then an hour later, toward other things, they each shared their hopes and the paths they intended to take. Mostly, the conversation turned back to the work of building the Mage Tower, and as the night wore on even further, Serah and Emma started hashing out a worryingly detailed plan of opening an amusement park on Psyche, complete with wyvern rides, bungee jumping into the rifts, and whitewater rafting through the Forest of Shadows.

Finally, at about three in the morning, everyone was beyond tired. As they stood outside the bar, Fergus wrapped an arm around Mira with a twinkle in his eye. "Same time next year?"

"I'm down," Lucian said.

"Me, too!" Serah agreed.

They lingered for a moment longer, basking in the camaraderie. Lucian and Serah promised to send save-the-dates as soon as they'd worked things out. Then, with hugs and promises to keep in touch, they dispersed into Archea Station, each walking their own path, but forever connected by the bonds forged in their shared quest.

As Lucian and Serah walked hand in hand down the station's main strip, they paused for a moment at a secluded overlook that offered an expansive view of the stars that sprawled endlessly above them. Lucian felt a profound sense of peace settle over him. The universe, vast and mysterious, still held infinite possibilities, but for the first time in a long time, he felt ready to explore them from a place of joy rather than duty.

"It's weird," he said. "Everything feels so different, yet exactly the same."

Serah leaned into him, and he wrapped his arm around her, his fingers resting on her ring. Her smile was reflective and tender. "That's because *we've* changed, right? The universe stays the same, but we don't. And that's a good thing. We've grown, learned so much about ourselves and each other. I'm just glad it's all over, that we get to just be ourselves. It's all I ever wanted."

"Same," Lucian said. "I can't even tell you how excited I am to build a future with you. It...feels like a dream sometimes."

"It's no dream," Serah said seriously. "The only thing that can get in the way is us. We need to allow ourselves to be happy, like Lakhmu said. In the end, that's all that matters."

Lucian then thought about Lakhmu. Often, late at night, he wondered how the old sorcerer had appeared to him in the Manifold, had told him the right thing to do just in the nick of time, had calmed him in the face of the Ancient One's terror.

Maybe it wasn't about Lakhmu being there physically. Perhaps it was because Lakhmu, despite their short time together, was within Lucian. He'd passed the mantle of sorcerer onto him and even undid the brand Vera had placed upon him. Maybe a part of Lakhmu's Focus had imprinted itself on Lucian's, and that was what Lucian had seen reflected to him in the Manifold.

He was struck by a profound sense of sadness, but he wasn't sad for long. He would see his old teacher again someday, along with all the rest who had stayed behind. Though his body would one day die, they would join the Manifold along with everyone else.

"Lucian? Are you okay?"

"Sorry. I was just thinking about Lakhmu. I just realized something. I saw him there in the Manifold because he's a part of me."

"He was always there," Serah said. "Our teachers always stay with us, don't they?"

Lucian nodded. "Yeah. Something like that."

Their conversation was interrupted by a pair of footsteps walking up. They both turned to see an elderly man of middling stature and deep brown eyes. Lucian recognized the man immediately, but what was he doing here?

"Nathi?"

"Aye, the same," Nathi responded, in the same archaic variant of the Ancient language that he had spoken before. "I see that thou hast achieved what thou didst intend. Verily well!"

"It wasn't easy, but we did."

"I am glad. I only came here to thank thee, Chosen, before I went away from this reality to new times and new realities that require my presence."

"What new times and realities?"

"New adventures. Adventures in which thou shalt have no part; the Manifold hath released thee from its command, and now it fixeth its gaze upon another. None whom thou knowest, yet it is important nonetheless."

"I see," Lucian answered, though he wasn't sure what Nathi meant. "While I have you, though, I have to ask."

"Ask what? Simply speak it, and I shall answer to the best of my abilities."

"It's something Enkius said."

Nathi's expression darkened. "Aye. What of him?"

"He said that Anlilta tricked you into going into the Shadow Realm with the Orb of Creation. That she poisoned you against him. Is that true?"

Nathi considered for a long moment. "Nay, I truly believed in her prophecy. I had little love for her, at least at the time. After all, Enkius left her for me, so we were not friends! I had no reason to trust her. And yet, I became convinced of her words, that the Manifold itself would fail if we did not act boldly. And I was the only one powerful enough to wield both Orbs, long enough, at least, to carry them to the Chosen. To thee." He gazed at Lucian sadly. "I can sense, from thy manner and thy heart, that Enkius hath perished. That in his grief, he sought to take from thee what I sacrificed myself to protect."

Lucian nodded solemnly. "That's what happened. We fought at the Heart of Creation itself."

"Then I can only pray that he knows peace and that the Manifold hath accepted him into its embrace. I shall join him one day, but for one such as I, who can travel forward, backward, and laterally, days matter not much. I shall make my way home, in time, and hope that my presence may heal his Focus, assuming the completeness of the Manifold is not a sufficient balm."

"I'm sorry you're stuck here," Serah said. "You probably just want to go home, huh?"

"Oh, I am far from stuck. I can return home now, though not in the manner Enkius desired. I can release myself to death once I deem it necessary, but that day hath not yet come. It shall not come for a while yet!" He checked an antique watch, a curious thing, probably from before the turn of the millennium. "I must take my leave, Lucian and Serah. I only wished to offer my congratulations—not only for the victory thou hast won, but for thy happiness. Many happy days lie ahead of thee both, and the future of humanity is indeed bright. Now, I must be off. Fare thee well!"

As soon as he said these words, he vanished, as if he had never been. Lucian blinked in surprise.

"That was...*interesting*," Serah said. "Who do you think needs his help?"

Lucian chuckled. "Another hero in another reality. Maybe even another version of me?"

"It's not so crazy if you think about it," Serah said. "But you know, when we talk quantum time travel stuff and the multiverse, my brain just turns to mush."

"Me, too. Let's head back."

They continued to walk in comfortable silence until they reached the airlock, beyond which *Blood Wyvern* awaited, still and quiet against the backdrop of bustling station life. Despite the late hour—or rather, *early* hour—Archea was a busy port.

Once they were on the ship, Lucian stopped in the entry area.

"You okay?" Serah asked.

He thought for a moment, trying to put his thoughts into words. "Just feeling nostalgic, I guess. We've all gone our different ways, but we're still a family, in a way."

Serah was quiet as she listened.

"I know I'll see everyone again," Lucian went on. "It's just hard *not* to feel like everything before was the good old days, even if it didn't feel like it."

"That's why we're making some more good old days," Serah said. "Good new days?"

Lucian smiled. "This is why I'm with you."

"Plus, there will always be bad guys to fight. You'll see."

"Not for a while, I hope."

Serah smiled sleepily. "Let's get out of here."

Once on the bridge, Lucian engaged the ship's AI to fly away from the station. He looked back one last time at the station fading against the backdrop of the desert planet Archea before switching the viewscreen to the bow. Ahead of them lay the quiet sanctuary of the stars, the vast unknown stretching before them. It was a familiar sight that strangely brought comfort where once it had only meant danger.

A sign, perhaps, of how much he had grown.

Inside, the familiar hum of the ship soothed him. They navigated the corridors toward the main cabin, their steps echoing softly, a stark contrast to the laughter and noise of the bar they had just left, and the Time Weaver's cryptic words.

Despite the strange encounter, Lucian was happy, and only part of that could be blamed on the alcohol. As he turned off the lights, lay down with Serah, and held her close, he felt the weight of the past year lift.

As impossible as it seemed, the Orbs were a thing of the past, but their legacy would live on. Even now, they were joined, beating in the Heart of Creation. The job was done. Even a year later, Lucian still couldn't believe it.

And now, it was time for the next chapter, the chapter he would share with Serah. They were one now, and they had been for a long time. The wedding was just a way to acknowledge it publicly. They had fought countless battles together, and the future promised new battles of a different sort.

Ahead of them was the rest of their lives—ordinary, beautiful, and filled with the potential of everyday joys and challenges. And, Lucian hoped, children of their own.

And, as Serah had hinted, maybe even new bad guys to beat up if things ever got boring.

He held Serah close, listened to her breathing as she fell asleep in his arms. The ship slipped silently into the expanse of space, a speck against the infinite. As he drifted off to sleep, his thoughts turned to the future. No matter what it held, they would face it together, with the same courage and love that had brought them through all the trials they'd faced so far.

Now, they were just two beings in the universe. And that universe wasn't just a place of endless stars, mysteries, new adventures, and dangers.

It was a place of magic, faith, and hope.

It was home.

THE END OF THE STARSEA CYCLE SERIES

ABOUT THE AUTHOR

Kyle West is the author of multiple science-fantasy series, including The Starsea Cycle, The Wasteland Chronicles, and The Xenoworld Saga. While his fiction is set on strange and alien worlds, he strives to write characters that are human and relatable.

He enjoys the outdoors, hiking, and all things sci-fi and fantasy. He lives in Oklahoma City with his family.

Please visit kylewestbooks.com to learn about his books and stay in the loop with future releases.

facebook.com/kylewestwriter

twitter.com/kylewestwriter

bookbub.com/authors/kyle-west

AFTERWORD

And here we are, at the end of a long journey. Ten books and approximately one million words later (that's over 3,600 pages).

I started The Starsea Cycle in late 2020. I'm not sure what my intentions were with the series. One question I'm most commonly asked is if I outline everything ahead of time.

The answer to that is a resounding "no!" I'm a discovery writer, meaning I find things out in real time, just like you.

I wrote the first books quickly. I loved the world and universe so much that I could release the first eight books in about two years.

Then around July 2022, our second-born came along, and chaos unfurled (delightfully, I assure you...mostly). With two under three, I had to adjust course and realize that finishing the series might become a bit more monumental than I'd previously thought...

As such, I'm beyond grateful for my fans' patience over the last couple of years. It might not have been easy waiting a year for each new book to come out, but trust me, it was way tougher for me.

At the same time, I've given a lot of my hours and attention to these books, to the point where I've had to make hard choices between spending time with family and getting more writing done. I'm grateful to the patience I've been shown from both sides.

Well, I've talked overly long about the trials of trying to get the books done. What about the books themselves? What do they mean to me as an author?

To be perfectly blunt, I'm still in the middle of it. Though the last words have been written, it doesn't feel like it's over to me. Everyone got their happy ending, even those I regrettably killed off early on (looking at you, Cleon. We could have used your humor beyond just Book 3!).

No doubt you're wondering: what's next?

As of this writing, I honestly don't know. The most common question I get is if there will be more Starsea Cycle-related stuff. The answer to that is: probably not in the near-term. After ten books and four years exploring the same universe, I need a bit of a palate cleanser.

The Starsea Universe is pretty vast, though, and from the ending, there's an opening for other stories being told, either with the same characters (though older) or completely new characters in different timelines.

From a marketing perspective, it's always better to go with the known characters. I also like the idea of Lucian getting to live happily ever after with Serah and getting his peace. If anyone deserves retirement, it's him!

Whatever I do next, you can bet it's going to be fantasy or sci-fi related.

If you want more, check out my website, kylewestbooks.com. There you can find signed copies for your shelf along with other series I've written. They're also good!

Thanks for reading. As an author, that you've spent ten books and hours upon hours of your life traveling this universe with me is the highest of compliments.

Keep exploring,

Kyle West
July 23, 2024

www.ingramcontent.com/pod-product-compliance
Lightning Source LLC
Chambersburg PA
CBHW011128190726
48289CB00012B/2948